Outstanding praise for the novels c

THE SUMMER NAI

"A satisfying and multifaceted story that For fans of similar works by authors such ...~~Sheney~~ Noble and Nancy Thayer." –*Library Journal*

THE SEASON OF US

"A warm and witty tale. This heartfelt and emotional story will appeal to members of the Sandwich Generation or anyone who has had to set aside long-buried childhood resentments for the well-being of an aging parent. Fans of Elin Hilderbrand and Wendy Wax will adore this genuine exploration of family bonds, personal growth, and acceptance." –*Booklist*

THE BEACH QUILT

"Particularly compelling." –*The Pilot*

SUMMER FRIENDS

"A thoughtful novel." –*Shelf Awareness*

"A great summer read." –*Fresh Fiction*

"A novel rich in drama and insights into what factors bring people together and, just as fatefully, tear them apart."
–*The Portland Press Herald*

THE FAMILY BEACH HOUSE

"Explores questions about the meaning of home, family dynamics and tolerance." –*The Bangor Daily News*

"An enjoyable summer read, but it's more. It is a novel for all seasons that adds to the enduring excitement of Ogunquit."
–*The Maine Sunday Telegram*

"It does the trick as a beach book and provides a touristy taste of Maine's seasonal attractions." –*Publishers Weekly*

Books by Holly Chamberlin

LIVING SINGLE

THE SUMMER OF US

BABYLAND

BACK IN THE GAME

THE FRIENDS WE KEEP

TUSCAN HOLIDAY

ONE WEEK IN DECEMBER

THE FAMILY BEACH HOUSE

SUMMER FRIENDS

LAST SUMMER

THE SUMMER EVERYTHING CHANGED

THE BEACH QUILT

SUMMER WITH MY SISTERS

SEASHELL SEASON

THE SEASON OF US

HOME FOR THE SUMMER

HOME FOR CHRISTMAS

THE SUMMER NANNY

A WEDDING ON THE BEACH

ALL OUR SUMMERS

BAREFOOT IN THE SAND

Published by Kensington Publishing Corp.

BAREFOOT IN THE SAND

HOLLY CHAMBERLIN

KENSINGTON
PUBLISHING CORP.

www.kensingtonbooks.com

Special book excerpts or customized printings can also be created to fit specific needs. For details, write or phone the office of the Kensington Sales Manager: Kensington Publishing Corp., 119 West 40th Street, New York, NY 10018. Attn: Sales Department. Phone: 1-800-221-2647.

The K logo is a trademark of Kensington Publishing Corp.

ISBN-13: 978-1-4967-1925-6 (ebook)
ISBN-10: 1-4967-1925-5 (ebook)

ISBN-13: 978-1-4967-1924-9
ISBN-10: 1-4967-1924-7

First Kensington Trade Paperback Printing: July 2021

10 9 8 7 6 5 4 3 2 1

Printed in the United States of America

As always, for Stephen
And this time also for Flick

While I loved, and while I was loved, what an existence I enjoyed!

—Charlotte Brontë, *Villette*

Chapter 1

At the head of the grand staircase, Victoria stopped to glance around the dark landing. By the dim light that was coming from the pendant globe just inside the front doors to the big old house on Old Orchard Hill, she could just make out that she was alone. At least, she prayed that she was.

She had to go on. She simply had to. Slowly, carefully, her slim hand firmly holding the wooden banister, Victoria made her way to the ground floor. There was only one phone in the house and that was in her father's study. She had been forbidden any contact with the outside world but simply had to try and . . .

In the center hall, to the right of which was Herbert Aldridge's study, Victoria glanced up at the portraits of Joseph, the brother she had never known. If he had lived, would he have come to her aid in this moment of crisis? Impossible to know. Victoria looked away and continued on, her slippers making only the tiniest brushing sound over the marble-tiled floor.

It had taken every ounce of her courage, a fortitude she hadn't been at all certain she could muster, to sneak out of her bedroom that night. She was desperately afraid of being found out. She dreaded that stern and disappointed look she was sure to receive from her father, that anxious and confused expression she was sure to perceive on her mother's face when she stood in front of them to accept her punishment.

It was a hot, still night in late August. Victoria was wearing her lightest nightgown but sweat was running down her neck and chest. Her parents refused to install air-conditioning for a reason that was obscure to Victoria. It couldn't be the cost. The Aldridge family was wealthy.

The door to Herbert Aldridge's study was always kept closed but not locked unless the family was out of the house. Slowly, wincing with anxiety, Victoria opened the heavy wood door. When there was enough of a gap for her to slip through, she stepped inside. Her heart was racing madly and the sweat continued to pour from her. No sooner had she begun to ease the door closed behind her than the sound of a footstep on the stair, the creak of a floorboard overhead, the rustle of a robe at the far end of the hall, made her freeze.

Someone was coming. Someone had heard her moving around. She couldn't be found, she just couldn't!

Without further thought, Victoria slipped out of the study, careful to close the door behind her, and back into the dimly lit hall. From there she fled toward the stairs. On the very first step she stumbled and smashed her toe. A small whimper escaped from her lips. Onward she raced, heart pounding, onto the second-floor landing and down the hall to her bedroom at the far end, where she threw open the door and closed it behind her. There was no lock on this door. Her parents didn't approve of children locking doors behind them.

With another whimper, Victoria hugged her arms tightly around her waist and waited for her father to find her, to demand to know what she had been doing in his study in the middle of the night.

A minute passed, and another, and another. No one came.

She was safe. But she had failed.

Had the footstep, the creaking of the floorboard, the rustling of a robe, been real, or had her weak and terrified mind conjured them to send her scurrying like a prey animal back to the safety of her room?

Shame flooded Victoria Aldridge, and in that moment, she knew without a doubt that she would never again find the courage to make that forbidden phone call.

It was over.

Chapter 2

Today

Arden Bell locked the door of the bookshop behind her and turned left toward home. She was a tall, slim woman; her long blond hair, threaded now with shades of silver and white, was coiled at the base of her neck in a casual chignon. Her eyes were blue, and aside from needing reading glasses, her vision was still strong. For a time when she was young, she had a habit of ducking her head in a way that had earned her the nickname Shy Di, but Arden had long since ceased to duck her head or to hunch her shoulders. If she wasn't the most outgoing resident of Eliot's Corner, she was also not the most retiring.

Arden waved to the owner of Chez Claudine, the Parisian-style bakery across the street, just closing his store for the evening. Not much stayed open past six or seven in Eliot's Corner, not until after the Fourth of July. The town wasn't a big tourist draw, unlike many other coastal towns in southern Maine, but it had its fair share of day-trippers in the summer months and right through leaf-peeping season. Visitors enjoyed poking around the craft and jewelry stores; eating lobster rolls at the waterfront seafood shack at the far end of town; and browsing Arden Forest, Eliot's Corner's beloved bookshop.

It was all of a ten-minute walk from the bookshop to Arden's cottage, but in the space of those ten minutes she exchanged greetings with three other residents of the charming little town she had called home for fifteen years. Harry Lohsen, principal of the grammar school. Emile DuPonte, whose family had owned the hardware store for generations. Judy Twain, whose law practice was known for the large amount of pro bono work it undertook.

Finally, Arden turned onto Juniper Road and a smile came to her face. A smile always dawned when home was in sight. While its official address was 10 Juniper Road, everyone in Eliot's Corner referred to the little house as Juniper End. Only two other houses were on Juniper Road, number 8 and number 9; house numbers 1 through 7 had disappeared into the mists of time. Ben and Marla Swenson had lived in number 9 for the fifty-two years of their married lives and continued to keep a spectacular garden. Number 8 was currently being rented by a young couple who were having a house custom built some miles away. Arden rarely saw the Harrisons; they seemed to spend a good deal of time at the building site or taking weekend jaunts to Portland and Boston.

As Arden approached Juniper End, she said a silent word of thanks to her dear friend Margery Hopkins. The former owner of Arden Forest, and an old hand at property deals, Margery had helped Arden, a first-time home buyer, through the endlessly detailed back-and-forth between buyer and seller. In this way and in so many others, Margery had been like a fairy godmother as well as a friend and mentor.

But Margery had died some time ago, peacefully, after a long and fruitful life. What mattered at the moment, Arden thought, as she opened the front door of the cottage, was the ecstatic greeting she was about to get from her cats. Ophelia was a long-haired gray-and-white mixed breed; Prospero was sleek, black, and short-haired; and Falstaff was a big tiger. Arden had adopted the motley bunch two years earlier from a shelter in Portland in a three-for-one deal, so eager were the shelter staff that the cats be adopted together.

"I'm home," Arden called out, and within seconds three large felines were meowing madly and circling her feet. She shuffled through to the kitchen, avoiding paws and tails, where she dished out food for her ravenous fur children. Side by side they settled to their dinner, noisily chomping and chewing.

While the cats ate, Arden removed the old leather cross-body bag she used for going to and from the bookshop and surveyed her home with satisfaction. The ground floor was a modest twelve hundred square feet, but with an open-plan layout the space seemed a good deal larger.

The cottage's kitchen and dining area was large enough for a table that sat four comfortably. For most of her adult life Arden had been on a stringently tiny budget. Dinner was often a cup of ramen noodles or a can of soup. Lunches consisted of a piece of fruit or a peanut-butter-and-jelly sandwich. Now, with a business that was solvent if not always thriving, Arden enjoyed cooking real meals for herself, as well as for her friends. And she loved to bake, especially at the holidays. Buttery shortbread. Super-chocolaty cookies. Spicy gingerbread. Fresh raspberry muffins. There was something so therapeutic about baking—the enticing smells, the comforting warmth, the delicious results.

Beyond the kitchen there was a bathroom, with a pedestal sink and a charming four-clawfooted tub equipped with a handheld shower attachment. A small window gave a view of green leaves on waving branches; Arden had painted the room white to make the most of the natural light.

The bedroom was at the back of the cottage; it was just large enough for a double bed, a tall dresser, and a wooden bookcase Arden had salvaged from the bookshop back when Margery had been making a few upgrades. The closet was ridiculously narrow and shallow, but for Arden this didn't pose a problem. Her wardrobe was small and she kept her coats and jackets on a clothes tree by the front door.

It was in the wooden bookcase that Arden kept her most precious possession, a rather battered, late-nineteenth-century edition of Charlotte Brontë's *Villette*. The book had been a gift from the only man Arden had ever truly loved and was priceless because of that. Some people might hide such a treasure in a locked safe, and that certainly made practical sense, but Arden liked to cast her eyes on the book each morning upon awakening and each evening just before sleep. Once a year, on a particular day in October, she reread her favorite sections of the novel in a tribute of sorts to a time in her past when, however briefly, like the heroine Lucy Snowe's spirit, her spirit had shaken "its always-fettered wings half loose."

Prospero suddenly lifted his head and made a throaty noise in Arden's direction. "You're welcome," she said with a laugh. Prospero went back to his meal.

The living room—more properly, the living area—was hands down Arden's favorite room in the cottage. When she had first arrived in town, the only material goods she possessed fit into two old hard-backed plastic suitcases, the kind that predated wheelie bags. A person on the move tended not to accumulate odds and ends. Now, the living room was the definition of supreme comfort. A couch covered in lots of cozy throws and pillows. A cushiony armchair she had found at an estate sale. Paintings of local scenes by local artists. Two occasional tables on which were stacked books and magazines. A collection of seashells in a basket on the coffee table, next to a vase of whatever flowers were currently in bloom, often a gift from the Swensons.

The focal point of the room was the large stone fireplace. Around Labor Day each year, the son of one of the bookshop's most devoted customers, now a young man of nineteen, helped Arden to replenish the woodpile at the side of the house. Replenishing the supply of wood each year was a task that had taken on the weight of a ritual, marking for Arden more than anything else did the inevitability of seasonal change and the passing of time.

A set of stairs in the far corner of the living room led up to a semi-enclosed landing, complete with a window that afforded a view of the small yard where Arden often sat in privacy to enjoy a colorful sunset or a pleasant afternoon breeze. There was just room enough on the landing for a high-backed armchair and a narrow sofa that could double as a bed should anyone need to spend the night. So far, there had been no such person. Everyone Arden knew lived in Eliot's Corner. People from her past remained in the past, that other country from which everyone came and to which none, if they were wise, ever returned.

Falstaff, having scarfed his dinner, was now trying to edge Ophelia from her bowl, but she was having none of it. Prospero gave way without protest; of the three cats, he was the least food motivated and the politest. Arden's own dinner could wait. Brent, her assistant at the shop, had convinced her that sharing a specialty sandwich from Chez Claudine for lunch was a good idea, and she still felt pleasantly full.

Another day coming to a close. Another day of comforting routine and familiar faces. Arden thought again of *Villette*. "The charm of variety there was not," Lucy Snowe had said, "nor the excitement of incident, but I liked peace so well."

Fifty-five-year-old Arden Bell was content. Juniper End was her castle and Arden Forest was her kingdom. After all the years of wandering, all the years of a peripatetic life during which she was always looking over her shoulder, expecting to be found out and punished, she was settled, safe, and secure. If life wasn't perfect— and she had wisely abandoned the expectation or hope of such a thing long, long ago—it was still pretty darn good.

Arden opened the door of the fridge and took out a pitcher of homemade lemonade. As she poured the lemonade into a glass, she was again reminded that the mundane pleasures in life were often the sweetest. A cold glass of lemonade on a warm afternoon in June. A new episode of her favorite British mystery series on Acorn to watch. A cat with which to cuddle.

For all of these blessings, as simple as they might be, Arden Bell was deeply grateful.

Chapter 3

Laura Huntington was a thirty-six-year-old, recently divorced woman of middling height and weight, with dark brown hair and large, dark brown eyes. She wasn't beautiful, nor was she pretty in the common way, but she was attractive, intelligent, and energetic. She looked people in the eye when she spoke to them. Her students listened to her and liked her. She had few friends but they were stalwart friends. She liked animals. She loved books.

On this early-June morning, Laura was genuinely trying to be an unbiased observer of Port George, Maine, but her emotions—curiosity, eagerness, even a tiny sliver of fear—were getting in the way. Of course, they would be. The task she had set herself was challenging.

After a hasty breakfast of toast and coffee, she had left the bed-and-breakfast into which she had booked herself the evening before. She had no particular route in mind, content for the moment to wander and take in the atmosphere of this Maine town. Before leaving her home in Connecticut, Laura had read up on Port George. It had been established in 1866. The Chamber of Commerce website stated that the population as of 2018 was just shy of ten thousand. Ninety-two percent of that population was Caucasian. There were a few Native American families, members of the Abenaki and

Penobscot tribes. A tiny percent of Port George's residents were black. It seemed always to have been a semi-important commercial hub, surrounded by thriving farms. Today, the majority of people still made their living in commerce. Some, not many, still farmed. A few commuted to and from larger towns for their employment. The streets were clean; this was a point of pride. The lampposts were old-fashioned, long since fitted with electric lights. It was a policy not to cut down trees for any reason other than that they were at risk for falling on someone's house.

The *Port George Daily Chronicle* had closed with little advance notice in 1998 due to falling circulation. No online archives were available to the public. The paper published in one of those larger towns in which residents of Port George had found employment provided local news.

Why the town, not actually on the coast, had been called Port George was lost to history.

So, what could possibly have drawn Laura Huntington to this decidedly average though charming enough town? The answer was both simple and not so simple.

Upon her death years before, Laura's adoptive mother, Cynthia Huntington, had left Laura a letter to be opened if she ever decided to try to locate her birth mother. Truth be told, Laura had never been interested in tracking down the woman who had given birth to her, not when she was thoroughly content with the people who had adopted and raised her so lovingly. And then, Jared Pence had come into Laura's life, promising to love, honor, and cherish her until death did them part. For a while longer, Laura continued to be content to let the woman who had given birth to her remain unknown.

But death had not parted Laura and her husband. Divorce had done that, and divorce had changed Laura. For the first time in her life she felt truly alone. Her parents were dead. Jared was gone. There was no other family. Except, maybe, for that anonymous woman.

So, Laura had finally opened Cynthia Huntington's letter to find that it contained the only clue Cynthia had been able to glean during the otherwise secretive adoption process. Laura's birth mother had been a teen living in the town of Port George, Maine. No name. No physical description of the girl. No clue as to the father.

Laura was not a professional investigator; she didn't even particularly like detective stories, but she had been an academic before she had let being a wife interfere, and she had been taught how to research. To an extent. Thus far, her research had involved only documents—obscure texts, handwritten letters, diaries crammed with hard-to-read scrawls, even the occasional legal document. She had absolutely no experience in knocking on doors and asking a complete stranger if he knew anything about a teenage girl who, back in the fall of 1984, might have been sent away to give birth to her child in secret.

Besides, only a very, very few people would know if such a thing had happened. That was the point. The birth and subsequent adoption had been a secret. And this woman who had given birth to Laura, whoever she was, assuming she was still alive and living in Port George, might not welcome the secrets of her past being made public. That was understandable. Laura had no interest in outing this woman.

But Laura did want to learn all she could about the past, and to do that, she had to have some reason for asking what might seem like pesky or irrelevant questions of the Port George residents. So, she had devised what she hoped was a believable cover. She would tell people that she was an advance member of a podcast team, going from town to town as part of preliminary research for a broadcast that would explore the effect on a small community of a member's having gone missing. Had anyone ever disappeared, say, back in the mid-1980s? Gone away and come back, oh, nine or ten months later? She might have to listen to lots of tales that began with "Back when my grandmother was a kid, that would be the 1920s, there was a guy who walked out of town one day and never came back, but I never heard tell it made much of a difference to anyone," or "Legend has it that back in the day the Indians snuck into the old settlement in the middle of the night and kidnapped a few of the young girls, but I couldn't say if that's true or not."

Be that as it may. Laura's birth mother—and, for that matter, her birth father—*were* indeed missing people, so she wasn't *really* lying, and anyway, missing-person stories were popular with the general public. Hopefully, the guise would serve as a way into Port George. And if not, she would just have to think on her feet.

Laura had come to the center of town. It looked much like the center of any old town you might find on a road trip through New England. A neatly kept green square, punctuated by beds of seasonal flowers, and in the center, a statue of a man wearing the uniform of the Northern Army. Iron benches placed at intervals around the park, each with a plaque of dedication. Maples. Oaks. And dominating the green space, on the north side of the square, a tall white church with a clock tower.

It was a Tuesday morning, post–rush hour (if there was such a thing in Port George), and Laura, lowering herself onto one of the iron benches, was alone except for an elderly man across the square, reading a newspaper.

She wondered what it would have been like to be a child in Port George twenty, thirty, even forty years ago, surrounded by farmland, only a short drive to the Atlantic Ocean. Where had the kids of Port George played? There might have been a public playground, and a ball field. There was always a ball field. Her mother would have passed that clock tower that soared over the square many times in her life. She might have sat under one of the ancient oaks, chatting with a friend, watching passersby. Had she been a cheerleader or a member of the debate team? Had she campaigned for a girls' sports team? As difficult as it was to believe, girls' sports teams weren't exactly ubiquitous back in the 1980s.

After a time, Laura continued her tour of Port George, passing a Methodist church set back on a neatly trimmed lawn. Had her mother's family attended this church, or one of the other local churches, the Episcopal, or the Catholic? The Chamber of Commerce website stated that these three denominations had been represented in Port George for over a century.

Where had her mother lived? In one of the big old houses that lined the streets perpendicular to Main Street? On one of the streets farther away from the heart of town—Laura had seen a few pictures online—in one of the smaller, newer houses? There were few economically distressed people in Port George now; had there been many at other times in the town's history? Her mother might have been terribly poor, maybe the daughter of a farmer who had come upon hard times, maybe one of several children being raised by a single mother barely able to meet her monthly expenses, let alone help her teenage daughter raise a child of her own.

And raising a child on one's own presupposed that the father would not or could not help. Who was this male who had contributed to Laura Huntington's life? Had he been a local boy, someone her mother had known from school? Had they gone to the prom together? Had they been going steady, or had their relationship been only a heated one-night stand after a wild, drunken party at a friend's house?

Or, Laura mused, passing a man about her own age dressed in a navy blazer, white shirt, and chinos, perhaps her father had been an older man of the community, a teacher or a minister going through a midlife crisis and finding a solution in a sexual relationship with a teenage girl. Maybe Laura's origins had been even darker. Maybe her birth mother had been raped by a stranger or even by a family member. It was possible. Sadly, evil always was.

Laura was no longer a wide-eyed romantic, but she still very much hoped that her mother had been in love with Laura's father, and he with her, even if the love was only teen lust in disguise. Laura didn't know if she could bear to learn that she was the daughter of a brutal cad. But she had set out on this quest knowing full well that she might discover joy as well as sorrow, happiness as well as pain.

And the one question that might truly bring pain with its answer was this: Why had her birth mother given her up?

Laura had never felt abandoned; from the moment she was born, she had been a part of a loving family. She had been chosen, pampered, and nurtured. She wasn't angry about what life had given her. But she did want to know the truth.

Might her mother have been eager to get rid of her unplanned child? Or had she been forced to give up her baby by her parents, assuming her parents had been alive at the time? For all Laura knew her mother had grown up with a grandparent; maybe she herself had been adopted. Laura understood that she might never know the answer to any of these questions. Even if she did locate her mother, and the woman agreed to meet, she might not want to admit to certain aspects of whatever had happened almost forty years ago. That was her right. That was okay. It would have to be okay.

Laura turned a corner and found herself in the path of a middle-aged woman, dressed plainly in cargo shorts and an oversized button-down shirt. "I'm sorry," Laura murmured as she stepped out of the woman's way. The woman nodded and smiled as she passed. For all Laura knew, she thought, glancing quickly over her shoulder, that woman in the cargo shorts could be her mother.

Had this anonymous person ever married? Had she gone on to have more children? If so, any of the people Laura might encounter in Port George between the age of about twenty and thirty-five might possibly be a sibling. Assuming her mother had stayed on in Port George to have a family. Assuming the children of that family had stayed on, as well.

Assuming this. Assuming that.

Laura felt her shoulders sag. It was all so frustrating, and yet, she had only just begun her quest. She should continue on, hope to glean some bit of emotional information from Port George itself, attempt to . . .

Maybe later. It was time, Laura decided, to return to the Lilac Inn. She was tired. Normally, she didn't take naps, but now wasn't a normal time. Life might not be normal for a long while.

Chapter 4

Arden loved being alone at the shop before the business day began. It was then that she often thought about Margery Hopkins, the former owner and founder of Arden Forest, the woman who was responsible in many ways for giving Arden the good life she now enjoyed. Margery had been thrilled that her new shop assistant was called Arden. "It was meant to be," she had pronounced happily at their first meeting. Maybe it had been. It wasn't long before the two women had grown close. Margery had found in Arden Bell a sort of surrogate daughter. Arden had found not only a friend but a mentor and, even, a sort of guardian angel. When Margery passed away, Arden found herself in possession of Arden Forest as well as the rest of her friend's modest estate.

Like most if not all independent bookstores, Arden Forest sold new and "used" books. It was a pet peeve of Arden's, that term *used*. There had to be a better word for a book that had been read by one person before being passed on to be read by another. You didn't hear of *used* paintings or sculptures or films. Old items that might be considered more utilitarian—china or furniture or even jewelry—were referred to as vintage or antique or estate pieces. Not *used*. Was *recycled* any better? Maybe not. *Previously owned*, as secondhand cars were described? Were library books *used*?

For a long time, Margery had resisted stocking items such as note cards, bumper stickers, and oversized pencils with erasers in the shape of maple leaves and lobsters. She had believed in the purity of a bookshop; she would sell books and only books, not even popular magazines or newspapers. While Arden tended to agree in principle, there was rent to pay and bills to meet and the competition of other bookstores in neighboring towns, let alone online venues such as Amazon, to consider. Eventually, Arden had convinced her mentor that integrity would not be lost if they broadened their offerings to include a few carefully selected book-related items. Hand-printed birthday and get-well cards; pretty bookmarks decorated with quotes from famous poems and novels; fancy pens; moleskin notebooks. Datebooks sold big in November and December, and miniboxes of chocolates made by one of the women in town were always a hit around the holidays. Popular impulse purchases such as magnifying reading glasses brought in a fair amount of cash.

Even more popular than the chocolates, however, was the Arden Forest Book Club, in existence since the 1970s. Membership waxed and waned. Men—mostly older and retired and often single—occasionally joined, but the majority of the members always were women. Discussions were routinely lively and inspiring, and not until everyone who wanted to speak had spoken did the wine and cheese, crackers and cookies, come out. The book was paramount. The socializing was important but less so.

Several times a year the shop hosted special events, such as the Fairytale Creating workshop, led by the Maine-based writer of fairy tales Deborah Eve Freedman. Last year's Children's Books for Adults miniseries had helped get people through a notoriously long winter. Philip Pullman's *His Dark Materials* trilogy had been everyone's favorite. The talk on memoir writing given by a lecturer at the University of Maine had drawn a huge crowd. Readings by local writers drew smaller crowds, but were always enjoyable.

The book club met in a corner of the shop where two low couches were draped with clean quilts to hide the badly worn upholstery, with a few mismatched ladder-back chairs and a tufted velvet armchair that had many years before been salvaged from a hotel lobby in Portland. The once-magnificent chair always attracted one member of the book group, Mrs. Shandy, who looked nothing less than a dignified monarch seated in its depths. Mrs. Shandy had been the English teacher at the local grammar school for over forty years before she retired. She was a formidable source of knowledge—her specialty was nineteenth-century American writers—and a stickler for proper grammar even in conversation. Only once in Arden's time did someone whom Mrs. Shandy had corrected midsentence have the nerve to argue that in conversation among friends the rules need not apply. Things had not gone well after that, but still, Mrs. Shandy attended the next meeting of the book club unbowed and ready once again to correct members who got the use of *lay* and *lie* mixed up, or those who insisted on adding an *r* to the word *idea*.

In spite of the shop's moderate success, Arden couldn't afford a full-time employee, but she was able to employ a part-time second-in-command. If the salary wasn't great, the working conditions and the perks (such as first read of hot new titles) seemed to make up for that. For the past two years that part-time employee had been a young man named Brent Teakle. Arden dreaded the day Brent had saved enough money to leave Eliot's Corner for a more cosmopolitan life in Boston. She would wish him well but she would sorely miss his energy, his attention to details, and, to be totally honest, his brawn. Boxes of books were heavy.

Each summer, following Margery's example, Arden chose two high school kids to intern. Interested candidates were asked to submit an essay on their relation to books and to provide two personal references, one from a teacher or counselor at school, and one from a friend or neighbor. This summer, Arden had chosen a fifteen-year-old boy from the public high school and a sixteen-year-old girl who was homeschooled. Zach was serious-minded and had decided to become a lawyer, and he seemed to be anticipating his responsibilities by conducting himself with a gravity beyond his years. In contrast, Elly had a bubbly personality, had no idea what she wanted to be when she grew up, and, though she was very intelligent, didn't much care about a career.

Arden hoped the two kids would get along. Though both voracious readers—Zach favoring nonfiction and Elly, novels by contemporary writers—they were so different in temperament. Arden knew she could rely on Brent to negotiate any tensions. Brent was tough but fair with the interns, doling out responsibilities as if they were rewards, which in a way they were.

"Bonjour, mademoiselle!"

It was Brent, wearing his usual black jeans, gray Converse, and white button-down shirt.

"Good morning," Arden replied. "You're in a chipper mood."

Brent patted his stomach. "Kurt made roast chicken for dinner last night. Roast chicken always puts me in a good mood for days."

"I wish something as simple as a chicken dinner had the same effect on me!"

"There's nothing simple about a roast chicken. It's Ina Garten's meal of romance."

Maybe that's why it didn't send her into ecstasies, Arden thought. No lover with whom to share the meal.

"Whoopie pies make me smile," she said, refusing to indulge in self-pity.

Brent grimaced. "Whoopie pies make me fat. But, oh, are they worth it!"

Chapter 5

A flight of marble stairs led up to the three-story, redbrick building that served as the Port George Public Library. The shutters of the front-facing windows were white; the large double doors of the building were red. The date on the cornerstone was 1901.

Laura climbed the stairs, passed through the doors, and walked into the impressive foyer. The floor was pale marble; the walls were painted white; darkened portraits hung at intervals, town mothers and fathers, no doubt. There was a faint smell of old books. Laura was never mistaken about that smell.

A middle-aged woman sat on a stool behind the circulation desk; a boy of about twelve lounged at the far end of the room, his nose buried in an oversized graphic novel; and an elderly man was seated at one of three reading tables, a huge volume of old maps opened before him. Otherwise, the place seemed empty.

Laura approached the circulation desk. She felt nervous, even though she had decided there was no need to tell the librarian her podcast tale.

The librarian smiled. "How can I help you?"

Laura cleared her throat. "I'd like to see back editions of the local paper. I'm researching a story, you see, and I couldn't find anything online."

The woman frowned. "I'm afraid I can't help you. We don't have that archive, in any format."

Laura was disappointed. "Do you know anyone who might have them?"

"You'll want to talk to Edward Meyer. He was the paper's chief editor for over thirty years. I hear he has print copies of every edition published from 1965 until the paper shut down in 1998. I can't guarantee he'll give you access to his archive—I've heard he's very protective of it—but you can ask."

The helpful librarian gave Laura directions to Mr. Meyer's house. Then she looked closely at Laura. "I'm sorry, but have I seen you before?"

Laura was startled. She hadn't expected this question. "No. This is my first time in Port George."

"It's just that for a moment you looked familiar. I can't really say how, but . . ." The librarian shrugged. "Oh, well."

Laura thanked the librarian and took her leave. Had the librarian seen in her a resemblance to a local man or woman, someone she had known long ago? Or, Laura thought, maybe she just had one of those faces, unremarkable, a bit like so many other unremarkable faces, common, familiar. It was better not to read into small incidents.

With Mr. Meyer's address in hand, Laura continued on her way.

Chapter 6

Arden yawned, glad no one was in the shop at the moment. She didn't want a customer to assume that she was bored. She wasn't. Only tired. The morning had dragged a bit; only two people had come in, and only one had bought anything. Traffic had picked up a bit after lunch but had fallen off again after three o'clock.

Oh, well, Arden thought. At least now she had a moment to consider the window display. She liked to change it every week, keep it looking fresh with new titles as well as old favorites. As she reached out to straighten a book that had gone awry, she spotted a teenage couple walking past the bookshop, hand in hand. She didn't immediately recognize them, which was surprising as she knew most everyone who lived in and around Eliot's Corner.

Then it came to her. The girl was wearing her hair differently but it was definitely Aria, daughter of Judy Twain. The boy was harder to place, but then Arden recognized the way he was loping along. It was Ben Jones, youngest son of a man who ran a catchall business that included dump deliveries, minor carpentry jobs, and dead-tree removal. Arden would never have imagined Aria and Ben as a couple, but then again, love didn't play by rules, had little to do with reason, and showed no respect for social barriers.

She knew that all too well.

Arden stepped back from the window display and touched the

pendant that hung on a thin chain around her neck. The small silver charm was in the shape of a foot, worn now with time and caressing.

Our time will come to walk together barefoot in the sand. Our time will come to be together always.

And suddenly, it *was* 1984 and she was right back in Port George. Ronald Reagan was president. The virus that caused AIDS had just been discovered and revealed to a panicked population. She had been enthralled with the British band the Smiths. After school, she had lived in high-waist, front-pleat jeans and bright polo shirts. Every other word out of the mouths of her classmates was *airhead* or *awesome* or *to the max*. The *Port George Daily Chronicle* had run a short-lived but popular advice and gossip column called Helpful Hattie. In June, she had graduated from high school. In July, she had turned eighteen.

Oh, that summer. It had been glorious in so many ways. And then it had all gone wrong. So very, very wrong.

As suddenly as the past had overtaken her, it was gone and Arden was a fifty-five-year-old woman in 2021. Owner of an independent bookshop. Owner of Juniper End. Caretaker of three cats. A woman on her own.

It had been a long time since this sort of emotional experience had occurred, a long time since she had been catapulted into the past with such immediacy and force. She felt a bit dizzy and was contemplating sitting down for a few minutes while she recovered when the door of the shop opened and in walked Etta Wolf.

Arden forced a welcoming smile. She liked Etta, a longtime customer. It wouldn't do to be rude. "Hi, Etta. How can I help you today?"

"It occurred to me only last night that in all the years of my life I have never read *Anna Karenina*! How could that have happened?"

Arden smiled politely. "All sorts of strange things happen."

"Well, I said to myself, 'Arden is likely to have a copy for sale,' and so here I am. I could, of course, have gone to the library, but, you know, the older I get the less I like touching books hundreds of other people have touched." Etta shuddered. "The strange stains on pages! Ugh!"

A first-world problem, Arden thought as she led Etta to the fiction section. But a problem for her customer nonetheless. "I have a nice, recently translated hardcover edition." Arden pointed to the Classics shelf. There was no use in mentioning that there was a "used" paperback copy available.

"Is the translation good?"

"I can't vouch for it myself, not knowing Russian, but the reviews are very positive."

"Well," Etta said firmly, "I'll give it a try. How bad can it be?"

When Etta had gone off, new purchase under her arm, Arden did finally sit. Funny, that as she was still reeling from her unwanted visit to the past, to the summer that had changed her life in so many ways, Etta Wolf should show up requesting one of the greatest and most tragic love stories in European literature. Poor Anna and Count Vronsky, Arden thought. So many great love stories were sad, short-lived things, doomed to failure. And therefore, popular. Not many people wanted to read about the other sort of great love stories, the quiet, mundane ones, the relationships built on affection and companionship as much as they were built on passion. Pain made stories interesting. That was just the way it was.

Enigma, too, compelled people, Arden thought, getting up and returning to the display window to gaze unseeingly out at Main Street. Like the ending of Lucy Snowe's great love story in *Villette*. Arden had always believed that Paul Emanuel had drowned in that terrible storm, not far from shore, not far from the woman who had been waiting three long years for his return. But others needed to believe he had survived the tempest and been reunited with the woman he loved.

The bell over the door of the shop announced another arrival. This time it was Arden's neighbor on Juniper Road, Marla Swenson. She was always a welcome sight, and Arden hurried over to greet her.

"I brought some of my famous homemade fudge!" Marla announced gleefully.

Saved from melancholy by the timely arrival of chocolate! "Fudge," Arden told her neighbor, "is exactly what I need right now."

Chapter 7

Laura knocked on the door of the large, well-kept house at 12 Broad Street. It was painted white, with black shutters; a front porch was reached by a broad set of stairs. The lawn was beautifully manicured. The azalea bushes that bordered the lawn were neatly trimmed.

A moment or two later, the door was opened by an old man, possibly in his mideighties, neat as a pin in a pair of pressed chinos and a short-sleeved dress shirt buttoned to the neck, a thin woolen vest, and a pair of clean brogues. He was wearing a slim gold wedding ring; Laura wondered if his wife was still alive.

"Mr. Meyer?"

"Yes?" The word was spoken with an unmistakable tone of wariness.

Laura introduced herself and explained that the librarian had given her his address. She presented herself as a researcher for a podcast about the effects on a small community of a resident gone missing. She was interested in perusing the archives of the *Port George Daily Chronicle* to see what she might find in relation to the topic.

Mr. Meyer was not impressed. He was suspicious of podcasts, he said. He thought them amateurish at best and dangerous at worst. Besides, he thought the topic somewhat flimsy.

Undaunted if a bit weak-kneed, Laura admitted that his concerns about podcasts were valid in many cases. About her topic being flimsy, she admitted nothing. Maybe it was the way she held his eye while speaking, but somehow she managed to convince Mr. Meyer of her seriousness of purpose.

Mr. Meyer sighed. "You might as well come in," he said not ungraciously. "It's been a while since anyone's shown any interest in my archive. I'd be lying if I didn't appreciate the fact that someone cares." Mr. Meyer finally smiled. "Even if that someone is working on a podcast."

Laura thanked him—and her lucky stars—and followed the editor to the basement of his house. It was a clean, dry, well-lit space. A washing machine and matching dryer were in one section of the room; another area was set up with a simple desk and straight-backed chair.

"I do most of my work in the den upstairs," Mr. Meyer explained. "But this setup is for when I need to hunt for a piece in the archive. I like to keep the papers all here and not risk an edition getting lost or damaged in transit."

The archive Mr. Meyer spoke of was a virtual wall of black storage boxes lined up on a series of shelves. Each box was carefully labeled with the dates of the enclosed editions.

"Take your time. I'll be upstairs in the kitchen." At the foot of the stairs, Mr. Meyer stopped and looked back to Laura. "I just remembered something. One of our own went missing in late summer of, oh, I think it was 1983 or '4. Never came back, never found. Maybe that will get you somewhere."

When Mr. Meyer had gone upstairs, Laura selected the box labeled *June/July/August 1984* and settled at the little desk to read. She didn't know what, exactly, she hoped to find, but even a snippet of gossip might be helpful, a stray comment made by the town busybody, something that might point in some way, no matter how tortuous, to one or both of the people who had given her life.

The first pages of each edition were devoted to important local, state, and federal government news. No big surprise there. Many of the advertisements had been placed by Port George businesses, as well as by a few businesses located in what Laura assumed were neighboring towns and villages.

Midway through each of these summer editions, Laura found a chatty column written by a person using the pen name Helpful Hattie, in which Hattie dished out advice and old-fashioned gossip in equal amounts. What eligible middle-aged bachelor was seen squiring what single gal around town on Saturday evenings. What to say to an overbearing mother-in-law when she insists on rearranging your carefully planned holiday table setting. How to get a lazy husband to get out of his favorite armchair on a Saturday afternoon and mow the lawn as promised.

In spite of the possibilities such a column suggested, Laura could find nothing that remotely touched upon real scandal, and in a small town such as Port George, a teen pregnancy might well have been considered scandal. The contents of each of the columns Laura perused were uniformly good-natured and earnestly helpful. In other words, dull.

Laura was getting ready to give up her search when finally, in the edition for a Wednesday in late August, she came across a story of a missing person. The story to which Mr. Meyer had referred? A well-liked and popular nineteen-year-old boy had disappeared. His parents had reported him missing when he failed to return home Sunday evening for dinner. This sort of behavior was completely out of character for Rob Smith. A manhunt was begun.

Laura followed the story in the editions for the following days. Search parties were mounted. Public appeals for witnesses to come forward were made by tearful members of Rob Smith's family. Interviews with the missing boy's friends and family revealed nothing other than the seemingly universal opinion that Rob Smith was a wonderful young man. A candlelight vigil was held in the town square, sponsored by the Smiths' church. Theories were floated and abandoned. Classmates and teachers at the local community college had been eager to speak to the paper, though not one of them had anything remotely resembling a clue to offer. Rob's employer, a John Willis of Willis Construction, gave glowing praise of the young man's work ethic: "He was a summer employee, going back to school in September, and I'd already promised him work at his next break."

Through all of this coverage, there was no mention of a girl-friend. Laura found this a bit odd. A popular, handsome nineteen-year-old without a girlfriend. Unless Rob Smith had been gay and closeted; in 1984 being closeted was not so unusual, especially in a small, parochial town in the midst of the worldwide AIDS crisis. And if Rob Smith had come out as gay, there was the dreadful pos-sibility that he had been the victim of a hate crime, or if he had tested positive for the virus, he might have taken his own life in despair.

Laura studied the grainy black-and-white high school gradua-tion photo of the young man. He was handsome and pleasant look-ing in an all-American sort of way. As with most if not all such portraits, little of the sitter's real character came through. At least, that was Laura's assessment.

When she had reached the last paper in the storage box, Laura retrieved the box labeled *September/October/November 1984*. The story of Rob's disappearance continued. A coworker at Willis Con-struction reported seeing a scruffy young man out along the high-way. The man was found; he turned out to be a harmless wanderer who had shown up in the area a week earlier. A psychic had offered her services to the Port George police. They had turned her down. Again, the Smith family issued a public plea for anyone with any information to come forward. Their hearts were broken. There was still no mention of a girlfriend. Another picture was published; this one showed Rob Smith with his three sisters. Now Laura could see a glimpse of the real person. His smile was open and genuine. He was square jawed and broad shouldered, but there was nothing ag-gressive about his bearing.

Laura read on. The psychic who had been rejected by the police approached Rob's older sister, Frannie Smith, with an offer of help. Frannie agreed. After ten days with no forthcoming information, the psychic was fired from the case. There was no further mention of Miranda Applebee in the *Port George Daily Chronicle*.

Suddenly, midway through the month of October, all mention of the case vanished. Laura went back through the September and early-October editions to be sure she hadn't missed something. She hadn't.

Laura thought it strange. As a researcher, she was used to coming upon dead ends; recorded history was notoriously full of holes and misdirection. Still, Laura made a note of the name of the reporter who covered the story, just in case she wanted to speak with him. He might know if the missing boy ever reappeared, or if he was indeed the person Mr. Meyer had mentioned, the one who had never been found.

But she wasn't in Port George to focus on a missing boy. She was there to search for an unknown teenage girl who had gotten pregnant. Old story. Why would a teen pregnancy make the news, especially one that had presumably been kept secret from the residents of Port George?

Laura looked at her watch; it had been a present from her parents on her college graduation, and though she knew she could sell it for some much-needed cash, she couldn't bring herself to let go of the timepiece. The inscription on the back of the face meant far more to her than any amount of money could: *To our lovely daughter. Mom and Dad.* Simple words. Big sentiment.

She had been in Mr. Meyer's basement for close to an hour. She replaced the old editions of the *Chronicle* in their storage box, returned the box to its proper place on the shelf, and hurried upstairs.

She found the former editor in the kitchen as promised, finishing a cup of tea. "Did you find what you were looking for? Anything about that old missing-person case interest you?"

"Maybe. Thank you for your assistance. You've been very kind. I'm sorry I took up so much of your time."

"That's all right. You showing up like you did got me thinking about the old days. That's not always a bad thing."

"No. Not always. Goodbye."

The editor walked her to the door. He was still standing on the front porch, waving, as Laura pulled away.

Chapter 8

Summer 1984

"I'm sorry, Rob. I just can't. It's . . . it's too risky."

Victoria was near tears. All they had wanted to do was see a movie together on a Friday night like a regular boyfriend and girlfriend. They didn't even care what they saw, though the options were limited to *Ghostbusters* and *Sixteen Candles*. What they really wanted was to sit together in the dark, side by side, to hold hands and maybe to kiss if the theater was empty enough.

But just as they were within a block of the movie theater in Waverly, the smallest of Port George's neighbors, Victoria had lost her nerve. She grabbed Rob's arm and pulled him into a darkened doorway.

"Please don't be mad," she begged. "Someone might already have seen us. Oh, I never should have—"

Rob took her hands in his. "Vicky, I'm not mad. How could I be mad at you? It just makes me sad you're not free to live your life the way you want to live it."

"They're not bad people, my parents. It's just that they're . . ." She bit her lip. Social snobs? "Old-fashioned," she said finally, lamely.

"It's all right. Really. Come on, let's get back to the car. I'll take the back roads to Port George just like before."

Rob kissed her, sweetly and firmly. Victoria returned his kiss with passion. She loved him so very much.

Half an hour later Rob left her at the very edge of the Aldridge property, by a rough gap in the hedge through which Victoria had escaped earlier that evening. Swiftly, the full moon lighting her way, she made her way across the property, finally reaching the house. No sooner had she put a foot on the topmost stair than the front door opened, revealing her mother.

"Where were you?" Florence Aldridge cried. "I was so worried. What with your father at the club and my being here all alone . . ." Her hands were clasped tightly at her waist. Victoria saw that her mother had been drinking.

"I'm fine, Mother." Victoria managed a smile. "You shouldn't worry so much. I just met a friend in town for ice cream."

"Who?" Florence demanded. "What friend?"

Victoria thought fast. "Jean Reynolds. You remember her? We took etiquette class together a few years ago."

A smile of relief dawned on her mother's face. "Oh, yes," she breathed. "What a lovely young girl. But still, you should have told me where you were going. I worry so."

Victoria was not a liar. At least, she hadn't been a liar before meeting Rob Smith. "I—I did tell you. I mean, I left a note in the kitchen. Didn't you see it?"

Florence frowned again. "Oh," she said fretfully. "Oh, but I didn't go into the kitchen, how silly of me, I should have . . ."

Victoria felt a pang of guilt and shame. "I'm sorry, Mother. Next time I'll be sure you know when I'm going out." Just not with whom, she added silently.

Florence reached out and laid her hand briefly on her daughter's arm. "Yes, thank you. I'll be in my room."

Together mother and daughter entered the house; Victoria closed and locked the door behind them. She watched her mother negotiate the grand staircase to the second floor with what remnants of grace she still possessed. Tears pricked at Victoria's eyes. She loved her mother. She didn't like disobeying or lying to her.

Glumly, Victoria climbed the stairs to her own room. Quietly, she closed the door behind her and sank into the comfortable armchair in front of the window. The moon was so bright, so startlingly white. It seemed to pin her to the chair, forcefully exposing her cowardliness. She hated that she lacked the courage to rebel against her parents and their strictures, that she lacked the courage to speak her own mind. It wasn't fair to Rob. It was insulting. How long would he put up with her insistence they live their romance in secret? True, he had never said a harsh word or in any other way given her cause to think he was losing patience with her, but a guy like Rob could have any girl he wanted. It stood to reason that before long he would get bored and frustrated being with a girl who didn't have the guts to be seen in public with him, a girl who wouldn't even allow herself to go anywhere near the construction site behind her home when Rob was working there, afraid that a keen-eyed observer would guess her motive.

Victoria hugged herself. How she longed to be with Rob right then! Starting tomorrow, she would try to be brave like the heroines of the great stories she knew by heart, Juliet and Jane and even Hester Prynne. She would make sacrifices for the man she loved, she would take risks for him without thought to her own safety.

"Oh, Rob," she whispered to the harshly bright moon. "I do love you."

Chapter 9

"Rare for Deborah and medium for you, Arden, right?"

"You got it," she told him with a smile.

Gordon Richardson was sturdily built and of average height. He had bright blue eyes made all the more vivid in contrast to his still-dark hair. He was amicably divorced from his wife of eight years. There had been no children.

After making a packet in the world of tech, Gordon had retired at the age of fifty-three and come to Eliot's Corner in a conscious effort to simplify his life, to seek quiet, to be in a place where he could work on his sculpture. That was five years before and he had never regretted his decision. Once a year he flew to California to visit with old friends from his career days, and though he enjoyed the laughter and the reminiscing, as he told Arden, he was always glad to be home in Eliot's Corner.

Deborah was setting out napkins and silverware. "What a nice evening. The humidity is mostly gone. I hate running around town when it's so humid. It's hard to look professional when your clothes are sticking to you."

Deborah Norrell was as petite as Arden was tall, with auburn hair she wore in a stylish pixie cut. She dressed well even when off duty, less out of a keen interest in fashion and more out of habit.

"Why were you running around town?" Arden asked. "Though

I'm not really surprised that you were." Her friend was a real estate agent. In Arden's experience, real estate agents were rarely still.

Deborah sighed. "Dealing with the craziness of the Coyne property. If I can close this sale, I stand a good chance of being made partner, and, boy, do I want to be partner. But so far, everything that can go wrong has gone wrong. Well, almost."

"You've managed the unmanageable before," Arden pointed out. "I have faith in you."

"Thanks. But what I really need are the real estate gods to kick in with their support."

"Dinner's ready," Gordon announced. "At least, my contribution."

The women joined him at the table. In addition to the steaks, there was a salad, freshly baked corn bread, beer, and wine.

"You spoil us, Arden," Deborah said. "Always having us for dinner."

"I enjoy it," Arden said truthfully.

The friends tucked into the meal. Conversation was light, allowing Arden's thoughts to wander yet again to the teenage couple she had seen walking hand in hand a few days earlier. She hoped that Aria and Ben wouldn't join the ranks of star-crossed lovers, but there were so many reasons to think that they might. Their youth for one, and that they came from very different social circumstances. The latter shouldn't matter, but too often it did and—

Suddenly, Deborah cleared her throat. "I don't mean to alarm anyone, but there's a fuzzy beast staring at me from that window."

Arden looked toward the house. "Falstaff. Of course. He wants some of our steak."

"A little meat won't hurt him," Gordon added. "He is a carnivore after all."

Deborah frowned. "I guess. Still, that stare is unnerving."

"Lots lined up for the shop this summer, Arden?" Gordon asked.

"Thankfully, yes. Several readings, book-group activities, and we'll do a Fourth of July promotion like always."

"If I can be of any help," Gordon said, "carting around books, setting up podiums, just let me know."

"Hey, that reminds me," Deborah said. "Did you hear that

Clyde Jones, the guy who carts people's stuff to the dump among other things, broke his leg on the job?"

Arden dropped her fork. Young Ben's father. "Sorry," she said with a bright laugh. "Clumsy me."

Deborah shook her head. "Poor guy can't drive for a while, let alone do much of anything else, so his older sons are taking over for the duration."

"That family has had a run of bad luck," Gordon said. "Clyde's wife had breast cancer two years back. Luckily, she's okay, but things looked pretty bad for a time."

"They have a third son, too. He's still in high school. I hope he doesn't wind up dropping out like the oldest boy did. From what I hear, Ben's the one with the brains."

Arden lowered her eyes to her plate. Just like Rob had been "the one with the brains," his parents' pride and joy, the one who would be the first to graduate college. Except that he hadn't graduated from college. He hadn't done anything but gone missing.

But the summer of 1984 was so long ago, she reminded herself. The past was the past. It mattered, it did, but it was no more important than the present. Sometimes, it was hard to remember that.

"Um, is there dessert?" Deborah asked suddenly. "Sorry, you know my sweet tooth."

"Chocolate chocolate-chip, French-vanilla, and cherry-swirl ice cream," Arden announced, glad for the change of subject. "Take your pick."

Gordon rose from the table. "I'll bring everything out."

"You okay?" Deborah asked when he was gone. "You seem a little, I don't know, spacey this evening."

Arden smiled. "I'm fine. Really."

Chapter 10

At seven o'clock on the dot, Laura woke up with the determination to call the reporter, Leonard Tobin, who had covered the disappearance of Rob Smith in August 1984. Fine, she wasn't here in Port George to follow the trail of a missing boy. But what could it hurt to have a chat with someone who had known the town back in the day?

After two cups of coffee in the breakfast room of the Lilac Inn, Laura was not so sure. It seemed a good bet that she would be wasting her time talking to Mr. Tobin. But that was the addictive thing about research, Laura admitted as she ate the last bit of her cereal, the thrill of the hunt. If you followed lots of leads, both thin and thick, you might just find the answer to the questions you had been asking, and maybe the answers to a few questions you had never even considered asking. Everything was connected to everything if you had the creativity to find those connections.

Laura pushed away her empty cereal bowl. She would go through with her plan to call Leonard Tobin, but first she would conduct a quick search online. She opened her laptop and within minutes learned that Mr. Tobin wrote for a reputable online political magazine and had published two collections of essays on American popular culture. He seemed no longer to be a newspaper reporter and for all Laura knew might not be eager to revisit those days, but the worst he could tell her was that she could take her questions elsewhere.

Leonard Tobin's contact information included a phone number. Laura sent him a text, and a few minutes later he responded. He would be happy to meet with her that very morning if it was convenient for Laura. It was. He gave Laura directions to his house in the next town inland from Port George.

Forty-five minutes later, Laura parked her car outside a bungalow-style house with the bright orange door. "You can't miss it," Mr. Tobin had told her. "My neighbors wish that you could."

The doorbell was answered by a tall man about sixty years old. He was wearing faded jeans, sneakers, and a T-shirt printed with the classic peace sign first introduced back in the 1960s.

"Welcome!" he intoned, in the booming but pleasant voice of someone who likely was a valued member of the church choir. "Come in, come in!"

Laura followed him into the house. Glancing quickly at the piles of books on every available surface, the open laptop on a desk, and the loose papers scattered over the floor, she wondered how Leonard Tobin had gotten along with Mr. Meyer, if they had clashed, as editors and journalists were wont to do, if they had remained in touch over the years or avoided each other entirely.

Mr. Tobin led her to a screened-in back porch. A large shaggy dog of mixed breed looked up briefly, thumped his fat tail twice on the floorboards, and promptly lost interest in the visitor.

"That's Otto," Mr. Tobin explained. "He's eleven. Hence his lethargy. Have a seat."

Laura lowered herself into a fairly rickety old wooden chair. It fit with the rest of the decor, which, if Laura was pressed to give it a name, might be called Intellectual Mess.

"You said on the phone that you were interested in the Rob Smith case in relation to a podcast in production. Where does your funding come from?"

Laura swallowed. She could not forget that this guy was a savvy media professional, bound to spot holes in her story.

"Well, Mr. Tobin—"

"Please, call me Lenny."

"Lenny, then. Our funding is private. We're, um, pretty much independent so . . ."

Lenny smiled indulgently. Maybe he believed her. Maybe he didn't. "So, what do you want to know?"

Laura smiled. "Everything?"

"Here goes. I was a cub reporter back in 1984, eager to make my mark with a big story, and big stories don't come along here in our neck of the woods like they do in a city. You're lucky if once every three or four years there's a home break-in or a fight outside a bar."

"And then Rob Smith went missing."

Lenny nodded. "Don't get me wrong, I wasn't glad the guy was gone, I knew him by sight, small towns you know, but I was glad for a chance to prove myself. I scrambled from family members to coworkers to kids he'd gone to high school with and pestered the police for details of their investigation. I watched and listened. And everything I learned, I wrote down as best I could."

"Yes. I read every bit of coverage in the *Port George Daily Chronicle*. Was the story picked up by other news sources? The Portland or Augusta papers maybe?"

Lenny shook his head. "No. They weren't interested. After all, there was no sign of foul play."

No sensationalism, no interest. Sad. "Did Rob Smith have a girlfriend?" Port George was a small town. Lenny had said so. There was a good chance Laura's mother, whoever she was, had known Rob Smith, if not personally then by sight. But if she *had* known the boy, what did it matter?

"Not that I ever knew of. No one I interviewed mentioned a girlfriend, and I did ask."

"The police investigation was thorough?"

"For a time, yeah. The police talked to everyone I had talked to, and more. Friends, family, coworkers, people at the community college. Searches were made of the wooded areas. Wells were looked into and ponds were drained." Lenny raised an eyebrow. "Herbert Aldridge, one of the bigwigs in town, even allowed the police to drain the pond on his property."

Laura recognized the name; she had seen it several times in her search through the newspapers in Mr. Meyer's archive, but she hadn't paid much attention to it. Well, she thought, this Herbert Aldridge, whoever he was, *would* allow the draining of the pond if he knew full well that Rob Smith's body—assuming he was dead— would not be found there. "Did the police search all of the Aldridge property?"

Lenny frowned. "Not as far as I know. There didn't seem to be a reason why they should, though I can't see how it would have hurt. The boy was working there as part of a construction crew; the Aldridges were having a swimming pool built. Anyway, after about six weeks, when no body was found, the case went quiet. No one had even been arrested on suspicion of foul play. It was as if Rob Smith had vanished into thin air."

Laura leaned forward a little. "Off the record, what do you think happened?"

"I think there was foul play behind the disappearance. And I think that things were hushed up," Lenny replied promptly. "A conspiracy of silence. I doubt I'm the only one who suspected as much. There are powerful people in Port George, always were. Maybe Rob Smith got in the way of one of them and paid the price."

"What exactly do you mean by powerful people?"

Lenny shifted in his chair. "People with money and influence, people like Herbert Aldridge. It's the same story everywhere. An old boy network. Intimidation used to keep people in line. I re- member one guy even lost his business because he knew some- thing he shouldn't have and threatened to talk."

"It sounds like a mob culture. That bad?"

Lenny shrugged. "I can't prove any of that, mind you. But it's pretty common knowledge."

Small towns, Laura thought. Not always what they appeared to be. "Does Herbert Aldridge still live in Port George?"

"Yup. He and his wife, Florence, are still at the big house on Old Orchard Hill. Not that they get around much these days. Word is that he's got a terminal illness and that Florence, never very strong-minded, is completely mad." Lenny smiled a bit. "Some even say she's been dead for the past ten years or so. But people with nothing better to do will make up the craziest stories."

Laura nodded. That was true enough.

"One more thing," Lenny went on. "About ten years after young Rob disappeared, his family had him officially declared dead. It called up the whole thing for me, and for a lot of people in Port George. Suddenly, it was like Rob had disappeared the day before. I covered the memorial service for the paper, and Ed ran that, but the background I'd written, about the disappearance all those years ago, the very reason for the memorial, was edited down to a line or two of just the facts."

"That is interesting. Do you think Mr. Meyer was prevented from running your entire article?"

"I'd hate to think badly of old Ed, but maybe he was intimidated into keeping the memorial low-key so as not to stir up interest in the case again. Ed Meyer ruffled more than a few feathers in the course of his career. Which means he might have had to pay the price now and again." Lenny smiled ruefully. "But that's all guesswork."

Sometimes guesswork was all a researcher or a reporter had to go on, Laura thought. That and gut instinct.

"Thank you for your time," Laura said. "I really appreciate your kindness."

With a slight groan, Lenny rose from his chair. "Like Otto"—he smiled—"I'm not as young as I used to be."

Lenny led her back to the front of the house and opened the door. "Let me know if there's any way I can help going forward."

"I will, thanks."

Laura headed back to Port George, her mind puzzling over all that Lenny Tobin had shared with her. On the surface, none of it had anything to do with an unnamed pregnant teenage girl. Still, Rob Smith's disappearance in the summer of 1984 was the only event of note she had discovered thus far. She would continue on his trail for a little while longer. What could it hurt?

When Laura reached Port George, she headed directly for City Hall. It was located on Main Street—no surprise there—and was a modest building compared to the library. A clerk directed her to a bank of computers, at which she was able to look up the declaration of "dead in absentia" for Rob Smith. What a strange concept, Laura thought. Dead because we don't know that you aren't.

It didn't take long to learn that the lawyer who handled the paperwork for the Smith family was Theodore Coldwell. Laura made a note of this in her notebook and logged out. On her way out of the building, she stopped to ask the clerk who had helped her earlier if he knew anything about Mr. Coldwell, specifically, if he was still practicing. He was. Mr. Coldwell, the clerk told her, had an office and a house in town. Then the clerk helpfully gave Laura the lawyer's phone number.

Laura thanked the clerk and left the building, momentarily blinded by the afternoon sun. She wondered what Mr. Coldwell could tell her about Rob Smith's disappearance. Maybe nothing more than Lenny Tobin had been able to tell her. But she had come to Port George to find the truth. If she made a nuisance of herself along the way, so be it. She would call Mr. Coldwell's office and ask for an appointment. What was the worst that could happen?

The phone was answered by a young woman with a singsong voice. Laura recited her podcast story. It was getting easier to lie. Not necessarily a good thing.

She waited a long moment while the young woman spoke to her boss.

"He can give you a few minutes tomorrow at ten a.m.," she said crisply when she returned to the phone. No more singsong voice.

Laura thanked her and ended the call. Clearly, Mr. Coldwell wasn't thrilled about meeting with Laura Huntington, one of those newfangled podcast people, but something had made him agree, and possibly it wasn't just politeness.

Suddenly, Laura realized that she was starving. She would treat herself to a decent meal in town. She had walked along Main Street for only a few yards when she came upon a small café. A handwritten sign in the window announced that the daily special was a platter of fish and chips. Laura realized she had never had fish and chips in her entire life. How had that happened? It suddenly seemed imperative to settle down with a meal of fried food, and maybe even to follow it with a rich dessert. Something chocolate.

With a growling stomach, Laura pushed open the door of the little restaurant and went inside.

Chapter 11

"We should charge admission to these events," Brent said, looking significantly at the old round-faced clock on the wall behind the counter. "What do people take us for, a nightclub?"

"Who knew a reading by a local poet would pack the house?" Arden smiled. "You know people are always reluctant to leave after a reading."

"Yeah. Because of the free wine and cheese."

"Or the air of warm conviviality."

"Harrumph." Brent was already heading off to retrieve a crumpled paper napkin that had found its way onto the floor.

Arden was pleased. The summer interns, Zach and Elly, had done a fine job of setting up chairs and the old wooden podium Margery had found at an auction an age ago; after the reading, while Sybella signed copies of her book, Zach wrote receipts, took money, and made change. Elly transported the unsold signed copies to a special display that would remain in place through the end of the summer.

"Sybella sold five copies of her book," Arden said to Deborah as her friend joined her, plastic cup of wine in hand. "I'm happy for her. I think she's got real talent."

"I think it's wonderful you give self-published writers a venue in which to hawk their wares."

"I wouldn't put it quite that way."

Deborah waved her hand dismissively. "You know what I mean. It's wonderful you support writers the way you do. There's no way people like Sybella can make back the money they spent on getting their work into print. I bet some unscrupulous store owners would demand a cut of any sale made."

Gordon joined them; he was one of the people who had bought a copy of Sybella's book. "I don't think independent bookshop owners are unscrupulous as a lot. Though they are required to be savvy about making a living."

"I'll say. If Margery hadn't taught me all she knew, I'd have lost the business several times before now."

"To Margery!" Deborah raised her cup in a salute.

"I can't find my mommy!"

The wail of distress had come from a little girl of about five, standing alone in the middle of the shop. Immediately, Arden felt the nasty sting of panic. She had seen the girl's mother only a few minutes earlier, but now she was nowhere in sight. She couldn't have gone off and left her child behind. Could she have? Who would do such a thing, abandon a helpless, defenseless little girl in such a cruel and . . . Arden realized her heart was beating too quickly and a cold sweat was pouring down her chest. She felt frozen to the spot, unable to approach the child, to offer help, to open her mouth to scream.

Then Gordon was kneeling at the little girl's side, speaking in a quiet and comforting tone. Though Arden couldn't hear what exactly he was saying, his message seemed to soothe her. She stopped crying and nodded solemnly.

"Gaby!"

"Mommy!"

The child's mother was dashing toward her daughter. Gordon stepped back as the child launched herself into her mother's arms. "I went to the ladies' room," the woman explained in a rush. "I told her to stand just outside the door. I didn't think she would wander off. I'm so grateful to you. Thank you."

"This is a safe space," Gordon said firmly. "Nothing bad would have happened to her here."

Holding her daughter in her arms, the woman left the shop.

Suddenly, Arden realized that she could move and quickly turned away from the others. Tears were pricking her eyes and she still felt a deep unease disproportionate to the actual event. Nothing terrible had happened. What was wrong with her lately? She had been thrown into fierce nostalgia by the sight of Aria and Ben the other afternoon, and now this scared child had excited a dreadful jumble of emotions, including guilt and shame.

With effort, Arden took a deep breath. It was no big surprise that she should be so hypersensitive. Summer was always a difficult season for her. Still, it had been a long time since two incidents in the space of as many weeks had elicited such a deeply emotional response.

"You okay?" Deborah asked. "That poor little thing. I was really worried for a moment."

Arden turned and smiled. "I'm fine, just tired. I think I'll go to bed the moment I get home."

Deborah frowned. "I haven't been able to sleep well with this sale hanging over my head. I just have to make it happen."

"Don't knock yourself out in the process. I know it's important, but is it really worth your health?"

"Maybe. No. Oh, I don't know." Deborah smiled as Gordon rejoined them, broom in hand. "Here's the hero of the hour."

"I didn't do anything special," he demurred. "Anyway, Brent had to dash so I told him I'd sweep up the crumbs."

"Well, as long as you have everything in hand," Deborah said, "I'll head home."

Deborah's leaving precipitated the exit of the final two guests, and then the shop was empty but for Arden and Gordon. Arden cleared up the business end of the evening while Gordon stowed the broom and dustpan. She badly wanted to ask him what he had said to the child to make her stop crying. Would it embarrass him if she did? He had dismissed Deborah's praise so definitively. She wished she could tell him what the incident had done to her, how it had made her feel, but that was impossible. That would come too close to the truth of the past, that other country from which she had fled.

"Ready to go?" Gordon asked. His copy of Sybella's book peeked out from the pocket of his cotton jacket.

Arden smiled and came out from behind the counter, keys to the shop in hand. "Yes. Thank you for being such a great help this evening. I really appreciate it."

"My pleasure. Besides, that jalapeño cheddar was awesome."

Chapter 12

Laura looked up at the narrow, redbrick building in which Ted Coldwell had his office. It was tucked between a hardware store, the good old-fashioned kind with a gumball machine for the kids accompanying their parents on a quest for a packet of bolts or screws, and a women's clothing shop called The Top Shelf. If the name alone weren't enough clue as to the shop's pretentions, Laura thought, holding back a smile, the items displayed in the window would confirm them. Who in Port George could possibly have need of a sequined cocktail dress?

Mr. Coldwell's office was one of two on the third floor. Laura opened the door to find who she assumed was the young woman who had answered the phone the day before. Her self-important air virtually smacked you in the face. Laura half admired the kid. She couldn't be more than twenty and yet she held herself with the self-assurance of a seasoned thirty-five-year-old professional. She probably shopped at The Top Shelf for her evening wear.

Laura announced herself. She noted a brass nameplate on the desk.

"I'll let Mr. Coldwell know you're here," Nadine West told her blandly.

Laura had to wait for only a moment before she was ushered

into Mr. Coldwell's office. He greeted her cordially but without a smile. He was a tall, broad-shouldered, handsome man of the William Holden mold, Laura thought. Masculine but not rough. He was wearing a good, sober suit with a patterned tie that hinted at a warmer, more relaxed personality after hours. He sat at his desk only after Laura had taken her own seat.

"How can I be of help?"

Laura, wondering how many times he had asked that question through the years, conquered her nervousness. "As I explained to Ms. West yesterday, and as I expect she told you, I'm researching a podcast about people from small towns who went missing and how their disappearance affected their communities."

Mr. Coldwell nodded slightly. His expression revealed nothing.

Boldly Laura went on. "I've been reading through copies of the local paper—the librarian pointed me to Edward Meyer, the former editor, and he gave me access to his archive—and I've also spoken to Lenny Tobin, a former reporter for the *Daily Chronicle*, and I'm intrigued by the story of Rob Smith's disappearance. I saw in the county courthouse that you helped his family have him declared dead in absentia."

Mr. Coldwell's expression took on a wariness. "Yes."

Laura pressed on. "I found it interesting there was no mention of a girlfriend in the articles Lenny Tobin wrote while the search for Rob was taking place."

"Why would that be interesting?" Mr. Coldwell asked neutrally.

"Because supposedly Rob Smith was well-liked by the entire population of Port George. It stands to reason he'd have a girlfriend and that any reporter worth his or her salt would have interviewed her along with Rob's friends and family."

Mr. Coldwell was silent for a long moment, long enough for Laura to wonder if she was going to be tossed out on her ear.

Finally, he looked Laura squarely in the eye and said, "I believe that Rob Smith was seeing a family friend of mine. Their relationship wasn't public, but some people knew in the way that they know things in small towns."

"Why wasn't the relationship public?" Laura asked, intrigued.

Mr. Coldwell cleared his throat. "Because the girl's parents would have found Rob unsuitable for their daughter. Her father was an investment banker. The boy's father drove a truck."

Good old-fashioned social snobbery, Laura thought. "What was the girl's name?"

Mr. Coldwell hesitated a moment, as if debating whether he would answer Laura's question. "Victoria Aldridge," he said finally, almost begrudgingly. "Her parents were Herbert and Florence Aldridge."

Herbert Aldridge. Lenny Tobin had talked about the man. "Does this Victoria Aldridge still live in Port George?"

"No. She left a long time ago."

"Do you know where she is now?"

"I have no idea." Mr. Coldwell's tone had become flat and dismissive. Abruptly he stood. "I've given you all the time I can give. I'm afraid this interview is over."

Laura stood. She knew better than to attempt another question. "Thank you. I can see myself out."

Deep in thought, Laura walked back to the Lilac Inn. The meeting with Mr. Coldwell had unsettled her. He had been both reticent and forthcoming, an odd combination of behavior, one she hadn't expected from someone who had been practicing law for so long. Could he have had something to do with the disappearance of Rob Smith? Or maybe . . . He was of the right age. Could Ted Coldwell be her biological father? Pretending to help her while leading her away from the truth? Because the last thing a respected lawyer would want was the sudden revelation of a love child.

Laura almost laughed out loud. Ted Coldwell. Victoria Aldridge. Herbert Aldridge. Rob Smith. You could go crazy making up stories featuring people about whom you knew virtually nothing. How did novelists do it? she wondered. All that conjuring stories out of thin air. She would stick to academic work. It seemed a breeze in comparison.

Chapter 13

Arden found Elly in the used-book section, her head bent over a copy of *My Love Affair with Jewelry*, a largely photographic volume about Elizabeth Taylor's beloved treasures.

"Elly?"

The young woman closed the book with obvious reluctance. "Someday," she said firmly, "I am so going to have a diamond ring as big as the ones Elizabeth Taylor got from Mike Todd and Richard Burton. And I'm going to go on vacation to big resorts on an island in the Pacific, and I'm going to have one of those really cool old cars, you know, like a Rolls-Royce or something, with a chauffeur to drive me around."

Arden smiled briefly. She refrained from asking just how Elly expected to afford such luxuries. She had no desire to burst her teenage bubble. And for all Arden knew, one day Elly would achieve her desires. Not that things were the real treasures in and of themselves; experiences were worth far more. But things didn't necessarily hurt.

"I think that the dusting is calling your name."

"Oh, sure!" Elly shoved the book back onto the shelf and dashed off.

Not for the first time did Arden wonder if Elly had given college any serious consideration. Elly was intelligent. She was a voracious reader with an amazingly retentive memory. But that didn't necessarily mean she was cut out for the academic demands of college. Some people were able to use their gifts to the full without the usual formal schooling. Maybe Elly would prove to be one of those rare types.

And, Arden supposed, she herself had been able to muster her talents without a degree. Not that at the age of seventeen she would ever have imagined such a possibility. No, at the age of seventeen she had been poised to attend Blake College, the school her parents had chosen for her. For the next four years, she would work hard and win enough academic awards to make her parents proud. Shortly after graduation she would marry a sober, steady, slightly older professional man. She would have children. It was what her parents had wanted for her since the day she was born.

Suddenly, Arden recalled a conversation with a classmate at Wilder Academy. Her name was Kathy or Katie; Arden had forgotten her last name entirely. Katie—that sounded right—was a scholarship girl, one of a handful of students from Port George and the surrounding towns whose parents couldn't afford the pricey tuition of Wilder Academy but who showed a degree of academic prowess. What had Katie looked like? Short? Well, every girl at Wilder Academy had been short compared to Victoria Aldridge.

"Did you get into your first choice?" Katie had asked one afternoon after classes had ended.

Arden hadn't bothered to explain that she had only applied to one college, and that it had been selected by her parents. "Yes."

"Radical. I'm not going on to college after all. It's okay. I never really wanted to anyway. My father is kind of bummed, though I can't figure out why. He's always thought I was kind of a ditz. My mother doesn't care what I do as long as I move out and pay my own way. I'm stoked to start working. And no more homework!"

Arden hadn't known quite how to respond. She had envied Katie. Arden wasn't allowed to make up her own mind about things. It wasn't cool that Katie's mother wanted her out of the house, but then again, maybe that was normal. Maybe it was right that parents should encourage their children to be independent. Maybe it wasn't right for parents to dictate their children's futures.

Before Arden could reply, another classmate, a guy whose blue hair was teased into a faux Mohawk and who mistakenly thought wearing black eyeliner was doing him a favor, came bouncing out of the building.

"Hey, girls," he shouted. "Either of you wanna do the nasty with me this weekend?"

Arden had blushed. Katie had rolled her eyes and called back, "Eat shit and die, Ralph. With a dickhead like you?"

Ralph had just laughed and bounded off.

A loud crash from the other end of the shop returned Arden to the twenty-first century.

"Sorry!" Elly yelled. "My bad!" A moment later she appeared, face flushed. "I knocked over that display rack up front but it's okay. No harm done."

"As long as you're not hurt."

"Nope." Off Elly went, feather duster in hand, to tackle another bit of the shop.

It could be heartbreaking to be around the young, Arden thought. They were so sure of so many things and, still, so terribly vulnerable, not yet made wise and toughened by experience. Life would inflict a beating on Elly—no one got out entirely unscathed; Arden was sure Katie had had her share of pain—but it could also bring Elly great joy, the kind of joy that had little or nothing to do with baubles and everything to do with peace of mind and emotional fulfillment. Maybe Elly would marry. Maybe she would have children. Maybe she would do neither. It didn't matter, as long as she lived her own, authentic life.

And how many people, Arden wondered, could say they were doing just that?

Chapter 14

Lenny Tobin had mentioned to Laura that Mr. and Mrs. Aldridge lived at the top of Old Orchard Hill, as they had done for close to sixty years. In one of the articles written at the time of Rob's disappearance, Laura had noted that the Smiths resided on Fern Pond Road, in a working-class section of town. It hadn't been difficult to learn that Mr. and Mrs. Smith lived there still.

That morning, Laura had decided to take a considered look at each house. What might they tell her about the two families? Certainly nothing that might provide a hard-and-fast clue as to the identity of her mother. But what could be the harm? Asking questions, following hunches, visiting sites of historical interest—it was all in a day's work for a researcher.

First, Laura drove to Fern Pond Road. She found the Smith family's home easily; their name was painted on the mailbox in large black letters. Laura stopped the car but kept the engine idling. The house seemed a small one in which to raise four children. Rob, as the only boy, had probably had his own bedroom, and possibly his older sister had had her own room, too, but the two younger sisters might have shared a bedroom. Laura wondered if the siblings had quarreled about that, the younger girls claiming it was unfair that Frannie and Rob were given special treatment. Laura shook her head. Making up stories again.

She could see there was property behind the house; once, it might have been home to a swing set or a plastic slide. A chimney indicated the presence of a fireplace. Lacy curtains on the windows were visible from the street. A wreath of dried flowers and herbs hung on the front door. Outside the small garage was parked a Subaru wagon that had seen better days.

The Smiths' residence was unremarkable, but from what Laura had been able to glean from Lenny Tobin's interviews with the family, it had been a happy home until Rob had gone missing. A wave of sadness flowed through Laura as she continued on past the house. It didn't feel right to loiter outside a home that had seen so much grief.

The Aldridge home was located on the other side of Port George, and it took Laura a full fifteen minutes to make the journey. What connected these two families—if anything—other than that a long time ago the daughter of the wealthy family had possibly been in a secret romantic relationship with the son of the poor family? A classic Romeo-and-Juliet plot, ending, of course, in disaster, at least for the hapless boy.

If Rob Smith's disappearance had had anything to do with his purported relationship with Victoria Aldridge. Laura reminded herself to be careful about making assumptions. Her habit of romanticizing had gotten her into trouble in the past. Her disastrous marriage was proof enough of that.

Suddenly, Laura realized that within the length of two or three streets the scenery had become vastly different. Here, the houses were larger and more ornate than the ones to be found in the other neighborhoods through which Laura had passed. Every house had a garage big enough for two or three vehicles. The cars that were parked in the driveways were new. Laura spotted a Mercedes, a Lexus, a Porsche. The land on which the houses sat was significant. She passed two trucks belonging to landscaping companies. People here didn't mow their own lawns or remove dead tree branches from their property. They had the money to call a professional to perform those chores.

Finally, Laura turned onto Old Orchard Hill. It was more of a gentle slope than a hill, and the apple trees that lined the way didn't look healthy. Not that Laura knew all that much about agriculture, but she could tell a healthy tree from a damaged tree and a McIntosh apple from a Cortland.

At the zenith, Laura parked and stared up at the house in which Ted Coldwell's friend Victoria had grown up. Although large and imposing, and in spite of the grand staircase that led up to the large double entry doors, Laura thought the house had a generally rundown look about it, as if it had been ignored for too long. As if it was unloved. The house was set back a considerable distance from the road. The property was surrounded by a tall iron fence with a formidable gate, though Laura noted that the gate wasn't quite shut. Maybe the lock was broken. Maybe nobody cared enough to keep it secure. Between the house and the gate was an expanse of slightly overgrown lawn. From the road, Laura couldn't see the garage or any other features that might be part of the estate, a greenhouse maybe, or flower gardens. Or the pool the Aldridge family had had built in the summer of 1984.

Was it possible, Laura wondered, sitting behind the wheel of her car, looking at that forbidding iron gate, that she, Laura Huntington, was the link between the Smiths of Fern Pond Road and the Aldridges of Old Orchard Hill?

She groaned. She was doing it again, creating silly fantasies. Laura started the car and turned back down Old Orchard Hill. Common sense told her that it would be far too neat and easy that the first age-appropriate female mentioned to her since she came to Port George should turn out to be the person for whom she was searching. So, of what value had this little excursion been? None.

Deciding that she needed a moment or more to calm her overheated brain, Laura set out for the coast. Twenty minutes later she came to a beach. It wasn't at all like the few she had seen on her journey north to Port George, like the beaches in Wells and Ogunquit. Here, rocks were layered thickly on the narrow strip of sand, making walking downright precarious. Laura wondered if the high tide had brought the rocks with it. She knew little about beach environments and how they worked. The coming and going of tides, the relevance and fragility of dunes, the types of seaweed and their uses, crabs, clams, and starfish, the busy life of tidal pools—all were largely a mystery. Maybe if she had grown up by the sea, she would have an intimate knowledge of coastal ecosystems, but she hadn't.

Oddly, Laura's ignorance made her feel somewhat lonely. That and the fact that as far as she could tell, she was the only human in sight. If she cried out for help, who would hear her? But why should she need to cry out for help? Why was she so acutely aware of her vulnerability in the world, of her aloneness? Why—

Suddenly, Laura whirled around. There was still no one in sight. The air was still; there was no breeze that might have gently caressed the bare skin of her arm. But something *had* touched her. Something or someone. Laura would swear to it. It had felt like a hand, a warm human hand, gentle, reassuring, and, strangely, somehow familiar. Could the touch have been her mother's, not her birth mother's (whoever that was), but the touch of the woman who had raised her so lovingly, the woman who had set her on this journey? Her mother watching over her? It was possible. But Laura couldn't say for sure.

What she did know was that whoever had made such a personal connection meant her no harm. None at all.

"Thank you," she whispered.

No one whispered back.

Chapter 15

"Pale ribbons of sand," a voice whispered. "Dim and murmuring sea."

The sky was the sickly yellow-gray that presages a thunderstorm. All else was drained of color, pale and lifeless. Her hands looked like the flesh of fish.

She could hear the dim and murmuring sea but it was far, far away.

A figure neither male nor female but also both and also possibly not quite human was moving toward her but not making any progress. What might have been its head was bent forward as if fighting against stiff winds.

But there was no wind. The air was still.

She realized now that she couldn't move. She wanted to run away from the dark, enigmatic figure that was coming relentlessly toward her but not. But coming. Coming.

Then a sudden lurid glare of light seemed to come from everywhere and nowhere, and hands with flesh like the flesh of fish covered her eyes. She tried to scream but no sound came from her throat but the—

Finally, with a cry that sounded even to her own ears like that of a terrified child, Arden shot up in her bed to find the cats circling her protectively.

"It's all right," she assured them with a shaky voice. "Mommy is all right."

It was just a dream. Just a horrible dream. If only she could understand it, discern the identity of that strange figure that had been coming for her . . .

Suddenly, Arden laughed out loud. Of course. Only weeks ago, she had reread the classic M. R. James ghost story "Oh, Whistle, and I'll Come to You, My Lad." Her brain had simply borrowed material from the terrifying waking dream the hero experienced in his hotel room after having found the ancient whistle on the beach.

Who is this who is coming?

Still, the dream had to mean something more than just a replay of the old story. It had to mean something unique to her, Arden Bell. And the most obvious meaning the dream seemed to suggest was that someone might be coming for her. Her parents? They had enough money to hire a private investigator, but after all these years why would they care to locate their daughter? To make amends before dying? No. Arden just couldn't believe her parents were capable of caring enough about the state of their eternal souls to atone now for their ancient sins. If they hadn't searched for her back when she had run off at the age of eighteen, they would not search for her now.

Arden rubbed her eyes. It was already close to four o'clock. There seemed little point in trying to get back to sleep for a mere two hours, considering the energy it would take to calm her mind and relax her body. Arden threw back the covers and got out of bed. Immediately, three cats began to crash their heads into her calves and weave their furry bodies around her legs.

"You're in luck," Arden told them as she put on her summer robe. "Breakfast time comes early today."

Chapter 16

A sign over the counter announced that the North Star had been in business since 1952. The design of its logo, the image of a radiating star, testified to its being a classic midcentury diner. A fair number of the floor tiles were missing; others were degraded; but the floor was clean. Most of the red Formica tabletops were chipped, and every one of the red leather seats on the stools at the counter was cracked, the fissures covered with silver duct tape. The banquette seats were similarly worn, but not a stray speck of food or spilled liquid was on any surface. The mirror over the grill was remarkably clean, given its proximity to grease splatters.

The hostess showed Laura to a table near the back of the diner, a perfect spot from which to observe the other customers. Within moments a smiling waitress was at her side. The waitress, Laura guessed, was in her mid to late fifties, about the same age as Laura's mother would be if she was still alive. She was a small woman, barely five foot, and wiry. Her eyes were pretty, a vivid green, and they drew attention away from the fact that the rest of her face was unremarkable. Her hair was badly dyed, probably with an at-home kit. Laura knew the look; she had suffered her own hair-coloring disasters.

"I haven't seen you in Port George before," the waitress said as she poured Laura a cup of steaming-hot coffee. "Visiting?"

Laura smiled and prepared, once again, to lie. "Yes, in a way. I'm doing research for a podcast. Basically, it's about people who go missing and how it affects their community."

The waitress put her free hand on her hip. "Is that right?" Her green eyes were wide with interest. "Nothing exciting ever happens around here, not usually anyway. And we rarely get interesting people visiting."

"At least you're not overrun by tourists in the summer months," Laura commented, though she wasn't sure that was a good thing. Tourists meant business. Business meant people could pay their bills.

The waitress shrugged. "I guess. My friend Kari lives down in Portland and she says you can't even walk down some streets in summer for all the people who come to shop and eat lobster. Anyway, what'll you have? Our blueberry pancakes are the best for miles around."

"Then that's what I'll have."

A few minutes later the waitress returned with Laura's meal. The plate was piled with three massive pancakes bursting with purplish blueberries. Laura hadn't eaten so large a breakfast since she was in college, when most Sunday mornings she and her roommates would go to the diner just off campus for a complete pig-out.

"Now, eat them while they're hot," the waitress advised. "Though frankly, I've had them cold and they're almost just as good."

Laura picked up her fork. She hadn't planned on asking about the Rob Smith case when she walked through the door of the diner—she had just wanted a good breakfast—but the waitress seemed inclined to chat so . . . "I don't suppose you remember Rob Smith?" she asked casually. "He was a teen in the mideighties. I'm asking in relation to my research."

The waitress, who now introduced herself as Kathy Murdoch, nodded. "I was born and raised in this town. Of course, I remember him, though I have to admit I haven't thought about him in ages. All that chaos when Rob went missing. His poor family. Every girl in town wanted to be Rob's girlfriend, and all the guys wanted to be his friend. He was one of those naturally popular types, no big ego but always everyone's favorite. It's a terrible shame what happened to him." Kathy paused. "Whatever it was."

"What about Victoria Aldridge? She was about Rob Smith's age. Did you know her?"

"I was in her class. I was a scholarship student at the Wilder Academy. I had a bit of a brain in those days, or I fooled someone into thinking I did. Victoria, though, she was the real deal, supersmart. I didn't know her well, but she always said hello when we met." Kathy shrugged. "Anyway, after high school, Victoria went on to some fancy private college. I think she came back once, but then she went away again, who knows where, while the rest of us—most of us, anyway—stayed right here and got on with life in Port George."

Ted Coldwell, too, had mentioned that Victoria Aldridge had not been back to Port George in a long time. It might be how Victoria was best remembered these days, by her absence. "You said you didn't know her well. Did she have close friends?"

Kathy frowned. "No, not really, though she got along with people all right. I think she was pretty shy. And her parents were rich. Her father did something in banking I think. I don't think they liked their daughter spending a lot of time with the locals, not the ones of us who weren't in their social set."

This bit of information, too, jibed with what Ted Coldwell had told Laura. "Do you know anyone I might talk to who could shed some light on Victoria?"

Suddenly Kathy frowned. "Wait a minute. Victoria didn't go missing, Rob did. Why do you want to know about her?"

Laura thought fast. "Well, when we're crafting a story, we ask all sorts of questions about all sorts of things that might seem irrelevant but which sometimes turn out to be important. We don't want to miss any, you know, er, angles." Laura managed a smile. She hoped Kathy bought her pathetic reply.

It seems that Kathy did. Her smile returned. "I get it," she said brightly. "And now that I think about it, my younger sister, Sarah, was good friends with one of the Smith girls, I can't remember which one, but she told me that Victoria had visited the Smith house once or twice with Rob. Why would Victoria have been there if she wasn't his girlfriend?"

Laura could think of a few reasons—for one, they might have been on a community youth group committee together. Still, it was another sort of confirmation that Rob Smith and Victoria Aldridge were an item or, at the least, knew one another as friends. It still meant nothing.

"I have to say it's a thrill to be talking to a real live journalist," Kathy went on. "You asked if I knew anyone who could shed light on Victoria before she went away. Well, you could talk to Renee Wilson. She and Victoria went to the same Catholic grammar school." Kathy smiled. "Like me, Renee never left Port George, but unlike me she doesn't have to wait tables for a living. She married some guy with his own accounting firm, and from what I hear she pretty much shops for a living." Kathy paused. "Not that there are many places around here to spend money. She probably buys a lot on-line."

Laura made a note, first asking if Wilson was Renee's married name. It was.

"And Jack McDonald. You could talk to him. He had a land-scaping company; in fact, his son runs it now. Anyway, I'm pretty sure Jack senior had the Aldridge account at one point. He was an okay guy. Funny, though. I haven't heard anything about him in years."

"What do you think Mr. McDonald could tell me about Victoria?" Laura asked dubiously.

Kathy frowned. "Hmm. You're right, that's a long shot. But his son, Jack junior, would have known Rob pretty well. They were the same age."

"Anyone else?"

"You'll definitely have better luck with our high school English teacher, Miss Thompson. She was close to Victoria, like a mentor or something. Tell her Kathy Murdoch sent you. Just remember that it's Miss, not Ms. or Mrs. She was always a stickler about that."

Laura promised that she would remember. "One last question if you don't mind. What did Victoria Aldridge look like?"

"Like a Viking princess, all that pretty blond hair and those bright blue eyes. And she was tall, too, like she could have been a model." Kathy laughed. "If she wasn't so nice, I might have hated her!"

Though Laura knew that not every daughter looked like her mother, she felt a teeny bit let down. She was not tall or blond. Nor did she have blue eyes, bright or otherwise. And why should this Victoria Aldridge be her birth mother, anyway? Victoria couldn't have been the only teenage girl in this small town who could have gotten pregnant in the summer of 1984.

"Nothing like me, then."

"You're pretty enough. Now, get on and eat your breakfast!" Kathy scolded good-naturedly before hurrying off to serve another customer.

Chapter 17

The cats had been fed, their water bowls refreshed, and their litter boxes cleaned. Arden had eaten breakfast; showered; and dressed. Her bag was packed for work.

Yet all she wanted to do was go back to bed. Ever since the strange dream the other night she had felt tired and out of sorts. The sense of being pursued had translated itself into her waking life, appearing at the oddest, most ordinary moments—while she was crossing the street to grab a coffee at Chez Claudine; reshelving books a customer had misplaced; even loading the dishwasher after dinner. If only she knew exactly what that ambiguous figure wanted from her.

Who it was. What it was.

Arden sank into a chair at the kitchen table. No matter how you tried to put the past behind you, it was never entirely gone. The past might be another country to which you could never return, but it was still right there on the map, stuck with pins to mark the location of the life-changing moments.

Like the summer of 1985. The summer she had finally escaped from her parents—the pursuing figure in her dream?—and from Port George.

So long ago! Arden had almost forgotten what her parents looked like, not the broad outlines but the details. How tall was her mother, exactly? Had her father's hair begun to turn gray before she left home? Her parents would have changed over the years, maybe drastically, but Arden felt sure she would recognize them. Of course, she would. They were her flesh and blood.

The better question might be, would Florence and Herbert Aldridge recognize their only surviving child? Would they want to?

Gently, Arden touched the silver charm that hung around her neck, one of a very few items from her past in Port George she had managed to hold on to through the years. Of course, along with the charm, she had succeeded in keeping her precious copy of *Villette*, the gift Rob had given to her on her eighteenth birthday.

There had been a scary incident once, many years before, when she had been working in the bakery department of a large grocery chain. She had brought the book to work with her, intending to read during her lunch break. Needing to use the ladies' room, she had gone off, carelessly leaving the book next to her half-eaten sandwich. When she returned only moments later, the book was gone. Arden remembered all too clearly the sense of panic that had overcome her, her heart racing, an acid taste rising in her throat.

Then a coworker appeared, holding the book in her hand. "I figured you wouldn't mind if I gave it a quick look," she said with a smile. "It's pretty old, huh?"

Arden had resisted the urge to yank the book from the other woman's hands. Still, her coworker had caught on to the depth of Arden's distress pretty quickly.

"Sheesh," the woman said with a frown, extending the book to Arden. "Excuse me for living. Take your stupid book."

After that incident, the book never left a locked apartment. Arden had even kept its existence a secret from Margery, her beloved friend and mentor, wary of questions she could not and would not answer. Where had she come by the book? Had someone given it to her? Why was it so special?

And who *was* Arden Bell, really?

It had been fifteen years since Arden had fetched up in Eliot's Corner and seen the hand-lettered sign in the window of Arden Forest: ASSISTANT WANTED. She had applied for the job the very next day, after concocting a personal backstory to go along with her generally unimpressive résumé.

She had been born in Ohio, she said. She had been orphaned when only a baby and sent to live with a much-older aunt and uncle who lived in a tiny town in upstate New York. They were not happy to become caretakers of a child and did the bare minimum—provided a roof over her head, clothes to wear, food to eat. She had moved out of their house when she was seventeen. They died when she was nineteen. She knew of no other family. The end.

Arden had been careful to keep her story bare of details that might catch her up in the retelling. She had rehearsed the delivery of this abbreviated tale in front of a mirror. A direct stare, no prevarication, no emotion, no room for questions. When someone did ask a question—"I have family in upstate New York. What town did you say you grew up in?"—Arden had a ready response at hand: "My childhood was not a happy one. I prefer not to talk about it."

This sort of closed behavior might have resulted in unpopularity, but it hadn't. Within months of her arrival in Port Eliot even those whose curiosity about the newcomer had taken the form of suspicion had accepted Arden Bell. So, the woman had secrets. Who didn't? And if Margery Hopkins liked her, she was okay. People hadn't seen Margery so energetic in years, and Arden knew her stuff when it came to books.

A lump of fur butted her leg and Arden shook herself back to the present, away from troubling dreams and bittersweet memories. Tired and out of sorts she might be, but the shop needed to be opened, and as Brent had a doctor's appointment this morning, the task was hers.

Arden got up from the table and put her satchel over her shoulder. "See you later," she told the kitties. "I'll be home as soon as I can."

Chapter 18

Laura Huntington was frustrated. She was also angry. Everyone had a story to tell. People needed to be heard. They wanted to be believed. That was okay. Really. What was not okay was when people chose to slander someone simply to aggrandize their own paltry importance or to fulfill a pathetic need for attention.

Her first stop that morning had been at the home of Renee Wilson. The house was singularly without charm or style, and that wasn't entirely the fault of the architect. The mistress of the house was no better. Renee immediately struck Laura as a vain and rather stupid woman, full of her self-worth but having little with which to back it up.

She was also unattractive, and it had nothing to do with the ill-fitting, garishly colored clothing she was wearing. If her personality had been warm and bright, or her manner of speaking smart and witty, one would easily overlook the rather bulbous nose, the too-small eyes, and the low forehead. One might even be tempted to call Renee Wilson a jolie laide, a magnificently ugly woman with her own strange attraction.

But her personality was not warm and bright, it was cramped and mean. And as for smart and witty, after about three minutes in the woman's presence, Laura was convinced Renee Wilson didn't know the meaning of either word.

But Renee was eager to talk to someone making a podcast. She had, she claimed (falsely), a famously melodious voice and would be more than happy to make time for the director when he needed an interview.

"I was told you knew Victoria Aldridge," Laura said, ignoring the woman's self-serving offer.

It was all the prompt Mrs. Wilson needed. "I knew the poor girl very well. From first grade on. I think she probably had autism or maybe some other disease that made her socially awkward. I mean, not just shy but, you know, like pathologically nervous around other people."

Laura kept her expression bland.

"Naturally, when I saw how backward she was, I made it my purpose to become her friend and help her to change. I knew she'd never be as popular as I was—not by half!—but at least, I thought, I could fix her enough so that she wouldn't be made fun of the way she was."

"And did you succeed?" Laura asked with a bright and false smile. *Backward? Disease?* Was this woman for real?

Renee seemed to consider. "You know," she said after a moment in a manner of great humility, "I think that I did. Better than any-one else could have, anyway. I have a gift with backwards people."

"Yes," Laura said, snappy replies racing through her mind. "I'm sure you do. And what about when Victoria went on to high school?"

Renee leaned forward and spoke in a conspiratorial tone. "The poor thing. If you could have seen how miserable she was all through high school without me by her side to guide her."

"When was the last time you actually spoke to Victoria Aldridge?"

Renee frowned elaborately. "Let me see," she said, thinking hard, "I think, yes, I think it was the day we graduated from our school. Back then the Catholic school was the only private gram-mar school around. It's sad to think the school was forced to shut down years ago. I—"

"So, you're saying that after graduation when you were about twelve or thirteen, you never spoke to Victoria again? You never actually knew her in high school, if she was miserable or not?"

Renee shifted in her seat. "Well, that's right. But I heard things."

"Like the fact that Victoria Aldridge was dating Rob Smith?"

Renee put her hand to her heart in mock horror. "Never! Rob would never have given Victoria the time of day! He was . . . Well, I don't know what he was, but he certainly wasn't dating anyone in Port George or I would have known."

"I'm sure you would have," Laura said, rising as she did. "Well, thank you for your time. It's been interesting."

Renee's practiced smile returned. "You'll let me know when I'm needed for my interview," she said, self-consciously touching her hair.

"Of course," Laura lied. "I'll call you myself."

She left the Wilson house feeling the need for a hot bath or a stiff drink. Maybe both.

Her next stop had been to McDonald Landscaping. Located on the outskirts of Port George, it looked like every other landscaping enterprise Laura had ever visited. Lots of greenhouses. The smell of fertilizer. Carts for customers to use as they collected their purchases. An office, located in an old clapboard structure, which doubled as a shop selling a variety of clippers, shears, hoses, and other gardening tools.

Laura went inside. She explained who she was and why she was there. At the word *podcast* the young receptionist sat up straight in her chair. Old Jack McDonald, Laura was told, had dementia and was unable to communicate with anyone and didn't even know who he was anymore, which was why he was in a nursing home up in Augusta. His son, Jack junior, however, might be able to help. If Laura would wait a moment, the receptionist would send him a text.

Jack junior appeared about three minutes later. He was overweight with a florid complexion; clearly, Laura thought, he wasn't doing any of the physical labor required of a landscape professional. She wondered if he ever had, or if he had always enjoyed the privileges of being the owner's son, overseer rather than worker.

Jack junior was more than happy to tell Laura what he remembered about the Aldridge family. He suggested they go outside. "That girl is as nosy as they come," he said, nodding back toward the receptionist.

Laura made no comment.

"I didn't know Victoria Aldridge," Jack junior said right off. "I mean, I knew who she was, everybody did. But it wasn't like she was hanging out with the other kids our age Saturday nights. Her parents were loaded. She was pretty aloof and stuck up."

"How do you know that if you didn't know her personally?"

Jack junior shrugged. "It's what everybody said about her."

"Everybody?"

Jack junior looked annoyed. "Yeah, you know, the people in town. Victoria Aldridge would go to pay for something in a shop and wouldn't even look the cashier in the eye. Too good for the likes of us."

"Maybe she was shy," Laura said, with a real effort at keeping her temper. She remembered that Kathy had considered her former classmate shy, not pathologically reclusive as Renee Wilson had opined.

Jack junior smirked. "Nah. My father said the mother was the same way. She'd stay in that big house and send someone out to tell him he was doing something wrong with the lawn or the flower beds, the maid or the housekeeper or whatever she was. Never spoke one word to my father in all the years he worked on their property. Too good for the likes of us."

Laura smiled blandly. "I'm guessing you don't have the Aldridge account now."

Jack junior's complexion grew even redder, if that was possible. "I wouldn't work for Herbert Aldridge if he paid me a million dollars a month. He fired my father back in 1986 or '7. No reason, just told him he wasn't needed. As far as I know, Aldridge never hired another landscaper. Could be a wilderness up there now for all I care."

Loath as Laura was to continue the conversation with Jack junior, she needed to ask more questions. "Did you ever hear of what happened to Victoria? Where she went after college or why she never came back to Port George?"

Another, nastier smirk appeared on the man's fleshy face. "Friend of mine who lives in Portland told me about, oh, fifteen or twenty years ago, that he saw Victoria Aldridge on line for a handout at one of the homeless shelters. Said he was one hundred percent sure it was her. She looked awful, a real mess. Serves her right is what I say."

Resisting the impulse to throttle the repulsive man, Laura forced herself to ask what Jack junior remembered about Rob Smith.

"He was a popular guy with just about everybody"—Jack junior stuck his thumbs in his belt—"but I saw through his act. Nobody is that nice and means it. No, underneath all that please and thank-you garbage Rob Smith was a schemer, out for his own good. What I think is he began to buy his own bullshit, got too big for his britches like my father used to say, went one step too far, and wham."

Laura knew in every fiber of her being that she should not encourage this weasel to go on, but a sudden sense of perversity forced her to open her mouth. "Wham?"

Jack junior nodded. "Wham. Someone taught him a lesson. Dumped the body somewhere out of town. End of Mr. Goody Two-shoes."

Laura could not get away from McDonald Landscaping and its pathetic owner quickly enough.

Now she was on her way to see the third person Kathy Murdoch had suggested she see regarding Victoria Aldridge. Hopefully Miss Thompson would prove at least a halfway reliable source of information. If she began to babble outrageously, Laura wasn't sure she could control a scream.

Finally, Laura turned onto Whippoorwill Way, literally around the corner from Fern Pond Road where the Smith family made their home. The small two-story house had seen better days; it was badly in need of a paint job, and a few of the window shutters were missing. The grass in the tiny front yard, however, had recently been mowed, and a pretty bed of blooming pink flowers was on either side of the front door. A mat on the tiny porch, perfectly free of any stray leaves or twigs, read WELCOME.

Laura knocked on the door. Almost a full minute later, the door was opened.

Miss Thompson, Laura thought, was a faded woman. It was an old expression but it was apt. Her clothes, though immaculately clean and pressed, were out-of-date—a dress a housewife in the 1950s might have worn while cleaning her home; a cardigan, the top button buttoned; her shoes, the sensible brogues of a screen Miss Marple. Her silvery hair was sparse; what there was of it was neatly arranged and held in place by small pins. Her eyes were a pale blue.

Laura introduced herself and explained her reason for being on the doorstep. Miss Thompson knew what a podcast was. She made a point of living in the present as well as in the past.

"Why do you want to talk to me?" Miss Thompson asked warily.

"Kathy Murdoch gave me your name. She attended Wilder Academy and graduated with the class of 1984."

"I'm sorry. I don't really remember her. So many students, so many years."

"Of course. Kathy works at the North Star Diner on Main Street. She was one of the scholarship students and remembers Victoria Aldridge with fondness. She thought you would remember Victoria, as well."

Miss Thompson suddenly became animated. "Oh, my, yes!"

"Do you think I might come in and we could talk a bit about what you remember?"

Miss Thompson ushered Laura inside. "Would you like a cup of tea?"

Laura didn't but felt that to say no would be rude. While her host scurried off to the kitchen, Laura glanced around the tiny living room. The decor was as faded as the inhabitant and as neat and tidy. China figurines of dogs lined the mantel above the well-swept hearth. Table lamps with frilly shades of pink and white were in abundance. On the walls hung framed prints of famous paintings—*A Girl with a Watering Can* by Renoir; *Madonna of the Chair* by Raphael; a landscape by Turner. The two armchairs were over-stuffed and covered in a chintz pattern of blooming cabbage roses.

Miss Thompson emerged from the kitchen carrying a battered silver tray on which sat a tea service. The tea service was old; Laura was no expert on china but could tell that much. The cup Miss Thompson handed her was nearly translucent and painted with tiny sprays of pink roses. On an equally delicate platter were five plump sugar cookies. Laura wondered if Miss Thompson had baked them herself.

Laura settled in an armchair across from Miss Thompson. The cushions were surprisingly firm and comfortable.

"So, tell me what you remember about Victoria Aldridge," she began, hoping Miss Thompson wouldn't question why Victoria Aldridge had anything to do with the subject of missing persons. Miss Thompson might be old but she clearly wasn't stupid.

"Victoria was my star pupil," Miss Thompson said promptly. "She wanted to be a professor of literature or a writer one day. She was an avid reader, always with her nose in a book. As far as I could tell, she wasn't at all like either of her parents, certainly not in temperament."

"What were Mr. and Mrs. Aldridge like?" Laura took a sip of the tea. It had a mild orange flavor.

"Cold," Miss Thompson said immediately. "Not people one could know easily. Not like their daughter. Victoria was shy but everyone liked her. She was friendly and kind. And how she loved Shakespeare. Her favorite play was *As You Like It*. Oh, and she was crazy for the Brontë sisters and Jane Austen and Charles Dickens and Shelley and Emily Dickinson, all those great writers."

"Did you keep in touch after she graduated?"

Miss Thompson's animated manner was gone as suddenly as it had come. "I lost track of her when she went off to college that September of 1984," she said, her voice softer. "We had agreed to write to one another, but she never answered my letters. I always thought that odd. I wrote her the most glowing recommendation." Miss Thompson smoothed her skirt over her knees and sighed softly. "I don't mind telling you I was hurt. I credit myself with being her mentor. Then again, the young can be fickle."

"Yes," Laura said gently. "They can be. When did you next see her?"

Miss Thompson's expression grew even more melancholy. "I never did. She came back to Port George at the end of the academic year—not for the Christmas holidays or spring break, which I thought was odd. I was waiting to hear from her but she never called. Next thing, she was off somewhere in about mid-June I think it was, and then on to school in the fall. And she never came back. Not once that I know of."

"What was the name of the college she attended?"

"Blake College. In those days, it was very prestigious, though in my opinion—and I shared my opinion with Mr. and Mrs. Aldridge— it wasn't academically challenging enough for someone like Victoria. But her parents had their minds set." Miss Thompson sighed. "Not a year goes by when I don't think about my star pupil and wonder where she is now, if she ever achieved her dreams, if she is happy, or . . . Well, if she ever does decide to visit Port George, I'd love to say hello. I hold no grudge."

Laura believed her. "Would you say that Victoria was at all socially awkward or stuck-up?"

Miss Thompson chuckled. "She was the least stuck-up young person you could ever ask to meet. As for socially awkward, well, as I said, she was rather shy, but she was thoroughly pleasant and well-liked."

So much for Renee Wilson and her backward theory, Laura thought. "Did you know Rob Smith?"

"Ah." Miss Thompson sat forward. "Now I see. You really want to know about that young man who went missing."

Laura smiled awkwardly. "Well, yes, but it often helps to know all sorts of things like who the missing person was friends with and—"

Miss Thompson put up her hand to silence Laura. "I understand all about thorough research," she said a bit archly. "Still, why would you be under the impression that Victoria was friends with Rob?"

"I don't know for sure that they were friends. It's just that two people have mentioned to me that Victoria and Rob might have been romantically involved."

Miss Thompson raised an eyebrow. "I know nothing about that,

I assure you. As for Rob himself, I didn't know him personally, but I knew him by sight and by reputation. He attended the public high school, you see, and the community college after that. He was a nice young man through and through. It was such a terrible shame when he went missing. And we never knew what happened to him. Some people said X and others thought Y, but nothing was ever concluded. A terrible shame."

Laura noted the sudden weariness on Miss Thompson's face. "I've taken up enough of your time," Laura said, rising. "I'll be on my way now."

"Will you take a few cookies with you? I made them myself."

Laura smiled and felt a prickling of tears. "I would love to. Thank you."

Miss Thompson walked her to the door and waited until Laura had buckled her seat belt and started the engine of her car before going inside.

Laura drove back to the Lilac Inn, her mind only half on the road. There was far more to the story of Victoria Aldridge than what was currently apparent. But there was still absolutely nothing to make Laura think that Victoria Aldridge, the girl who looked like a Viking princess, was Laura's birth mother.

Because, Laura reminded herself, Victoria Aldridge hadn't been the only teenage girl living in Port George the summer of 1984. What about the others? Kathy Murdoch—once one of those teens—might be able to help even more than she had already. Laura decided she would approach Kathy again as soon as possible.

What a day it had been! If only she had met with Miss Thompson first . . . But she still would have needed to meet with that horrid Renee Wilson and that obnoxious Jack junior, just in case either had any vital tidbit to offer.

Laura parked in the small lot next to the bed-and-breakfast. What she needed now was wine to go along with Miss Thompson's sugar cookies. Good thing a bottle was waiting in her room.

Chapter 19

It was Brent's day off. Zach was on duty but he was a quiet worker, entirely focused on the tasks at hand. Arden might as well have been alone in the bookshop, an experience she usually enjoyed, but this morning she yearned for Brent's sarcasm or Elly's ebullience. Anything to take her mind off the memory of the dream.

It had come again, but with differences. The enigmatic figure, neither man nor woman, human or otherwise, but maybe all at once, had seemed to make some advancement toward her. The sky had not been sickly yellow-gray but a medley of dark and dusky blues, and there had been no lurid glare of light to frighten her. The words she had heard spoken aloud in the first dream were now repeated several times in a singsong way. *Pale ribbons of sand. Dim and murmuring sea.* Rather than attempting to scream, her dream self had opened her mouth to call out to the dark figure, when suddenly, she had woken with a start.

Only later, over breakfast, had Arden allowed herself to face a possibility she had been denying since the occurrence of the first dream. Could the enigmatic figure coming toward her with such difficulty represent her long-lost child?

The idea had immediately produced a wave of sadness. Arden—Victoria—had been allowed only a tiny glimpse of the baby before she had been taken away. She was never to know what color eyes her daughter was to have, what color her hair would turn out to be, if she would grow to be tall like her mother, or broad shouldered like her father. Not a day had gone by when Arden hadn't thought about the daughter she had lost. Passing little girls in the street—babies, then toddlers, grammar schoolers and middle schoolers, teens—she would wonder, Could that be my child?

That morning, sitting at the kitchen table with her coffee growing cold, Arden had tried to dismiss the idea of being reunited with her child as wishful thinking, the pathetic fantasy of a lonely middle-aged woman. The chances that someone could find her after thirty-six years were remote. Whoever had adopted her child had been told absolutely nothing about the birth mother's identity. Nothing. Herbert Aldridge had made sure of that.

Besides, the thought of being discovered frightened her. A reunion would not be a reunion but a first-time meeting between two strangers, related by blood and bone, but not by so many things that mattered as much if not more. Daily rituals of loving behavior; long-standing family traditions; mutual friends; common interests. What if the child born to Victoria Aldridge had become a woman her mother wouldn't much like? Narrow-minded. Hateful. Cold. Anything was possible.

And what if her daughter should appear with a score to settle? Arden would be called upon to beg her daughter's pardon, to defend a decision that had not freely been made. In theory, Arden would have the choice to engage or not to engage. In actuality, she could never turn her back on her child. No. She would have to steel herself to withstand whatever slings and arrows her daughter chose to hurl at her and work to build a good mother-daughter relationship for the future.

But could she succeed at such a monumental undertaking?

That question had led Arden to get up from the kitchen table, go into her bedroom, and open her copy of *Villette*. It hadn't taken her long to find the line she sought.

With self-denial and economy now, and steady exertion by-and-by, an object in life need not fail you.

Self-denial. Economy. And always, steady exertion. Arden had returned the book to the shelf, heartened. Like Lucy Snowe, she *had* succeeded in making a life for herself, and until she met Margery Hopkins, she had done it entirely on her own. She would make yet another life for herself if she had to—a life with her child?

"Ms. Bell?"

Arden returned to the moment to find Zach standing before her. He explained that the shipment of new blank journals they were expecting had still not arrived. "I've tried tracking them online, but I got nowhere. I could make a call to the supplier if you want?" Zach's eyes fairly shone with excitement.

Zach was the most responsible young man Arden had ever encountered, and while responsibility was all well and good, Arden hoped he occasionally found the time to let go and be a teen— illogical, irrational, even reckless.

As she had once been, if only for a brief moment. But that brief moment had radically changed her life.

Arden smiled. "Thanks, Zach, I'll take care of it. But I want to thank you for the excellent work you're doing here at Arden Forest."

Zach nodded almost solemnly. "Thank you, Ms. Bell. I do my best."

Chapter 20

"I met with Renee Wilson, Jack junior, and Miss Thompson yesterday." Laura had returned to the North Star Diner in the hopes of speaking with Kathy Murdoch. Luckily, she found Kathy on duty. "Jack senior, by the way, is suffering from dementia."

"I'm sorry to hear that about Mr. McDonald. He's a nice man. Jack junior is a bit of a jerk, though. I kind of remembered that after I gave you his name." Kathy was holding a pot of coffee in one hand and a customer's check in the other. "Was anyone of any help?"

"Miss Thompson was charming. Renee Wilson was, well, never mind. Look, do you by any chance still have your high school yearbook? The one from 1984?"

Kathy nodded. "Of course, I do. That's not the sort of thing you get rid of, is it, not unless you had a terrible time in high school, and that wasn't me. In some ways, those years were the best of my life. Hey, I'm getting off my shift in fifteen minutes. If you want to hang around and have a cup of coffee, you could come home with me and take a look at it. Gosh, I haven't cracked it open in years. It'll be fun."

Laura agreed. Half an hour later saw the two women seated in Kathy's living room. The house, within walking distance of the North Star, was small, with, as far as Laura could see, nothing exceptional about it other than its extreme tidiness.

They sat side by side on a couch that was upholstered in a pleasant shade of green. Kathy had opened a bottle of white table wine and poured them each a generous glass. With the yearbook opened on her lap, Kathy began to chatter on, telling Laura more than she would ever need to know about the graduating class of 1984. Some of the information, however, was potentially relevant, such as that three of Kathy's classmates had gotten pregnant in senior year. Two of them married right after graduation; the other had had the baby on her own. "Luckily," Kathy said, "her parents were cool about it. I mean, as cool as you can be when your seventeen-year-old kid gets pregnant and refuses to name the father."

"So, she kept the baby?"

"Oh, yeah. Little Mikey will be in his late thirties by now. He never married either, just like his mother. He's a terminal charmer, always got a woman hanging off his arm. But he's okay. Always leaves me a good tip when he comes into the diner. And here's Victoria Aldridge, the girl on the far right. I almost forgot how pretty she was."

Though the group shot—it was a photo of the Honors Society—was a bit blurry, Laura could see that Victoria Aldridge was indeed pretty. More than that really, she was beautiful, with good bone structure and even features. But such beauty could put people off; they might see it as intimidating and prejudicially suppose it went hand in hand with arrogance.

One hundred students were in Kathy's graduating class, and Kathy seemed to know what had happened to each and every one of them. Who had died. Who had moved away. Who were grandparents now. Who had gotten divorced. Who had never married. Who had been arrested; who was currently in jail. Who had made it big, or relatively so. Who was always out of a job because he had the worst luck in the entire world. Whom Kathy had made out with a few times. Her ex-husband, Kathy explained, had been two classes ahead of her, so his picture wasn't in the 1984 yearbook.

Kathy turned another page. "Here are the formal portraits. I don't think I've ever seen a good one in all of my life."

So many forced smiles from kids too aware of the camera, uncomfortable in their cheap caps and gowns. Laura thought of Rob

Smith's graduation photo. These photos, those of the class of 1984, shared that same air of blandness, of sameness, and yet, behind each and every one of these faces there had been a real, three-dimensional kid with hopes and dreams and plans.

Laura noted an interesting thing. Under every graduate's portrait was his or her full name as well as a nickname in quotes. A girl with flyaway hair had been called Breezy. A large boy had been dubbed Moose. "Our class president came up with the idea of a nickname for everyone," Kathy explained. "If you didn't already have one, you could choose one or he made one up for you. Silly."

Kathy flipped forward in the yearbook. "Here are the portraits of the teachers. Look, here's Miss Thompson."

"She looks almost the same as she does now," Laura said in surprise. "Some people really do look old before their time. Kathy? You mentioned the other day that your sister was under the impression that Victoria Aldridge and Rob Smith were a couple. Miss Thompson said she knew nothing about a relationship, and Renee Wilson swears Rob would never have given Victoria a second look."

Kathy laughed. "Renee's just jealous. Everybody knew she had it bad for Rob, but he never gave her the time of day. Anyway, I never saw Victoria and Rob together, so, who knows? One thing I do know, those Aldridges wouldn't have been happy their daughter was spending time with the son of a truck driver. They were the most stuck-up people in Port George, still are, I suppose. Not that anyone sees much of them these days." Suddenly, Kathy's expression turned serious. "Last time we talked you said you asked all sorts of questions when you're getting ready to do a story because you never know what might be important in the end. I think I get it now. You've been asking all these questions about Victoria because you think she might have had something to do with Rob's disappearance, or that maybe she knew something about it, like maybe that someone hurt Rob, and that's why she never came back to Port George after going off to college because she was afraid."

Laura was impressed. Kathy Murdoch had a keen intelligence. "Something like that, yeah. Do you think I could borrow your yearbook for my research? I promise to return it."

"Sure, I'm glad to help. So, do you think I could be interviewed if this podcast really happens? I've never been quoted before." Kathy laughed. "That's probably because I've never said anything very interesting!"

Laura felt that too familiar twinge of guilt. She hated lying to this smart and openhearted woman, self-effacing and hardworking and generous with her time.

"Would you like to have dinner at that Italian place one night?" Laura asked, sidestepping the idea of a formal interview. "My host at the bed-and-breakfast told me it's the best Italian food in miles. My treat," she added hastily.

"Do you have an expense account?" Kathy asked excitedly. "You must, working on a podcast and all. Sure, I'd love to go to Enio's. I've been wanting to go forever!"

Laura—who did not have an expense account—arranged to meet Kathy at Enio's two nights from then at six thirty, and, yearbook under her arm, she left Kathy's pleasant home.

Chapter 21

Thank you again for providing such an enjoyable shopping experience. The next time my husband and I are passing through Eliot's Corner we'll be sure to stop in!

Arden smiled and closed her laptop. It wasn't terribly often that customers sent e-mails via the Arden Forest website, but when they did, the messages were always positive and confirmed—as if it needed confirming!—that Arden was exactly where she was meant to be. Surrounded by books.

Oh, the countless hours she had spent as a child reading alone in her room or under a shady tree on the Aldridge property! Every penny of her allowance had gone toward books, and her library card—paper in those days—was soft with use. Once she had even walked into a wall while reading a well-worn copy of *Oliver Twist*. "She was too fond of books, and it turned her brain," her nanny had intoned afterward, putting a cold cloth on young Victoria's forehead to help prevent swelling.

Books were one of the many things she and Rob, two kids from opposite sides of the track, had had in common.

"My family teases me about being a bookworm," Rob had told her not long after they had met. "I've got stacks of them in my room. Neither of my parents went to college. In fact, my father didn't even finish high school. But they both love to read. My father has a subscription to *Reader's Digest*. And my mother likes *Good Housekeeping* for the recipes. We also have a Bible that belonged to my great-grandmother. She got it as a wedding present, and it gets passed down to the oldest child of each generation when he or she gets married. That means Frannie will get it pretty soon. She's tying the knot next year or the one after that, as soon as she and her fiancé have saved enough money."

Victoria hadn't told Rob that her father's study held leather-bound sets of the novels of Charles Dickens, the plays of Shake-speare, and poems of Longfellow, along with a set of encyclopedias and a massive dictionary. She thought the information might sound like a brag, given the lack of books in Rob's home. She had no idea if her father had bought the books himself, had inherited them, or even if they had come with the house. He never protested when his daughter borrowed a book; sometimes she wondered if he even noticed a gap in the rows of dark blue and maroon leather stamped with gold writing.

Suddenly, the door to the shop opened and twelve-year-old Tami Mogan came striding in. She was robust and healthy looking, and a great reader. Today, she went directly to the Classics section. Arden, knowing that Tami liked to talk, joined her there.

"Ms. Bell," Tami said excitedly, "I just saw a really awesome movie about the Brontës. It's really, really old, from 1973. But it's really good, and poor Branwell! I think anyone could go mad living in such a gloomy place. At least, I probably would. Anyway, one day I want to visit Haworth and see for myself the house where they all lived." Tami frowned. "I think it's still there. I hope it is. I wonder if Charlotte's and Anne's and Emily's spirits haunt the house? Or maybe their ghosts roam the moors at night, thinking about how their lives would have been different if they'd grown up somewhere else, like maybe London. Maybe they're still sad they never really found true love." Tami rolled her eyes. "I mean, I know Charlotte got married eventually, but, please, that wasn't romantic. I bet Branwell was cute. In real life, I mean."

"I remember seeing *The Brontës of Haworth* ages ago," Arden told her when Tami had stopped to catch her breath. "I'll try to find it on Roku. Do you know about Charlotte's time in Brussels?"

"Not really."

Briefly, Arden explained how Charlotte had fallen in love with the married man in charge of the school at which she had been hired as a teacher. "*The Professor* was Charlotte's first novel, but it wasn't published in her lifetime. In some ways, this book"—Arden turned to the shelves for a copy—"*Villette*, her last novel, is a reworking of the earlier novel. Both are assumed to be pretty autobiographical."

Tami's eyes shone with excitement. "Cool. I'll get it, thanks. Oh, and I forgot." Tami followed Arden to the checkout counter. "My mom and I watched a good miniseries adaptation of *Jane Eyre*. Ruth Wilson plays Jane, and this guy named Toby Stephens plays Mr. Rochester. You should check it out. I love Ruth Wilson."

Arden thanked Tami for her recommendations and watched as the girl left the shop and joined her mother, who was just emerging from Chez Claudine, holding a large white bakery bag.

The exchange had been bittersweet for Arden. She might have had similar conversations with her daughter had she been given the chance. But *did* her daughter, whoever and wherever she was, like to read? Did she enjoy the works of the Brontë sisters? Was she a writer, herself? Arden would probably never know.

The sudden ache in her heart was keen, and Arden was briefly tempted to close the shop early, go back to her comfortable cottage, and hunker down with her cats.

But she would do no such thing. Instead, she would follow the example of Lucy Snowe. Only through steady exertion were results achieved.

Sometimes, it was almost impossible to remember that.

Chapter 22

Shortly after breakfast, Laura returned to her room at the Lilac Inn and got down to work.

She had learned that Victoria had not come back to Port George for Christmas or spring break her freshman year of college. Most kids did come home. At the least it was a chance to have someone do your laundry and see high school friends. Was it possible that Victoria hadn't been away at Blake College or any other school from September 1984 through the spring of 1985? If not, then where the heck had she been?

Laura opened her computer and found a phone number for the alumnae office at Blake College. As nutty as it seemed—and it did seem nutty—Victoria Aldridge was shaping up to be the most likely candidate to be her mother.

"I'm looking for information about my aunt," Laura told the woman who answered the phone in a pleasant voice. "My family lost track of her ages ago, and I'd very much like to find out more about her. I thought perhaps that you could tell me her current whereabouts, assuming she's an active alum, or maybe the name of a former classmate who might still be in touch with her."

It was a feeble story (if it merited the title of *story* at all), but lying was fast becoming a habit. Laura hoped it wasn't indicative of a total decline in morals.

The woman politely told Laura that the only information the college would release about a student, even a former one, was when she had attended the college. Laura had half expected as much, as she had half expected what she learned next.

Victoria Aldridge had not registered for the academic year of 1984–85.

"There's a note here that indicates she was accepted for matriculation back in the spring of '84," the woman explained, "but that she never actually registered as a student at Blake."

Laura felt a frisson of excitement, thanked the woman, and ended the call.

"Where were you, Victoria?" she whispered aloud. Even if Victoria Aldridge was not her birth mother, she had been a flesh-and-blood young woman, and Laura had become intrigued by what she had learned of her story.

So, Laura wondered, what next?

Once again, Laura turned to her laptop and chose a search engine with which to look for anyone with the name of Victoria Aldridge residing in the New England states. There were only three people with the name, and none fit the age of the former Port George resident. Of course, the Victoria Aldridge Laura was seeking might be living anywhere in the United States or even abroad. She might have married and changed her name. She might, for all Laura knew, have become a nun—she had, after all, attended a Catholic grammar school. She might, indeed, be dead.

Exasperated, Laura turned again to the Wilder Academy yearbook. Those awkward formal photos, under which the student's name was printed, followed by a nickname in quotes. Silly names. Cute. Possibly meaningful. Possibly not.

French toast. There was no obvious clue in the photo of that pretty girl to explain why she was called or had chosen to be called a piece of bread dipped in egg and fried.

Mouse. The boy had large ears. Like Mickey Mouse? That wasn't very nice.

Grumpy. This boy was grinning widely. Irony? Affection?

Puff. Laura sighed. The photo of the ordinary-looking girl offered no clue as to the relevance of her nickname.

Kathy Murdoch's nickname had been Cheesy; she had told Laura it was because she ate a bag of Cheez Doodles every day with her lunch.

Under the photograph of Victoria Aldridge—the Viking princess— was the word *Arden*. *Arden* had a note of seriousness about it. Didn't it?

Laura sent a text to Kathy: *What did the name/word Arden mean to VA?*

Kathy responded almost immediately: *No idea. An in-joke?*

Laura turned again to her laptop and searched the word *Arden*. What did it mean? Would she find a clue in its etymological origins as to why Victoria had chosen the word, or why it had been chosen for her? Though the Internet hadn't yet been in existence in 1984, research certainly had. A curious student would have had access to reference books at the library and might uncover the origin and subsequent history of a word.

Arden. Possibly from the Hebrew word for Garden of Eden. Now that might be a clue, Laura thought. Anytime the Bible was referenced there was a wealth of information and opinion to review.

Elizabeth Arden, the queen of cosmetics. Nothing there, not given what Laura had learned about Victoria Aldridge, a girl who had cared more for her studies than for makeup.

John Arden was an important British playwright in the 1950s and '60s. Laura had never heard of John Arden, but maybe young Victoria Aldridge had and was a fan of his work. It wasn't impossible. But it didn't seem likely.

In Hindi, *arden* meant valley of the eagle. Laura nodded. There might be something there. In many cultures the eagle held great symbolic meaning. It represented mankind's connection to the divine. It stood for courage and honesty. Yes, this might be something to think about.

Laura scrolled on. There was a village in Delaware called Arden. Unlikely to be a lead.

Was there a town in Maine called Arden? Not according to this search engine.

The Ardennes, or Ardennes Forest, was located in southeast

Belgium and extended into Luxembourg, Germany, and France. Sadly, it was the scene of terrible battles in both World War I and World War II. Laura couldn't imagine even a serious young woman such as Victoria Aldridge choosing such a depressing moniker. Besides, *Arden* was obviously an English version of *Ardennes*; why make the change?

Suddenly, Laura's fingers began to fly over the keyboard even before her mind had fully remembered that Miss Thompson had told her that Victoria Aldridge's favorite Shakespearean play was *As You Like It*. The play was set in the Forest of Arden. There was such a place in real life, Laura learned, extending from Stratford-upon-Avon in Warwickshire to Tamworth in Staffordshire. But Shakespeare's Arden was a forest of fantasy, a place where the spectacular might happen, where happy endings were possible.

Laura took a deep breath. Could that be why Victoria had chosen the nickname Arden? Or was that stretching things just a bit too far? How, Laura wondered, putting her hand to her aching head, did one go about this sort of detective work without making a fool of oneself several times along the way? Leaping to conclusions based on the flimsiest of connections, imagining solutions to puzzles that might prove to be unsolvable.

Still, Laura pressed on and began a targeted search for people and businesses—anything, really—employing the word *arden* in the state of Maine. And if nothing helpful came to light, well, she would start on the next forty-nine states. Where else did she have to be? she asked herself grimly. No family, no husband, on leave from her job—

"Oh, my," Laura breathed.

A bookshop in Eliot's Corner, Maine, was called Arden Forest.

Laura easily found the shop's website. It was professionally done. The home page showed a picture of the storefront with its two large display windows and old-fashioned awning over the center front door. Arden Forest: A Haven for Book Lovers.

Laura clicked on the About page. The shop had been founded in 1971 by Margery Hopkins. In 2008, Margery had passed away. There was a photo of the current owner. Her name was Arden Bell.

She looked to be in her fifties. She was blond. Her eyes were blue. The only biographical detail was that the owner was a native Mainer.

Laura stared at the photo of the woman. Every nerve in her body was tingling. Arden Bell wasn't necessarily Victoria Aldridge. She wasn't. Laura reached for Kathy Murdoch's yearbook and opened to Victoria's formal portrait. The resemblance between the two faces was strong. Very strong.

Hands shaking, Laura placed a call to Lenny Tobin. He was a journalist. He would know how to proceed from this point. He had better know, Laura thought, because she was too shaken to think clearly.

Lenny Tobin didn't answer his phone so Laura left a message on the voice mail. She hoped she had been coherent but she couldn't be sure. Mr. Tobin didn't return her call for an interminable hour and a half. If he was curious as to why a podcast journalist didn't know how to proceed in a simple investigation, he didn't say. Generously, he provided Laura with information he thought might be helpful.

"Good luck in your quest," he said finally. "For whatever it is you're really after."

Laura gulped hard. She had been right. Lenny Tobin had known from the start that she was keeping her real purpose from him. "Thank you," she said unsteadily. "Thank you."

Referring to the notes she had taken during the call with Lenny, Laura went to Whois Lookup & IP, a reputable database of domain names, registration possibilities, and availability.

The owner of Arden Forest's website was listed as Arden Forest LLC.

All right, Laura thought. Onward. Now she accessed the State of Maine's database of registered businesses in search of a license. And there it was, right on the screen in front of her.

Victoria Aldridge DBA Arden Forest LLC.

Laura's heart began to beat madly. She squinted at the screen through a mist that had suddenly come over her eyes; yes, she was reading correctly. She had found Victoria Aldridge. She had found her.

Still, there was nothing to prove that Victoria Aldridge was Laura's birth mother. But . . . But this woman and her bookshop were all Laura had at the moment. She had no choice. She would go to Eliot's Corner, no matter how far from Port George it was, and see this Arden Bell. And with any luck . . .

Laura buried her face in her hands and sobbed as she hadn't done since the deaths of Marty and Cynthia Huntington.

Chapter 23

"Success," Arden announced to herself as she replaced the receiver of the landline on its base.

She had just persuaded a young, Maine-based, African-born novelist to give a reading from her first published work. Already the book was being praised as the effort of a significant young immigrant voice. Arden had read the debut novel in one sitting, impressed by its beautiful combination of harsh realism and genuine hopefulness. The way the author handled the relationship between the protagonists, a young brother and sister from the Democratic Republic of the Congo who had lost their parents to one of the many armed groups that routinely resorted to violence, committing atrocious abuses of human rights, was particularly deft. The siblings, now living in Portland, Maine, with an aunt and uncle, faced the unique challenges of asylum seekers in a strange new culture, as well as the universal challenges of childhood. Arden was sure the October event would be popular with the residents of Eliot's Corner.

"Rats!"

Arden looked toward the back room where Brent was unpacking boxes and seeing to it that this storage area for everything from toilet paper to light bulbs didn't descend into utter chaos.

"You okay?" Arden called.

"Yeah." Brent sounded frustrated. "This stupid old box cutter was jammed again. I got it unstuck but managed to nick my finger in the process."

"You know where the first aid kit is, right?"

"Exactly where I put it the last time this happened. I'm fine."

Arden believed him. Brent was an extremely competent young man, used to taking care of himself. Probably, Arden thought, because he had experienced more than his fair share of woes while still a child. His father, a rough sort who routinely spent too much of his salary on beer and the lottery, had been furious when he learned that his only son was gay. He had treated Brent, only twelve at the time, badly, more than once resorting to physical violence. Finally, tired of trying to talk sense into her brute of a husband and unable to protect her child, Mrs. Teakle had threatened to leave the marriage, taking Brent and his siblings with her, if her husband didn't get his act together. Mr. Teakle hadn't reformed overnight, but he had come around enough to keep his hands off his son and his mouth shut when the mood to say hateful things came over him.

As soon as Brent had graduated from high school, he moved out on his own. It took him six years to put himself through college but he had done it, graduating with honors. Two years earlier, he had met his partner, Kurt, and they were now living together and planning to marry. If Brent still suffered the psychological and emotional effects of his father's abuse, he didn't say. He couldn't have forgotten, but Arden believed that he had forgiven.

Brent had been lucky to have at least one parent who loved and supported him. So many children were left to fend for themselves either in an unsafe home or out on the streets. Arden thought of the two orphaned children who were the protagonists of the novel that had so moved her and found herself hoping yet again that her daughter had grown up in a safe and loving home. Biological parents, adoptive parents, aunts and uncles, grandparents, friends—it didn't matter who cared for a child as long as the child was cared for, loved, protected, and championed.

The bell over the door of the shop announced an arrival. It was

Deborah. Arden literally sighed in relief. Her thoughts were beginning to take a gloomy turn.

"I came to steal you away for a bit," Deborah announced. "How about we get something to eat at Chez Claudine and take it to my place? Brent is here today, isn't he? And everyone is entitled to a lunch hour."

"True. Hang on just a moment."

Arden found Brent taking inventory of printer paper. A Band-Aid was on his right forefinger. "I'm going to pop out with Deborah for lunch. Hold the fort?"

Brent pushed a lock of hair away from his forehead. "Only if you promise to bring me a croque madame." He smiled. "And a large coffee."

Arden promised and returned to her friend. "Let's go. And whatever you do, don't let me forget to get a sandwich and a coffee for Brent. Really, I don't know what I'd do without him."

Chapter 24

Laura had changed her date with Kathy to a day earlier so she could be on the road to Eliot's Corner as soon as possible. She had been sure to return the Wilder Academy yearbook with many thanks.

Kathy had been good company at dinner, and Laura had learned more about life in Port George than she might ever have thought to ask. The Christmas festivities put on by the Episcopal church were always a big hit, even with members of other congregations. For years, there had been no movie theater, and if you wanted to go to a fancy multiscreen cinema, you had to drive over thirty miles to Spurlink to see the latest *Batman* or the next in the *Star Wars* series. The historical society had lost its building to a notoriously greedy landlord about ten years back; since then it was located in the basement of the public library, though every few years the society was rumored to have somehow found enough money to relocate to their own, freestanding space. People bought a good deal of their produce directly from farms in the surrounding area, and much of their day-to-day needs at the mom-and-pop grocery store in town, traveling to the chain store one town over for all other needs.

When, at the end of dinner, Laura told Kathy that she was leaving Port George, possibly not to return, her new friend was disappointed. Laura didn't say where she was going or why; she let Kathy assume she was returning home to resume work on the podcast with her colleagues.

"Well, if you have to come back to Port George," Kathy said, "I hope we can get together again. I'll cook. I make a mean mac 'n' cheese with bacon."

Laura had thanked her with tears in her eyes.

Now, Laura was fast approaching her destination, and with each mile she covered her nerves grew more strained. Finally, there it was up ahead, a sign announcing that she was entering Eliot's Corner, founded in 1782. It didn't take long for Laura to see that the pretty little town was not all that different from Port George, past and present living side by side, mostly in harmony. Eighteenth- and nineteenth-century homes, some humble, others grand, sat next to low-ceilinged houses built in the 1940s and '50s. The tallest brick building seemed to be no more than four stories high. There was a town square. The sidewalks were virtually empty of people at this time of the morning. Laura wondered if they were ever really busy, even in high summer.

It hadn't been difficult to find Arden Bell's home address, and that was where Laura was headed. Arden Bell might not be at home. She might be almost anywhere. At the bookshop, at the dentist, taking a walk with her dog. If she had a dog. On vacation up north with her partner. If she had a partner.

GPS led Laura to Juniper Road and then, to number 10. A painted wooden sign announced that this was JUNIPER END COTTAGE; under these words was the date 1923. It looked very much as one imagined cottages in fairy tales to look, Laura noted, without the thatched roof. A chimney announced the presence of a fireplace. A small front garden was alive with pink, yellow, and purple flowers.

Laura brought her car to a stop. This was it. The moment she had been pursuing since she had decided weeks ago to seek out the woman who had given her life. Now, that moment having arrived, Laura felt reluctant to seize it. Juniper End Cottage. This was a quiet, almost-magical-seeming spot. It felt somehow wrong to be disturbing the peace of the place and, more important, the peace of the inhabitant. Even if she, Laura Huntington, was indeed Arden Bell's biological daughter, she was still an outsider here, an interloper, an intruder.

Maybe, Laura thought, tightening her hands on the steering wheel, it would be better, kinder, to send Arden Bell a letter, explaining who she was and whom she thought she had been born, to give this woman a chance to absorb the monumental suggestion that her biological child—if Laura was indeed her biological child— might have found her.

But Laura wanted what she felt that she deserved. She was seeking a simple answer. Yes or no. She needed to look this woman in the eye and find out for sure whether Arden Bell was Victoria Aldridge—and maybe also Laura's birth mother. She was not at Juniper End to reproach or to blame or to punish. She was there to . . .

Laura's throat tightened. She was there to be welcomed into her mother's life.

Still, her hand shook when she opened her car door, and again when she lifted the old-fashioned knocker on the door of the cottage. A moment later she heard footsteps approaching the door, even, unhurried footsteps. Laura's heart began to race as the door began to open.

A tall, attractive woman with blond hair pulled into a loose ponytail stood before her.

Before Laura could say a word, the woman fell heavily against the door.

"It's you," she gasped. "You've come at last."

Chapter 25

"I'm all right now, really."

Arden wasn't really all right, but the younger woman leaning over her was clearly distressed and needed to be put at ease.

"If you're sure I shouldn't call a doctor or—"

Arden managed a trembling smile. "I'm sure."

She was seated in the armchair in the living room; she wasn't sure how she had gotten there. A glass of water was on the small table by the side of the chair. The younger woman must have fetched it for her.

Now, this woman, a stranger who was no stranger, sat on the couch across from Arden and placed her hands on her knees. Her expression was hesitant, almost wary. "I'm sorry. I should have called first, not just shown up. I didn't know the right thing to do. I mean, no one tells you how you're supposed to . . . And I wasn't even sure you were my mother until you . . ."

"It's okay." Arden's smile was wobbly. "My daughter. My child. You said your name was—"

"Laura. Laura Huntington."

Arden nodded. "Huntington. Was that your—" She couldn't finish the question.

"Yes. My parents' name. Their first names were Marty and Cynthia." Laura attempted a smile. "I never expected you to know me like that, in an instant."

"I always knew that I would recognize you the moment I saw you. If that day ever came. And it has." Arden shook her head. "The dreams. Recently, I've been having dreams. . . . Now I know what they meant."

"What sort of dreams?"

"Dreams that made me wonder." Arden leaned forward a bit. "I was on a stretch of sand and I saw a figure, I couldn't tell if it was male or female or even human, coming toward me, but at the same time making no progress. It's hard to explain. The first time I had the dream everything was gray and murky, sand and sky and ocean, except for a sick yellowish color that flared up. The second dream wasn't quite so frightening, though it still left me puzzled. I thought that maybe . . . Now I know for certain that I must have known my child was coming for me."

"I hope I'm not frightening to you," Laura said earnestly. "I don't want to be."

"I'm sorry. I didn't mean to imply that you're one to fear. It's more—what happened back then." Arden managed a less wobbly smile. "No one from my past has ever come looking for me before. At least, no one has ever found me. Until now. How *did* you find me?"

"It's a bit of a long story, but it started when my mother passed away—my adoptive mother. Among her effects, I found a sealed envelope addressed to me. On the outside of the envelope was a short note instructing me to open the envelope when and if I ever needed to find my birth mother. For a long time after that, I didn't need to know. I'm sorry if that sounds harsh, but it's the truth. Though I'd been curious at times in my life about my birth parents, the need to know who exactly they were had never been strong."

Oddly, at that moment Arden was more fascinated that there had been a stray clue as to her identity all along, than hurt by her daughter's admission of disinterest. "Go on, please."

"It was only when my marriage was falling apart—I'm recently divorced—and I realized just how alone in the world I was, with both Mom and Dad gone and my husband having proved completely unreliable, that I began to feel a real need to look for my roots. I had no expectations of success, but I had to know, or at least I had to try to find out who had brought me into this world."

"So," Arden said, attempting to conceal how eager she was to learn more, "you opened the letter."

Laura nodded. "Yes. In it my mother had left me the only clue in her possession, that my birth mother had been a resident of Port George, Maine. She had overheard this bit of information while in the lawyer's office when all the paperwork was signed, and she'd kept it a closely guarded secret. She said she'd never even told my father. I'm not sure why. Anyway, I took that one little clue, and a few weeks later, here I am."

"She wanted you to find me one day," Arden said with conviction. "That's why she held on to that clue so tightly."

"I think," Laura said after a moment, "that my mother might have felt some guilt about the adoption. Not regret, I don't mean that. See, she knew that my birth mother was young and unmarried. She had to have supposed there was a good chance the girl had mixed feelings about giving up her baby. That she was vulnerable, maybe even that she had been coerced. I think that's why she left me the clue, so that I might find you one day, and that the young, vulnerable girl who gave birth to me would finally know that her child was all right."

Arden sighed deeply. "I'm so grateful to her. And your biological father?" she asked hesitantly. "Have you found him, as well?"

"I think I have," Laura said gently. "Was he—is he—Rob Smith?"

Hearing his name spoken aloud after all the years of silence sent a shock through Arden's body that caused her to jump in her seat.

Laura quickly got up and came across to Arden. "Please, do you want to lie down?"

"No," Arden said firmly. "I'm all right. Yes, your father is Rob Smith. Do you know—" But she couldn't go on.

"About his disappearance?" Laura asked, sitting once again. "As much as there is to know, at least, all that was in the papers at the time."

Arden put her hand over her heart; it was racing madly. "How did you make the leap from Victoria Aldridge of Port George to Arden Bell of Eliot's Corner?"

Laura smiled. "By playing amateur sleuth. Figuring out that Arden Bell was Victoria Aldridge took some real creativity though. And luck."

"I chose the name Arden from my favorite Shakespeare play."

"Of course. Arden Forest. Miss Thompson remembered that *As You Like It* was a favorite of yours."

"Miss Thompson? You saw her?"

"I did. She thinks of you with fondness even now."

A wave of shame overcame Arden, making it difficult to speak. "Miss Thompson was so good to me," she said after a long moment. "I've always felt bad about not keeping up with her, but how could I have? Like everyone else in Port George she thought I was away enjoying my first year of college, not . . . If I wrote to her, I'd have had to lie, and it was too much. . . . When I came back to Port George briefly after you were born, I could have visited Miss Thompson, but . . ."

"I think I understand. And what about Bell? Where did that come from?"

"Currer Bell. It was the pseudonym chosen by Charlotte Brontë, one of my favorite writers."

"I should have guessed that. Arden Bell has a nice ring to it, pardon the pun."

Arden smiled briefly. "What do you want from me?" Her tone was not combative.

"Please believe that I'm not here to make you feel bad for having given me up," Laura replied earnestly. "But I would like to know what happened to you and to my father back in the summer of 1984."

Arden nodded. "All right. I'll tell you everything, but not right now, not today. What else do you want from this . . ." She didn't know how to define this strange moment.

"I'd like us to get to know one another. If that's possible."

Arden swallowed hard. "Yes. That's possible."

"I'm glad. By the way, I also spoke to Ted Coldwell during my search."

Arden started. "Ted? You spoke to Ted?"

"Yes, I did. He didn't or couldn't tell me much, but I got the impression that he feels bad that he didn't try to learn what happened when you left Port George for good in June of 1985."

Arden put her hand to her head. She felt slightly dizzy. Events she had willed herself not to think about, people she hadn't consciously thought about for so long, it was all coming back, and but for those two recent dreams, harbingers of a crisis, she had had no preparation.

"I'm sorry," Laura said. "I didn't mean to upset you, but of course it can't be otherwise."

Suddenly, there was a thundering sound and the cats came charging into the living room, where they stopped directly at Laura's feet.

"Oh!" Laura cried. "What an entrance!"

Arden laughed. "Let me introduce, from right to left, Prospero, Ophelia, and Falstaff."

Laura smiled. "You named them well. Prospero looks wise. Ophelia has the air of tragic heroine about her. A drama queen? And Falstaff, well, he's a big boy, isn't he?"

As if to prove Laura's observation, Falstaff plopped to the floor and showed his impressive belly.

"You'll stay here with me, won't you?" Arden said suddenly.

"I'd planned on finding a bed-and-breakfast locally. Or a motel would be fine, if there's one not too far away. I really don't want to put you out."

"Please. I don't have a guest bedroom but there's the loft. There's plenty of room. And . . . I'd like it very much if you'd stay with me. If you would feel comfortable."

Laura nodded. "Thanks. I will stay with you. To be honest, my budget is pretty strained at the moment."

"That's settled. I'll make up your bed right away."

"I can do it if you point me in the direction of the sheets."

"Let me," Arden said almost pleadingly. "It would be my pleasure." To make up a bed for her child. A simple task she had never had the chance to perform.

"All right. Is it okay if I pet the cats?"

Arden smiled. "Only if you agree never to stop."

Chapter 26

Laura had shared a meal with her mother, the first of what might be many to come. It had felt surprisingly comfortable sitting across the table from the woman who had given her life, passing the salt and pepper, toasting to the future with a glass of wine. That Arden Bell was an excellent cook made the experience all that much more pleasurable.

Over dinner, Laura had explained the ruse under which she had elicited information from the residents of Port George, assuring Arden that no one had learned her real identity.

"I guess I didn't know my real identity, either," she said with a laugh. "Not until earlier today."

Arden had told Laura a bit about how she had come to be the owner of Arden Forest, and about the woman who had been her mentor and friend. "Finding Eliot's Corner, and then Margery Hopkins, was a great bit of luck. For the last fifteen years, my life here has been pretty peaceful."

Laura had hoped that her mother wasn't beginning to regret her daughter's sudden appearance. But clearly, regret was not what Arden was feeling. She had reached across the table, palm open, and waited for Laura to put her hand in hers. "Today is a miracle," she said, tears shining in her eyes.

Both women had decided upon an early bedtime. It had been an exhausting day, wonderful, startling, unreal. Barely had the dishes been cleared away when Laura found her eyelids closing.

Now, tucked into her makeshift bed in the loft, she spoke silently to her adoptive mother, thanking her for having preserved the clue that had led Laura to Arden Bell—and to Victoria Aldridge. It had been an act of true generosity on the part of Cynthia Huntington.

But that was no surprise. Marty and Cynthia Huntington had been wonderful parents. Interestingly, Laura didn't remember a time she hadn't known she had been adopted, but she would always remember the moment when her situation had become something to question.

"My mommy says you're not natural."

Those words had been spoken by a classmate of Laura's one day at recess.

Laura, who didn't know what the other seven-year-old had meant by that remark, had immediately retorted, "I am, too, natural." Contradiction came easily to a child.

"No, you're not," Polly had insisted. "You didn't come out of your mommy's belly."

Laura knew that. Sort of. Maybe not really. She knew she was adopted. But what did that mean? The understanding of human biology had not yet taken hold in Laura's seven-year-old brain.

When she got home from school that day, Laura told her mother what Polly had said. Laura had been confused and upset. Her mother had been reassuring and comforting. Within days the issue had become a nonissue.

Laura pricked up her ears. She thought she heard a sound from below. It might have been the cats, but it might also have been her mother. Arden had been so greatly affected by Laura's arrival. For all Laura knew, her mother wasn't in good health. Maybe she had a heart condition that made a shock of the sort she had encountered earlier potentially harmful. Suddenly, Laura felt a bit anxious. There was just so much she didn't know about the woman in whose home she had agreed to stay.

But before she could debate the wisdom of her decision, she was asleep.

Chapter 27

Arden stared at the ceiling over her bed. She was happy. She was frightened. The past that she had buried so carefully but never for one moment forgotten had been resurrected and was here in the shape of a fresh young woman with a straightforward manner and a hearty appetite—just like her father.

Laura and Rob had other traits in common, too. They had the same coloring, darker than Arden's, though not quite olive in tone. Laura's eyes were shaped like Rob's, large and long. And their daughter shared her father's strongly made medium height and build. Arden supposed she saw herself in her daughter, as well, though it was more difficult to identify those physical similarities. As for similarities of personality and character, they would show or not in time. So much about whom a person became had to do with nurture, and Laura had been nurtured by people who were strangers to Arden. Strangers to Victoria and Rob.

Arden sighed. She was desperate to tiptoe up to the loft and watch Laura as she slept, as a mother would most naturally do when her child returned from a journey. To resist the temptation took every ounce of Arden's formidable self-control. What if Laura woke to find a woman she hardly knew, a virtual stranger, hovering over her? The last thing Arden wanted was to scare off her child, not after all the long years of their separation.

Together. It was finally how it should have been, or could have been if Arden had been strong enough to defy her parents' order that she give up the child. But what sort of life would she and the baby have had, cut off financially, alone in the world? Countless women had faced just such a grim future, but Arden hadn't been strong enough to take the risk—especially with Rob gone missing. Maybe, if she had known for sure that he was alive and well, that while he had abandoned her, he hadn't been hurt or killed . . . But all that was speculation. Things were the way they were.

And all because she had gotten pregnant at the age of eighteen. Arden's—Victoria's—initial response had been panic, followed immediately by denial. She couldn't be pregnant. She and Rob had taken precautions—but perhaps not as completely as they should have. A second test revealed the same result, and by that time Victoria didn't need a medical professional to tell her that she was carrying Rob's child. Their child.

She hadn't been the least bit afraid of telling Rob. She knew he would be happy, not walk away leaving "it" for her to "fix" like the cads she had so often seen in movies. She had never seen Rob cry before and had realized in that moment that she had fallen in love with him all over again. Here was a real man, her very own hero, the father of her child! And though she had not planned for this child, and though the idea of becoming a parent while still a teenager filled her with an understandable dread, she felt happier than she had ever before felt.

Rob had immediately asked Victoria to marry him. "I love you and you love me. I'll quit school and go to work full-time. We'll live with my parents and sisters until we can afford a place of our own. Our baby will have all the love he or she could ever hope for."

Victoria had hesitated. Her parents needed to be told. Her parents, who didn't even know their daughter had a boyfriend, let alone that he was the son of a working-class family, let alone that he was employed on their property. How would they react to the news that their daughter was not only pregnant but engaged to that young man?

But the look of love and devotion in Rob's eyes overruled all of her fears, and she had gladly agreed to become his wife. Surely her parents would want their only child to be happy. Surely, they loved her and would support her. They had to. It was their job as parents. Wasn't it?

Enough, the adult Arden commanded. What had happened had happened and could not be altered, not all these years later. But the joys of the future—of a future with her daughter—might conceivably outweigh the pains and deprivations of the past.

It was possible.

Wasn't it?

Chapter 28

"I hope sleeping on that sofa wasn't uncomfortable," Arden said when Laura made her appearance in the kitchen. Arden was already dressed for the day in a pair of jeans and a cotton blouse.

Laura, who was still in her pajamas and robe, smiled. "It was just fine."

"Were you warm enough? Too warm?"

"It was perfect. Really. And one of the cats visited me. I couldn't tell who it was, but I woke feeling this weight on my chest and guessing it wasn't an incubus, I assumed it was a cat."

"Probably Ophelia." Arden smiled. "That was her way of telling you that you're welcome here. I hope you didn't mind."

"Not at all. We had a cat for a while when I was very young. His name was Oscar. He was already five or six by the time I came on the scene, and he died when I was ten. I guess that's a decently long life for a cat."

"Decently long, yes. But I know of a kitty who's turning twenty-one in the fall. And another who's nineteen."

"Wow." Laura took a seat at the table, already set with breakfast things. "I wanted an animal companion when I was married, but Jared, my husband, wasn't keen on the idea. He claimed he had allergies, but I never saw him sneeze when he was around a friend's pet. I suspected he just didn't want the bother."

"You said your divorce was recent?" Arden hadn't taken a seat. Laura thought she seemed a bit nervous. Well, if so, that was to be expected.

"It was finalized this spring. It wasn't pretty, and I'm still knee-deep in debt. But you don't want to know the nasty details of that."

"I do if you want to tell me."

Laura smiled. "Thanks. Maybe some other time."

"Do you drink coffee in the morning?" her mother asked hurriedly. "Tea? I have a variety of teas. Do you eat breakfast? I've always been a breakfast person, but I know plenty of people don't care to eat in the morning. I could always—"

Laura smiled. "Arden. It's okay. We'll figure things out and you're not to wait on me. And coffee will be fine."

Arden clasped her hands in front of her. "It's just that I know so little about you. Nothing, really. It's . . ."

Laura quickly stood and went over to her mother. "And I know nothing about you, either"—Laura placed a hand on Arden's shoulder—"so we're both in the same boat. Well, different boats but the same sea. It will be exciting getting to know one another."

But maybe not all sunshine and roses, Laura added silently.

Arden wiped at her eyes and reached for the coffeepot as Laura took her seat again. "I haven't asked what you do," Arden said, pouring two cups of steaming coffee.

"Not much of anything at the moment, I'm afraid. I got my master's degree in literature years ago with the intention of continuing on for my PhD. But I got married and I let being a wife get in the way of my work. See, Jared wasn't keen on my burying myself in academics; he needed all of my attention." Laura smiled a bit embarrassedly. "I don't blame him. I blame myself. Anyway, for the past years I've been teaching writing to freshmen at our local college, you know, honing—more often, introducing—the basic skills, that sort of thing."

"It sounds challenging. Teaching someone to write is teaching her to think."

"It is challenging. But it can be rewarding. Well, not so much financially!"

Arden smiled. "So, what *would* you like for breakfast?"

"Just toast would be fine."

"I have butter and a jar of blueberry jam made locally."

Laura smiled. "The famous Maine blueberries. I had blueberry pancakes at the North Star Diner in Port George."

"It's still around? That's good to hear. You know, you might get sick of blueberries after a time. They show up on tables all year long as people freeze great bags of them to use in the long months of winter."

Laura felt a sliver of anxiety. Would she still be in Eliot's Corner come winter? Did her mother already expect her to stay on? It wasn't wise for either Laura or her mother to make assumptions about their relationship, but it was difficult to ignore the possibility of a future.

Arden brought a plate of toast to the table and finally took a seat of her own. As if on cue, the thundering of feline feet began and stopped only when Falstaff, Ophelia, and Prospero were standing at Laura's feet, balefully staring up at her.

"They've already had their breakfast." Arden rolled her eyes. "Don't fall for the pitiful looks of starvation."

"Not even a bit of butter on my finger?"

"It will become a habit. If you're okay with being hounded for food every time you take a seat at the table, be my guest."

"Sorry, kitties," Laura said to the bundles of fur. "You'll just have to hold out until later."

Chapter 29

"Tell me about my father," Laura said suddenly, but softly.

Arden tightened the grip on her coffee cup. She had been silent about her past for so long, she could hardly believe she finally had the opportunity to speak. It was a gift, and a challenge.

"We met in the library. We bumped into one another and Rob dropped an armload of books."

Laura laughed. "That's so charming!"

"I fell in love with him at once. Words aren't enough to give you a good idea of how special he was, not only to me but to everyone he knew."

"Do you have a photo? I've only seen pictures the *Port George Daily Chronicle* printed at the time he went missing. They were grainy but I got the general impression of a nice-looking young man with a great smile."

"No," Arden said shortly. "What photos I had got lost a long time ago. I'm sorry."

The photos had not been lost. Her parents had thrown them out along with pretty much everything else Rob had given her during their all-too-brief relationship.

Laura nodded. "That's okay."

"When I met Rob, everything began to change. He opened my eyes to laughter. To love. I was seventeen; he was nineteen. We had to keep our relationship a secret, and Rob accepted that. If my parents were to find out I was dating . . ."

"The son of a truck driver?"

Arden sighed. "Yes. They were snobs. But it was more than that. In some ways, it was as if I was being raised in another time entirely, not 1984, the year when Prince released 'When Doves Cry' and when doctors were making ground-breaking discoveries about the cause of AIDS, and *The Burning Bed* caused such a sensation. I mean, it was not a time of cultural stagnation, but you would never have known that from the way my parents behaved. I was exposed to the real world at school, but when I got home every day, I was right back in this sort of cocoon." Arden smiled ruefully. "Being groomed for marriage to an eligible man."

Laura frowned. "It sounds pretty awful. Did you ever meet any of Rob's family?"

"Yes. When we'd been together for about a month, Rob persuaded me to come to his home to meet his family. It took a lot of courage for me to agree, but I didn't want to disappoint him. At first, the Smiths were wary. I think they wondered what I was after, maybe just the thrill of dating a boy from what my parents would say was the wrong side of the tracks. But the second time I visited we were all more comfortable with each other. Except for Frannie, Rob's older sister. She never took to me and clearly wasn't happy that I was dating her brother."

"I'm sorry about that. Look, I told you that I read about the investigation into my father's disappearance. I spoke to Lenny Tobin, the reporter who covered the story for the *Chronicle*. He told me he believes the investigation was prematurely halted by one of the town's powerful men, maybe someone involved in the disappearance."

Arden just nodded. She couldn't bring herself to tell Laura her suspicions about her father's involvement in Rob's disappearance. Not yet, anyway.

"You should know," she said, "that after leaving Port George for good, I kept Rob and the child we'd had together a secret."

Laura's eyes widened. "No one else knows about me? Really?"

"Other than my parents and anyone involved with the adoption.

Some in Port George speculated, but no one knew for sure." Arden hesitated. "Frannie Smith confronted me when I'd returned to Port George after. . . . She knew in her heart that Rob had a child, but I was too scared to admit the truth. Too scared of what might happen when my parents learned I'd revealed their shame. Too scared of what Frannie and her family might do to me if they knew I'd given Rob's child to a stranger."

"Is that why you left Port George? Because you felt pursued?"

"Only partly. But the rest of my story will have to wait." Arden reached across the table and gently touched Laura's hand. "I'm sorry."

"No." Laura placed her hand on Arden's. "I'm sorry. It's a lot all at once, for the both of us. So, if my father and I don't exist as far as anyone in Eliot's Corner is concerned—well, who are you? I mean, what have you told people?"

Arden sat back in her chair. "Before I settled in Eliot's Corner I never stayed long enough in any one place to need much of a back-story. When I did need to *be* someone, I created a very simple narrative. I realized that the fewer details I had to keep track of, the less likely I'd trip myself up."

"And now?"

"Now I want to share the whole truth with my two closest friends here. Deborah and Gordon. And eventually, at least part of the truth with others."

"People will ask about my father. Where he is now. If you two were married. What will you tell them?"

"I don't know."

"It might be easiest to tell the truth as far as you know it. That Rob went missing not long after you discovered you were pregnant. End of story."

"Won't that give rise to a lot of wild speculation?"

"Yes. But no matter what you say or don't say, people are going to speculate."

"The only people whose opinions I care about are Deborah and Gordon.," Arden said firmly. "I'm afraid they might not be pleased with me for having lied to them all this time."

"If they're truly your friends, they'll understand why you kept certain parts of your past a secret. Everyone keeps something back. No one is entirely an open book." Laura smiled. "And speaking of books, I'd like to see your shop. But maybe not today. If you don't mind, I'd like to spend the day here, resting. These past weeks have left me feeling exhausted."

Arden rose from her seat. "Of course. Brent, my assistant, will open if I'm not there, but I should get going. Oh, and don't let the cats con you into giving them more food! They'll eat when I get home."

"You know, the apple didn't fall far from the tree. We've both devoted our lives to the written word in one way or another."

Arden smiled. "For a long time, I regretted not having been able to go to college."

"You could do it now. There are reputable online degree programs."

"I know. But I'm okay with the way I've educated myself over time. Not having a degree doesn't make me a less literate person."

"Of course, it doesn't!" Laura followed Arden to the door of the cottage. "That was another thing about my ex-husband that should have set off warning bells. He didn't read. Well, he said he did and he kept a few tomes around as if to prove his claim, but ask him a basic question about a particular work, and it became clear pretty quickly he had no idea what lay between the covers. For a while I thought it didn't matter to me. I figured he was intellectually curious in other ways. But he wasn't."

"I'm sorry," Arden said feelingly. "I'm sorry you were made so unhappy."

"Me, too. What a waste of time! I think that's what gets me most about the marriage, the fact that I'll never get back those years I wasted with Jared."

Arden fought back new tears. She would never get back the long years she had lived apart from her child. But the future . . .

"Well," she told her daughter as she opened the door of the cottage, "call me if you need anything today. I'm only a few minutes away."

Chapter 30

When Arden had gone, Laura cleaned away the breakfast things and then began a tour of the cottage. She didn't, however, go into Arden's bedroom, though the door was open and Arden hadn't asked her to stay out. That seemed an intimacy too far even though it was clear that her mother trusted her—a stranger, a woman who claimed to be her daughter but who, for all Arden Bell knew, might be an impostor.

What was behind the trust? Laura wondered. Guilt over having given up her baby? Or a real, deep-down certainty that Laura was who she said she was? The bottom line was that Laura was dying to know all that her birth mother had to tell. Stories were a person's heritage, even her birthright; stories were the real riches of inheritance. But her mother might not want to provide anything more than a bare outline of the events that had marked the progress of her life. Burying one's painful memories was a valid coping mechanism, if not the healthiest method of getting through life, and Laura was in no position to criticize. Besides, Arden had asked for patience, and Laura would proceed carefully and with respect for her mother's feelings and all that she had endured since that catastrophic summer of 1984.

Laura looked from the lovely stone fireplace to the wooden slatted blinds on the living room's windows; from the neat-as-a-pin kitchen to the small but cozy loft. Evidence of her mother's character and personality was likely to be in her home, unless, Laura thought, a person who had lived the majority of her life in secrecy and silence might not want to speak through inanimate objects that might invite penetrating questions. Still, it couldn't hurt to observe.

On the coffee table, for example, there sat a basket of seashells in shades of ivory, creamy white, taupe, and mottled brown. Perhaps Arden had collected the shells over years of walks along the shore. Or perhaps she had bought the shells as a collection; Laura had seen packaged seashells for offer in high-end home-goods shops.

A small signed oil painting depicting a line of rowboats at dock caught Laura's eye. The technique was good; the textures of the paint expressive. Did the painting evoke a memory for Arden? Had she—when she was Victoria—gone rowing with Rob one idle summer afternoon?

Though no one piece was overly bright or garish, the cottage was full of color. Various shades of blue and green. Salmon pink. Touches of crimson. What, Laura wondered, was her mother's favorite color? That morning she had been wearing a cotton oxford blouse and jeans. Did she always dress simply and casually? When a little girl, had she enjoyed dressing up in her mother's jewelry and high heels?

A set of three narrow shelves attracted Laura's attention. The centerpiece of the top shelf was a painted fan, Japanese or Chinese, Laura couldn't determine. It might have been a gift. It might have been a flea market find. A quick glance around the room proved that it was the only item of Asian origin, which, again, might mean nothing much or something significant.

Laura smiled. Next to the fan was an iron doorstop in the shape of a comically fat sheep. Found at a yard sale? Laura looked more closely. The top shelf and the two below it were thoroughly free of dust. Arden was a good housekeeper. Had she learned this out of necessity or did she enjoy cleaning and tidying? Laura did not enjoy such things.

No framed photographs were in the living room, or in the kitchen, not even of the friends Arden had mentioned, Deborah and Gordon. That wasn't especially unusual; these days lots of people kept their favorite photos in their phones or on their computers. But Arden didn't strike Laura as being particularly into technology and its constant so-called advances. Then again, all she possessed of her mother were first impressions, and their worth was limited.

But as for books! The cottage was crammed with them. Paperback novels piled high against a wall of the loft. Cookbooks tightly packed on a shelf in the kitchen. Large photographic books lined up on a low shelf in the living room. And Laura had glimpsed a standing bookcase in Arden's room. There was no doubt where Laura had come by her love of reading. She had left Connecticut for her journey to Maine with a satchel of titles she didn't like to be without, old friends, comforting presences, the best traveling companions. *The Historian* by Elizabeth Kostova. *Albion* by Peter Ackroyd. Toni Morrison's *Song of Solomon*. A book of poems by Elizabeth Alexander. Six or seven other volumes. The satchel weighed enough to cause Laura to grunt when she lifted it into the back seat of her car. Getting it up to the loft had been a chore.

After a while, Laura ventured into the yard, careful not to let the cats out, per her mother's firm instructions. It was a beautiful day, the sun shining hotly but cool enough in the shade of the maple tree. Laura sat in one of the four cushioned chairs at a square table and allowed her body to relax. She realized that she felt oddly at ease, even though she was poised at the threshold of what would most likely prove to be the biggest adventure of her life.

Within moments, Laura was asleep.

Chapter 31

Maybe, Arden thought, for about the tenth time that morning, she shouldn't have bothered to come in to the shop today. Maybe she should have stayed home with Laura. Brent was more than able to run the shop on his own, and Zach—or was it Elly? One of them—was due in after lunch. But Laura had said she was tired, and no doubt she needed some time alone after the emotional drain of yesterday's reunion.

Suddenly, Arden became aware of Brent frowning at her. "What?"

"You moved that pencil holder from one side of the counter to the other and back again three times for no reason that I can fathom. And I've asked you twice if you want me to weed out the used-book section, and you either didn't hear me, which means you might be going deaf, or weren't paying attention, which means something's up. Are you feeling okay?"

Arden opened her eyes wide. "Me?" she asked coyly.

Brent dramatically surveyed the otherwise empty shop. "Um, yeah. You."

"I'm fine."

"Hmmm." Brent eyed her more closely. "Are you coming down with something? There was that awful Milton kid in here the other day, coughing up a storm and not bothering to cover his mouth. I had to restrain myself from using a mop handle to push him out of the shop. What sort of parents let their sick children out and about like that?"

Arden laughed. "No, really, Brent, I feel fine. And the Miltons aren't exactly the brightest sparks in Eliot's Corner. I'm not sure we can blame them for that."

Brent still didn't look convinced, but he went off, no doubt to clear from the used-book section the titles that had been there for over six months. They would be donated to the charity shop run by the Baptist church on the edge of town.

The moment Brent was gone, Arden's mind returned to Juniper End's new resident. She wondered what Laura was doing at that very moment. Exploring the cottage perhaps; assessing Arden's book collection; seeing what she kept in the kitchen cupboards. Napping on the couch. Playing with the cats. Speaking to a friend back in Connecticut, relating the story of her reunion with the woman who had given birth to her. What would she tell this friend about Arden Bell? What were Laura's *true* first impressions of her mother?

Hopefully, not that Arden was a liar. She had promised to tell Laura everything about what had happened between the summer of 1984 and June of 1985, but now she wondered if she could keep that promise. Some things were so dark and unpleasant—like, for example, her suspicion that Herbert Aldridge had had a hand in Rob's disappearance.

Arden sighed. She would have to wait and see how things developed between Laura and her. Hopefully, they would grow close and Arden would feel safe in sharing the thoughts and feelings she had kept to herself over the long years since leaving Port George.

Brent suddenly reappeared. He did not look happy. "Elly just texted to say she's running late today and won't be in until two. That girl is impossible."

"Not the most responsible person, I agree, but I think she's harmless."

Brent put his hands on his hips. "You're a softie, that's your problem. She should be thankful she got this internship—why did you chose her, anyway? Don't answer that—and learn to pull her weight around here. She's taking advantage of you, that's what she's doing."

Arden sighed. Brent was probably right. She did have a soft spot for the young. "Okay. Talk to her if you feel you must. But be nice. Maybe she should be thankful for the internship, but she's also under no compulsion to stay, and some Elly is better than no Elly."

"Hmmph." Brent frowned. "That's debatable. I'll be in the travel section if you need me, dreaming of foreign lands."

When Brent had gone off, Arden looked up at the big round clock over the counter. It was only a bit after eleven. Darn. She couldn't wait to go home to her daughter. Such a simple thing—to go home to a loved one—parent, partner, child, friend.

Such a simple and marvelous thing.

Chapter 32

"I'm sorry there's not more for dinner. I really need to do a big shop," Arden explained. "I didn't know . . . I mean, I need to restock on a bunch of things."

"Don't apologize," Laura said firmly. "You didn't know I would suddenly show up on your doorstep. If you want to give me a list, I'll do the shopping tomorrow while you're at work."

Arden took a sip of her wine before going on. "You know, I have to tell my friends who you are very soon. You were probably seen driving into town, and people will have noticed an unfamiliar car parked outside the cottage. And if someone sees you bringing groceries into the cottage, well, the gossips will be having a field day. See, I've never had a visitor from out of Eliot's Corner. I never told anyone where I was going when I left one place for another."

Laura made no comment but wondered how a woman who appeared as friendly and, well, as normal as Arden had managed to remain so unattached for all the years since leaving Port George and fetching up in Eliot's Corner. Maybe one day Laura would know the answer.

In spite of Arden's protests, she had created a delicious and filling meal of pan-fried chicken with savory rice and fresh broccoli. For dessert, there was a choice of vanilla-bean or dark chocolate ice cream.

Finally, Laura put down her spoon and leaned back in her chair in satisfaction. "Have you always been a good cook?"

"I never tried my hand at cooking until I was almost thirty. I found I enjoyed it and I guess I got better as I went along. It wasn't until I came to Eliot's Corner and made friends that I learned how to cook for more than one."

Laura smiled. "I'm hopeless. Jared did the cooking in our marriage, if you can call dumping a jar of red sauce on a pile of pasta and frying hot dogs cooking. But not having any skills of my own, and not having any intention of acquiring those skills, I couldn't complain."

"Good thing you're not a fussy eater. Your father had an enormous appetite for whatever was put in front of him."

"So that's where I got it from. I've eaten a box of Apple Jacks for dinner and been satisfied. My lack of culinary discrimination used to drive my mother crazy."

Arden laughed. "Now that's something else we have in common! I love Apple Jacks! It's the child in me."

"Did you have any other children?" It was a delicate but fair question, Laura thought.

"No. I made a decision a long time ago not to. I felt it would be wrong somehow, an insult to the child I had given up. Some people might think that foolish, but that's how I felt. I don't regret my decision."

"It's not foolish," Laura said firmly. "And I'm glad you don't have regrets. What were *you* like as a child?"

"Do you really want to know?" Arden asked doubtfully.

"Absolutely. I want to know everything about you. Well, everything you're willing to share."

"All right then. I was a pretty solitary child. I never had many friends, and the ones I did have were less confidants than just other girls to pass the time with between classes. You know that old expression 'still waters run deep'? That's what people said about me. I didn't mind. I guess they were right. Only with Rob, your father, did I begin to know what it was like to have a friend, someone with whom I could be really honest. Someone with whom I could be silly or serious, with whom I could laugh or cry. Then that relationship was abruptly cut short."

"I'm sorry. That sounds so inadequate but it's sincere."

Arden smiled. "I know it is. But being totally on my own all these years wasn't as difficult as it might have been if I'd been a really social person. When at times I did feel the need for sympathy, the need for someone to know what I'd been through, some innate survival instinct told me to be quiet."

"Even when you came to Eliot's Corner? I'll admit I've been wondering how you managed to stay so aloof from personal entanglements for all those years."

"That's when my habit of silence began to become a burden. Once here, I began to feel safe, comfortable, even happy. Then it seemed silly not to tell the people I was coming to love about my past. But the habit of caution was so ingrained. And there was always the fear that I might be rejected for—"

"For what? For giving up your baby when you yourself were only a kid?"

Arden nodded. "Maybe. Anyway, I convinced myself that the more people who knew about the past, the more difficult it would be ever to put it to rest. Trust, you see, isn't easy. At least, for me it hasn't been."

"And yet, you trust that I'm your flesh and blood, without any hard proof."

"A mother knows her child. And I never gave up hope. 'I believe while I tremble; I trust while I weep.' That's a line from Charlotte Brontë's *Villette*." Arden smiled. "I'm in the habit of quoting it."

Laura leaned forward. "That reminds me of something I've been wanting to tell you. A week or two ago I went to the beach near Port George one afternoon. I was totally alone, I'm absolutely sure of that, when I felt what I can only describe as a reassuring touch on my arm. I was startled but not afraid." Laura smiled. "You see, I believe the living aren't alone here. At the time, I thought it might be my adoptive mother comforting me, but now I can't help wonder if it might have been my father. Maybe he was telling me that I was close to finding you."

To finding home, Laura added silently.

"It's possible," Arden said. "I told you about the dreams I had. It's not unheard of for family members to be intimately connected across miles, so why not through different planes of existence and states of consciousness?"

Laura glanced to the cats, who were in a wrestling match at the edge of the living room. "Some people believe cats can see ghosts, all sorts of things, really, that we can't see or even sense."

Arden looked to the ball of felines and laughed. "I'm not so sure how aware of otherworldly presences Falstaff might be—he's firmly rooted in the here and now, as in, what's in his food bowl—but there have been times when I'm sure Ophelia and Prospero have sensed the spirits of people who made the cottage their home long ago."

"Why?" Laura asked, genuinely interested. "What did the cats do?"

"Tried to bite their ankles, of course."

Chapter 33

"Welcome," Deborah said, standing back to allow Arden to enter. "You're just in time. The tea is ready to pour."

Arden was nervous, not the least because she had lied to her friend yet again. Last evening, in response to Deborah's question about the car with Connecticut plates parked outside Juniper End, Arden had said that an old friend was visiting. She simply hadn't been prepared to share the truth of Laura's identity over the phone.

Deborah Norrell had a talent for decorating; she achieved a sense of harmony that was a lot more considered than it appeared. Now the two women sat on the sleek, pale gray couch in a living room that was a study in neutrals. Several milk-glass pieces from the mid-twentieth century provided pops of white against the palette of taupe, cream, and cool grays.

"You look worried," Deborah announced. "What's up? Does it have anything to do with this old friend you mentioned? Where'd she come from, anyway? I've never heard you talk about anyone from your past."

Arden took a deep breath. It was best to just dive in. "I lied. I'm sorry. Laura Huntington, the woman staying with me, isn't an old friend. She's my daughter."

Deborah's eyebrows shot to the skies. "Holy moly, you'd better start from the beginning."

Arden did. She told Deborah about growing up in Port George, and about meeting Rob Smith, the first and only love of her life, when she was seventeen. She told her about learning she was pregnant and about Rob's disappearance soon after. She told her about being sent away to have the baby, about the baby being adopted at birth, about coming back to Port George, and about her running away from her name, her home, her old life.

"I knew there was something big you weren't telling us!" Deborah exclaimed when Arden had completed her tale. "But I couldn't bring myself to ask questions. I assumed a tragedy and I was right. Damn, how did you keep this to yourself all this time? Did Margery know?"

Arden smiled feebly. "Nobody knew. Silence becomes a habit like anything else. Inertia, too."

"A body at rest stays at rest. But still, I'd have blabbed to the first person I met after leaving Port George! I'd begin with 'You'll never believe what happened to me!'"

"Not if you were afraid of being found and brought back."

"Oh. Right. And major kudos to you for taking charge of your life at such a tender age! Sheesh." Deborah frowned. "I feel a bit like a slug now. How can I ever bitch and moan to you about a fussy client or the fact that the grocery store doesn't carry my favorite low-fat yogurt anymore when you've shouldered such big burdens without a complaint?"

Arden laughed. "Trouble is trouble. A person's burdens feel huge to her, no matter how insignificant they seem to others."

"Yeah, I guess." Deborah reached for her friend's hand. "Arden, I'm so happy for you, being reunited with your child after all these years. Wait. You're not going to go back to using Victoria, are you? Not that it's not a pretty name, but I'm so used to calling you Arden . . ."

"No. I'm not going back to Victoria. And I'm not going to talk about the details of my past with anyone other than you and Gordon. At least for now. If someone grabs you in the post office and wants to know everything you know, please say nothing. This is all too new and overwhelming for me to make public yet. Maybe I never will."

"I promise. Mum's the word." Deborah laughed. "Mum! Mom. Oh, my gosh, you're a mom! Maybe we'd better ditch the tea and break out the bubbly!"

Chapter 34

"How did your friend Deborah take the news?" Laura asked as she helped Arden to set the table for dinner that evening.

Arden smiled. "She was happy for me. She said she always suspected I was keeping something from her, from everyone. I never meant to set myself up as a woman of mystery, but I guess that's what I did when I settled in Eliot's Corner."

"A woman of mystery. It sounds so romantic, even glamorous. But too often the reality doesn't match the glossy movie image we have of a tragic, beautiful heroine bravely soldiering through life while tightly holding a dark and painful secret in her heart."

"Indeed."

After a meal of pasta with mushroom sauce, Laura excused herself and returned a few minutes later holding a photo album.

"I wonder if you'd like to see these. I put together a small collection of photos before I left for Port George, just in case I did manage to locate you and you wanted to know me. It's a collection of highlights of my childhood, up through my wedding. I know my marriage was a bust, but doesn't every parent want to see her child on their wedding day?"

"Of course," Arden said readily. "I'd love to see it. Let's sit on the couch and you can explain everything as we go."

"Before we get to that, I've been meaning to ask you about your photo on the shop's website. Did you ever consider that someone from your past might come across it and recognize you? Or that someone from Port George might come into the shop one day and realize that you were Victoria Aldridge? I mean, the towns are only a few hours apart."

"Maybe I wasn't as careful as I should have been. But by the time I had the website set up, I guess I felt strong enough not to care if someone found me out. Even my parents. Besides, it's been so long since I was last seen in Port George, and I was never well-known, not like your father. I doubted many people, if anyone, would put two and two together."

"I guess you were right."

"There's another thing about that photo. When I left Port George, I didn't take much with me, and that included pictures of myself. And for all the years before I settled in Eliot's Corner, I was careful not to let myself be photographed. Not that anyone wanted to take my picture; I had no friends by choice. So, after Margery passed and I set up the Arden Forest website, I found I really wanted to proclaim myself, Arden Bell, as *here*. Does that make sense?"

"Absolutely." Laura opened the album. "Ready?"

Arden nodded.

"This one was taken just after my parents brought me home."

Tears sprang to Arden's eyes and she reached into her pocket for a tissue.

"I'm sorry." Laura laid a hand on Arden's arm. "Are you sure this won't be too difficult? We could look at it some other time, a week, a month from now."

Or, I could leave it with her when I go, Laura thought. *Because I won't be here forever.*

"No," Arden said resolutely, dabbing at her eyes. "I want to do this now."

Next, Laura showed Arden a photo of Marty and Cynthia Huntington taken a few years after the adoption. "And here are my parents," she said quietly.

Arden smiled. "They look like kind people. I think I would have liked them."

"They were kind." Laura turned a page. "This is me on my first birthday. I really was a chubbums, wasn't I?"

Arden laughed. "Skinny babies make me nervous. Rob showed me a few photos of him as a toddler. You look so much like he did!"

"That's nice to know," Laura said feelingly. She continued to lead them through the mandatory first-day-of-school photos, from kindergarten through ninth grade. "After that I'm afraid I declared I was too mature for another first-day-of-school picture. Teens can be so selfish. I'm sure my refusal to have my picture taken hurt my mother, but she said nothing."

They continued on through high school and college graduation, with a stop along the way for senior prom—"What a hideous dress!" Laura commented, to which Arden said, "No, no, you looked very nice"—and for a backpacking trip around Europe with friends.

"And here's the day I was awarded my master's degree," Laura said softly. "I hadn't planned on attending the ceremony, but my mother insisted. It meant a lot to her to be there. Dad was too weak by then to attend."

"I wish I could have been there myself." Arden shook her head. "I'm sorry. That was a foolish thing to say."

"Not foolish." Laura turned a page to a formal portrait of a bride and groom. "The big event. My wedding. I spent so much time working with the florist and the photographer and selecting readings and music. I wanted everything to be perfect, to really describe me." Laura laughed ruefully. "Jared wasn't interested in the planning. I'd hoped he would be, that he'd want to add his tastes to the day, too, but he insisted that I should do whatever I wanted and he'd do his part by showing up on time. Not a fantastic sign of the state of our relationship, if I'd had the brain to see it."

"You were a beautiful bride," Arden said warmly. "What happened later on doesn't take that away."

"Thanks. My parents were both gone by then, so there was no first dance with Dad. My mother had died not long after him. Once Dad passed, she seemed to wither. She had been so in love with him."

"Well, your father was very handsome. Not that looks count in the end, not like character and kindness."

"Looks shouldn't count as much as they do in the beginning," Laura said dryly. "I know if Jared had been a below-average-looking guy I might not have fallen as hard as I did. Ridiculous. In retrospect, I see that my money was the real draw for him. It certainly wasn't *my* looks. Oh, well, lesson learned."

"Forget about Jared. Tell me more about your father."

Laura closed the album and considered for a moment how to describe Marty Huntington. "In a way," she said finally, "he was what I would call a classic man of the old school. Strong, silent, hard-working, devoted to his family." Laura smiled. "He was genuinely in love with my mother, and she with him. We were well-off thanks to Dad's being CEO of a big engineering firm. When he retired, he continued to consult and that was pretty lucrative. I adored him as a little girl and came to really admire and respect him as I got older. Not every daughter can say that about a father. I was lucky."

Arden took Laura's hand. "I'm so very glad you were cared for so kindly."

"I was. You know, my father had a chronic heart condition. It's what killed him in the end, but while he lived, he tried never to let it get in the way of being there for us." Laura smiled fondly. "He taught me how to ride a bike and how to swim. He was my date for the father-daughter dance in seventh grade, and when I was bullied in tenth grade by a girl in my class, he taught me how to rise above the situation."

"You loved him."

"I did. It's interesting. I never knew why my parents didn't have a child of their own, or why they waited so long to adopt. My mother was forty-seven and my dad fifty-three when they brought me home. Neither ever offered that sort of personal information, and for some reason, I never asked." Laura shrugged. "I guess it doesn't really matter now."

"No, I guess it doesn't. Are there any more photos in this album?"

Laura shook her head. "No. I didn't want to include anything from the years of my marriage." Suddenly Laura had an idea. "I understand if this sounds . . . I mean, if you'd rather not, but maybe we could take a selfie of us together?"

A radiant smile broke out on Arden's face. "That would be lovely! But you'll have to be the photographer. I've never taken a selfie. I'm not sure I know how!"

Laura laughed and fairly leaped off the couch. "I'll go and get my phone. And I'm going to teach you how to turn the camera on yourself. After all, it's about time you come into focus."

Chapter 35

Gordon opened the front door of his home wearing his uniform of cargo shorts and a black T-shirt. "Hi," he said brightly. "I didn't expect you. Come in."

"I hope I'm not interrupting anything important," Arden said. "I should have called first. I don't know why I didn't."

"Not at all. It's a beautiful day. Let's go out to the yard."

Gordon's house was bare of knickknacks and decorated instead with mounds of books (mostly nonfiction), several computers (and all the wires and gadgets that went with them), a large-screen television (Gordon was a fan of soccer), a vintage pinball machine (he had sold all but this one of his collection before coming to Eliot's Corner), and furniture that defined the word *mismatched*. The decor might fairly be described as Random Convenience. For example, Gordon had wanted a couch, so he had bought one, with absolutely no thought as to size or style. It was far too large for the living room and upholstered in a pink-and-green cabbage-rose pattern that clashed badly with the round glass-and-chrome coffee table he had bought at a yard sale thirty years before. Deborah had tried to give Gordon a few tips on home decorating, but the lesson hadn't been a success.

"I've been procrastinating all morning," Gordon admitted. "I should have been in my workshop but . . ."

A large shed in one corner of the yard was where Gordon created his wood carvings and scrap-metal sculptures. The lawn—which hadn't been mowed in a while—was home to various works in progress, some of which were draped with cloths while others remained exposed to the elements.

Gordon and Arden sat across from each other at an old-fashioned picnic table that Gordon had painted bright purple.

Arden folded her hands in her lap, then placed them on the table before her. She was nervous. Gordon's friendship meant an awful lot to her, more, she suspected, than she was able or willing to acknowledge. It was vitally important that he understand she had never meant any harm with her lies.

"I need to tell you something. I want to tell you."

A look of concern came to Gordon's face. "Is anything wrong?"

"No, in fact, things are pretty wonderful. It's just that . . ." Arden took a deep breath. "I lied about who I am. Something's happened that makes that lie meaningless and unnecessary now."

"Does it have anything to do with the owner of the car that's been parked outside Juniper End for the past few days? The one with Connecticut plates?" Gordon smiled. "People talk."

"Yes." Without further hesitation Arden told Gordon what she had told Deborah. Telling was no easier or less exhausting the second time around, and when she had finished, she felt the need for a long nap.

Gordon whistled. "Now that's something I never expected to hear when I woke up this morning. Arden, I'm thrilled for you. I—I have so much to say, but maybe I'd better let you do the talking now. You said that things were pretty wonderful. There must be some level of stress, as well."

A surge of relief and gratitude swept through Arden. She should never have doubted Gordon's capacity for understanding. "There is. When I opened the door the other day and was suddenly face-to-face with my daughter, I felt sheer panic. I almost passed out. Was she there to punish me? To demand answers that I couldn't give? But now I don't believe that Laura has any hurtful intent toward me. Still, I'm afraid I'll say the wrong thing—and what could possibly be the right thing?—and make her angry, and the new and fragile relationship will shatter."

"But there's more present in your heart than fear."

Arden nodded. "There is. There's happiness. And I'm so grateful to Laura's adoptive mother for giving her the clue that led Laura to me."

"That was very generous of Mrs. Huntington. She sounds like a good woman. Now, when do I get to meet your daughter?"

"We'd like you and Deborah to join us for dinner tomorrow. I told Deborah about Laura just yesterday. And I'm only sharing the entire story with the two of you. The people in Eliot's Corner will come to know that Laura is my daughter, but the past will stay in the past."

Gordon smiled. "Got it. So, does Laura look a lot like you?"

"Not much that I can see. I think she resembles her father pretty strongly. It's a bit unsettling, but I guess I'll get used to—"

"To seeing a ghost?" Gordon suggested gently. "You said Rob went missing. You assume he's dead?"

"I believe he's been dead since August of 1984. So, yes. In a way, I'll have to get used to seeing a ghost."

"You loved him very much." It was a statement, not a question, and spoken gently.

Arden nodded and felt tears pricking at her eyes. "I did. He was my first real friend as well as my first love. In a way, I've never gotten over him. It's the way he just disappeared. If he had dumped me for another girl, if he had been killed in a car accident and decently buried, it would have been easier, I think, to let him go. But the not knowing was cruel. It *is* cruel."

Gordon reached across the table and took Arden's hand in his own. "I'm sorry. I truly am." He released her hand, then nodded for her to go on.

"As bad as it's been for me, imagine what his family has gone through. Rob was the only son. His sisters and parents adored him. Laura told me that about ten years after Rob disappeared they had him officially declared dead, and maybe that brought some closure, but I doubt it. And at least one of Rob's sisters suspected that there was a baby. I'm sure she's always held me responsible for her brother's disappearance. If Rob had never gotten involved with me . . ."

"I don't understand. Why do you assume his disappearance has anything to do with you?"

Arden felt her lips tighten. She couldn't admit to her friends that she believed her father was responsible for Rob's disappearance. At least, not before sharing that doubt with Laura. "Nothing. I was just being dramatic."

Gordon didn't press her. "You've been honest with me," he said after a moment, "so I'll be honest with you. It's always been clear to me that you were keeping something back. Not only from me, but from Deborah, and from the rest of Eliot's Corner. Of course," he added hastily, "that was your right."

"Deborah also said that she knew there was something I was withholding. And yet you both trusted me as a friend, knowing I wasn't exactly who I said I was. I don't really understand."

Gordon smiled. "Who is ever entirely who they appear to be? Who is only one person for her entire life? There are as many Gordons as there are people who claim to know me. And if I were to describe myself, I'd probably paint a picture my friends would hardly recognize! For one, I'd call myself a great artist, but I doubt anyone else would."

Arden laughed. "Thank you," she said gratefully.

"Which doesn't mean I'm not much happier now that you've shared the truth with me. I'd like to think it brings us closer."

Arden felt a flutter in the region of her heart. Maybe it was foolish to continue denying her romantic feelings for Gordon, the increasingly strong desire for intimate connection. She suspected—maybe she even knew—that Gordon was in love with her and had been for some time so . . . But no. Arden suppressed the flutter. She would never allow herself the joys of another romance. Not after what had been done to Rob.

"I'm glad," she said, aware that her voice wasn't entirely steady, "that you aren't upset with me for lying all these years."

"You weren't lying. Not in my opinion. So, are your parents still alive?"

"Laura tells me they're still living in the house in which I grew up. It's odd to think of them having stayed on for all these years. But maybe they felt they had no place else to go. Or maybe they just love the house itself. It is pretty impressive, and that sort of thing appealed to them. Social status. Wowing the neighbors."

"Maybe they thought you'd come back one day. Maybe they were waiting for you in a place you could easily find them. Home. Or is that being too romantic?"

Arden laughed. "Way too romantic! At least in terms of my father. My mother . . ." Arden paused and thought for a moment. "I suppose it's possible my mother hoped I'd come home. She was always emotionally fragile, at least in my memory. My running off without a word of farewell or explanation might have hurt her badly. I guess I knew that at the time, but I truly felt I had no choice. It's possible that over the years my mother came to accept my absence as normal; she was always good at pretending. Or maybe she *has* been waiting for me to knock on the door the way Laura knocked on my door."

"You could find out the answers to those questions," Gordon said gently. "If you wanted to."

Arden smiled. "Some questions are better left unanswered."

"I agree. But I don't claim to know which ones."

Chapter 36

"Moses smell the roses!" Brent cried. "Your daughter? I didn't know you had kids."

"I don't." Arden smiled. "Just this one."

Brent shook his head. "It just goes to show, don't assume anything. Good to meet you, Laura."

"And you as well," Laura assured him. The two shook hands. "Arden tells me she wouldn't be able to run this place without you."

"That's a lie! I'm sure she'd do just fine without me, but I'm in no hurry to leave."

The bell over the door of the shop tinkled, and Brent glanced over his shoulder to where a chubby middle-aged man was standing. When he turned back to Laura and Arden, he rolled his eyes. "It's Steve Baker," he whispered to Laura. "He's nice enough, but he can't get it through his head that I haven't read every single book we sell. He asks endless questions about a particular title even when I've told him all I've done is read the cover copy."

Brent went off to greet Steve Baker and, hopefully, to satisfy his endless curiosity.

"It's true," Arden said quietly. "Steve's one of Eliot's Corner's characters. Totally harmless but, at times, frustrating. Still, he's one of the shop's greatest supporters and I can't complain about that."

"I guess not. You know, this is really wonderful, my mother owning a bookshop."

Arden smiled. "Friends and family discount, you mean?"

"I wasn't thinking about a discount. I was thinking about how it demonstrates our similarities, like I said the other day. We're both avid readers, and writers. Well, I assume that you write, too, maybe keep a journal or write poetry?"

"Honestly, I haven't written in years. I kept a journal until the time I got pregnant. I took it with me when I was sent away, but suddenly I wasn't able to put my thoughts and feelings on paper. Since then, the only things I've written, aside from grocery lists, are synopses of books and discussion questions used by the book club."

"I'm sorry. I did it again, brought up something upsetting. There's a minefield under our feet and we just have to step as carefully as we can."

The conversation was interrupted by the entrance of another customer. The tall, slim woman looked to be in her early thirties. Her hair was cut close to her head in a style that flattered her face and brought attention to her large blue eyes. She was dressed in a flowing linen top and matching pants, giving her a wraithlike appearance. She came—or rather, Laura thought, flowed—toward them with her hand extended.

"Hello, Arden," she said in a low and breathy voice, "how are you? I had to come in as I'm absolutely dying for a new mystery. I'm sorry, am I interrupting?" The woman turned to Laura with an openly inquisitive smile.

Arden introduced the woman as Lydia Austen, a devoted member of the Arden Forest Book Club. "And this"—Arden gestured to Laura—"is Laura Huntington, my daughter."

It didn't take a genius to realize that Lydia Austen knew very well that the woman standing beside Arden Bell was her child. Word was probably all around Eliot's Corner by now.

"Oh, it's a pleasure to meet you." Lydia extended her hand to Laura, the compelling blue eyes boring into her as if hoping to unearth every clue as to Laura's character. "I hope you enjoy your stay in our charming little town. Will you be here for long? Are you stay-ing with your mother?"

Laura was dying to glance at Arden but felt it might result in a chuckle, and that would be rude. "Eliot's Corner is lovely," Laura said dutifully. "I'm not sure how long I'll be here, and, yes, I'm staying at Juniper End."

The brief and to-the-point answers seemed to satisfy the woman, and with a nod she went off in the direction of the mysteries—a large area and arguably the most popular of the shop—but was gone mere moments later, with a wave but no purchase.

"It seems," Laura said, "that in spite of 'absolutely dying' for a new mystery, Lydia Austen stopped by just to see the new attrac-tion in town."

Arden smiled. "She means well. I don't blame people for want-ing to meet you. It's a small town. In a way, it's one big family, com-plete with bossy great-aunts and ne'er-do-well brothers-in-law and overbearing mothers. They consider you a member of our family."

Whether she wanted to be or not, Laura thought. It was too early to tell.

Laura glanced to where Brent and Steve Baker stood by the table of new releases. Brent, seeing he had Laura's attention, dis-creetly ran his forefinger across his throat. Laura hid a smile. Brent might complain about Mr. Baker and no doubt about other difficult customers, but Laura had the distinct feeling that he enjoyed his job immensely.

"So," Laura said to her mother, "put me to work."

Chapter 37

After a dinner of cheeseburgers and salad—during which Arden discovered that she and Laura shared a preference for Swiss cheese on their burgers and mustard rather than ketchup—the women retired to the yard with cups of coffee. It was a beautiful evening, and Arden thought it would be almost sinful to miss an opportunity to enjoy the warm weather when a long, long winter was inevitable.

"I'd like to talk more about my father, if you feel able," Laura said when they were settled. "About what happened in August of 1984."

Arden nodded. "When I told Rob that I was pregnant, he immediately asked me to marry him. He was so excited. I said yes. It was crazy, of course, we were young and had no money of our own, but we were in love. I knew my parents would object, but I really believed my happiness would mean more to them than their ideas of social preeminence."

"You were wrong," Laura said shortly.

"I was. The night I told my parents was the worst night of my life. My mother got hysterical. My father was coldly furious. I was never to see 'that boy' again. I was basically put under house arrest. A few days later, Rob was reported missing by his family. I was in a state of shock. I wondered if I could have been wrong about Rob. I wondered if he really had abandoned me. I remember my father saying to me something like 'That young man is a piece of trash. No doubt he's left town for good.'"

Laura frowned. "I'm so sorry. It must have been an awful time."

"I truly wanted to believe that Rob would never willingly leave me and our unborn child. But where was he? Could something terrible have happened to him? And then I thought, 'My father can be ruthless in business, or so everyone says. Maybe he can also be ruthless in other parts of his life, too.' And then I remembered something my father had said the night I told my parents that I was pregnant with Rob's child, something like, 'I'll make that boy pay.' Maybe it was an empty threat, just one of those things people say in the heat of the moment, but from that moment on it loomed large in my mind."

"So, there you were, barely eighteen years old, wondering if your own father had orchestrated the disappearance of the boy you loved, and all the while being held prisoner."

"Not literally. I wasn't being kept under lock and key. I was held in place by the habits of obedience and fear. And I was depressed. Numb. Rob had opened the door into a warmer, brighter world. Now, with him gone, I sank back into the cold and gray world from which I'd only begun to emerge that summer. I found that I had no capacity to protest being sent off to a home for wealthy unwed pregnant girls. I had no capacity to protest the plan for my baby to be adopted."

"It's a nightmare," Laura murmured. "Like something you'd find in a classic Gothic novel."

Arden nodded. The same thought had occurred to her often enough. "This is the first time I've told anyone about my suspicions of my father."

"Thank you. Not that it's so great to hear that your grandfather might have been responsible for the disappearance of your father, but I'm glad you trusted me enough to share your concerns."

And she did trust her daughter, Arden realized. Her own flesh and blood. "I loved Rob so much. If he hadn't gotten involved with me, he wouldn't be . . . He would still be here, alive, with his family."

"You don't know for sure that he's dead, or that if he is dead, it was your father's fault. But either way, you're not the one to blame. You were in love with Rob and he was in love with you. You each risked being together because you wanted to. You needed to."

"Yes," Arden murmured; she went on almost as if talking to herself. "Even if Rob hadn't disappeared that day, it wouldn't have changed the fact that I was forbidden to see him and that I would have been sent away to have my baby in secret. He would have lost access to his child."

Laura leaned forward and spoke urgently. "Stop thinking about what-ifs and alternative scenarios. That sort of thinking can drive you crazy fast."

"I know. But sometimes it's hard not to wonder, especially when I'm alone with my thoughts at the end of the day."

"I still can't believe you kept everything about your past a secret until now. How could anyone keep such a tragic story to themselves and not go mad? I know I couldn't."

"You never know what you're capable of until you're tested. That really is true, though not necessarily of much comfort." Arden paused. "To be honest, my father wasn't the only one I suspected of being involved with Rob's disappearance. My family were friends with the Coldwells. We knew each other since we were kids. Ted himself told you that. I knew that Ted liked me in a way I didn't like him, but he never said or did anything to make me feel afraid or uncomfortable. Not until that summer of '84."

Laura frowned. "What happened then?"

"I wasn't there when it took place; Rob told me about it after. It seems he ran into Ted in town one afternoon not long after my eighteenth birthday. Rob told me he'd never spoken to Ted before that incident, that he hadn't even known him by name. But Ted approached Rob, told him he was a friend of the Aldridge family, and that he'd known me since I was a baby. Nothing physical happened, just Ted being vaguely verbally threatening, but Rob got the message: 'Don't mess around with Victoria. If you hurt her, there will be consequences.'"

"Sort of like what your father said about Rob," Laura noted darkly.

Arden nodded. "I was so upset when Rob told me this. I'd always trusted Ted, but after Rob's disappearance I began to wonder if he'd been in league with my father, if together they had made Rob go away."

"And now? Do you still think Ted had something to do with my father's disappearance?"

"No," Arden said firmly. "A long time ago I stopped suspecting that Ted had been involved. I remembered the fun times we'd had together when I was young. He was like a big brother to me, kind and protective. I believe Ted's warning Rob not to hurt me was just what it appeared to be—a big brother flexing his muscles. Nothing more and nothing less."

Laura smiled. "I have to admit that for about half a second I wondered if Ted could be my father. I was all over the place with theories! Anyway, I liked him. Not that he was super–welcoming, but he rang true. I've always had good instincts about people. Except, of course, when it came to the man I married."

"I'm sorry. I know all too well that romantic attraction clouds judgment."

"Yes, but I suspect we're stuck with romance." Laura smiled. "The heart wants what it wants."

The women went inside soon after to find the cats munching from their bowls of dry food. Suddenly, Prospero left his bowl, went over to where Ophelia was eating her own snack, and with his head pushed her out of the way. Immediately, Ophelia whacked him hard enough to cause him to jump away from her bowl. The look on Prospero's face was pitiful: *What did I do to deserve that?*

Arden hid a laugh. Cats didn't enjoy being laughed at. "If you didn't try to steal her food in the first place," she told Prospero, "you wouldn't have gotten smacked."

"Boys." Laura shook her head. "Always causing trouble and then wondering how it happened."

Chapter 38

"I splurged and got us lobsters. This is, after all, a celebration."

"You shouldn't have!" Deborah cried. "But I'm awfully glad you did!"

Gordon nodded. "Me, too!"

Laura smiled. She had met Deborah and Gordon only moments earlier but already felt at ease with them. Her mother, it seemed, was skilled at choosing friends, in spite of the largely lonely life she had been leading.

"I got a great deal," Arden explained, "because I bought them right off the boat from Tommy Harper this morning."

"Always buy direct from the farmers and fishermen when you can," Gordon agreed. "It's good for everyone."

It was almost seven when the four sat down to dinner around the table in the yard. Laura had spent a good part of the day exploring Eliot's Corner on foot and was famished.

It was too early in the season for local corn, so Arden had made a corn salad using frozen kernels. There was bread from Chez Claudine. There were individual pots of drawn butter for the lobster (Laura had never before seen drawn butter prepared; it seemed a bit of a culinary miracle), and two bottles of a Portuguese *vinho verde*.

Deborah raised her glass. "To friends and family."

The toast was seconded, and all dug in to the meal.

"Your mother is a very good cook," Gordon said, passing the corn salad to Laura. "And she's generous with her friends who can barely boil water. That would be me."

"I don't know about being very good," Arden demurred, "but I do enjoy cooking."

"And baking," Deborah added. "Don't get me started on her apple pie!"

Laura smiled. "I don't seem to have inherited the kitchen gene. Like Gordon, I can barely boil water. I mean it. Every time I've attempted to make pasta, it comes out too hard to properly chew or so soft the noodles disintegrate in the pot."

"You'll need a few lessons from Arden then, before you—" Deborah broke off in obvious embarrassment.

"That's okay," Laura said quickly. "At this moment, I have no idea how long I'll be staying in Eliot's Corner. I'm taking it one day at a time." She looked to Arden. "I think we both are."

Arden nodded but said nothing. Laura thought she saw a flash of sadness cross her mother's face. Maybe she had imagined it.

"Where are you stationed at the moment?" Gordon asked.

"For the past ten years or so I've lived in Chester, Connecticut. First, with my former husband until we separated last spring, and after that, in a charming little rental a friend found for me. The lease was up just before I left for Maine, so now my things are in storage in a colleague's garage."

"Arden tells me you teach?" Gordon asked.

"Yes. I had to take a second job as a private tutor to help pay off some of the debts Jared had accrued, but my main gig is teaching writing to freshmen at the local college."

"Is the divorce final?" Deborah asked.

"Thankfully, yes." Laura hesitated. "With my parents both dead, and Jared finally out of my life, I realized just how alone I was in the world and that it was time to locate the woman who had given birth to me." Laura looked to Arden and smiled. "I can't tell you how glad I am that I undertook the search."

Arden reached for Laura's hand. "Me, too."

"I can see your mother in the shape of your nose. And there's something about the shape of your mouth. Can you see the resemblance, Laura?" Deborah asked.

Laura nodded. "Yes. I saw it immediately."

"I see it now as well," Arden admitted. "But I see a stronger resemblance to Laura's father. Laura has her father's coloring, and his smile, and his eyes."

Deborah turned to Laura. "Okay, tell me to shut up, but I have to ask. Now that you've succeeded in locating your mother, do you have any intention of trying to find out once and for all what happened to your father?"

Laura nodded and told the others an abbreviated tale of her adventures in Port George. "I intend to go back and see what else I can find. An old family friend of my mother, Ted Coldwell, might be able to shed further light on events that took place in the summer of 1984. I'd like to meet with him again and see what he has to say. If he's willing to talk, that is. I'm afraid I wasn't honest with him when I presented myself as a scout with a podcast research team."

"Would anyone like anything more before I bring out dessert?" Arden asked.

"Yes," Deborah said promptly. "Another teensy-weensy helping of corn salad."

Gordon laughed. "You wouldn't know teensy-weensy if it bit you on the nose!"

Deborah looked up from the mound of corn salad she had just loaded onto her plate. "It's all about perspective," she said haughtily.

"In that case," Laura said, "I think I'll have another teensy-weensy helping myself!"

Chapter 39

For dessert, Arden had made individual strawberry shortcakes with homemade biscuits and hand-whipped cream.

"Heaven on earth," Deborah sighed when Arden brought the dessert out to the table.

"I'm with you there," Laura said. "I have a mighty big sweet tooth."

Arden joined the others and dug into her dessert. She was glad that Laura had kept their agreement not to reveal Arden's suspicions about Herbert Aldridge just yet. After all, it was just a suspicion; there was no need to blacken a person's name when he might be innocent of wrongdoing.

"I feel the need to be the voice of caution here," Gordon said suddenly. "Digging into the past can be a dangerous undertaking. When you set out to find your birth mother, Laura, I'm sure you realized that things might not go well, but miraculously, they did. A miracle might not happen again."

Laura nodded. "I know. But this is something I have to do."

"I'm scared of what we might find," Arden admitted. "Nothing at all, or, worse, evidence of a crime or a terrible accident. But Laura strongly feels it's time to make an effort to find out what happened that Sunday afternoon in August of 1984, the last day Rob Smith was seen in Port George."

"The more time passes, the colder the trail goes," Deborah pointed out. "And an awful lot of time has passed. But if this is something you guys are determined to do, I'll help in whatever small way I can, even if it's just to say prayers."

Arden smiled. "Prayers are hardly a small thing."

"Amen to that," Gordon said.

The evening wound down after coffee had been drunk and dessert demolished. When Deborah and Gordon left, with promises of getting together again before long, mother and daughter cleared the table, set pots to soaking, and began to put away the few leftovers.

"Always save lobster bodies," Arden instructed. "They're perfect for making broth for risotto."

Laura sighed. "I could get fat living here."

The idea made Arden smile. There was such joy in feeding her child after all the years of separation!

"I really like your friends," Laura said. "They seem entirely themselves, if you know what I mean. No airs."

"They're the first real friends I've ever had, with the exception of Rob and, of course, Margery. What about you? Do you have a best friend? Or a tribe, if that term is still being used."

"No tribe. But there is a woman named Sara. We met in grad school. We don't need to live in one another's pockets, but we're very close." Laura reached for the sponge and began to wipe the counter next to the sink. "Gordon likes you," she said in an overly casual way. "It's pretty obvious. How do you feel about him?"

"I like him, too," Arden replied promptly.

"What about getting romantically involved with this man you like?"

"I couldn't . . ." Arden winced. The words had come of their own volition.

"Why?" Laura turned to look directly at Arden.

Arden shrugged. "No real reason. Just because."

Laura grinned. "You sound like a kid. What you mean is that you *won't* get involved with Gordon."

In a delaying tactic, Arden reached for a plastic container and lid in which to store what was left of the corn salad. "The truth is," she said finally, "that on some level I've always felt I don't deserve to be happily in love after what happened to Rob."

"I see," Laura said gently. "I'm sorry. I should have guessed it was something like that."

Arden waved her hand dismissively. "Now isn't the time to talk about such things. We've got to put the food away before Falstaff hauls himself onto the counter and digs in."

As if to prove the strong possibility of this happening, Falstaff crashed his considerable bulk into Arden's calf. "Yes," she said with a laugh, "I'm aware that you're here."

Chapter 40

Dusting was an oddly soothing task, Laura had discovered just that morning. It had the added benefit of allowing her a close look at the titles currently available at Arden Forest. There was a broad selection of fiction, contemporary and classic, from writers based in both Western and Eastern cultures, with a solid selection of African authors both renowned and just starting out. She hoped the readers of Eliot's Corner appreciated the wealth that Arden Forest offered.

Still, the health of the bookshop was only one topic on Laura's mind as she worked. Brent was manning the front of the shop, so if she spoke quietly, there was little chance of his overhearing what she said.

"I've been thinking a lot about the Smiths," Laura said quietly.

"In what way?" Arden was wielding her own feather duster a few feet away.

"Well, I'm torn. I believe they have a right to know about me. On the other hand, I'm afraid of what such a revelation might do to them, maybe cause too much pain."

"It's a difficult situation. Why don't we see what Ted advises? Assuming he agrees to help us."

"That sounds reasonable. He knows them better than either of us do, even if he's not a personal friend of theirs."

Brent suddenly appeared at the end of the aisle. "Heads up," he whispered dramatically. "Mrs. Shandy just came through the door. She's a nosy one is our Mrs. Shandy. No bad intentions, just nosy."

Nosier than Lydia Austen? Laura wondered. "Thanks for the warning."

Mrs. Shandy was a large woman who wore her weight well. Her hair was a striking shade of silver, waved and styled in a way that reminded Laura of a 1940s screen matron. She wore a cotton skirt that came to well below her knees, and an old-fashioned twinset. She stood squarely in sturdy brown brogues. Around her neck was a strand of pearls Laura took to be genuine. They had that unmistakable luster.

"Let me introduce Mrs. Shandy." Arden gestured to the woman. "She's a long-standing member of our book group and for years before that was a very respected and well-loved teacher here in Eliot's Corner."

Mrs. Shandy regarded Laura frankly. "So, this is the long-lost daughter."

"I wouldn't say I was lost," Laura replied evenly. "But, yes, I'm Arden's daughter."

"Where have you been all this time? Arden, why have you never told us that you have a child? Laura, will you be staying on in Eliot's Corner?"

Brent, who was standing behind and to the left of Mrs. Shandy, rolled his eyes dramatically. Laura restrained a laugh. Brent would get her into trouble one of these days.

"The answer to your last question, Mrs. Shandy"—Laura wondered if Mrs. Shandy had already conferred with Lydia Austen—"is that I'm just not sure. The answers to your other questions will have to remain between my mother and me. I'm sure you understand."

The expression on Mrs. Shandy's face—suspicious? At least, doubting—proved that, no, she did not understand, but she gave up on her inquisition. Not that Laura didn't anticipate more questions at a later date.

"What happened to Mr. Shandy?" Laura asked when the woman had gone on her way, off, she said, to lend a hand washing and ironing clothes at the charity shop.

"Rumor has it," Brent said, "there never was a Mr. Shandy. The grand dame just showed up in Eliot's Corner one day ages and ages ago, all on her lonesome and calling herself Mrs. Over the years some have dared to ask about the missing husband, but few have lived to ask again."

Laura laughed. "Slight exaggeration? And does Mrs. Shandy have a first name?"

Arden worked to hide a smile. It was never right to laugh at a person's name; as she knew too well, a name was in some ways inseparable from the deepest self-identity.

"Her name," Brent said, with barely suppressed glee, "is Foundation."

Laura burst into laughter. "I'm sorry," she gasped, "but all I could think of for a moment was 'foundation garments.' Why would a parent burden an innocent child with such a ponderous name?"

"Maybe she chose it herself along the way." Arden looked meaningfully at her daughter.

Maybe, Laura thought, because Mrs. Shandy had realized the only person on whom she could build her life was herself. "Certainly possible. Stranger things."

"The Puritans used to name their kids after virtues. Patience. Constance. Fortitude. Maybe Mrs. Shandy's parents belonged to some strict religious sect."

"Well, I, for one, have never had the nerve to ask her about her first name," Arden admitted.

"I know who it is she reminds me of," Laura said suddenly. "Margaret Rutherford, that great British actress who played Miss Marple and a whole host of eccentric and formidable ladies of a certain age. I wonder if she'd take that as a compliment? I adore Margaret Rutherford, but Mrs. Shandy might not like the comparison."

"Better keep it to yourself," Brent advised. "We wouldn't want to get on her bad side."

"As bad as all that?" Lauren asked, eyes wide.

Arden smiled. "Not at all. Now, let's get back to chasing dust."

Laura was more than happy to abandon the subject of Mrs. Foundation Shandy, return to work, and let her thoughts turn once again to Geraldine and Robert Smith.

Rob Smith's parents.

Laura Huntington's grandparents.

Chapter 41

Arden sent Laura off to take a hot shower—she had complained her back was hurting her, possibly the result of all of the lifting and reaching she had done at the shop earlier—while Arden cleared away the dinner things. As she loaded the dishwasher, she found herself thinking about the discussion she and Laura and Brent had had regarding Mrs. Shandy's first name. Burden or benefit? Gift or curse?

Arden had been named after a great-great-aunt on some distant branch of the Aldridge family tree; presumably, this had been her father's choice. Victoria was a grand name to bear, largely but not entirely thanks to Queen Victoria and her considerable cultural influence.

Victory. Victorious. A winner. Winners vanquished others. Winners were not losers.

After *Victoria*, *Arden* was a great relief. For one, you could hardly "live up to" a forest, and besides, forests were (or they could be, outside of the Grimm Brothers' fairy tales) places of peace and tranquility, shade and sun-dappled grass, singing birds, and cute woodland creatures. They could also be, like Shakespeare's forest, a place of fantasy.

Laura returned to the kitchen just as Arden closed the door to the dishwasher. "I feel much better. A hot shower and an ibuprofen can work wonders."

Arden suggested they make themselves comfortable in the living room. "There's more I think you should know before you go back to Port George," she began when they were comfortably settled. "More about my family dynamic."

Laura nodded. "I'm listening."

"My parents lost a baby not long before I was born. His name was Joseph, after my mother's father, and he was only three months old when he died. My mother never got over it. His loss haunted her. In some ways, it came to define her. 'If only your brother hadn't died,' she would say to me when something had distressed her, and things often did, 'everything would be okay.'"

Laura put her hand to her heart. "How very sad. How did Joseph die?"

"It was called a crib death. Only a few years later the term *sudden infant death syndrome* came into use to describe a baby's death from unknown causes. In my brother's case, there was no evidence whatsoever of foul play, but my mother was crushed by guilt. And it didn't help that her own mother was convinced that her grandson's death could be laid at Florence's door."

Laura shook her head. "Oh, Lord. What a nightmare."

"When I was very young, I used to think a lot about the brother I never knew. I used to wish he had lived so I would have a friend, an ally. But maybe he would have found me just a bothersome little sister. Eventually, I gave up imagining what might have happened if Joseph had survived."

"Poor little guy. Gone before he had a chance to experience joy— and sorrow. Life can be terribly difficult, but it's so very worth it."

"Yes. You should probably also know that until I was twelve, I had a nanny. I adored her. When I was with Mrs. Clarke, I felt safe and happy. She read to me when I was little, and then, when I'd learned to read on my own, I would read to her. She taught me how to identify the various flowers in our garden, and on nights when I couldn't sleep, she would point out the constellations in the sky and explain how they'd gotten their names."

"She sounds like a gem. What happened to her after she left?"

"She died three years later. We kept in touch, birthday cards and little notes, and then one day I got a letter from the cousin she'd gone to live with, saying that Mrs. Clarke had died suddenly. I remember bursting into tears. It felt like a terribly important part of my world had collapsed. I was bereft." Arden sighed. "But I didn't say anything to my parents about the note. Honestly, I half believed they'd forgotten about Mrs. Clarke by then."

"Out of sight out of mind," Laura said grimly. "Too true for too many people."

"The opposite can be just as sad. If only my mother had been able to forget Joseph just a little, she might have found some happiness or peace of mind. But that's just speculation after the fact."

Laura nodded. "Thank you for telling me these things," she said after a moment. "If it's okay, I'm going to turn in early. I want to be on my game tomorrow when I meet with Ted Coldwell."

When Laura had gone up to the loft, Arden stepped outside into the garden and looked up into the night sky. She was reminded again of Mrs. Clarke—and, also of Margery Hopkins—and of how safe and cherished she had felt with each. Arden wanted her daughter to feel the same with her, safe and cherished, but Laura was an adult now with a mind and will of her own. Arden wished she could convince Laura to let go of the need to find the truth about what had happened to her father. So many things could go wrong. So many terrible facts might be uncovered. But it would be selfish to try to hold her daughter back from this quest.

Arden went back inside and began to turn off the lights in preparation for retiring to her room. Whatever the future held, good or bad, mother and daughter were at least safe for the moment at Juniper End.

Chapter 42

Laura pulled into the small parking lot of the Lilac Inn. She wished there were a motel in Port George, or even one within a ten-mile radius. The Lilac Inn, while charming, wasn't inexpensive. After stowing her bag in her room, she set out for Ted Coldwell's office on Main Street.

She was glad that Mr. Coldwell had agreed to see her again and surprised that he had agreed so readily. Why? She would find out soon enough.

Ms. West, no warmer than she had been on Laura's last visit, ushered Laura into Mr. Coldwell's office. Laura hadn't paid much attention to her surroundings when here before; now, she made note of it all.

The centerpiece of the office was a massive oak desk, on which stood a classic brass lamp with a green-glass shade. One entire wall of the office was covered in shelves, on which rested thick books bound in tooled red and blue leather. On another wall were three framed maps of the world; the fantastical creatures shown emerging from the seas dated the maps to well before the modern age. Framed photos of a woman Laura took to be Mr. Coldwell's wife, as well as photos of three young people she thought must be his children, sat on his desk and along the room's deep windowsill. Along with those were framed photos of two border collies.

Mr. Coldwell must have noticed Laura smiling at the latter. "Our fur children. I never had a pet growing up, but my wife has lived and breathed dogs since she was a baby. She converted me pretty quickly."

A bouquet of summer flowers in a cut-glass vase sat on a small occasional table by the side of a high-backed leather armchair; next to the bouquet was a copy of *National Geographic* and a recent members' magazine from the Museum of Fine Arts in Boston. In one corner of the room a fishing pole rested against the wall. A large tackle box sat on the floor beside it. Ted Coldwell was a man of interests outside of his professional life.

"What can I do for you, Ms. Huntington?" he asked when Laura had taken a seat across from the commanding desk in a beautifully upholstered chair with impressively wide armrests.

"First, I'd like to thank you for seeing me today. I wasn't entirely honest with you when we last met. There is no podcast."

Mr. Coldwell gave a small smile. "I suspected as much. You don't spend all these years as a lawyer without learning how to spot a lie or a prevarication."

"And yet, you agreed to meet with me again."

"I was curious. You see, I agreed to see you in the first place because I was intrigued by your theme of the negative effects missing persons can have on a small community. And I know that sometimes a popular podcast can lead to new information coming to light and, on occasion, even the conviction of a guilty party. Assuming a crime was committed. I agreed to meet with you today because I have a—let's say a vested interest in the Aldridge family."

Laura smiled briefly. "I'm afraid that what I have to tell you is going to come as a shock, and I have to ask that it remain between us, at least for a time. There's a good reason for secrecy, I promise."

Mr. Coldwell frowned. "Are you going to tell me that you've committed a crime or that you know someone who has? Because if you are . . ."

"No," Laura said hastily. "Sorry. Let me start again. The thing is, I'm the daughter of Victoria Aldridge and Rob Smith. I was adopted when I was born. I always knew that part of the story, about the adoption I mean, but until just a few days ago, not the identity of my birth parents."

For a moment, Mr. Coldwell looked as if he might cry. Instead, he cleared his throat and spoke. "I always thought there was a child. It was just a feeling I had. And now, to know that I was right . . ."

"There's something else." Laura smiled a bit. "I've found my mother. She lives only a few hours from here. We've met."

Much to Laura's embarrassment, a sob broke from her and she put her face in her hands. A moment later, Mr. Coldwell was patting her shoulder and offering a wad of tissues. Laura accepted them and began to mop up her tears as Mr. Coldwell returned to his seat.

"Sorry," Laura mumbled.

"There's no need to apologize," Mr. Coldwell said soothingly. "This is a stirring time in your life, revolutionary even."

Laura nodded and took a deep breath.

"How is she? Victoria. Is she well?"

"She's fine," Laura assured her mother's old friend. "She goes by the name of Arden Bell now and she owns a lovely little bookshop in Eliot's Corner. It's called Arden Forest. She lives in a charming cottage, which she shares with three cats. Their names are Prospero, Ophelia, and Falstaff."

Mr. Coldwell laughed. "That's Victoria all right! Well, Arden I mean. My God, this is so hard to take in. Is she . . . Did she ever marry?"

"No. At least, not that I know of. I do know she never had any other children. But we've hardly had time to learn much of anything about each other. I also know for sure that she never heard from my father after he went missing. I—I don't think he's alive. Neither does my mother."

"No," Mr. Coldwell murmured. "Neither do I."

Briefly, Laura told him about Victoria's being sent off to have the baby in secret. "Everyone or almost everyone assumed she was away at college. But she wasn't. She only returned to Port George after I was born in late spring of 1985."

Mr. Coldwell shook his head. "I saw her not long before she left Port George for good. It was at one of those ghastly parties her parents used to throw. I was there with my own parents. I'm not sure why they agreed to go other than good manners, but I do know the only reason I went along was in hopes of seeing Victoria." He smiled sadly. "But she wanted nothing to do with me that evening. I never knew exactly why but . . ."

"You see, she believed that her father had played a part in Rob's disappearance, and she just couldn't have anything more to do with either Florence or Herbert, so she left."

Mr. Coldwell sighed. "We all thought she'd gone back to school a bit early, maybe for a summer session, and when she never came back, most people assumed that life had taken her in a more exciting direction than what she would have found back here in Port George."

"My guess is that my mother's parents never bothered to look for her. If I could find her today, with virtually no information and absolutely no financial resources, Mr. and Mrs. Aldridge could have hunted her down easily back then."

"Yes." Mr. Coldwell was silent. "I've told you that my parents were friends with the Aldridges. But the relationship wasn't close. And not long after that awful party I mentioned, my parents retreated from any association with Herbert and Florence. I know they both felt bad for Florence; she was never emotionally strong. It was more Herbert they had no time for, but Florence and Herbert came as a package deal as it were. As for me, without Victoria, the Aldridge family held no appeal."

Laura nodded. "I can see why. I mean, from what my mother has told me about her parents, they don't seem very likable. They're still living in that big place out on Old Orchard Hill, I hear."

"Yes, but hardly anyone sees Herbert and Florence these days. In fact, it's been years since he quit the golf club, which was the main source of their socializing when he was in Port George and not traveling on business. Every once in while you see that big old Cadillac they've had forever passing through town, with either Florence or Herbert in the back seat, rarely the two together. Who knows where they're headed. A skeleton staff takes care of their shopping and other chores. Rumor has it that neither Herbert nor Florence is in good health."

"Be that as it may, I want to know if Herbert Aldridge did have anything to do with my father's disappearance and the shutting down of the police inquiry. Because from what I could tell from the articles in the *Port George Daily Chronicle*, the investigation came to a complete and abrupt halt with no official explanation of why."

Mr. Coldwell frowned. "You'll need to be careful. Even now, retired for many years, largely reclusive, Herbert Aldridge is seen as formidable."

"I'll be careful. But the man doesn't scare me." It was not a lie.

"I'll do what I can to help you, as long as it's within legal bounds."

"Thank you," Laura said feelingly. "That means a lot to me. The first thing I'd ask is that you would keep my real identity a secret. I feel bad about lying to people in Port George, pretending I'm working on a podcast, but I think the pretense might be helpful. I don't want to give anyone a chance to slip away."

"By 'anyone,' you mean your grandfather."

Laura frowned. "Yes. If Herbert Aldridge is responsible for my father's disappearance, I'm the last person he wants meddling around, trying to dig up the past."

"Yes, you're probably smart to keep your real identity quiet for now." Mr. Coldwell paused. "Your mother—Arden—knows you've come to see me?"

"Oh, yes. And she sends you her love as well as her apologies. It seems that for a brief time after Rob's disappearance she wondered if you were in cahoots with her father. She was just so scared and confused."

Mr. Coldwell smiled sadly. "No wonder she didn't want anything to do with me at that party. And I understand why she might have thought I had a hand in making Rob go away. It was no secret that I'd been in love with her for years, though I was well aware she thought of me only as a brother. And though I'm ashamed to admit it, I did take it upon myself to, er, have a talk with Rob that summer of '84. Kind of warn him that if he didn't treat Victoria right, there would be consequences. I guess I was a bit of a macho idiot back then. But please believe, I would never do anything to hurt Victoria—Arden—not then and not now."

"She knows that."

"Are you prepared to come up empty? Maybe Herbert Aldridge is guilty of having a hand in Rob's disappearance and maybe he's not. We just don't know and we might never know. Sometimes the past is best left to itself."

"I'll deal with what comes," Laura said firmly. The butterflies in her stomach belied her outward display of confidence. "I plan to spend a few days a week here in Port George—I'm booked at the Lilac Inn—and the rest of the time with Arden in Eliot's Corner. Here's my contact information." Laura passed him a piece of notebook paper on which she had written her cell phone number and e-mail address. "I'm old-fashioned. I suppose most people would have asked for your phone number and sent you this information electronically."

Mr. Coldwell smiled. "There's nothing wrong with pencil and paper. They worked just fine for thousands of years. So, what's your first step?"

"I'd like to speak with Frannie Smith. But given what I know of her stance against my mother's family, I'm not sure she'll agree to go into the story of my father's disappearance again. After all, she had her brother declared dead. End of story."

"Not for Frannie," Mr. Coldwell corrected. "By the way, her married name is Armitage. Let me talk to her first, let her know you're legitimate—Well, you know what I mean. I'll call you when I've spoken to her."

Laura rose from her chair. "Thank you, Mr. Coldwell."

"Please, call me Ted. And remember me to your mother."

"I will."

Ted walked her to the door of his office. "Laura, it's so good to finally know for sure that you exist."

Laura felt tears threatening again; all she could manage in return was a nod before she hurried out of the office.

Chapter 43

Summer 1985

Victoria stood in front of the full-length mirror in her bedroom. It was strange, she thought. On the outside, she hadn't changed. She was still tall and slim and blond. Her eyes were still blue. But on the inside . . . A stranger looked back at Victoria from the depths of the mirror. A new Victoria, older, not necessarily wiser, chastened by misfortune and heartache.

With a sigh, Victoria turned from her image. She had been back in Port George for almost two weeks, but not once had her parents mentioned the baby. Her mother seemed incapable of looking her daughter in the eye as she reminded Victoria that Ted Coldwell had always been interested in her and would make a fine match. Her father was even more formal and distant than he had been before he had sent Victoria away. That was all right. Victoria didn't want to talk to him anyway. She didn't even want to see him.

What she wanted, at least in that moment, was to get out of the house. The weather was fine. There was no reason why she had to continue her self-imposed isolation. No reason other than the fear of being found out.

But how could she be? She weighed less now than she had last summer; stress was an effective reducer. Nothing about her body would give away the truth. Her face, however, was another matter; it was etched with sadness. But she would wear sunglasses and avoid as best she could any conversations with passing busybodies. She couldn't stay in the house forever. There had to be a first time and it might as well be now.

Before more doubts could assail her, Victoria reached for her sunglasses and shoulder bag. She encountered no one on her way out of the house or all the way to the bottom of Old Orchard Hill. The sun on her head felt comfortably warm. Her stride was strong.

Not until she had reached an isolated stretch of road that led into the heart of town did trouble appear, in the form of Frannie Smith, Rob's older sister.

Victoria came to a halt, her stomach flipping. It was one of her worst nightmares come true. Why couldn't it be one of Rob's other sisters, or, better yet, a distant friend, an acquaintance? Why Frannie, of all people, the one member of the Smith family who hadn't taken to Victoria?

Frannie Smith, too, had stopped in her tracks, effectively blocking the way forward. Her expression was dark, suspicious. Victoria felt a shiver of fear run through her. Would Frannie resort to physical violence against the girl she suspected of having led her beloved brother into trouble? If she turned around and ran, would Frannie fly after her?

Slowly, not knowing what else to do, Victoria continued on her way until Frannie was only three or four feet in front of her. Frannie was wearing jeans and a Kiss T-shirt. She looked much older than the last time Victoria had seen her, less than a year ago. Her eyes looked hard.

"You're back."

"Yes," Victoria said simply. She could feel panic rising in her and prayed her fear didn't show.

"How's college?" Frannie's tone of voice made it clear she had absolutely no interest in the answer.

Victoria smiled nervously. "Fine. You know."

"No," Frannie said sharply. "As a matter of fact, I don't know."

Victoria cringed. It had been a stupid thing to say, but she was so nervous. "Sorry," she mumbled. "Rob. Has he come home?" Why was she asking such a ridiculous question? She knew the answer. Everyone in Port George knew the answer.

"You know he hasn't," Frannie snapped. She took a step closer to Victoria. "Did you know that the case was declared cold, that it was closed months ago? Did you hear that when you were away at your fancy college?"

Victoria swallowed. "No," she said quietly. "No, I didn't know." And who would have told her if she had asked? Certainly, not her parents.

"Did you ever even think about Rob once you'd gone off?" Frannie demanded. "Or was he just a distant memory, an insignificant part of your past? Was he just a temporary plaything for a rich girl who wanted to see what it was like to slum it before going off to an exclusive private college to earn her Mrs. degree?"

Victoria clutched the strap of her pocketbook. "No!" she cried. "No, that's not it at all. You're wrong about me, about all of it."

"Rumor has it that your father used his influence to get the investigation dropped." Frannie had fairly spat the words.

"But why would he do that?" Victoria asked, though in her heart she knew the answer.

I'll make that boy pay if it's the last thing I do.

Herbert Aldridge was behind Rob's disappearance. He had to be. In spite of the early-summer sun, Victoria felt suddenly chilled.

"You tell me," Frannie spat.

"I can't." Victoria could hear the desperation in her voice. "I don't know anything. I don't know where Rob is or why he left—"

"Maybe your father did even more. Maybe he 'took care' of my brother. And don't say you don't know what I mean." Again, Frannie came toward Victoria; her stance was unmistakably threatening. "There had to have been foul play. Rob would never have willingly left his family."

"Maybe there was an accident," Victoria said frantically, "a terrible accident. Maybe Rob was hit by a truck passing through town or . . ."

"Then why was a body never found? A bit of bloody clothing, the bike he was riding? Anyway, we'll never know, will we? Not now that the case has been closed."

Victoria took a deep breath. It didn't much help. "Rob said nothing about where he was going or who he was meeting that day?"

"Nothing. Was it you he was going to meet?"

"No," Victoria said firmly. "It wasn't, honestly."

"Do you know why he was on his bike that day? Why he didn't take his car wherever it was he was going?"

Victoria shook her head. She wanted so badly to run away, but she was still too scared to move.

"It was because he had loaned the car to a friend who wanted to take his mother to see a sick relative a few towns away. That's the sort of person my brother, Rob, was, kind and caring and generous. That's the sort of person your—" Frannie swiped at her eyes with the back of her hand. "In the day or two before Rob went missing, he was moody and upset. I asked him what was bothering him, but he denied anything was the matter. He was lying. Something was wrong. Are you sure you don't know what it was?"

"No," Victoria cried. "I mean, yes, I'm sure, I'm totally sure." But that was a lie. Rob had been worried about her. He knew she had told her parents about the pregnancy. Her ensuing silence had to have signaled that there had been trouble.

Frannie looked at Victoria with deepened suspicion. "You know I don't believe you were off at college. I'm sure I'm not the only one in Port George who thinks there was a baby. There was, wasn't there? Rob's baby."

"No," Victoria cried more desperately now. "No there wasn't, really. You have to believe me!"

"I don't have to do anything of the sort. All I can say is that if there was a baby, my brother's child, and you did something despicable with it, I'll—"

"I didn't do anything! There wasn't a baby, I swear!"

Frannie looked at her with unmistakable contempt. "Don't expect any sympathy from me. Poor little rich girl. You have no idea what you've put my family through."

Victoria began to tremble.

I'll make that boy pay if it's the last thing I do.

Those words. Those awful, threatening words!

Suddenly, it was all too much. "I've got to go," she gasped. Rather than attempt to push past Rob's sister, she turned and fled back the way she had come.

Frannie did not pursue her.

Victoria ran straight for home, her thoughts keeping pace with her pounding feet and racing heart. Poor Rob! If he hadn't loaned his car to his friend . . . Cars were much harder to hide or to make disappear than a bicycle. Assuming someone had hidden the bike. And Rob himself? Could someone have hidden his body?

No. It couldn't be.

Victoria had barely taken a step onto the Aldridge property when she fell to her knees and was violently sick to her stomach. When the crisis was over, she crawled to her feet. She couldn't go on this way, lying, keeping secrets, haunted and hunted. She stared ahead at the house, that massive brick structure with its impassive facade. She had to go inside. She couldn't stand in the drive forever. But every fiber of her being fought the necessity of entering that building at the top of Old Orchard Hill.

She took a step and then another, up the long and curving drive, under the old apple trees, past the towering oaks, up the stone stairs until the front door was in reach. She extended her right hand to the doorknob. It felt icy cold.

What, she wondered, had happened to her life?

Chapter 44

Laura didn't want to meet Frannie Armitage at the North Star Diner. Kathy was a gem but she might be inclined to eavesdrop (with no malicious intent), and Laura wanted to be as alone with Frannie as she could be in a public place.

Laura was nervous. She wondered if Frannie was going to mention her suspicions of a child having been born to Victoria Aldridge in the spring of 1985. If she did, Laura would do her best to remain calm and keep her expression impassive, professional. But it wouldn't be easy.

The moment Laura stepped through the door of the Rosebud Café she spotted a woman sitting on her own at a table for two. Laura knew in her gut that this was Frannie Smith Armitage. Her aunt. Her father's sister.

Life had been hard on Frannie if her appearance was anything to go by. She looked much older than her age of about sixty-one or -two, and she had an air of weariness about her. Not defeat, exactly, but great weariness. The disappearance of her only brother so long ago had to have changed the course of Frannie's life forever, just as it had changed the course of so many other lives in Port George and beyond.

Frannie blew a stray lock of gray hair away from her face—an oddly youthful and carefree gesture. Somehow, it gave Laura the encouragement she needed to approach.

"Mrs. Armitage?"

The woman nodded.

"I'm Laura Huntington. Thank you for meeting me."

Laura took the seat across from her aunt. A waitress appeared, and following Frannie's lead, Laura ordered a cup of coffee.

When the waitress had moved off, Frannie said, "Your stomach had better be lined with lead. The coffee in this place is notorious."

A smile was in her words if not on her face. Laura nodded. "Thanks for the warning."

Neither woman spoke again until Laura's coffee had been delivered. She took a sip and her eyebrows shot to the sky. "I see what you mean. But it's good."

Frannie now offered a real smile. "Mr. Coldwell called me. He handled everything when my family had my brother officially declared dead. Anyway, he told me about you. He said I could trust you, that you weren't a phony or a scam artist."

Laura hid a cringe behind a polite smile. "So, he explained my involvement with the podcast?"

"Can't say I knew what a podcast was until Mr. Coldwell explained it. But I understand now. You're trying to tell the story of what happens to a community when one of their own goes missing and never comes back." Frannie took a sip of her coffee and was silent for a long moment. Finally she said, "One of the cases you might want to feature is my brother's."

Laura nodded. "Yes. I know this might be difficult for you, to talk about it again, and I'm sorry if I—"

Frannie put up a hand to silence Laura. "It is difficult. It always was and it always will be. But I talked it over with my husband, and we agree that there doesn't seem to be any harm in someone taking another look at what might have happened to Rob."

Laura felt her stomach clench. "I'm not really leading an investigation. I hope Mr. Coldwell was clear about that. I don't want to mislead you."

"He was clear." Frannie nodded. "I know what I'm doing."

"Okay. Good. So, what I'm looking for in this early stage of development is anecdotal evidence. It can be very helpful in painting a complete picture of a person and a place in time."

Frannie took another sip of her coffee. "Okay."

"I've learned that Rob might have been involved with a local girl, someone named Victoria Aldridge. What can you tell me about her?"

Frannie sat back and placed both hands flat on the table. "They were involved all right," she said tightly. "Rob brought her around to the house a few times. It made us all uncomfortable at first, this privileged girl sitting in our tiny living room on furniture that my parents had had since the day they were married, and nibbling on oatmeal-raisin cookies, not some fancy pastries she was probably used to getting at home. The Aldridge family had staff, you see. The father was some sort of moneyman, big banking or something like that. I never really knew."

Laura nodded. Her heart began to beat painfully. "Go on."

"But soon enough my parents and sisters were fawning over her. You should have heard them once Victoria had gone home. How polite, how pretty, the way she gazed at Rob with such affection." Frannie shook her head. "I was the voice of reason. I was the one who pointed out that nothing but trouble could come from the only daughter of the town's wealthiest and most powerful man dating a mere local boy, son of a truck driver and homemaker, neither of whom had gone to college."

"Didn't your parents share your reservations at all?" Frannie's parents. Laura's grandparents. She felt a bit dazed for a moment, as if she had drunk one too many glasses of wine and now had to stand up.

"My mother did at first. But even she went over to Victoria's side. She was a romantic at heart. She said she knew real love and affection when she saw it, and that only time would tell if her son would make a life with Victoria Aldridge." Frannie took her hands from the table and let them fall into her lap. "Only problem was, there was no time, not much of it anyway, for anything to develop or not. By the end of the summer Rob was gone and it was all over."

Laura just knew she was going to cry. With supreme effort, she got control of herself. "I'm so terribly sorry. I really am. I know that even after all this time has passed—"

Frannie didn't seem to need encouragement to continue with her story. "I hated Victoria Aldridge for a long time. I blamed her for what happened to Rob. But as I got older and Rob's disappearance began to register as a reality and not a nightmare, I guess I didn't hate her anymore. She was nice enough, sweet really, and I think she probably did love my brother. It was those parents of hers, manipulating everything, with their love of money and status. No, I don't hate her. In fact, I hope she's had a decent life since she left Port George. None of us deserve to suffer more than we have to in this life. That's my belief."

At that moment, Laura badly wanted to reveal herself to Frannie, to reach out and hug her long-suffering aunt, to ask for her forgiveness. After a moment, she said, "Thank you for your time. I appreciate your talking with me."

Frannie eyed her carefully. "You seem like an honest enough sort, like Mr. Coldwell said. Do you really think this podcast thing will change anything?"

"I don't know," Laura said quietly. "I really don't know."

"Fair enough." Frannie shrugged. "Never make a promise you can't keep."

"Yes. Though we go ahead and do just that, don't we? We believe we can honor our promises, we make them in good faith, most of us anyway, and then, so often we just can't stick to our word."

Frannie nodded. Her expression thoughtful, she looked closely at Laura again. After what seemed an age she stood, nodded, and began to walk toward the door of the café. Laura noticed that Frannie—her aunt—walked with a slight limp but also with a great deal of native dignity.

Laura sat alone at the café table for a while; she still felt too shaky to get up and leave. Shaky and raw and sad. She was eager to tell Arden what she had heard from Rob's oldest sister, though Laura would withhold that Frannie had long hated her. Arden suspected as much already. Only after the waitress approached Laura with the offer of a refill—an offer Laura declined—did she get up from the table and make her way back out onto the streets of Port George. Suddenly, the sweet little town seemed not so sweet, replete with dark shadows and dangerous secrets. Like every other small town everywhere, Laura thought. If only people would admit that.

Chapter 45

"Are you sure you don't want me to dump that water out back?" Deborah asked, eyeing the brimming bucket with something akin to suspicion.

Arden shook her head. "It's all right. I've already gotten rid of two buckets. A third won't kill me."

"Good. What I mean," Deborah added hastily, "is that it looks darn heavy."

The bucket was heavy. There had been a big rain during the night, and Arden had come into the shop that morning to find several puddles on the floor; the ceiling above each of the puddles was visibly damp. She had immediately called Deborah and Gordon, more for moral support than for practical assistance. By the time they arrived at the shop, Arden had finished mopping. Luckily, stock had not been damaged, but luck didn't hold out forever.

Gordon joined them; he had been talking on his phone to the roofer who had dealt with a problem at Gordon's house the year before. "Matt says he's tied up for the next six weeks at least. Unless the roof is on the floor, he's not available."

Arden shook her head. "I knew I'd need to have the roof fixed before long. Why didn't I do something before now? What if the roof fails and I can't afford to keep . . ."

Deborah reached out and put a firm hand on Arden's arm. "We

won't let you lose the shop," Deborah said calmly. "I'll start a Go-FundMe campaign. Believe me, no one in Eliot's Corner wants Arden Forest or you for that matter to go away. Or, God forbid, to have the shop replaced by a corporate giant, though to be sure they must have their uses. Just not here."

"I can't ask my neighbors for money!" Arden protested.

"Why not?" Deborah asked. "You're not planning a jaunt on the Riviera with your Mediterranean lover, you're raising money to fix the roof of an important building on Main Street. Everyone in town is invested in the future of this place."

"She's right, Arden," Gordon said. "This is not about charity. This is about you being able to continue to offer all that you offer to your neighbors. Essential stuff. Books. Conversation. Free cookies at Christmas. And it's about continuing to honor Margery's legacy."

"Let me think about it," Arden begged. "Please. Don't do anything just yet."

Deborah shrugged. "If you say so."

"Let me ask around," Gordon suggested, "talk to a few other roofing guys and see what they say. Maybe there's a temporary option, a stopgap as it were. I mean, we don't even know what exactly is going on up there until we have an expert take a look."

"You're right. Maybe it's not as bad as I'm imagining it to be." Arden managed a smile. "Thanks, you two."

Gordon and Deborah went on their way after that, Deborah to her office and Gordon to a parts shop—more of a dump, really—in a neighboring town to source material for his work.

Arden put her hands over her eyes and sighed. She wouldn't know how to go on if she lost this shop. It had always been so much more than a source of income. A home. A haven. A passion. A reason to get up in the morning. A place in which to meet with other members of the Eliot's Corner community, young and old, and share hopes, tell personal stories, seek advice or solace, and, of course, to talk about books.

And for it all Arden had Margery Hopkins to thank. Though, like Arden, Margery had kept much of her life before coming to Eliot's Corner a secret, she had shared enough of her story to be an inspiration to Arden, an example of a woman who refused to give in to tragedy.

"When my fiancé was killed in action during the Korean War," Margery had told Arden, "people said, 'You're young, you have your whole life ahead of you, you could marry some other nice man, have a family, be happy.' But they were wrong. Carl was the only man for me."

"You *are* happy though, aren't you?" Arden had ventured. "In spite of your loss."

"I am," Margery had promptly replied. "I'm proud that I've been true to Carl, and I know I'll meet him again when I die." Here, Margery had smiled. "And I love my bookshop. I have everything I need."

Arden took her hands from her eyes. Margery had understood the need for secrets, for a past to be kept inviolate. Still, Arden wished she had been able to be honest with her friend; she wished she had been brave enough to tell Margery about her child.

But she hadn't, and at the moment what mattered most was the future of Arden Forest.

Arden looked lovingly around the shop, at the books neatly shelved; the table of new releases; the display of paperback versions of last year's hardcovers; the standing racks of leatherbound diaries and notebooks; and finally, at the counter behind which Arden stood as if at the wheel of a ship, the commander and caretaker of this vessel.

"I promise you, Margery," Arden said aloud, her voice determined, "that I won't allow Arden Forest to close its doors. I promise."

Chapter 46

Laura was walking along Main Street when suddenly she knew with absolute certainty that she was being followed. Her skin began to tingle and her heart to race. She was furious. She was curious.

Laura halted and turned around. Not very gracefully, a figure several yards away scuttled around a corner. She was sure it had been a woman, middle-aged, maybe in her sixties, though it was hard to be sure. It had definitely not been the elderly, frail Florence Aldridge. The woman had been wearing a bucket hat and large sunglasses, an effective if clichéd means of hiding the details of her face. Laura thought she had been tall, at least average height.

The woman was not a threat, at least not a physical threat. Laura knew that in her gut.

She turned around and resumed her way along Main Street. In spite of the woman's almost comic performance, the incident had left a nasty taste in Laura's mouth. Not long after she had left her husband, he had begun to stalk her, lurking in a doorway across the street when she came home from an evening out with a friend, leaving nasty voice mails on her phone, even showing up in her classroom one memorable afternoon. Campus security had seen to him then. Finally, Laura had been compelled to get a restraining order against Jared.

During the nightmare weeks of Jared's pursuit, Laura had gone from being dreadfully frightened to being supremely angry. By the time the restraining order was issued, she was reveling in fantasies of clobbering Jared over the head with a lamp or a baseball bat (not that she owned a baseball bat) until he had learned his lesson.

The cowardly pest did stop his vicious little campaign of intimidation—and Laura's anger did abate so that she no longer dreamed of acts of violence—but not before any shred of affection for her soon-to-be ex-husband she might still have been holding on to was gone, obliterated, buried forever.

Laura had almost reached the Lilac Inn when fear finally began to make its insidious way through her defenses. Damn, she thought. Maybe someone had discovered her true identity. Maybe someone knew the podcast story was a pretense, a cover for another more important goal. She half regretted she hadn't dashed after that woman and demanded to know who she was and what she was after.

The honk of a car horn made Laura jump. She felt exhausted. The meeting with Frannie earlier had taken a lot out of her. And there was no shame in retreating when it seemed wise to retreat. To rest. To be still. To recover. To slide under the cool, clean sheets of a bed and sleep.

Moments later, Laura pushed open the wrought-iron gate that kept passersby from trampling on the beautifully kept lawn and garden of the bed-and-breakfast she was calling home for a time. When she reached her room, she fell onto the neatly made bed and was asleep within moments.

Chapter 47

The cats were taking one of their daily naps. Quiet reigned in the cottage and the sun was shining brightly. For this, Arden was especially thankful because since the morning she had discovered the puddles of water on the floor of the bookshop, she had lived in dread of rain. One big summer storm, the kind that knocked out power lines and caused the Eliot River to flood, and she could be in big trouble. Of course, her mind might be somewhat put to rest if only she could find a roofer with five minutes to spare.

As good as his word, Gordon had gotten estimates from a few local contractors; unfortunately, without having identified the exact problem, the estimates were all over the map. Even so, the lowest figure was prohibitively high. After sharing this information with Arden, Gordon had offered to loan her the money himself; there would be no interest and she could set the terms of the repayment plan.

Arden's immediate reaction had been to accept. It would be a quick and easy solution to her problem. But reason came to the rescue before she could commit herself to a folly. She remembered Gordon saying that he felt closer to her now that he knew the truth of her past. Accepting Gordon's offer of a loan might give him the false impression that she was ready to take a further step in their relationship, and she wasn't.

And what if she couldn't stick to the repayment plan? Money could destroy even a healthy relationship between friends. Polonius might have been an annoying babbler, but he was right when he advised that one should neither a borrower nor a lender be.

She had thanked Gordon sincerely and declined. He didn't protest her decision, and since then things had gone on as usual. Still, Arden wondered if she hadn't inadvertently issued a death blow to the relationship. She sincerely hoped she had not because other single women in Eliot's Corner would be more than happy to walk hand in hand with Gordon through life. How long would it be before Gordon, a human being with the human need for companionship, turned his attentions to, say, Jeanie Shardlake, a forty-five-year-old artist whose work was shown in galleries in Portland as well as Boston, or, say, to Martha Benbow, fifty-two, who had inherited her family's construction business and taken it to greater heights than her forebears could have imagined? Both women were intelligent, hardworking, creative, and kind. If Gordon entered a romantic relationship with either of those women, or, indeed, with any other woman, Arden's friendship with him would be dealt a blow.

But she was not in control of Gordon's emotional life. She was only in charge of her own. And right then, Arden's foremost concern was that she hadn't yet heard from Laura, who had been planning to meet with Rob's sister Frannie that morning. Arden hoped the meeting hadn't been difficult for her daughter—or, indeed, for Frannie. Arden remembered Rob telling her that even as a small child his older sister had displayed a level head and a strong sense of responsibility. "Sometimes," Rob had said, "I wish she would lighten up a bit and have some fun. But that's Frannie."

Certainly, Arden thought, Rob's younger sisters, Maureen and Abby, had been much more inclined to fun. They had seemed absolutely delighted to be included in their brother's big secret romance. Maureen, only a few months younger than Arden, had been totally into the new wave scene—which made her a bit of a standout in Port George—dressing like Cyndi Lauper and never without her Walkman. Maureen's dream was to move to New York, that mecca for both high and low culture, get a job in Tower Records, and hang out in the dance clubs at night.

Abby had been sixteen the summer of 1984. Unlike Maureen, she seemed uninterested in pop culture, at least, as far as Arden—Victoria—had been able to tell. Abby had had her heart set on going to art school. She was rarely without a pencil and sketchbook. Victoria had seen some of Abby's work and had found it impressive.

Arden filled the kettle with water, placed it on the stove, and went to the cupboard for a tea bag. She had often wondered what had come of Maureen and of Abby. She supposed that Laura might find out in her investigation. They might have married, had children, become grandmothers. Abby might have gone to art school, and Maureen might have made a career in the music industry. Or, like their brother, they might have—

Arden put her hand to her forehead and frowned. She wished Laura would hurry back from Port George. She realized that she felt genuinely lonely, something she hadn't experienced for years. It was because for the first time in an age she hadn't been on her own. She had been living side by side with her child. Her home, her castle and safe haven, had always felt so full and complete, but now it felt empty of an essential element. Another human being.

A particular human being. Laura.

Chapter 48

"So, until I can get a roofer to tell me exactly what's going on, I'm kind of stuck." Arden paused. "Gordon offered to loan me the money for repairs. He said there'd be no interest and that I could set my own repayment plan."

Laura's eyes widened. "Wow. That's very generous. What did you say?"

"I said no. Money can come between friends."

Laura didn't press for a further explanation. She remembered what Arden had told her about not feeling she had a right to be happily in love. To accept Gordon's generous offer might create a bond her mother might not be able to accept.

The two women were sitting at the table in the yard after a dinner of pasta and salad, during which Laura had told her mother about her meeting with Frannie Armitage.

"How does Frannie look?" Arden asked suddenly. "Can you tell that she's a person who has suffered?"

"Who among us hasn't suffered? But, no." Laura went on, lying for her mother's peace of mind, "I wouldn't say she looks particularly worn. Aging comes to most of us."

"Well, I'm grateful she didn't mention the idea of my having had a baby. That's a blessing. It would have made things even more awkward for you."

"And they were awkward enough, believe me. I caught her looking at me pretty intently at one point. I couldn't help but think she was seeing a resemblance between me and my father. But she said nothing."

"Frannie probably thinks about her brother every day, about their childhood together. From what Rob told me, it was pretty idyllic." Arden shook her head. "What are you supposed to do with memories of childhood? The good stuff, like Christmas mornings, and birthday parties, and trips to the beach? Is it dangerous to cherish them, to relive them, to memorialize them? What's the point? The past can't actually make the present any better or worse, but it can, if you let it, taint or distort what's decent about the present. Always remembering. Those happy memories of early times can make the bad or challenging times that came after that much darker." Arden sighed harshly. "Oh, I don't know. I guess thinking about Frannie and the Smiths has put me in a melancholy mood."

Laura reached across the table and gently squeezed her mother's hand. "Memories matter. Why don't you tell me about some of the good times when you were little?"

Arden was silent for a long moment. When she spoke, her voice had softened. "Christmases were pretty magical. My mother went all out with decorations. We had three or four real trees, with lots of glittering and glistening ornaments. The house felt alive then, like it never really did for the rest of the year. Our cook made all the traditional dishes, from plum puddings to roast goose, cookies of all sorts, and even homemade candies. I can still taste her caramels when I close my eyes!"

"Taste and smell are such powerful carriers of memories." Laura smiled. "Proust reminds us of that."

"Yes." Arden paused. "My mother was so glamorous. She was always dressed to the nines, heels, pantyhose, designer bag. And always makeup. She never, ever left the house without lipstick." Arden smiled. "Sometimes, not often, I wonder what she would think of me going around the way I do, no makeup most days, sneakers and jeans, an old leather satchel I've had for ages. But maybe she wouldn't be surprised. Maybe by the time I left Port George she'd given up on my ever being the sort of daughter she wanted me to be. Whatever that was. Like her? Or not like her at all, not an emotional wreck."

"Maybe she would be genuinely proud of you and all you've accomplished."

"Maybe. I just don't know." Arden smiled. "I remember, too, that she had a large collection of jewelry but wore a few pieces on repeat. There was one particular piece that fascinated me; I'd only get to see it on very special occasions, and only once did she let me try it on. It had come down through her own mother's family. It was a Victorian snake bracelet, gold with turquoise and garnet."

"So, supposedly the bracelet would have come to you eventually?"

"And then to you, yes."

"I'm not really fond of snakes, to be honest." Laura smiled. "They scare me. Anyway, what do you remember about your father? I mean, before . . ."

Arden nodded. "I understand. My father was tall, six foot two inches, and he stood very straight, shoulders back, like he was a high-ranking officer in the army. But he never was in the army. And he had very thick hair that waved back from his forehead, the way the hero's hair does in romance novels."

"What color were his eyes? I don't know why I want to know. I don't like your parents very much, not surprisingly. But I suppose they are my family, so my curiosity is to be expected."

Her mother looked closely at Laura. "Yes," she said firmly. "They are your family, in spite of everything."

Laura felt chastened. "Tell me more about your father." She still would not say "my grandfather."

"His eyes were blue. His hair was blond, like mine. My mother, too, was a golden girl, blond and tall and slim. Her eyes were also blue, but that icy blue that can be so unnerving. I thought she looked exotic, I don't know, like Freyja from the Norse myths."

Laura shook her head. "You talk about your parents with kindness, even fondness. After all they put you through."

"Do I speak with fondness?" Arden said after a moment. "That's interesting. Maybe all—or a lot of—the anger I held toward them has lost its power over me. I don't feel actively angry about what happened to me. Not now, anyway."

"But aren't you still angry about what might have happened to my father?"

"Yes. Angry and frustrated. I think I'd like to know the truth, no matter how unpleasant, but at the same time I'm not sure I do want to know. It would be devastating to learn that Rob ran off to escape his responsibilities as a father."

"He didn't run off," Laura said firmly. "Don't ask me why or how I know that, but I know."

Arden smiled. "I know, too. But it would also be devastating to learn that he was hurt by someone who wanted him out of the way."

"And the only people who would have wanted him out of the way are your parents."

"We don't know for sure that Rob didn't have other enemies. Though I can't bring myself to believe that he did."

"So, an accident was never officially ruled out. The case was closed due to lack of evidence. Anything and everything might have happened to Rob Smith, but nothing at all could be proved. Well, if I do find out that your father did have something to do with my father's disappearance, I'll—" Laura stopped talking, alarmed by the look of concern on her mother's face.

Arden reached for Laura's hand. "I won't allow you to ruin your life by doing anything stupid," Arden said fiercely. "When I told you my suspicions about my father, I didn't intend to create a vendetta."

"Don't worry. I won't do anything stupid. But justice needs to be done."

"What would justice look like now?" Arden let go of Laura's hand.

"It would look like the criminal going to jail," Laura said promptly. "It would look like some sort of restitution for my father's family, for me, too, and for you."

"Restitution. What would *that* mean at this late date?" Arden shook her head. "Money? No amount of money can bring Rob back to life. An apology? That would be good, assuming it was genuine, but maybe not enough."

Laura sighed. "I can't imagine ever forgiving the person who hurt my father."

"We're different people. I think you're . . . I think I'm not as tough or as—"

"As unforgiving as I am? You're probably right. Frankly, I've had enough of forgiveness for a while. I've been hurt and I don't much like it."

"You shouldn't like being hurt, of course not. But that doesn't mean it's a good idea to abandon the possibility of forgiveness."

Laura smiled. "We're getting ahead of ourselves. At this moment, we know nothing about what happened to my father other than the fact that no one in Port George has seen him since that Sunday afternoon in August 1984." Laura rose from her chair and stretched her arms over her head. "On that note, I'm going to bed. Good night, Arden."

As Laura prepared for bed, she decided that she would tone down her talk of justice and retribution. Clearly, parts of their conversation that evening had upset her mother, and Arden Bell—along with Victoria Aldridge—had suffered enough distress in her life. There was no need for her own child to add to that distress.

Chapter 49

It was Arden's afternoon off, and while what she really wanted to do was go to the beach and soak up some sun, the fridge and kitchen cupboards hadn't been entirely cleaned out in almost two months. Two months was too long.

"I have to admit I've never done such a thorough cleaning in my own kitchen," Laura said, reaching into the cupboard over the oven. "Don't get me wrong, I don't live in squalor! I'm just not as good a housekeeper as you are."

"I hope I didn't pressure you into helping me." Arden smiled. "But it does make the chore less time sucking."

"I volunteered, remember. Um, what do you want to do with this?" Laura held up a glass jar that contained something gray and lumpy. "I'm not sure what it is, exactly."

Arden grimaced. "Toss it!"

After an hour, the chore was completed to Arden's satisfaction, and the two women took tall glasses of iced tea into the living room for a well-deserved rest.

"When you were pregnant with me," Laura asked when they were settled, "did you know you were having a girl? I mean, you had the option to know, right?"

"I did have the option, but I didn't want to know. I wanted to be surprised. I know that sounds kind of crazy, especially since the baby was going to be taken from me right away. . . . I can't really explain it. I'm sorry."

Laura nodded. "There's no need to be sorry. Had you and my father chosen a name before—"

"We had." Arden smiled at the memory. "We had decided on Elizabeth if we had a girl. Rob liked the old-fashioned nickname Betty."

Laura smiled. "I can see myself as a Betty. And for a boy?"

"Robert, of course. Rob's father was a Robert, and his father before him. Neither of us wanted to break family tradition."

"Arden?" Laura paused a moment before going on. "How did you feel about the pregnancy once Rob went missing and your parents sent you away? Did you regret having met my father in the first place?"

"No," Arden said firmly. "I didn't regret anything. But it was a very strange time for me. Rob and I had shared next to nothing of the pregnancy. That experience had been stolen from us. So, there I was, on my own with this huge, life-changing thing happening to me. I felt like a stranger to myself. Only a few months earlier I'd been planning to start college in the fall, unhappy about having to go to Blake as it was my parents' choice, not mine, but looking forward to the academics, and to being away from home, and by the end of the summer everything had changed. I'd met Rob, fallen in love, and gotten pregnant. Now, Rob was gone and I was being sent off to have the baby in secret." Arden shook her head. "It was all so disorienting."

"I honestly can't imagine. Did you ever attempt to find me? I mean, once you were settled."

Arden smiled sadly. She hoped she could make her daughter understand. "No," she said quietly. "At various times in my life I did think about hiring a lawyer to see if I had any grounds on which to sue my parents for having coerced me into giving up my child. I'd agreed to the adoption under mental and emotional duress, partly because I assumed the adoption was legal. But what if it wasn't legal?"

"Why didn't you speak to a lawyer, then?"

"I had no close friends from whom I could seek advice before taking such a big step," Arden explained carefully. "And I was too frightened to act on my own. At one point I even worried that a lawyer might discover I had committed a crime in acquiescing to the adoption. I was always so afraid. And then I wondered what good going to court ten, fifteen years after the adoption would accomplish. Even if the adoption was found to have been illegal, the ruling wouldn't change what my parents had done." Arden paused and looked fondly at her child. "But there was a more important reason for my holding back. Concern for you. What if you had never been told you were adopted? How would you feel learning the truth as the result of an acrimonious court case? Even if you had known that you were adopted, to discover the adoption was illegal would cause all sorts of chaos, for you and for your parents. There were so many what-ifs, so many variables. In the end, it seemed to me that too many people could get hurt. So, I kept silent."

"I think your decision not to pursue the matter was very selfless," Laura said robustly.

Arden smiled ruefully. "I don't know about selfless. Cowardly? Maybe."

A toot from a bicycle horn announced that the mail had arrived. "I'll be right back," Arden said, grateful for the interruption. Telling the truth was tiring.

When she returned, a frown was on her face. "There's something here for you. It's addressed by hand. Who knows you're staying here, other than Ted?"

"I don't know. I certainly haven't told anyone and I don't think he would have, either. What's the return address?"

"There is none."

Arden handed the letter to Laura. She felt cold. She didn't recognize the handwriting. It looked old-fashioned, something about the neat slant of the letters.

"It's postmarked yesterday. That was quick. A local sender?" Laura frowned and slit open the envelope. Inside there was one sheet of paper, unlined. The white of the paper was a bit yellowed around the edges.

Arden watched as her daughter read the few lines. The hand-

writing, Arden could see, was the same as the writing on the envelope. "Well," she said after a moment, "what does it say? Who is it
from?"

Laura looked up, her expression grim, and held out the piece of
paper. "I think you'd better read it yourself."

With slightly trembling fingers, Arden took the letter. *If you
know what's good for you, you'll stop asking questions about the past. I
mean it.*

For about half a second Arden wanted to laugh. *If you know
what's good for you* . . . It was straight out of an old black-and-white
gangster film. But the letter, she felt sure, was no joke. She was
frightened.

"We've opened a Pandora's box," she said, giving the letter back
to Laura. "Clearly, someone who was involved in whatever happened in 1984 doesn't want the truth coming to light."

Laura was frowning at the letter. "Mmm. The last time I was in
Port George I caught a glimpse of a woman following me. It wasn't
Florence Aldridge, of that I'm sure."

Arden felt the chill that had come over her harden to ice. "I
think we should stop this search," she said tightly. "I don't think
you should go back to Port George. It's not safe."

Laura shook her head. "I'm not going to be intimidated. This
note doesn't threaten anything specific, certainly not death. It's
one big cliché. I don't think the threat is real."

"I know my default is to keep my head down. After so many
years of hiding in plain sight it's all I really know how to do. But
don't you think we should go to the police with this?"

"No," Laura said decisively. "Whoever is the author of this note
doesn't scare me. He or she is a coward. I was married to a coward.
I know how to handle them. But I will tell Ted. Frankly, I'd like his
opinion."

"It's just that . . ." Arden felt the words stick in her throat, but
they had to be spoken. "What if the letter is from my father? He's a
lot of things, but not a coward, not the man I remember."

"Well, if the letter is from Herbert Aldridge, he's finally met his
match." Laura looked down again at the piece of paper in her
hand. "Black ink. That tells me nothing. I wish I knew something

about handwriting analysis. I can't even tell if this is from a man or a woman."

"It was written by an older person."

Laura studied the letter for a long moment. "I see what you mean. The hand is strong, it's not that, but I'd bet whoever wrote this had penmanship lessons in school." Laura folded the letter and stuck it back in its envelope. "I say we try to put this out of our minds for the moment and enjoy the rest of the afternoon. Dinner outside this evening?"

Arden nodded, but the last thing she was concerned about was dinner. She knew she would have no appetite, not with knowing for sure that someone wanted to silence her daughter. Why, oh, why, had they agreed to go down this road?

Chapter 50

Laura sat across from Ted in his office. She had told him about the letter and texted him a photo of both it and the envelope in which it had come. Ted was inclined to agree with Laura that the threat, being so vague, was not to be taken all that seriously.

"I'm not saying you shouldn't proceed with caution." Ted smiled. "If you get a call from a blocked number asking you to meet 'a friend' in an abandoned parking lot at three a.m., don't go."

"Don't worry. I've watched a few detective dramas. I know to avoid empty houses and dark alleys. So, why did you ask me to come by?"

Ted cleared his throat. "Because of an old friend. Let me explain. James Barber and I went to kindergarten and grammar school together. He and his family lived around the corner from us. As we got older, we'd just climb the fence that separated our yards when we wanted to hang out. Our parents weren't close, they moved in slightly different social circles, but everyone got along. Anyway, James and I remained friends over the years. We were at each other's weddings. We have dinner several times a year. That sort of thing. Yesterday morning James paid me a visit at home. He told me he'd heard about the woman researching a podcast and that it had gotten him thinking. And remembering."

Laura felt the proverbial butterflies of excitement take flight in her stomach. "Remembering what?"

"Remembering his brother. James and his older brother, Jake, were the complete opposites right from the start. James was a by-the-rule kind of guy, and Jake broke every rule he could just for the hell of it. James did well in school; Jake was suspended more times than I can count. Mr. Barber, the boys' father, came down extra-hard on his firstborn, wayward son, while Mrs. Barber lavished Jake with affection. Neither parent did Jake any real service. There was no consistency in the home, and a heck of a lot of fighting. James sort of sailed through it all without visible scars, whereas poor Jake wasn't so lucky. He got into drugs and alcohol before he was in high school and never looked back."

Ted paused to take a drink of water. Laura, though itching to know where this background story was leading, waited patiently for him to resume.

"I suspect James still harbors a sense of guilt concerning Jake, a sense that he should have been of more help to him than he was. Frankly, I don't know what else James could have done for his brother. He tried to get him into rehab more than once and bailed him out of endless scrapes. But nothing worked. Jake was one of those people who seem bent on self-destruction, whether they want to be that person or not."

"I'm not sure I see how this has anything to do with my father's disappearance."

Ted smiled ruefully. "It might have absolutely nothing to do with it, or it might have a great deal. I don't know, yet. James told me what I'd guessed years ago, that Jake was not above earning a dollar through illegal means. Sadly, he became one of those types a powerful, ruthless man might use to do his dirty work, then get rid of if he caused trouble."

Laura sat up straighter in her seat. Now, she thought, they were getting somewhere. "And your friend James thinks that his brother might have worked for Herbert Aldridge."

Ted nodded. "While he has no concrete evidence, offhand re-marks his brother made through the years led James to believe that

Jake knew Herbert better than he should have done. Why would a powerful investment banker like Herbert Aldridge want anything to do with a dubious character like Jake Barber unless it was for using him to take care of—of unpleasant messes."

"Where is Jake now?"

"Dead," Ted said simply. "He died of an overdose in late 1985. The police never learned from what source Jake had acquired the drugs. It was a sorry end to a sorry life."

Laura frowned. "This is still all very conjectural. I don't see how a fictional podcast about the ramifications of a missing person on his community is connected to Jake. . . ." Laura halted. The connection, however tenuous, was beginning to come clearer.

"James believes that his brother was hired by Aldridge to do several bits of dirty work over the years," Ted went on. "Now he wonders if Jake could have been involved in something underhanded involving Rob Smith. He remembers as well as I do how the police investigation into Rob's disappearance was squashed, and he also remembers the rampant cronyism that went on in Port George back in the seventies and eighties. Aldridge was a key figure in the power circle that included the mayor, the chief of police, and a retired lawmaker in the state government. And he had lots of connections in Augusta, the state capital. James thinks that if he could somehow help to bring Herbert Aldridge to justice for a crime, any crime, he will have gotten justice for his brother in some small way."

"I see. But why not take his concerns to the police? Why bring them to you? Unless the police today are as corrupt as they were back then."

Ted cleared his throat. "No, today's force is clean, but James came to me for two reasons. First, he has no real evidence of any kind to offer the police. You can't ask for an official investigation based on the hints of a man long dead."

"Oh. Right."

"Secondly, James knew you and I had met a few times. He thought that my having a connection to a member of the investigative podcast crew . . ." Ted sighed. "Don't worry, your secret is safe—James has no idea you're Rob's daughter. Anyway, before he left he gave me this old videotape from his brother's effects. As you'll see in a minute, it shows Herbert Aldridge rubbing elbows with the rest of the Port George power elite at a party at the country club in the spring of 1984."

Laura felt a rush of emotion she couldn't quite identify. She would now see for the first time her maternal grandfather. A man she was loathe to claim as kin.

Ted got up and inserted the videocassette into an archaic video player Laura hadn't noticed until then. "Luckily, James had this old machine at home, otherwise I'm not sure how we'd have been able to watch."

As the four-minute video played out, Ted identified the party-goers. The chief of police. The mayor. An alderman, whatever that was. The owner of the biggest car dealership north of Portland. The retired state lawmaker. A state representative, in Port George who knew why. One by one the men acknowledged whoever it was recording the moment, some with brief nods, another with a thumbs-up, yet another with a rude gesture.

"There's Herbert Aldridge," Ted said.

Laura hadn't needed Ted to identify him. Reluctantly, she admitted that he was a handsome man of the Gary Cooper school, as her mother had told her, but something about his face was cold and mean. Sure, the quality of the tape was poor and she was prejudiced against the man, but Laura was sure she could detect the look of a criminal character.

As the tape continued, and in spite of the difficult feelings elicited by the image of her grandfather, Laura couldn't suppress a smile at the awful way these self-important small-town men were dressed. One wore an oversized pastel-blue suit with a black T-shirt; this might have been acceptable if he had left the brown wing-tipped shoes at home. One was wearing sunglasses; again, this hot trend might have been bearable, if it the man weren't also wearing what was clearly a badly fitting toupee. Another man had pushed the sleeves of his jacket up to his elbow, not a good look for an overweight man in his fifties. Three others wore fat pinstripes. The lone woman at the gathering looked no better than her male associates. Her hair had been sprayed into a virtual helmet; her earrings were bright blue plastic circles; the shoulder pads of her shiny orange dress were enormous; her black lace stockings were criminal. Forget the 1970s, Laura thought. Were the 1980s the decade that good taste forgot?

"Who is the woman?" she asked when the video had ended.

"I don't know. Maybe a girlfriend, maybe someone hired to entertain. If you know what I mean."

Laura nodded grimly.

"Again, this is no proof of anything other than the fact that Herbert Aldridge knew and socialized with the other bigwigs of Port George and beyond back in the day. And that, for some reason, Jake Barber got his hands on the tape. For all we know, he might have been paid to be the videographer. If the sound was better, we might have been able to hear something incriminating, but that's wishful thinking."

"It was good of Mr. Barber to bring this to you, though. I just hope he's not too disappointed if we can't uncover a crime that links Herbert Aldridge to Jake Barber. After all, there is no podcast team. There are no researchers. There is no real investigation."

"I warned him about harboring false hope. And about the possibility of learning that his brother was involved in a crime far more serious than James already suspects. But he's determined to keep digging through his own files and what's left of his brother's possessions in the hope that something of use to us will emerge."

Laura nodded. "A man obsessed. I can understand that."

"At some point, I will have to tell him the truth, that you're Rob Smith's daughter. But not until—"

"Not until this has all been put to rest."

Shortly thereafter, Ted walked Laura to the door of the reception area. "There's been a lot of bad feeling about Herbert Aldridge in this town for a very long time. I'm willing to bet my friend is not the only one who would like to see Mr. Aldridge pay for his sins. Rather, his alleged sins."

And that group, Laura thought, would include Frannie Armitage.

Laura took her leave. On the way back to the Lilac Inn, she found herself thinking about Ted's choice of the word *sin*. People didn't think much in terms of sin anymore, or of evil. There were social and psychological reasons for people doing bad things; society or genetics took the burden of responsibility for most crime. That was fine, a civilized way to consider the problems that plagued the human condition. But what if evil was real in the sense that it used to be considered real, alive, a powerful force, apart from human consciousness or unconsciousness? And what if that sense of evil resided in the mind and heart of Herbert Aldridge, her grandfather?

Laura soon abandoned the troubling thoughts. She wasn't a philosopher or a theologian, just a tired sort-of academic playing amateur detective and not doing a very good job at it, either. And what this tired sort-of academic needed was a large cup of ice coffee and a sugary cookie.

Chapter 51

Arden was curled up on the couch in the living room, talking with Laura, who was still in Port George. The cats were lumped on the floor nearby, Falstaff snoring loudly as was his usual habit.

"I knew my father hobnobbed with so-called important people," Arden said when Laura had finished telling her about the video James Barber had unearthed from his brother's things. "Every time he came back from a business trip to Boston or New York, he would regale my mother with stories of the exclusive restaurants he'd eaten in and the fancy parties he'd attended. But it doesn't mean he was involved in cover-ups or graft or political fixing back home. Assuming that sort of thing even went on in Port George."

"According to Ted it did. And I suspect that sort of thing goes on in just about every city and town, large or small, all across the world. But maybe I'm too much of a cynic."

A cynic or a realist, Arden thought, realizing she had had enough talk of Port George and its politics.

"I know you'll enjoy the Fourth of July here in Eliot's Corner," she said brightly. "There's the parade of course. It takes about four minutes from beginning to end, but everyone loves it. After the parade, everyone mills around the center of town and the fire department gives the kids tours of the station, and there are always one or two groups, Girl Scouts, the choir from the Baptist church, selling cupcakes and lemonade. Eventually, people move off to their homes and their private celebrations."

"What about fireworks?"

"Eliot's Corner doesn't have fireworks, but there are plenty of places within an hour's drive that put on a show. I don't like fireworks. Ever since I was small, I've hated loud noises, loud music, even the television turned up too loudly."

"Funny, I don't like loud noises, either. Jared knew that, but I swear he seemed to enjoy crashing about the house and blaring his music. I might not have minded the music so much but we had totally opposite tastes. Techno-pop at high volume might be some people's idea of happiness, but not mine."

"His behavior was cruel," Arden said passionately. And protectively. For so many years she had not had the opportunity to protect her child. It wasn't too late to start now, she thought. Though she wished she could shake that Jared Pence. "What are your plans for tomorrow? I hope you're being careful."

"I'm not entirely sure about my plans. But I'm being as careful as I can be. I haven't seen that woman again, the one who was following me. I suppose I could ask Mr. Meyer if I could look through the *Chronicle* archives again, though I'm not sure where that would get me."

"Didn't you tell me that a psychic had offered to help in Rob's case? And that Frannie had hired her at one point, after the police had rejected her help?"

"Yes. What of it?"

"Well, do you think we should consider contacting her? Maybe she has something useful to tell us after all."

"But if what the *Chronicle* said was true, Frannie dismissed her as being of no help. Besides, I think turning to a psychic should be one of our last resorts. A few years back a colleague hired a reputable psychic to help her with a family matter and it cost a small fortune, something neither you nor I have."

Arden sighed. "That's for sure."

"I guess I'll just try to get a good night's sleep and hope the morning brings a bright idea."

"It often does. Good night, Laura."

Arden got up from the couch and stretched her arms over her head. A good night's sleep seemed like a perfect idea for her, as well. But first, she would read a bit from *Villette*. It always brought her comfort, knowing that Rob had once held the volume, seeing her name in his handwriting, remembering the night he had given it to her.

A huge snort from Falstaff caused Arden to startle, and then, to smile. She was so lucky to have found these three balls of mayhem. And so very, very lucky that her daughter had found her.

Chapter 52

Summer 1984

Even though she was on her family's property, Victoria felt a bit scared. Maybe scared wasn't the right word. Maybe, she thought, she was just nervous. Waiting for Rob always made her feel jumpy, and not in an entirely good way. Always, there was the element of risk, and Victoria had never been comfortable with risk-taking of any sort.

Still, she wouldn't have said no to meeting Rob this evening, the Fourth of July, for anything. They wouldn't have long to spend together; Rob was working for the company in charge of the Port George fireworks display and needed to be at his post fifteen minutes before the show was to begin. Victoria hated loud noises, but she would bravely have endured the chaos and commotion just to be near him.

If she had been allowed to attend the town's celebrations.

Herbert and Florence Aldridge had invited a couple they knew from the country club for drinks at eight. When Victoria had left the house at eight thirty, the four adults were comfortably settled in the living room, a drinks trolley near to hand, Dean Martin crooning softly in the background. Mr. Mitchell's unpleasant bray of a laugh had caused Victoria to jump as she slipped past the open door of the room on her way out to the far edge of the Aldridge property to meet Rob. She desperately hoped she would be back at the house before any of the adults noticed she was gone.

Victoria sighed. The air felt heavy, oppressive. Though rain wasn't expected until well after midnight, she felt sure the skies would open before that. Maybe, she hoped, the fireworks would be canceled at the last minute. People would be disappointed and Rob probably wouldn't get paid—no work, no money—but at least he and the other guys would be safe.

There he was! Victoria felt her heart begin to race. How she ached for his touch! He jogged closer through the waning evening light.

"Rob!" she called.

His face broke out into a broad smile as he caught sight of her. He was wearing a red bandanna around his head. She knew it was to absorb sweat, a thoroughly practical item, but Victoria thought it gave him a rakish air. His T-shirt advertised his love of the band the Police; his jeans were almost completely worn through at the knees.

"I brought you a sparkler," he said when he had reached her. "Here, let me light it and we'll have our own celebration."

"Not yet." Victoria pulled him close to her and they shared a long and passionate kiss.

"I'm sorry I can't be at the celebrations with you," Victoria murmured.

"It's all right. I'll be so busy we wouldn't have had much time together anyway." Suddenly Rob pulled away. "I wish I could stay here with you all night, but I've got to get back. The show starts at nine."

"Be careful, Rob. I don't know what I would do if anything happened to you."

Rob laughed. "You worry too much. What could happen? We take every precaution. Besides, I've been helping out with the fireworks for the past three years. I know what I'm doing. Here, let me light the sparkler for you now."

They shared another kiss before Rob broke away and hurried

off through the dark. When he was barely visible, he turned and waved. Victoria waved back. Her heart was brimming with happiness. That one human being could bring so much joy to another was still so new to her. So new, and so wonderful.

All too soon, the sparkler fizzled to an end. It was time to return home.

Rather, to the big old house in which Victoria resided with Mr. and Mrs. Aldridge.

Chapter 53

Laura was not the only one at breakfast that morning. The hostess of the Lilac Inn was run off her feet after the late-night arrival of a family party of two grandparents, a mother and father, their three children under the age of ten or so, and a middle-aged woman who might be an aunt or a cousin or a sister. She was certainly no nanny, as neither she nor any of the other adults bothered to check the antics of the three kids. In fifteen minutes, a sugar bowl had been overturned, a glass of milk spilled, and the flowers in the tiny vase on the neighboring table thrown onto the floor.

Laura finished her breakfast as quickly as she could without inducing indigestion and retreated to her room. She had confessed to Arden the night before that she had no plans for the day, and in spite of a good night's sleep, she had woken with nothing more on her mind than food. Now, having eaten and drunk two cups of coffee, Laura's brain began to work, if slowly at first.

A fairly comfortable armchair was in one corner of the room, and Laura sat there now, laptop at hand. Was it possible to review a person's police record after that person's death? Would she need to contact the police department to do so? She hadn't trained as a journalist. She had never thought about this sort of thing before.

But there was no time like the present to start learning. Within minutes Laura discovered that most court information was public record. Not long after, she learned from the Maine State Police, State Bureau of Identification website that Jake Barber, born in Port George in 1956, had quite the record. Petty theft. Involvement in drunken brawls and creating a public nuisance. Driving without a license. Laura merely scanned the rest of the lengthy list. There seemed nothing at all to link Jake Barber to Herbert Aldridge and the sort of misdeeds he might want committed.

Laura didn't doubt the exactness of this official information, but she did wonder if she might find any interesting editorial comments in the *Daily Chronicle* from Jake's most prolific years. She decided to contact Edward Meyer and ask once again for access to his archive.

Mr. Meyer was amenable and Laura set out right away. She had learned from Kathy Murdoch that he was a widower. He and his wife had been married for close to fifty years when she passed away suddenly from a massive stroke. They had been a good couple, Kathy had told her. Popular, too. The funeral had been mobbed.

Laura arrived at Mr. Meyer's home to find him wearing gardening gloves and wielding a spade. Once settled in the basement, Laura scanned every Crime Beat column published between January 1983 and December 1985. As expected, Jake Barber was frequently mentioned, but as his official record had already shown, not in association with anything particularly outrageous. It just didn't make sense to Laura that a petty thief with a drug-and-alcohol problem was the sort of person you would hire to perform a murder or a kidnapping or any other major crime that would involve planning or stealth or real intelligence.

After thanking Mr. Meyer for his kind assistance—after which he offered her access to the archives anytime she wanted and asked her to call him Ed—Laura headed back into town where she'd left her car at the Lilac Inn. A long walk was what she needed. Her legs were feeling twitchy after having spent the morning on her butt.

Laura had not gone far along Main Street when she spotted Miss Thompson coming her way. For a second, Laura considered darting into a shop to avoid the former schoolteacher. Laura felt like such a lowlife, lying to this kind older woman, someone who had once loved and believed in young Victoria Aldridge. But Laura was no coward. At least, she tried not to be one.

"Hello, Miss Thompson," she said with a smile as they drew close. "I hope you're enjoying this lovely afternoon."

Miss Thompson returned Laura's smile. She was wearing a light-weight cardigan over her flowered dress and carried a string bag of groceries. "How is your research going?"

"Fine. I just spent a few hours at Ed Meyer's house, reading through the newspaper's archives."

They exchanged a few further pleasantries, and when Miss Thompson had proceeded on her way, Laura mentally shook off her feelings of guilt and set off for the green square in the center of town, the square she had visited on her very first day in Port George. Her walk could wait. She felt the need to hear her mother's voice.

Laura found a seat on a bench in the shade of a large maple tree. The sound of birds singing in the branches overhead was soothing.

Arden was pleased to hear from Laura. "So, what have you learned today?"

Laura related her findings regarding Jake Barber. "Nothing at all sounded an alarm." Laura sighed. "Not that I expected anything to. I ran into Miss Thompson when I got back to town. She asked how my podcast research was progressing. I felt like such a heel continuing to lie to her." Laura sighed again. "Clearly, I'm upsetting people. For one, the person who sent me that note. Maybe also that woman who was following me. And how many other people am I hurting by lying and by digging into the past? Innocent people who might suffer from what I might uncover."

"I know. It all feels so distasteful, what we're doing. Cruel, almost."

"But think of what was done to you. Far more cruel and distasteful. I'm going to have to swallow my scruples and carry on."

"Are you sure? This quest is upsetting you, too, and you're the most important person here."

Laura felt tears come to her eyes. "Next to you," she said feelingly. "I'll be okay. And I'll be home tomorrow."

Only after Laura had ended the call did she realize she had referred to Eliot's Corner and Arden's house as home. That felt about right.

Chapter 54

Gordon's purple picnic table was laden with summer foods—sliced watermelon; potato salad; hot dogs; cupcakes. A few of Gordon's pals from around town had stopped by earlier, bearing bottles of wine or six-packs of beer. After downing a glass and scarfing a hot dog, they left for another, probably more raucous venue. The only people left at the moment were Gordon, Arden, Laura, Deborah, and Brent and his partner, Kurt Wallace.

"Who remembers what Fourth of July was like when they were a kid?" Brent asked, reaching into one of the coolers set by the table for a beer.

Laura laughed. "I remember dressing up as Betsy Ross for a town parade. I think I was about seven or eight. The mobcap was far too big for my head and kept sliding down over my eyes. Between that and the long skirt I pretty much stumbled my way from one end of Main Street to the other. But I had a blast. I felt so important! What about you, Deborah?"

Deborah shrugged. "I don't remember my family ever making a big thing out of July Fourth. Some years we did absolutely nothing to mark the occasion. Other years we'd visit my cousins in the next town for a barbecue. My uncle always had a few fireworks on hand, no doubt illegal, and he'd set them off just before we were to head home. Gordon?"

"I had a bad experience with fireworks once. I must have been about five or six. My parents and brothers and I were at a neighbor's house. One guy got pretty drunk, and before anyone could stop him, he blew his hand off with some sort of incendiary device. I remember people screaming and my mother grabbing me and running toward the street. I don't think I understood exactly what had happened until years later, but from that moment on I've never been a fan of fireworks, near or far."

Brent shivered. "Yikes. What I remember most about Fourth of July when I was a kid were those cheap, paper Uncle Sam hats my mother would buy and make us kids wear, the hats and the red, white, and blue streamers and the bunting. What my mother lacked in taste she made up for in enthusiasm. Kurt?"

"Red-white-and-blue-iced cupcakes," he replied promptly. "Red punch. Blueberry ice cream. In my house, every holiday focused on theme food. And that's not a complaint! At Thanksgiving, my mother would dye the mashed potatoes orange, as if the pumpkin pie and the sweet potatoes weren't enough. What about you, Arden?"

Arden shrugged. "My Independence Days were uneventful." Except, she thought, for the one she had spent with Rob. "My parents might attend a dance at their country club. Very sophisticated, from what I was told. Sit-down lobster dinner, cocktails. There were fireworks over the golf course at the end of the evening."

"What did you do while your parents were at play?" Kurt asked. "Watch Jimmy Cagney in *Yankee Doodle Dandy*?"

"I don't remember," Arden said honestly. "I probably spent the night in my room reading."

"Tell me you at least went to the town parade?" Brent asked. "There must have been one. The single fire truck, the local Boy Scouts troop, members of the Rotary Club? A lot like our parade this morning."

"I did, when I was old enough to go on my own. My parents never got involved in the more pedestrian town events. Pardon the pun! I remember my father being asked one year to be a judge in a baking contest sponsored by the church we occasionally attended. He and my mother got a big laugh out of that and declined the offer."

Deborah turned her eyes heavenward. "Judge in a baking contest! My dream job."

Only when Brent and Kurt had gone on to another party did anyone mention Laura's investigation.

"Hardly an investigation," she said ruefully, in answer to Gordon's question. "More like aimless meandering. You can't get very far with rumors and innuendos."

"Tell that to the tabloids," Deborah said. "The general public is all too willing to believe any hint of juicy scandal."

Suddenly, the sound of distant fireworks broke the relative peace of Gordon's backyard party. Gordon and Laura flinched. Deborah looked up again as if in hopes of seeing a flash of color in the night sky.

Arden thought again of that one and only Fourth of July she had spent with Rob, of their meeting in secret, of the sparkler he had lit for her before going off to help out at the town's official celebrations. She hadn't known it at the time, but the sparkler had been a metaphor for their love. How quickly ignited, how beautifully it had burned, and how quickly it had died.

But that wasn't quite right. The love between Victoria and Rob hadn't burned out; it had been denied the oxygen it needed to live. A wave of sadness threatened to overwhelm Arden, and she wished it were still light enough to warrant sunglasses. They would hide the tears she was sure would soon be falling.

As suddenly as the fireworks had begun, they ended. Gordon turned to Arden and frowned. "Did the noise bother you that much? You look shaken."

"Yes," she lied. "But I'll be fine now."

Chapter 55

Laura mopped her forehead with her bandanna. The temperature was near ninety and the humidity at 85 percent. She felt swollen with heat, as if her skin would burst open and release great waves of fire, but Arden had suggested this walk on the beach and Laura hadn't wanted to disappoint her.

"You don't really feel the heat much, do you?" Laura asked now, noting that her mother appeared almost as fresh as the proverbial daisy.

Arden shrugged. "I'm not a big fan of hot weather, but it doesn't really bother me the way it does some people. My father was like that, I remember. It just occurred to me that maybe that's why we didn't have air-conditioning when I was growing up."

"What about your mother?" Laura asked, using the bandanna to wipe the back of her neck.

"She was hypersensitive to both heat and cold, but if I remember correctly, she was tolerably comfortable in the spring and fall."

Laura couldn't help but imagine those two elderly people in that big house on top of the hill, rattling around in empty rooms, the woman, her grandmother, wrapped in a heavy shawl, while the man, her grandfather, went about in his shirtsleeves, his baggy pants held up by ancient suspenders. . . . She smiled to herself. She really did have a flair for the dramatic.

"I've been thinking about getting in touch with Lenny Tobin," she told her mother, "the reporter who covered the story of my father's disappearance."

"How do you think he could help? You've been through the *Chronicle* archives twice now."

"I'm not really sure. I told you it turned out he never believed my podcast cover, but he was nice enough to help me that second time I approached him. And he didn't charge me for asking a few questions, like a psychic would. But maybe you're right. I guess I'll spare Mr. Tobin another call.

"Hey," Laura went on after a moment, "I've been meaning to ask about that necklace you're wearing. I don't think I've seen you without it since I showed up in Eliot's Corner."

Arden touched the small silver charm that hung on a delicate chain around her neck. "You haven't. I wear it always."

"Was it another gift from my father?"

"Yes. I'll never forgot the afternoon he gave it to me. It was just after we had tried to go to a movie in another town. I say tried because before we'd even reached the theater, I got too scared to go on. Rob understood—he always understood—and took me home, careful to keep to back roads so as not to draw attention to ourselves." Arden paused to sigh. "I felt so bad for having ruined our time together, and Rob knew that. The next time we managed to sneak away to meet, he gave me this necklace. I'll never forget what he said as he fastened it around my neck. 'Our time will come to walk together barefoot in the sand. Our time will come to be together always.' All we wanted was to be a normal couple, free go anywhere we wanted to go, to the beach in summer, ice-skating in winter, to Boston to see a Red Sox home game." Arden smiled. "Rob loved the Red Sox. He played baseball in high school. I never saw him play, of course. Our worlds hadn't yet collided."

Laura shook her head sadly. "The whole thing is heartbreaking. Such prejudice, in this day and age!"

"And such a simple dream, to walk barefoot together on the beach. But it never came true because of the need to keep our relationship a secret. As long as we weren't seen together in public, our romance was just a rumor."

Laura linked her arm through her mother's. "Try not to be too sad. Try to be grateful for what time you did have with Rob. My father." Laura laughed quietly. "I'm certainly grateful. I wouldn't have a life if you and Rob Smith hadn't found each other."

"I am grateful. Being able to walk on the beach with my child—barefoot or not!—makes up for every moment of pain Rob's disappearance caused me."

"Did your parents ever question you about the necklace?"

Arden laughed. "I'm pretty sure neither of them noticed it. I suppose if they'd asked, I would have said I'd bought it at one of the shops in town."

"I can't imagine the courage it took for you to make the decision to leave home and take your chances out in the world," Laura said after a time. "And you never wavered in your determination."

"Oh, I wavered lots of times. Like whenever I was feeling particularly vulnerable, when my boss at whatever awful job I had was harassing me or when I was sick with a bad flu. But I could never stomach the idea of putting myself back into the hands of the two people who had shown me so little support or compassion. Assuming, of course, they would have accepted me back." Arden paused for a moment. "As for leaving Port George, it was more of an impulse than a well-thought-out decision. I suspect if I'd taken a day or two to really consider what being on my own might entail, I probably wouldn't have gone at all. I probably would have sagged back into the inertia and sadness that had come to define me and done whatever it was my parents wanted me to do with my life."

"I'm so very glad you didn't think things through," Laura said feelingly. "I'm so glad you found the strength to make such a fine life for yourself."

"Me, too."

Laura felt a drop of rain on her shoulder. Thank God, she thought. Now maybe the air would cool down. "We should get back to the house. It's beginning to rain."

Arden smiled. "I actually like walking in the rain." A clap of thunder immediately followed. "But not in a thunderstorm."

A flash of forked lightning caused Laura to wince. "Yikes. Let's run!"

Chapter 56

Prospero, like his namesake, was undisturbed by the storm; Arden wondered if he had summoned the tempest for his secret feline reasons. Falstaff was hiding under a chair and probably wouldn't come out until hours after the storm had passed. Ophelia was slinking around the perimeter of the first floor, nose working furiously, as if seeking the source of the disruption. "I call her the director of Homeland Security," Arden told her daughter.

Laura, who, like her mother, had gotten a good drenching before she had reached the car, was drying her hair with a towel. "I'd trust Ophelia more than I'd trust any human appointed to the role." She laughed.

Only after the women had finished dinner and were settled in the living room with cups of ginger tea did the conversation return to the Aldridge family.

"Where did your parents meet?" Laura asked. Ophelia was taking a well-deserved break from her security duties and was curled up on Laura's lap.

"They met in college and got married right after my father graduated. My mother didn't go on to her senior year. Probably fairly typical at the time. My father, though, went on to earn an MBA, and after that his career really began to take off."

"So, what went wrong?"

"I'm not sure anything went wrong." Arden took a sip of her tea. "My parents stayed together when lots of other couples of their generation got divorced."

"And we know they're still living in the same house. Too big for them now, I'd think."

"It was too big when I was living there. Perfect for parties, but not for much else."

"What did your parents do for fun, besides give fancy parties?"

It wasn't lost on Arden that Laura never claimed Florence and Herbert as family members. It was never "my grandparents," but always: "your parents." Arden thought she could understand why that was.

"My father loved golf. When he wasn't working, and he worked an awful lot, he was at the country club. My mother joked she was a golf widow. Not that she seemed to mind when he was gone. Well, maybe she did and she just didn't tell me."

Laura frowned. "No doubt he did a lot of business deals over drinks at the clubhouse after nine holes. Isn't that the cliché?"

"I suppose. I remember being out on the green with my father once when I was small, sitting in the golf cart where I would be out of the way. I remember feeling so proud of him. He was taller than the other men and more handsome. At least, I thought he was."

"Meanwhile, your mother was probably back at the clubhouse sipping martinis with the other golf widows."

"Probably," Arden said sadly. "She did a lot of that over the years."

Arden took another sip of her tea and considered. She and Laura had grown so close these past weeks. Surely, there was no reason to keep back another strange aspect of the Aldridge family's dynamic.

"I've been reluctant to tell you something else about my family."

Laura nodded encouragingly. "Go on."

"I've told you how the death of my brother haunted my mother. And I told you that her mother blamed her for what happened to Joseph."

"Did your father blame her as well?"

"I don't think so, no. He treated my mother with kindness, with a sort of exaggerated gentleness."

"That sounds demeaning."

Arden frowned. "Please, just listen before judging too harshly. This is difficult for me to talk about."

"I'm sorry," Laura said sincerely.

Arden took a breath. "My mother commissioned portraits of what my brother might have looked like at the age of five, and then ten, and finally, at the age of eighteen. I don't know where she found an artist to undertake such a strange project. I imagine she paid well. And she probably provided photographs of other family members as a clue to what Joseph might have looked like, photos of my father as a child and young man, her own photos, maybe pictures of her parents, as well."

Laura's expression betrayed her shock. "Wow. So, were the portraits hung in a private room, a place where only Florence could view them? Sort of like a shrine?"

"Oh, no. That might have been—acceptable. The portraits—they were oil paintings—were hung in the big entrance hall where they couldn't be ignored."

"I should say not. What did your father think of your mother commissioning so strange a project? Was that one of the times he was exaggeratedly gentle with her?"

"I don't know what he thought in the beginning, but I remember when my mother told us one night at dinner that the newest addition to her gallery was going to be finished soon. Joseph at eighteen. My father suddenly got very angry. He slammed his glass on the table and asked when this nonsense would end. I don't remember my mother's reaction, but a week later the newest portrait was hanging in the front hall. If she commissioned more after I left home, I don't know."

"I think the whole dynamic is pretty macabre. Your father's complicity feels almost cruel."

"He couldn't very well forbid an expression of his wife's grief."

"Maybe not. Do you think your mother ever talked to anyone outside the family about Joseph?"

Arden shook her head. "I'm pretty sure she never saw a therapist. As for my mother's friends, I could tell that she wasn't close to any of them. No, I think my mother was a very lonely woman. I wouldn't be surprised if she still is."

"Maybe her husband forbade her to talk about the tragic loss of her baby son," Laura suggested grimly.

"He wasn't a demon, Laura. And he loved my mother, he really did."

"Maybe so," Laura replied after a moment. "I know very little about romantic love, or domestic love, or whatever you want to call it. I mean, I had the example of my parents, but sometimes an example, good or bad, just doesn't stick. You know what I mean?"

Arden nodded. "I do."

"Where is your brother buried? My uncle."

At least, Arden thought, Laura could claim one other member of her family without hesitation. "In the Montgomery family plot in a cemetery a bit further north. I never visited the grave. I don't know if my father did, either, after the funeral, I mean. My mother used to go alone. You didn't approach her when she got back to the house, not if you knew where she'd been. She'd go straight to her room and not come out until the next morning."

"She had her own bedroom?"

Arden nodded. "Yes. I don't ever remember my parents sharing a bedroom. It was only years later when I realized that most couples did and that some parents actually let their children sleep in bed with them."

"Were you allowed to ask questions about your brother? About what happened?"

"I learned early on not to ask my mother about my brother. If she wanted to talk about him, she did, but if I mentioned him, she'd get upset. It didn't take me long to figure out it was a topic I shouldn't bring up."

"What about your father? Did he ever talk about the son he lost?"

"No, at least not to me, except for one occasion when my mother was in a particularly bad way." Arden paused. "I was about twelve at the time," she said finally. "My parents had gone to a party at the house of one of their friends, and something happened to upset my mother—I never knew exactly what—because they came home early and I could hear my mother sobbing. I was worried, so I crept down the stairs. The door to my father's study was closed and they were inside. What I managed to hear made me think someone at the party had mentioned a child who had recently died, maybe from SIDS, and that the remark had sent my mother over the edge. My father was trying to calm her down, but her hysteria went on and on. And then I heard a crack. My father must have slapped my mother's face to get through to her. It worked. There was silence. I dashed back to my room before my parents could find me eavesdropping. I felt sick to my stomach. I'd never seen or heard either of my parents raise a hand to the other."

Laura's face looked drained of color. "How terrible."

"The next morning my mother didn't appear for breakfast. It was a Sunday and my father hadn't gone off to the golf course yet. I remember sitting in my usual seat at the table, feeling miserable, when suddenly my father blurted that it was my grandmother's fault my mother was such a wreck. I was shocked, but somehow, I found the nerve to ask him what he meant. He told me that my grandmother had blamed my brother's death on my mother; she said my mother had been neglectful. But she hadn't been, not according to my father." Arden took a deep breath. "Finally, after what seemed like an eternity, my father stopped speaking and left the table. He never mentioned the subject again."

"Poor Florence," Laura said fiercely. "What a nightmare *her* mother must have been."

"My memories of my grandmother are pretty vague. She died when I was nine. And she only came to visit once a year from her home in Quebec. Her husband, Joseph, was Canadian, and when my mother married, my grandmother and grandfather went back to his hometown. He was sickly by then. I never met him. He died shortly after my brother did."

"Ah! I see now. Your grieving grandmother hoisted her anger and frustration onto her daughter. She probably blamed her for both deaths."

"I never thought of it that way, but you could be right." Arden sighed. "My, what a mess! My mother must have been pretty damaged already to collapse so completely when her baby died. Instead of being able to stand up to her mother, she just accepted the blame inflicted on her."

Laura put her empty cup on the side table and, looking deeply troubled, stared down at the cat in her lap for some time.

"I'm sorry. Maybe I shouldn't have told you about the paintings."

"No," Laura said quickly, looking back at her mother. "I'm glad that you did. It's just . . . Do you think we can escape from the crazy cycle we were born into, mother harming daughter?"

"Yes," Arden said promptly. "I believe we can. We're not Regina and Florence, or Florence and Victoria. We're Arden and Laura."

"What *about* Victoria?" Laura asked gently. "What happens to her in all this craziness?"

Arden considered for a moment. "She was only a child when I put her aside. I suppose she needs to be forgiven for any wrongs she committed. They wouldn't have been done intentionally."

"And she needs to be honored for her courage and perseverance."

"'With self-denial and economy now, and steady exertion by-and-by,'" Arden quoted with a smile, " 'an object in life need not fail you.'"

Laura smiled back. "Let me guess. Lucy Snowe."

Chapter 57

"Pink lemonade?" Laura asked. "Really?"

Laura and her mother were at the bookshop preparing for a special event on the topic "Star-Crossed Lovers in Literature." Together, they had created a program that, they hoped, would engender lively discussion and introduce the attendees to doomed literary lovers they might not have known about, such as, for example, Stephen Gordon and Mary Llewellyn in Radclyffe Hall's *Well of Loneliness*, and Joseph Asten and Philip Held in Bayard Taylor's 1870 novel, *Joseph and His Friend: A Story of Pennsylvania*. A whopping twenty-five people had signed up for the event, which meant that additional seating had been borrowed from dedicated members of the book group.

Arden laughed. "I know. It's kind of cheesy, pink for romance. We should be serving Bloody Marys and devil's food cake. Much more appropriate."

"You said it." Laura sighed dramatically as she continued to set out napkins. "Tristan and Isolde. Anna and Count Vronsky. Romeo and Juliet. I nearly drowned myself in those tales of doomed love. In fact, I'm convinced it tainted my idea of true romance and contributed to why I chose to marry a guy around whom there were so many obstacles. Somehow, I managed to convince myself that my love would cure him of his soul sickness or whatever lofty thing it was that made him act badly." Laura paused. "It was almost as if the obstacles themselves made my efforts worthwhile and my love more valuable."

"When there is affinity between two people, 'the threads of their destinies are difficult to disentangle.' That's something Paul Emanuel tells Lucy Snowe in *Villette*."

Laura smiled. "So, it all comes down to fate? I used to believe that, but now I'd like to imagine I'm in control of my life, at least parts of it. I'd like to think that if I ever fall in love again, it will be with someone completely unobjectionable. Sure, we could be torn apart by forces we can't control, but that's life. A plane crash like the one that took JFK Jr. and Carolyn Bessette, or some dread illness that separates us, like with poor Keats and Fanny Brawne. Or like what happened to poor Abelard and Héloïse, for that matter!"

"My, you've got it bad, haven't you? Years ago, I came across a quote supposedly by Frida Kahlo. It really struck me. Part of it goes, 'You deserve a lover who takes away the lies and brings you hope, coffee, and poetry.' I guess I've always felt that Rob could have been such a lover, if we had been allowed to live our lives together. But who knows what might have happened to us over time?"

"There are so many factors that can conspire to keep lovers apart. It's amazing that lovers ever manage to stay together."

"Can you tell me more about your marriage?" Arden looked up from the vase of white roses she had just placed next to the pitchers of pink lemonade. "Or is this a bad time?"

Laura looked at her watch. Guests wouldn't be arriving for another twenty minutes or so. "Sure. Why not? It was a mistake from the start, but try telling me that at the time. My friends at the college had a bad feeling about Jared. They said he was too obviously charming. I'm embarrassed to admit it, but I thought they were just jealous. None of them were in a relationship, and two of the women were divorced. One was a single mother. The father of her kid had gone off with his secretary, if you can believe that old cliché. What those women *really* were, was smart."

" 'The heart wants what it wants.' How old were you?"

Laura frowned. "I was old enough to know better. Who knows?

Maybe I would never have gotten involved with Jared had my parents been alive. Sometimes I get so angry with myself for taking on such an obviously damaged person. And angry with him for being who he was. Which is not really fair, is it? People are who they are."

Arden nodded. "Yes. But some people are predatory. It's legitimate to be angry with them for luring you into their dramas. I'm not sure how legitimate it is to be angry with yourself for being vulnerable to a predator."

Laura nodded. "You're right, of course. If only I hadn't made the mistake of agreeing to a joint bank account. Before we married, I had no idea Jared had a gambling problem. I'm not condemning Jared for being a gambler; I know it's an addiction. But I should have been smart enough to keep apart at least some of what my parents had left me as security for my future. At the time, I really believed it would be like announcing to the world that I didn't trust my husband." Laura sighed. "Too many old-fashioned romances and not enough practicality."

"I'm sorry. If I thought it would really make you feel better, I'd suggest you have one of these decadent cupcakes I got from Chez Claudine."

Laura smiled. "A cupcake always makes me feel better, especially one with a mound of icing. But I'll wait until later. You know, the thing I feel most bad about is that I let Jared squander the money my parents worked so hard to earn for my sake. It's like throwing Mom and Dad's gift in their faces."

"You didn't mean any disrespect. They would know that."

Laura knew that Arden was right. Still, she thought, she would probably always feel a bit guilty.

"I lost my inheritance by running off the way I did," Arden said. "It was only much later that it dawned on me what I'd given up. Money. A lot of it, certainly more than I could ever earn on my own. The contents of the house, my mother's jewelry. The house itself and the land on which it sits."

"Who do you think will get it all now?" Laura placed the stack of handouts she and her mother had prepared by the tray of cupcakes.

Arden shrugged. "I have no idea. For all I know my parents

latched on to some young person along the way, a distant relative or maybe someone who worked for my father, and made him the heir to the Aldridge fortune."

"Which is rightly yours."

"Is it? I'm not so sure. And what if a portion of it is ill-gotten gains? After all, I never really did understand what exactly my father did for a living. Something with high finance. Could I in good conscience accept money come by in an underhanded way?"

Laura half smiled. "Right now, I'd say yes to any sort of financing someone wanted to give me, from a fistful of cash to stock in some hot company. Who cares how they came by any of it?"

"You don't really mean that, do you?"

Laura sighed. "No. I don't. Having a conscience can be so inconvenient. But I'm stuck with one and so are you. We'll just have to go on making the best of it."

The bell over the door alerted the women that their guests were beginning to arrive. Mrs. Shandy and Lydia Austen led the way, followed by, among others, Arden's neighbor Marla Swenson; Judy Twain; Elly and her mother; Jeanie Shardlake; Martha Benbow; and Tami and her mother.

"Pink lemonade!" Tami exclaimed. "My favorite!"

"Cupcakes!" Elly cried. "Awesome!"

"No men, I see," Laura murmured under the excited chatter of the growing crowd.

"Did you really expect any?" her mother asked.

"No." Laura smiled. "Not for a moment."

Chapter 58

Summer 1984

Somewhere in the house the housekeeper was running a vacuum. Victoria was glad that she was not alone. She had never been afraid of her parents before, not really, certainly not afraid of their physical wrath, but at that moment she felt sure that anything at all could happen to her, that her father might grab her arm and throw her to the floor, that her mother might slap her face, the sharp bits of one of the large diamond rings she wore causing blood to ooze from her daughter's cheek.

"Stop it," she scolded under her breath as she slowly descended the main staircase. "You're being dramatic." For a moment she wondered if she should turn around, go back to her room, and accept Rob's offer to be with her when she broke the news to her parents. But something, she didn't know what, made her continue on.

Victoria found her parents in the living room.

"What is it, Victoria?" her father asked when she entered. He was leaning against the mantelpiece, a glass of Scotch in hand, dressed in one of his white Brooks Brothers oxford shirts, complete with gold cuff links. The crease in his pants was as sharp as a knife.

Her mother, seated in her favorite armchair with a fashion magazine, was wearing an aqua silk dress printed with a pattern of tiny pink flowers. Pinned to the dress was a platinum-and-diamond brooch, a family heirloom.

Suddenly, Victoria wondered if she should have dressed more appropriately for the occasion. A peach-colored linen blouse, a pair of jeans, and Keds sneakers seemed far too youthful and even silly for what was sure to be a weighty confrontation.

A confrontation that would change the course of her life.

"Well, dear?" her mother urged without looking up from the fashion magazine on her lap. "What is it?"

Victoria took a deep breath and clasped her hands together. "I've been seeing Rob Smith," she said with as much bravado as she could muster. "From town."

"What do you mean by 'seeing'?" her mother asked, a vague smile on her face, eyes still on the glossy page.

Her father remained silent. His expression was fixed.

"I mean that we've been dating."

Her mother chuckled. "You can't be. You're not allowed to date."

Victoria fought a wave of anger. Her mother was doing it again, blocking a bothersome truth, pretending that all was well when it was most certainly not.

"Yes, Mother, I have been seeing him. He's my . . . He's my boyfriend. You know him. I mean, he's one of the part-time workers building the pool. You must have seen him. He's—"

"He's our employee?" Florence interrupted, her tone puzzled, finally looking up from her magazine.

"Well, yes, but he also goes to the community college and—"

Her father now stood away from the fireplace and trained his formidable countenance on Victoria. She felt herself begin to tremble.

"You'll stop seeing this boy at once," he said tightly.

Florence had returned to her fashion magazine. The diamonds on her fingers winked each time she turned a page.

Victoria felt a sickening buzz start in her head and begin its journey through her entire body. She felt dizzy, wobbly, as if the ground were falling away from her. Somehow, she managed to take a step closer to an armchair and grabbed on to it for support. "I . . .

I can't." The buzzing now seemed almost to energize her. "I won't. I'm pregnant. We want to get married," she continued in a rush. "We *are* getting married."

Suddenly, her mother closed her magazine. "No," she said softly. "No, no, no."

"We're in love," Victoria stated boldly. But even to her own ears the words sounded foolish and clichéd. She was a child. Rob was one, too. What had they been thinking? "Mother?" she begged. "Can't you at least understand?"

With a surge of energy Victoria had never witnessed before, her mother rose from her chair and tossed the magazine to the floor. "I'll go to the police! I'll tell them to keep that boy away from you! He's corrupted my daughter, my only child!"

"That's enough, Florence," Herbert said sternly. "There's no need for the police. I'll handle this." Herbert turned to his daughter. "From this moment on, you will have nothing to do with this boy. You will not call him or receive calls from him. You will not leave the house without someone accompanying you. Needless to say, he will never set foot on this property again. Who else knows about this?" her father demanded.

"No one." Victoria's voice trembled. "Only Rob. But—"

"But nothing. You will go away to have the baby. It will then be adopted. The lawyers will handle everything. No one in Port George will be the wiser."

It. It will be adopted. A thing, not a child.

Florence suddenly made a dash toward the door.

"Mother! Wait!" Victoria reached out to grab her mother's arm as she passed, but Florence was too swift. Seconds later, Victoria could hear her mother's footsteps hurrying up the stairs. Then, a door slammed.

Victoria looked back to her father. He had finished his Scotch. "Go to your room and stay there," he said evenly.

"But—" she began, unsure of what she could possibly say after what had just transpired.

"Do as I say!" her father roared. He had never before raised his voice to Victoria.

Victoria lowered her head as if to protect herself from a blow and hurried past her father. She had only just reached the hall when she heard him utter the most terrifying words she had ever heard spoken.

"I'll make that boy pay if it's the last thing I do."

Had he meant his daughter to hear the threat? He must have. Why else would he have spoken so loudly? Heart pounding, Victoria fled up the stairs and into the relative safety of her room.

"Please," she cried aloud, "help me. Someone help me!"

What had she expected? Her parents to smile, gather her in their arms, congratulate her on having found true love? No, not that. But also, not this. Not being separated from Rob, not being sent away, not being denied her baby . . . How had it all gone so wrong? What had she done? Everything was a mess now. . . .

Victoria stumbled across the room and sank onto her bed, her father's last words resounding through her head.

I'll make that boy pay if it's the last thing I do. I'll make that boy pay.

Chapter 59

Laura had gone for a walk; much to her mother's delight Laura was genuinely interested in getting to know every bit of Eliot's Corner and always returned from these walks eager to share observations and ask questions. At times, Arden joined her daughter on these excursions, but today Arden had opted to remain at the cottage and work on the notes she had taken during last evening's "Star-Crossed Lovers" event. It had been a great success. Not a few tears had been shed, lots of laughter shared, a few ribald comments made sotto voce, and lots of pink lemonade drunk. Elly and Tami, besides having consumed an impressive number of cupcakes, had contributed a few thoughtful remarks to the discussions, earning praise from several of the long-standing members of the Arden Forest Book Club.

Arden had decided that the topic of star-crossed lovers deserved another visit, maybe in February to counteract the commercial excesses of Valentine's Day, and to that end she was eager to get her thoughts on paper before they fled. She took a seat in the living room, a glass of ice tea by her side. The cats were sprawled in a large patch of sun and would likely remain oblivious of her presence until one or more got hungry.

Eager as she was to begin the planning of "Star-Crossed Lovers Redux," Arden found herself revisiting the story of a real-life doomed romance. She wondered if she had been in her daughter's life at the time Laura had met Jared Pence, would she have been smart enough to see what Laura's colleagues had seen, that Jared was not to be trusted? Would she have been capable of giving good, solid advice to her daughter? Arden had little experience offering advice. She had never gotten close enough to anyone to be sought out when trouble was looming or when a difficult decision was to be made.

But there was always the future, wasn't there? Maybe, as the relationship with her daughter grew and deepened, she would find herself not only capable of giving but eager to give Laura genuine guidance and support.

Arden looked down at her notes and smiled. She had copied one of Tami's comments word for word. "I think," Tami had said rather boldly, "I think that even if you fall in love with someone and things don't work out, it's worth it because at least your life won't have been boring, and boredom is pretty terrible. At least, that's what I think." Tami's mother had fairly beamed with pride, and one of the attendees had actually clapped her hands in appreciation of Tami's observation. Childish? Maybe. Innocent, naïve? Yes. True? Quite possibly.

How foolish she herself had been all those many years ago, eager to believe that her parents, wanting their child to be happy, would welcome her having gotten pregnant with a boy she had known only a few short months! In hindsight, Arden could admit that their reaction had, at least in part, been justified. Herbert and Florence Aldridge had been responsible parents, protective, concerned, conscientious. That was more than could be said for too many parents.

That said, Arden wondered if she had ever really appreciated her parents before her pregnancy had torn her apart from them. Had she been truly grateful that they had provided a comfortable home, good food, sturdy clothing, and a decent education? She honestly couldn't remember. She hoped that she had been appreciative; she certainly had been dutiful, until, that is, she had met Rob Smith.

Whatever harm her parents had done to her, the good they had performed before the harm had to count for something. To be un-grateful for what care she had received would make her less than a decent person. Arden remembered what Laura had said about a conscience being inconvenient. But they were both in possession of one and—

Arden's phone alerted her to a call from Gordon. They chatted for a few minutes—about the recent event at Arden Forest, about the shop's leaky roof, about the rumor around town that Harry Lohsen, the principal of the grammar school, might be retiring after the coming school year—before Gordon related his big news. He had been approached by the owner of a gallery in Alcott, a fairly large town an hour to the west, about including a few of his pieces in a show opening at the end of September.

"That's fantastic, Gordon! I'm so happy for you."

"I wanted you to be the first to know. You've always been so supportive of my efforts."

"But I didn't know you were interested in showing your work. You never said a word."

"Every artist is interested in making his work available to oth-ers. I just didn't want to make a big deal out of my efforts to gain at-tention in the likelihood I met with rejection. Which I have, several times. But for some crazy reason, the owner of the Fry Gallery likes my work."

"Not for a crazy reason. He likes your work because it's good. And you can count on me to be there on opening night."

They talked on for a bit more, and when the call had ended, Arden finally focused on her notes from the night before. Gordon, she thought, was such an important, even a necessary, person in her life, steadying her when she felt wobbly, making her laugh when she felt sad, helping her in practical ways that could often mean so much. She knew that rejecting his offer of a loan for the repair of the shop's roof had been the right thing to do. Nothing must be al-lowed to damage their friendship.

As Arden put pen to paper, a strange thought came to her and she scribbled it down. "Gordon and I," she read when she had lifted her pen, "are not star-crossed lovers."

Then what, Arden wondered, were they?

Chapter 60

"Port George has changed a lot since I was a kid," Kathy Murdoch said as she and Laura emerged from a shop that couldn't seem to decide what it was, exactly, a crafts venue or a tourist trap. They had spent the better part of the morning window-shopping along Main Street, and though Laura had virtually no expendable income, she had enjoyed the outing.

"We never had an art gallery," Kathy continued, "before Burt Ransom opened his framing shop fifteen years ago and started to show the work of local artists. And there was no such thing as a gelato shop, either! I never knew ice cream could taste so good. Still, in some ways I liked Port George better the way it was back then. Simpler. Less fancy." Kathy laughed. "Maybe that's because I've never been a big fan of change."

Laura nodded. "Nostalgia is comforting, but it can be dangerous."

"Don't I know it! Like what I said about liking Port George better in the old days. To be honest, things weren't always all that great. There was a lot of bullying in school when I was in the lower grades, tough kids pushing around the younger kids, girls being what today we'd call sexually harassed, their skirts flipped up, being grabbed. No one ever reported anything, though I'm sure the teachers knew what was going on. How could they not know?"

"Turning a blind eye is way too popular an option. Sometimes I think that will never change."

"You might be right. I remember there were some really awful guys a few years older than me, like a gang, though as far as I knew they used their fists instead of knives or guns. They were real thugs. I can't remember their names—I never wanted anything to do with any of them!—but I do remember that at least two of them died pretty young, not long after I got out of high school."

"Didn't anyone stand up to them? If not the police, then, well, I don't know, other guys?"

"No, not that there weren't a lot of good guys in town, but they were smart enough to stay away from the creepy ones. Rob Smith, now he was one of the good guys, right from the start. He was super-popular but always totally nice to everyone, especially the shy, nerdy kids. I remember once in second grade I fell and cut myself up pretty badly. I had these big bandages over my knees and shins and the palms of my hands. My mother wouldn't let me stay home more than a day, so back to school I went. I remember being only about a block away from my house when suddenly Rob Smith came running up to me and offered to carry my books. He even helped me get up the stairs when we reached the school. I felt like a princess or something. I mean, who does that sort of thing but someone really special, right?"

Before Laura could respond, Kathy grabbed her arm. "Look, there goes the Aldridges' car!"

The car was long, sleek, and black. Even to Laura, who wasn't at all interested in cars, it was recognizable as a Cadillac, and an old one at that, dating from the years when cars were the size of small boats.

Laura watched as the car moved slowly through the intersection. It had the air of a hearse about it, she thought. Somber. Unhappy.

"I wonder who it is who drives them around?" Kathy said. "They used to have a chauffeur, the kind who wore a fancy uniform and a cap and all that, but I don't think they need one now. They hardly leave the house. They're like recluses." Kathy shuddered. "I bet the house is all dirty and dusty, piles of old newspapers in every corner, empty soup cans rattling around the hall-ways, rats running wild up and down the stairs. Ugh."

Laura recoiled from the macabre image Kathy had painted. Whether Laura liked it or not, Herbert and Florence Aldridge were her grandparents, her flesh and blood. The thought of them living in an atmosphere of deterioration and decrepitude was depressing.

Suddenly Kathy looked at her phone. "Yikes, I'm going to be late for my shift if I don't dash now."

"Thanks for showing me around. It was fun."

Kathy waved and hurried off in the direction of the North Star Diner. Laura continued to stroll along Main Street. Without Kathy's companionship, though, window-shopping in Port George rapidly lost its appeal. Just as she was considering turning toward the Lilac Inn, two women just getting out of a car up ahead caught her attention.

The younger one was Frannie Armitage. Frannie was holding the arm of the older woman. The older woman was using a cane but otherwise looked hale and hardy. Her hair was a bright shade of silver. From where Laura stood she couldn't tell if there was a resemblance between the two women. Still, it struck her that she might well be looking at her grandmother Geraldine Smith. Laura was overwhelmed by a sense of love and affection. It was a genuine struggle not to approach the women, not to blurt out the truth, that she was their flesh and blood. This family that she had never known were now close enough to touch, to hold in an embrace, to . . .

Laura watched as Frannie and the older woman went into the post office. Immediately, Laura turned and walked quickly in the direction of the Lilac Inn. One supposed grandmother in the post office. The other possibly in the back seat of that creepy old Cadillac. She was surrounded by a past that both did and did not belong to her. She both was and was not a child of Port George, an outsider and an insider. She thought of her father's kindness and realized that she deeply missed a man she had never known. Laura felt almost sick with emotion and was glad for the relative privacy her sunglasses provided.

When she reached the Lilac Inn, she hurried up to the sanctuary of her rented room and curled up on the bed. She had intended to spend a few days in Port George, but would instead return to Eliot's Corner the next morning. She could leave now and be home in time for a late dinner, but she felt too emotionally agitated to get behind the wheel of a car. She would sleep if she could and for as long as she could.

Tomorrow would be a new day.

Chapter 61

It sometimes amused and sometimes annoyed Arden how many people who visited Arden Forest didn't feel the need to put the books they had considered back on the proper shelves. She routinely found paperback mysteries in the science section and ponderous biographies of people long dead on display tables featuring current novels about topics such as climate change and trans lives.

At the moment, Arden was taking back to its proper place a large book of photographs she had found in the children's section. A few people in Eliot's Corner used Arden Forest rather like a library, most notably a genteel older woman who spent at least an hour each week going through this very volume, an expensively produced coffee-table book featuring elegant New England homes. If the book ever sold, Arden knew she would feel compelled to replace it for Edna Rogers. Rumor had it that Edna had grown up in an elegant home in Lexington, Massachusetts, and that this hefty tome served as a bittersweet reminder of a lifestyle she had lost.

Before replacing the book with its fellows, something compelled Arden to open it at random. She found herself looking at a photograph of a meticulously preserved wood-burning stove.

And suddenly it was the summer of 1984, and she, Victoria, was preparing for her first visit to Rob's family home. She had been so terribly nervous, but Rob had assured her there was nothing to fear.

"But what if one of your family tells someone I was at your house and it gets back to my parents?"

Rob had promised her he had sworn his family to secrecy. "I explained that your parents are very strict. Don't worry so much."

So, the date for the visit was settled. She would meet Rob at his home on Fern Pond Road, after taking a lengthy, circuitous route. She had never felt more anxious. She had been so eager to make a good impression on Rob's family.

Rob had opened the door and led Victoria inside. She remembered being struck by the vast differences between his home and her own. The living room, for example, with its wood-burning stove, the faded embroidered samplers on the wall, the couch and plushy chairs draped with colorful crocheted blankets—all this was the antithesis of the living room in the grand house at the summit of Old Orchard Hill. That room was cold and forbidding, a showplace, not a room in which to relax. This room felt eminently warm, cozy, and welcoming.

Mrs. Smith had been particularly gracious, if a bit formal on that first visit. Mr. Smith had seemed slightly ill at ease but polite. Rob's younger sisters hadn't said much but stared at Victoria in awe, as if she were an exotic creature, something never before seen in Port George. Their attention made Victoria nervous until Maureen had blurted, "You're so pretty!" Her exclamation broke the ice, and both Maureen and Abby chatted nonstop from then on.

The only person in the family who had not warmed to Victoria was Rob's older sister, Frannie, but that, Victoria had thought, was understandable. Older siblings were often protective of their younger siblings. Victoria had liked that about Frannie.

When it came time for Victoria to leave, she had trouble holding back tears. "I love your family," she said to Rob the moment they stepped out the front door. "They're so nice and they made me feel so welcome and . . ."

Rob had smiled. "I told you it would be okay. I really wish you'd let me drive you home."

"I'm sorry." She had placed her hands on his broad chest. "I'm so sorry."

Rob had drawn her close. "Stop apologizing," he whispered. "One day it will be how we want it to be."

Well, Arden thought now, sliding the book of photographs onto the shelf, trying to shake off the strength of that poignant memory, Rob's hopeful prediction hadn't come to pass, at least not for the two lovers. But a united family might still be possible, if not for Arden then for Laura. The Smiths were Laura's flesh and blood, and she deserved the gift of family. And the Smiths deserved their granddaughter.

The tinkling of the bell over the door to the shop caused Arden to turn to offer assistance to her customers, but Vincent and Kevin knew exactly what they were after and made a beeline for the graphic novels. There was a good chance they wouldn't buy anything today—they were only about eleven and probably had little money of their own to spend—but if history was anything to go by, they would be back within a week with a parent in tow.

"This is the most awesome place in town," Kevin suddenly exclaimed to his friend.

"I know," Vincent replied solemnly.

Arden wasn't sure she had been meant to hear the praise, but it brought a smile to her face.

Chapter 62

Laura had asked Deborah to join her for a drink at Martindale's. Arden would be home late that evening; there was a staff meeting at the bookshop, and Laura didn't feel like being on her own. Martindale's was a splurge, but after the emotional impact of her most recent experiences in Port George, Laura felt she deserved a treat. Well, maybe she didn't actually deserve a treat but she wanted one.

"It's pretty swanky in here," Laura noted when they were seated at a table for two. "How long has this place been in business?"

"For about three years now. It's the only upscale restaurant in Eliot's Corner, so it's the go-to stop for special occasions, anniversaries, and engagements, that sort of thing. By the way, what's the occasion tonight?"

Laura shrugged. "Nothing. Just a change of pace."

The waiter took their drink order, a vodka tonic with a slice of lime for Laura, and for Deborah, a cosmo.

"What do you think they mean by a Roli Poli?" Deborah asked, studying the list of appetizers available that evening.

"I have no idea, but it's got cheese, so how bad can it be?"

When the waiter returned with their drinks, Laura gave their food order. "Cheers." She raised her glass to Deborah's. "Here's to summer. Don't mention this to Arden, okay?" Laura said after a moment. "But I got another threatening note from the anonymous sender."

Deborah frowned. "That doesn't sound good. What did it say?"

"The message was similar to the first one, only slightly re-worded; the threat wasn't any stronger and it wasn't any more specific. To tell you the truth, I got the feeling that the writer of this second note—and, presumably, also of the first—might actually be trying to protect me from someone or something."

"I suppose that's possible. But why keep the note from Arden?"

"Well, when I told her I'd seen the Aldridges' car in Port George the other day, she got really frightened and wondered if her parents had somehow found out my real identity and were following me themselves. I tried to assure her that their car driving down Main Street meant nothing, that whoever was in the back seat—if anyone—was probably just out for an airing."

"But she wasn't reassured."

"No. And after seeing how she reacted to my sighting of her family's ancient Cadillac, I just couldn't bring myself to tell her about seeing Frannie and the older woman I told you about, or about the second note. Do you think I'm wrong keeping these things to myself?"

Deborah shook her head. "You're being kind. Sometimes a person doesn't need to know every detail of a situation to understand its overall nature."

"Thank you," Laura said feelingly. "But enough about me. I know so little about you. I do know that you were married twice. Arden told me. Do you mind if I ask what happened?"

Deborah shrugged. "Not at all. Both marriages were mistakes. I was only twenty-one the first time. He'd been my boyfriend all through college, and we got married the summer after graduation. It was just like in a magazine—lots of guests, tons of flowers, ridiculously expensive bridesmaid dresses, enough food to feed a small nation." Deborah cringed. "Which, I suppose, made the end of the short-lived marriage all the more upsetting for my parents, who had paid for every canapé and bottle of champagne."

"Ouch. What do you mean by 'short-lived'?"

"Two years, barely enough time for my parents to pay off the bills. It was such a cliché, really. He cheated on me. Worse than that, he actually fell in love with the woman and couldn't wait to get away from me. Seems he'd rushed into our relationship before he'd had time to sow his wild oats."

"Ah. So, it came down to sex, as it so often does."

Deborah nodded. "He married the woman—her name was Tricia—and five years later, they were divorced. I wasn't in touch with him, but we still had a few mutual friends from college. They told me."

"Poor Tricia. What's this stellar specimen of manhood up to these days?"

"I have no idea. I lost contact with the old college gang years ago. If I had to guess, I'd say Alan—that was his name—is making some other woman miserable."

"And the second time around for you?"

Deborah paused for a moment. "That was a very different story. In fact, how about I tell that tale another time? We could make getting together a regular thing. If you're interested?"

Laura smiled and raised her glass. "I'm very interested." At least, for as long as she was a resident of Eliot's Corner. And from what she could tell so far, being a resident of Eliot's Corner was not a bad thing at all.

"Ah, here come our appetizers!" Deborah announced.

"Heaven. I'm starved. Oh, and look at the Roli Polis! They're oozing cheese!"

Chapter 63

It was Brent's day off and both interns were down with summer colds. Arden was alone in the shop, and that suited her just fine as it allowed her to take an appreciative stroll through the eclectic collection of titles Arden Forest offered its customers, something she never tired of doing.

Books about art and history and fly-fishing and furniture making. Books about books and books about the people who wrote them. Books about cooking and baking and sewing. Novels and poems and essays, many in translation. Volumes that included maps of the ancient world or maps of Maine's current coastline.

Arden stopped and slid a book from the shelf. *Popular Day Trips in Maine*. She felt a bit of a frown come to her face as she remembered Laura's having seen her grandfather's old Cadillac on the streets of Port George. Other cars had been in the Aldridge garage at any given time, but the Cadillac had always been her father's favorite, his and his alone. Had he, then, been the passenger the day Laura had spotted the car? The thought made Arden shudder, and she abandoned her stroll to return to the stool behind the counter, where there was paperwork to be done.

But before she could focus on business, an image of Rob's car, a Dodge Coronet from the 1970s, came to her mind's eye as clearly as if the car were parked just outside the shop. The car had once belonged to a friend of Rob's father's. Rob used to joke that the engine was held together by string and wire coat hangers, and for all Arden knew it was, but Rob had kept the inside of the car neat and clean—no empty soda cans rolling around underfoot or dirty tissues stuffed in the armrests.

She had been in the car so rarely, but there had been one memorable time when Herbert and Florence Aldridge were away from Port George on a rare overnight visit to Portland. Victoria had mustered the courage to agree to an afternoon drive along back roads. It hadn't been difficult to slip out of the house without the housekeeper knowing, or to take a path through the wooded area on the Aldridge property until she had reached a little-used dirt road, dappled with sunshine, making its way through a thick canopy of trees.

At first, Victoria had been too tense to enjoy the outing, wondering how quickly she might duck to the floor should they pass another car. But after half an hour or so, she had relaxed. Neither spoke much. The windows were open to the warm summer breeze; the radio was playing pop hits. Rob's perfect profile inspired fresh waves of love in young Victoria. She had felt so mature and adult sitting next to Rob in the front seat of that big olive-green vehicle, as if she really did have, or at least could have, a life of her own apart from her parents, as if she could be her own person, no longer just Florence and Herbert Aldridge's daughter. Sitting at Rob's side as they traveled those lonely dirt roads, Victoria had longed for the day when they could be seen together by all of Port George, when they would maybe even be Mr. and Mrs. Smith with a house of their own and a future they could determine for themselves.

The arrival of a customer jolted Arden from her reminiscences. She was about Arden's age, wearing a pink-and-green floral-pattern sundress and espadrilles that tied around her ankles.

"I don't think I've seen you in town before," Arden said with a smile.

"No, I'm actually passing through. My wife and I are headed north for a vacation. We stopped for a bite to eat at that adorable little French bakery across the street, and I saw your sign. Thank

God, too. Can you believe I forgot to bring my books with me? They were all packed and ready to go, in a bag sitting right by the front door, and yet somehow I managed to walk out without them."

"That does sound like a nightmare!"

"Especially since the place we're staying has no television or Internet service. Which is fine by me, as long as I have my books! Ah, the fiction section!" The woman hurried off.

Arden was happy to be of help to this avid reader. Arden Forest was her personal haven, but it was also a vital resource for so many of her neighbors and even for the occasional visitor to town, such as this woman. It was essential that Arden find the money for a new roof. She had been putting off visiting the bank to see if she was eligible for a loan, and she wasn't sure why. Fear of being turned down? Suddenly, Arden felt supremely annoyed with herself for not having acted before now. She was not the sort to indulge in self-sabotage. With "steady exertion by-and-by," a goal might be achieved. Procrastination accomplished nothing. There and then, Arden vowed to call the bank that afternoon and make an appointment to meet with a loan officer. There was no way she would allow Arden Forest to close its doors.

After almost twenty minutes, the traveler came staggering to the counter, no fewer than twelve books in her arms. She thanked Arden profusely for having such an excellent selection of titles and, satisfied, went on her way.

The woman's bill had come to a hefty sum. If only there were more customers like her, Arden thought, able to spend a few hundred dollars per visit, the roof repair might not be such a financial burden. She lifted the receiver of the shop's landline and placed a call to the local branch of her bank. There was no time like the present.

Chapter 64

Summer 1984

"You look beautiful," Rob whispered.

"Do you really think so?" Victoria glanced down at the pale blue ankle-length concoction she was wearing. "My mother picked out the dress. It's not really my style."

"Well, I think you look great, really. The blue matches your eyes. And you're wearing the necklace."

"Of course." Victoria touched the small silver charm in the shape of a foot. "I never take it off."

Today, July 12, was Victoria's eighteenth birthday. Her parents had insisted on giving a party in her honor. A party to which Victoria knew she couldn't invite Rob. A party to which she didn't have the courage to say no. Though she had mustered the courage to sneak out of the house about an hour before the party was to begin and make her way to this secluded part of her family's property.

"I have something for you," Rob said now as they stood in the evening light filtering through the branches of dark pine trees. He sounded a bit nervous. "Here."

Victoria, hands trembling, accepted the object wrapped in white tissue paper.

"I found it in an antique shop in Waverly," Rob explained as she removed the tissue paper. "I'm sorry it's in such bad condition, but it was all I could afford. Someday I'll be able to get you a really good copy, I promise."

Through tears, Victoria gazed down at the late-nineteenth-century edition of *Villette* she held in her hands, a novel by her favorite author, Charlotte Brontë. "It's perfect," she breathed. She felt happier in that moment than she ever had before. Carefully, she opened the cover of the old volume. Rob had written an inscription on the title page.

To my Vicky. Happy Birthday. Love always, Rob.

"After I wrote that, I thought that maybe I shouldn't have. You know, maybe it ruins the value of the book or something."

"But I'd never sell this, ever!" Victoria clasped the volume to her heart. "Rob? I'm ready. I want to be with you."

Rob looked surprised. "Are you sure, Vicky?" His voice was a bit high. "Really sure? Because it can't be . . . It has to be . . ."

"Yes," she promised. "I am."

And though terribly naïve for her age, Victoria truly was sure. She had overheard stories about sex as she and her classmates changed for gym class, tales that ranged from the matter-of-fact to the downright clinical, from the absurd to, on one occasion, a tale that came too near to violence. But none of those stories had at all mentioned the sheer physical and emotional ecstasy she experienced that evening with Rob. This, she thought while thought was still possible, was *love*, this was the ultimate communion of two soul mates, and it was more beautiful and thrilling than anything she could ever have imagined.

Afterward, they lay in each other's arms on a bed of soft pine needles, their hearts still beating fast, the cooling evening air caressing their skin.

Rob kissed the tip of Victoria's nose and smiled. "I didn't really want our first time to be, um, under a pine tree."

"It was perfect. Better than anything I ever dreamed it would be."

"It was for me, too. And you know why? It's because we love each other."

Victoria snuggled deeper into Rob's arms. "And we do love each other," she whispered, "totally and completely."

"So, who's going to be at this party?" Rob asked after a moment, tucking a stray strand of her hair behind Victoria's ear.

"My parents' friends." She sighed. "Honestly, I could disappear after an hour and nobody would know I'd gone."

"No one your own age?"

"I don't think so. The Coldwells might bring their son, Ted, I suppose. They're old family friends, about the only decent people my parents know."

"This Ted. You like him?"

"He's nice," Victoria said readily, looking up at Rob. "He's always been like a big brother to me. But I don't know why he'd want to be there tonight. I'm sure he has something better to do."

A strange look flitted across Rob's face, something like fear, and Victoria wondered if he could be jealous of Ted. There was no reason he should be, no reason at all. She wondered if she should assure Rob that she only had eyes for him—as if what they had just done wasn't proof enough—but maybe mentioning the possibility of a rival, even an imaginary rival, might make him think she was protesting too much.

So, she said nothing but kissed him one last time before brushing any pine needles or dirt from her party dress, thanking Rob again for the best gift she had ever been given, and hurrying back to the house—not without a backward glance and a final wave.

It wasn't difficult to sneak in through the back door and to dash up to her room. There, she hid Rob's precious gift under her mattress, sure it would be safe until she could return to the peace of her room later that evening.

When she joined the party a few minutes later, Ted Coldwell was the first one to greet her and kiss her cheek. "Happy birthday," he said with a smile. "If you want to duck out at any time, I'll be your partner in crime."

Before Victoria could imagine what Rob might think of Ted's offer, her father was calling the room to quiet and beckoning her to his side. Blushingly, she joined her parents and silently endured her mother's fond smile, the toast her father made in her honor, and, finally, the polite applause that followed. As she stood there in her pale blue dress, a glass of champagne in hand, a smile fixed to her face, Victoria was torn both by the urge to sob and the urge to laugh. She was miserable without Rob at her side, absolutely miserable. And she was also blissfully, madly happy.

She was in love. She was loved. Victoria Aldridge was the luckiest person in the room.

Chapter 65

It was the eve of her mother's birthday, and Laura still hadn't been able to think of an appropriate birthday present for the woman who had given her life—the woman she hardly knew. If inspiration didn't strike soon, Laura thought, she would simply have to apologize abjectly and promise to spend the rest of the summer searching for the perfect gift.

Laura was sitting on the couch; her mother had gone to her room to fetch something. The cats were sleeping off their dinner and the bit of cream Arden had given them as a treat. Lucky kitties, Laura thought fondly. Adopted into a life of comfort and security. Much as she herself had been.

Arden came back into the room, holding a small object against her chest. "I'd like to show you something. I've never shown it to anyone before now."

Laura reached out to receive the small, hard-backed book her mother now offered her. Without opening the volume Laura could see that the pages were soft and yellowed and the spine weakened with age.

"Open it."

Laura did so, carefully. " 'To my Vicky,' " she read aloud. "'Happy Birthday. Love always, Rob.' " Laura looked up in surprise. "He called you Vicky."

"No one else ever did."

Laura felt her heart swell. Her father had held this book. "He must have seen the lively young woman behind the prim and proper facade."

Arden laughed. "And I was prim and proper all right! Rob gave me that on my eighteenth birthday. It was the only birthday we ever celebrated together."

"It's a terribly thoughtful gift." Laura looked up to her mother. "I have to admit I never read *Villette*. I know you quote from it often enough, so it must be special to you for all sorts of reasons."

Arden held out her hand and Laura returned the old book. "I love the passionate voice." Arden opened to a particular page. "Listen to this: 'I could not go in: too resistless was the delight of staying with the wild hour, black and full of thunder, pealing out such an ode as language never delivered to man—too terribly glorious, the spectacle of clouds, split and pierced by white and blinding bolts.'"

"My," Laura said, her eyebrows raised, "that is highly wrought language!"

"I recommended the book to one of my young customers a few weeks back. Tami. You met her at the 'Star-Crossed Lovers' event. She's young but I think she's mature enough to make her way through to the end. And if not, she can return to it when she's older."

Arden placed the book gently on the coffee table and took a seat next to Laura.

"The night of my eighteenth birthday was the first time Rob and I had sex," Arden said softly. "The book is a marker of that moment when what I thought would be my real future began. My future with Rob."

Laura felt tears prick at her eyes. Her parents' story was so romantic, but had ended so sadly, as so many romantic stories did.

"My parents insisted on giving a party in my honor. Of course, no one my age was invited, the guests were all their cohorts from the country club, and of course, Rob couldn't be there. I felt guilty about that, but to invite him would have been a disaster."

"Yes. I can imagine what your parents would have thought had Rob Smith shown up at the front door, having to explain who he was and why he was there."

"So, I met Rob first in the wooded area on our property." Arden smiled. "I was wearing this awful froufrou dress my mother had chosen for me, and Rob, I suppose in an effort to look nice for my birthday, was wearing a dress shirt and a tie with his jeans. He gave me the book, and then, well, we made love. Finally, I had to hurry back to the house before I was missed. First, I hid the book in my room and then I joined the party. There I was, pretending to be the good and dutiful daughter, when I held this enormously exciting secret. I was in love. I had a lover. There were moments when I thought I'd burst out in gleeful laughter, and other moments when I wanted to break down in sobs, I missed Rob so much. I don't know how I got through that dreadful evening, but I did."

Laura sighed. "Your eighteenth birthday was a milestone in more ways than one. Did you . . ." It was an oddly difficult question to ask. "Did you get pregnant with me that night?"

"I think I must have, yes. If not, it was soon after. Rob and I didn't have much more time together at that point."

Suddenly, it was all too much for Laura. She put her hands over her face and sobbed. A moment later, she felt her mother's arm around her shoulders, heard her mother's voice whispering comforting words. She relaxed into the embrace, and only some time later did Laura lift her head, wipe her eyes, and take a deep breath. "I'm sorry. Imagining the two of you, so young and happy and hopeful . . ."

Arden gave Laura's shoulders a final squeeze. "That's all in the past now. We'll talk about something else. You know, Deborah told me she had a really good time with you the other evening."

"I'm glad." Laura gave her eyes one final swipe. "I enjoyed our conversation. And misery loves company, doesn't it? We've both been through the marriage wars, but at least we've made it out alive. Battle-scarred, slightly shell-shocked, but alive. It brings us together."

"I hope you talked about more than just the painful times."

Laura smiled. "We did. We had a really good chuckle over the antics of some of our worst colleagues. Did you know that Deborah once shared an office with a woman who changed her nail polish at her desk twice a week? Deborah said the smell of nail polish remover was overwhelming!"

"That makes the odd troublesome customer seem bearable. Hey, how about a glass of wine? We can put on a funny movie, or maybe an old screwball romantic comedy and forget everything else."

"I vote for *My Man Godfrey*!"

Arden sighed and put a hand over her heart. "William Powell! You get the wine and I'll cue up the movie!"

Chapter 66

Deborah had insisted on hosting Arden's birthday party and had gone all out with lovely decorations, which included balloons in pearlescent mint green and pale blue, two of Arden's favorite colors. Deborah had found the balloons online from a company based in Luxembourg.

"You had balloons shipped from Europe?" Arden exclaimed.

"Nothing too good for my friend! And I got the cake at Chez Claudine. I wanted it to be something really special."

The table on Deborah's backyard patio was beautifully set with real china and glassware. A vase of a dozen white roses served as a centerpiece, and from a silver ice bucket peered a bottle of chilled champagne.

Deborah suggested they begin the festivities by presenting their gifts to Arden, who was seated at the head of the table.

Gordon went first. His gift was a small, elegant carving of a cat in highly polished wood. "It looks more like Bastet than your three massive felines," he noted, "but I hope you like it."

Arden thought it was lovely and said so. Since Deborah's gift was the party, Laura was next.

"I really didn't know what to get you. Please consider this a token, or a placeholder, until I can come up with something more significant."

Arden opened the beautifully wrapped box to find inside a hand-painted silk scarf just long enough to tie jauntily around the neck. The colors were mint green and pale blue.

"I asked Deborah to tell me your favorite colors. And I got it at the little boutique in town, so if you want to exchange it—"

"Never," Arden said firmly. "It's perfect. But would it be too corny to say that the best birthday present I could ever have is my daughter being here with me?"

"Corny, yes. But I'm okay with that."

Arden reached for Laura's hand. This was the first birthday they were spending together as mother and daughter. To suppose it might be the last was impossible. Even if they were physically apart on the exact day, from this time on they would always be united. They had to be.

Next, the birthday song was sung, the cake was cut, and the champagne was poured.

"Do you remember a particular birthday from your childhood?" Gordon asked after a time. "Mine all sort of blur together."

Deborah frowned. "I remember being taken to an amusement park with some friends for a birthday outing. It didn't go well. I got totally sick from one of the rides, two of the other girls went missing for over an hour, causing my parents to completely freak out, and then, when we were finally all back in the car heading home, another girl threw up all over the back seat. It seems the hot dogs, cotton candy, and ice cream she had eaten were a bit too much."

"Ugh," Laura said.

"What about you, Arden?" Gordon asked.

"As a matter of fact, I do remember one birthday in particular. I was nine. I was going through a ballet phase, obsessed with the costumes and glamour, the idea of the handsome prince and the lovely princess. Ballet lessons weren't an option, I remember, not at that time in Port George. But my mother had a few old recordings of some of the classics, and I played them over and over. The sound mustn't have been very good, but I wouldn't have known the difference. Anyway, that summer my parents surprised me with tickets to see *Swan Lake* in Boston. It was so exciting. We got all dressed for the occasion and spent the night in one of the big hotels close to the Public Garden. The performance itself had me transported. I went around in a sort of trance for what seems now like weeks, humming the tunes, envisioning myself as Odette." Arden smiled. "It was the best gift my parents could have given me."

"I'm glad you have that memory," Gordon said sincerely.

"I know that things between you and your parents went south after a time," Deborah offered, "but it's good to know your youth wasn't entirely spent in misery."

"Are you sure you're not being a bit overly nostalgic?" Laura asked.

"No, I don't think that I am. My parents weren't always wrong. They weren't evil people."

Deborah shook her head. "I'm never comfortable when the term *evil* comes into the conversation. I can't get my head around what it means in this day and age. Maybe the same as it always did? I just don't know."

"I suspect it means different things for different people," Gordon said. "No longer entirely involved with a satanic being or force. Maybe having something to do with psychological illness and cultural mores."

"Ted Coldwell used the word *sin* in reference to Herbert Aldridge's criminal deeds," Laura told them. "Not that he was ever charged with a criminal offense, but according to Ted lots of people in Port George assume Aldridge is dirty, corrupt."

Neither Deborah nor Gordon responded.

Arden shifted in her chair. Maybe Laura's grandfather was "dirty" and "corrupt," maybe he was guilty of criminal behavior—hadn't she herself suspected as much for years?—but to hear the supposition from the mouth of her child, Herbert's granddaughter, felt deeply unpleasant, especially today of all days.

"I don't think we should be passing judgment," Arden ventured. "Bandying about terms like *evil* and *sin*, *guilt* and *punishment*."

"Well," Laura responded forcefully, "be that as it may, the bottom line is that parents shouldn't get a medal just for doing the right thing, like for ensuring their child enjoys her birthday. That's just basic stuff in the job description. Food, clothing, education, a roof over their heads."

Arden could feel the anger emanating from her daughter but had no idea how to calm it.

"I have a policy," Gordon said suddenly. "Never talk about sin, evil, or even plain old meanness after six in the evening. It's not conducive to a good night's sleep."

"Nor is a second piece of that decadent chocolate-hazelnut cake," Deborah declared. "As much as I want another piece."

Laura said nothing but looked appropriately chastened.

The party wound down soon after, and as Arden made her way back to Juniper End with Laura, she felt a sliver of melancholy winding its way through her. If Laura sensed her mother's unhappiness, she respectfully ignored it, for which Arden was glad. It had been a lovely evening overall, and if there had been moments of tension, well, that was only to be expected.

Life, Arden thought, opening the door of Juniper End, was not all a night at the ballet.

Chapter 67

Laura was having difficulty getting to sleep. Her conscience was bothering her again. She was sorry she had been so negative about Herbert Aldridge earlier. He was Arden's father, and in spite of what he had put her through she clearly retained some warm feeling toward him. After all, Arden had known the man far better than Laura had—which was not at all—and most people were complicated, an ever-shifting mix of positive and negative qualities.

Even her parents—Rob Smith and Victoria Aldridge—weren't perfect human beings, no matter the almost-mythic proportions they had been taking on in Laura's romantic imagination this summer. She pictured her teenage parents making love among the trees, her mother in a party dress, her father in jeans with a shirt and tie. The imagined picture was both touching and heartbreaking, sweet and a wee bit ludicrous, as romantic love was always seen from the outside.

Laura sighed aloud. She had never enjoyed a true, life-changing romance. She had talked herself into thinking that Jared and a few others before him were her soul mates, but deep down she had known—hadn't she?—that she was kidding herself, willing something beautiful to sprout from rotten seeds.

Some might consider Laura lucky to have achieved the age of

thirty-six without having endured the messier, painful aspects of true, life-changing romance. The realists, the practical, the cold-hearted. How many of them were there, really? Laura suspected not all that many, in spite of claims otherwise. Romance was a human addiction; it fascinated and compelled while it tore apart anyone even remotely involved in the story. Laura thought again about the famously ambiguous end of *Villette* Arden had told her about. Had Monsieur Paul been shipwrecked in that mythic seven-day storm—a destroying angel—or had he been returned safely to his dear Lucy? The narrator was vague, almost taunting: "There is enough said. Trouble no quiet, kind heart. . . . Let them picture union and a happy succeeding life."

Desperate readers had written to Charlotte Brontë, begging to know the fate of these fictional lovers. Had Lucy Snowe married Paul Emanuel after all, or had she gone bravely into her future alone? Charlotte had told her publisher she had never meant for Lucy Snowe to have a happy ending. She had written the book during a time of her physical decline and depression. Arden had explained that some scholars thought that Lucy's troubles were a reflection of the author's own.

Suddenly, Laura wondered why Arden hadn't included *Villette* among the books discussed at the "Star-Crossed Lovers" event. The novel meant so much to her. But maybe that was the very reason to exclude it from open discussion.

That dreadful ambiguity, Laura thought. What *had* happened to Rob Smith? Would he have married the mother of his child had he not gone missing? Would Victoria have gone through with the wedding, facing the possibility of being cut off from her parents, on whom she had always been so dependent? There was no way to know.

Laura shifted under the covers. The night was warm; she wished she had thought to open the window before climbing into bed but was too groggy from cake and champagne to get up. The sound of padding footsteps came to her attention. Her mother wasn't yet asleep, either. Laura hoped Arden wasn't upset about her daughter's earlier harsh remarks. In so many ways Arden was still a mystery to Laura, still a person very much apart.

For example, that morning Arden had met with a loan officer at her bank. Laura would have been more than happy to accompany her mother, for moral support if nothing else, but Laura hadn't even known that Arden had made an appointment. Laura wasn't a part of her mother's life, not in a day-to-day, reliable way. Arden Bell wasn't used to having someone on whom she could rely—at least, not a family member. Would she ever need her daughter?

"Oof!" Laura cried, as a heavy object covered in fur landed on her stomach. It was Ophelia. "You're getting as big as Falstaff," she murmured as the cat made a job of settling for the night.

Within moments, both Laura and Ophelia were asleep.

Chapter 68

"I'm sorry again about the things I said at your birthday party."

Arden smiled. She had never seen a person look so contrite. "It's all right. Emotions run high on special occasions. It's to be expected."

"Still, I hope I didn't ruin your good time."

The two women had finished dinner—salmon; green beans; roasted red potatoes—and were settled in the living room with the cats, Laura in the comfortable armchair and Arden curled in a corner of the couch. Arden had put on a CD of Ella Fitzgerald's songs; it seemed that Laura, too, was a fan of the old standards. The windows were open to the balmy evening air. Arden sighed in contentment. There was little that could improve this moment, other than the physical presence of Laura's father.

"You haven't told me about the place where you were sent to live out the pregnancy," Laura said suddenly.

"It's odd you should ask about that today of all days. Only this morning at the shop I was thinking about someone I met there. I remembered that her favorite book was *The Secret Garden*. It's been years since I last read the story. Did you read it when you were young?"

"Of course. And I loved it. So, what was this place you were sent to called?"

"The Two Suns Retreat and Spa."

Laura laughed. "You've got to be kidding me. What a ridiculous name for a—for a prison!"

"I won't argue with you there. Anyway, it was more like an exclusive boarding school, with the cool-girl clique, and the random bully, the nerd faction. We had a large communal bathroom and ate our meals together in a cafeteria, but luckily, we each had our own room.

"The main building had been a private residence once, in the style of Le Corbusier but executed by someone without the talent. Courses were offered but not required, things like basic geometry and current affairs. As far as I know, the courses didn't count for anything back in the real world. But I guess it was important to keep up the pretense of this—incarceration—being a character-building, educational time. There were walking trails and a tennis court and an indoor pool. And I read voraciously, as always. There was a library and I'd brought some of my own books, including, of course, the copy of *Villette* Rob had given me for my birthday."

"And you were there almost your entire pregnancy?"

"Yes, from late August until shortly after you were born. I spent Thanksgiving and Christmas there as well. I couldn't go home, of course. There were some very dark days that fall and winter, but I never totally despaired. I clung to Lucy Snowe as a sort of predecessor in pain. 'Life is still life, whatever its pangs.'"

"Thank God for fiction. Did your parents call you? Send letters?"

"At first my father called every Sunday at four o'clock on the nose. After about five or six weeks of miserable, clipped conversations, he told me he thought I didn't need checking up on any longer, and that if I wanted something, I should call him. I never did."

Laura shook her head but made no comment. "What about your mother?"

Arden hesitated. It was difficult to reveal the extent of Florence Aldridge's deteriorated mental state to anyone, let alone to the granddaughter she had never known. "Mother," Arden began finally, "would send me letters in which she chattered on about what was happening at the country club and tell me about the new hat she had bought, or the holiday parties she and my father were attending. She never once mentioned the pregnancy. It was as if she had blocked out the truth of where I was and why. At first, I was devastated by what I saw as a lack of concern with my welfare. Then, I reminded myself that pretending was my mother's way of handling—unpleasantness. I remember wondering how she was dealing with the women in her social set. I'm sure she was terrified of the truth being found out."

Laura sighed. "I'm so sorry," she said feelingly. "For both you and for Florence. Please believe that."

"I do."

"Tell me about that girl you mentioned earlier, the one who loved *The Secret Garden*."

"Her name was Alice Davidson. She was from the San Francisco area. She was younger than me, sixteen to my eighteen. She had the most gorgeous hair. It was dark red and thick and wavy. Thinking back now, I realize we didn't really get to know each other well, but what we did know was enough to make us care. Other than Rob, Alice was my first real friend."

"Did you talk about the fathers? Did you tell her about Rob?"

"Yes," Arden said after a moment. "But I couldn't bring myself to tell her about his disappearance from Port George. I couldn't bear to make it more terribly real than it already was. I just said that my parents had broken us up and that neither of us was happy about it."

"Do you think she believed you?"

"Yes. She was very young in some ways, even more naïve than I was." Arden frowned. "She had been seduced by an older boy she had met at church. She told me she had liked him a lot but wasn't ready to get serious." Arden frowned. "He didn't care for her refusal and . . ."

"Disgusting." Laura shook her head.

"Yes. Still, she wanted to have the baby, so her parents sent her to Two Suns. Poor Alice. It was so much more horrible than what had happened to me. I had found true love. I couldn't bring myself to show her my birthday present from Rob, not after I heard her story. It seemed cruel."

"What happened to Alice? I mean, she had the baby and then what?"

"She didn't have her baby," Arden said quietly. "She suffered a miscarriage. She was mad with grief. I was allowed to visit her in the infirmary, and even though she had known all along that her baby was going to be taken away from her the moment he or she was born, she had counted on that birth. I didn't know what to say to make her feel better. Maybe there was nothing I could have said. A few days later someone came to fetch her. Maybe a parent, I don't know. Anyway, one morning she was just gone."

"You must have been devastated," Laura said gently.

"Nearly. Alice and I thought we still had a few months to spend together. I don't recall either of us planning anything specific for the future, the days post life at Two Suns. We never talked about keeping in touch. The moment seemed enough, until it was torn away from us."

Laura sighed. "It's like Jane and Helen in *Jane Eyre*. Two orphans— you both might as well have been—finding solace within an institution of misery. And you've never heard from Alice afterwards?"

"No. I've thought often of her through the years, but I never actually considered searching for her. What if she had worked hard to put that part of her life behind her? What if my contacting her only brought her pain?"

"How would you feel if she reached out to you? I found you. Others could, too."

"I'd be glad to hear from Alice," Arden said after a moment.

"You can't know for sure she wouldn't feel the same."

"True. But sometimes the past is best left to itself."

"Sometimes. What kept you going all those months? Besides Alice, of course."

"The thought of you," Arden said firmly, "the child Rob and I had created. And the belief that Rob would write to me, apologize for having gone away. I swore to myself that I would forgive him anything, as long as we were reunited. In that way as well, I related closely with Lucy Snowe. 'My hour of torment was the post-hour.'"

"But he never did write to you."

Arden laughed weakly. "No. He never did." Suddenly, the memories were all too much. Arden put her hands over her eyes and sighed deeply.

A moment later, she was wrapped in her daughter's arms.

Chapter 69

"Before we get down to business," Ted said, "I want to share with you something I remembered the other day. A nice memory."

Laura smiled. "I could use one of those right now."

"There was a pond on the Aldridges' property, as you know. One afternoon I was visiting with my parents and I came upon Victoria kneeling by the edge of the pond. When I asked what she was doing, she said she was trying to catch a frog. She'd begun to put together a terrarium in her room. Of course, this was all top secret. Florence would have been horrified to learn there were slimy creatures living in her impeccably clean home. Anyway, I managed to catch the frog for Victoria, but she was suddenly terribly upset when she realized that the little guy was being kidnapped from his home and family, and she begged me to release him."

Laura smiled. "So, my mother had spunk even before she started to date Rob in spite of her parents' rules! Building a terrarium behind their backs."

"And she was always kind, letting the frog go free."

"I wonder if Arden remembers that afternoon? I'll ask her when I get back to Eliot's Corner. So, why did you ask me here today?"

Ted took a seat behind his desk. "James Barber has come up with something—interesting. I think I mentioned that until the past few weeks he had never bothered to go through his brother's belongings; he figured there was nothing of any real worth in the few cardboard boxes Jake had left behind, and the brothers hadn't been close in Jake's final years—but neither could James bring himself to throw the boxes away."

"He found something more significant than an old videotape?" Laura felt her heart begin to race—just a bit—with excitement.

"Possibly. James is still hoping to find something that might eventually lead him to proving that Herbert Aldridge employed Jake to perform illegal activities." Ted paused. "James found a gun."

Laura startled. She didn't like guns. She didn't want anything to do with guns. "Oh," she said after a moment.

"This gun is what some might call a lady's gun. Very small, with a mother-of-pearl handle, and, most potentially interesting for us, an inscription. The initials F.A. and a date, 1982. James, taking an understandable leap of imagination and supposing that F.A. stood for Florence Aldridge, brought the gun to me. It's currently in my safe."

Laura tried to process what Ted had just told her. It wasn't easy. "May I see it?" she asked finally.

Ted got up from his desk and retrieved the gun from his safe. He brought it back to the desk and placed it on the blotter. It was in a sealed plastic bag.

Laura stared at the thing. It was almost pretty. "Where are the initials?" she asked flatly.

Ted pointed them out. Laura looked away. No. Guns were not for her.

Ted sat back in his chair. "When James had gone, I suddenly remembered a conversation I'd overheard between my parents about a year before Rob Smith went missing. We were all in the living room after dinner. I remember my mother looking up from the book she was reading and saying something like 'I can't believe Herbert bought Florence a gun. The only person she needs protecting against is herself.' To which my father replied with something like 'The last thing I'd give that woman is a gun. She'll blow her own hand off one of these days, shooting at shadows.'"

Laura shook her head. All that her mother had told her about Florence Aldridge's precarious state of mind had been too true.

"Was the gun ever registered?" she asked finally. "You must be able to find out if it was and to whom."

"If Herbert gave his wife a gun back in 1982, he was under no legal obligation to have it registered." Ted paused. "Anyway, even if we knew for sure that the gun once belonged to the Aldridge family, the gun, like the video clip, doesn't prove anything, but it is a possible link between the Aldridge family and a known lowlife with a record."

Laura laughed helplessly. "I don't know what to think at this point. I really don't."

"There's one more thing. I have a friend in ballistics. I asked him to examine the gun. There were no fingerprints other than Jake's; James used gloves when he handled it. And my friend determined that the gun hasn't been fired in over thirty years. Not much use to us, sadly."

"Why would this Jake character have the gun?" Laura mused aloud after a moment. "Do you think Herbert Aldridge hired him to kill my father?"

Ted frowned. "With Florence's gun? No."

"So maybe . . ." Laura shook her head. "I'm very confused. What the heck happened that Sunday in August of 1984?"

"Damned if I know. One idea: Herbert Aldridge killed your father and hired Jake to dispose of the body and the evidence. For some reason, Jake kept the gun instead of tossing it."

"But why would Herbert Aldridge use his wife's gun to kill my father? Surely he would have used a gun that couldn't be traced. And if no gun was available to him, he would have had access to another means of murder, like—"

Suddenly, another possibility struck Laura like a slap across the face. "Do you think that *Florence* Aldridge could have killed my father? And that her husband hired Jake to get rid of the evidence that would lead back to her?"

"I honestly don't know. Maybe Jake stole the gun from the house at another time, before or after Rob went missing. We don't know for sure how Rob was killed or even if he *was* killed."

Laura shook her head. "So, we have no evidence of anything other than the fact that when Jake Barber died he left behind this particular gun, which might or might not have belonged to Florence Aldridge."

"I'm sorry," Ted said feelingly. "Still, I thought you should know what my friend found."

"I'm grateful. What will you do with the gun now?"

"Return it to James." Ted walked her to the door of his office, thanked her for coming in, and wished her a safe journey back to Eliot's Corner.

The meeting had disturbed Laura; it had brought a sense of violence too close for comfort. Maybe that was why she had a sudden and strong—if macabre—desire to take another look at the house atop Old Orchard Hill before returning to Eliot's Corner. She brought the car to a stop about half way up the drive and willed someone to appear, to open the front door, to peer out a window, to come striding from around the back of the house. But there was no sign of human life, and no sign of the old black Cadillac. The spot at the end of the road seemed somehow more lonely and isolated than it had on her last visit, though of course the change was in Laura, not in the big house on an expansive bit of property.

Abruptly, Laura restarted the car. She couldn't get out of Port George fast enough.

Chapter 70

"So, what did you learn on this latest trip to Port George?" Arden asked.

Laura had returned to Juniper End late that morning, with no explanation for her unexpected appearance. Arden, who had been about to leave for the shop, hadn't pressed her daughter then, but now, as the day was nearing its end, Arden could no longer quiet her curiosity.

Laura, on whose lap Falstaff had made a bed, smiled as she related the childhood memory Ted had shared with her. "He said your mother would not have been happy to learn she was housing crawling creatures."

"He was right, she wouldn't have. I remember that day, as well. I think it was the first time it really occurred to me that it was possible—even necessary—to feel empathy with nonhuman lives. It was a turning point in my emotional development. It's odd to think that Ted remembers that moment, too."

"Well, he did have a crush on you back in the old days."

Arden nodded. "Yes. But tell me. What else did you find out while in Port George? And why did you come home so abruptly?"

For a long moment Laura lowered her eyes to the cat on her lap. Arden wondered if Laura was drawing comfort from Falstaff's warmth and steady breathing. Finally, Laura looked up.

"There's something not so pleasant I need to tell you," she said evenly.

Arden felt her stomach clench. "Go on."

She listened with close attention as Laura spoke about the gun Ted's friend James Barber had unearthed among his brother Jake's effects. The name Jake Barber was vaguely familiar to Arden. She thought he might have run with a small group of thugs who had occasionally been a public nuisance when she was a teen.

"And that's the whole story," Laura said finally. "A lot of what-ifs and maybes."

"I can't believe my mother would own a gun," Arden said raggedly. She felt as if she had been running for a long time, weak at the knees, exhausted. "Why would she want one?"

"Maybe she didn't want one. Maybe your father insisted she keep a gun for protection. I told you about the conversation Ted remembers. His parents knew that Herbert Aldridge had given his wife a gun."

Arden struggled to take a clean breath. Had Mr. and Mrs. Coldwell known for a *fact* that Herbert had given Florence a weapon? What if Herbert had lied to his friends? . . . But why?

"What would have been her motive in killing Rob?" Arden said almost pleadingly. "It was already decided that I would be sent away and the baby adopted. And she knew that my father would handle any other details that needed handling. He always did. Why would Rob be a threat to her? No, the idea of my mother hunting Rob down to exact revenge is ridiculous. My father, maybe. But he'd hire someone to do his dirty work."

"Maybe Florence didn't have to hunt Rob down. Maybe he showed up at the house, wanting to see you."

"But he didn't. I would have known about it. I was there the whole time, from the night I told my parents that I was pregnant until the day I left for Two Suns."

"Would you really have known if Rob had come to the house? Isn't it possible you were asleep when he came to the door, or taking a shower?"

Arden put her hand to her head. "Yes," she said quietly. "It's possible."

"So, what if Rob showed up one afternoon and confronted your parents?"

"My father would have turned him away immediately."

"What if Florence was alone when Rob showed up?"

"Assuming he did," Arden snapped.

Laura nodded. "Always assuming. What if Florence lashed out? You've said she was unstable and that she could get out of control when she felt threatened."

Suddenly Arden stood and began to pace. "I suppose that anything is possible. You always hear that in an extreme situation a person can do the unthinkable, something totally out of character, something insanely heroic or unspeakably violent." Arden shook her head. "But, no. No, not my mother. She was a gentle person. Troubled, yes, but fundamentally loving. Thwarted, shame ridden, depressed, but I know she loved me and would never do anything to hurt me."

"Except to send you away and force you to give up your baby," Laura said quietly.

"But that wasn't an act of physical violence. And we don't know for sure that the gun James Barber found in his brother's things belonged to my mother. Other people have the initials F.A."

Laura nodded. "You're right. Let's put this topic to rest for now. I'll go put a pot of water on to boil. I thought I'd make pasta primavera for dinner using the tomatoes and sweet peppers you got at the farmers' market."

Arden nodded vaguely as Laura extricated herself from Falstaff's bulk and went off to the kitchen. When Arden felt her breathing return to an almost normal rhythm, she asked herself why she was defending her mother so strongly against the possibility of having committed a crime. Had she learned compassion for Florence Aldridge without realizing it? Was that possible? Had she come to forgive her mother, if not her father, for her part in the terrible things that had happened in August 1984?

Anything was possible. Anyone could commit a murder. A long-lost child could turn up on her mother's doorstep. A man she had loved but thought long dead could—

With a sigh of exhaustion, Arden sank back onto the couch.

Chapter 71

"Never a dull moment around here, is there!" Deborah shook her head. "And I thought there were some strange happenings in my family."

After a lengthy discussion over dinner the night before, Laura and Arden had agreed to tell Deborah and Gordon absolutely everything they had learned concerning the summer of 1984 as it pertained to the disappearance of Rob Smith, everything they believed or suspected might have happened, every rumor they had been privy to since Laura had begun her quest for the truth.

Earlier, Arden had spoken to Gordon. Now, gathered in Arden's yard with a pitcher of cold lemonade, Laura and her mother had filled Deborah in as best they could. Deborah was not happy to hear about the latest factor—the gun couldn't be called evidence—to come to light, nor was she surprised to learn that Arden had long suspected her father of being involved in Rob's disappearance.

"So, where do you go from here?" Deborah asked.

Laura sighed. "I wish I knew. Let's face it, as an amateur detective, I'm terrible. What little evidence I've stumbled upon is purely circumstantial, if that."

"I've been wrestling with the idea of letting the matter drop," Arden admitted. "Of accepting that we might never know what happened to Rob and moving on with our lives. And, of course, of going to the Smith family with the good news we do have, that Rob's daughter is alive and well."

"How will you know when it's time to let the investigation go?" Deborah asked.

"I don't know," Laura admitted. "I've got to get back to my teaching job. I can't afford to be without income for much longer. And long ago I put my academic career on hold because of Jared's overwhelming neediness. Now that he's gone, I'd like to return to graduate school as soon as I can." Laura smiled and held her hand out for Arden to take. "At least I found my mother. My quest wasn't entirely a failure."

"And there's still a possibility the truth about what happened to Rob will out," Deborah said robustly. "Can you at least give it until the end of the summer before you go back to Connecticut?"

"Yes, but no longer." Laura released Arden's hand. "The semester begins right after Labor Day."

"We've gone on long enough about our woes," Arden said suddenly. "How's the sale going, Deborah?"

Deborah frowned. "We've hit another snag. I'm not the sort of person who gives up without a good fight, but I swear, there are moments when I want to throw in the proverbial towel and walk away. But I won't. Too much depends on my closing this sale."

"What got you into real estate?" Laura asked.

Deborah took a drink of her lemonade before replying. "Not even Arden knows this part of my life. After my first marriage ended in such a tawdry way, I swore I'd never walk down the aisle again. But a few years after my divorce I met a truly lovely man. His name was Charles, and he had his own business as a finish carpenter. We dated for about three months before it was obvious to both of us that what we had was really special. I was serenely happy, which felt like a big improvement on the sort of frantic happiness I'd felt with Alan. A month later, we were married. This time, I opted for a quiet ceremony. Besides the minister and our two witnesses there were only my parents and Charles's mother. After the wedding, Charles and I traveled through Italy for three weeks and it was bliss. I'd never felt more at peace with myself and the world."

Deborah paused to take another drink from her glass. "We'd been back home about six weeks when I began to notice that Charles was acting strangely. He was absentminded and rarely smiled. His appetite began to dwindle and he got into the habit of taking a long walk on his own each evening after dinner. At first I thought there was a problem at work, but he said that everything was fine. Then, I considered that he might be physically unwell, but I was wrong there, too. Finally, I worked up the nerve to ask if he was unhappy in our marriage—and I got the shock of a lifetime. Charles had decided he needed to devote the rest of his life to contemplation, specifically as practiced by a lay Carmelite order he'd visited when we were honeymooning in Italy." Deborah gave a grim smile. "I don't know where I was that day, probably shopping. Anyway, I was stunned even though I knew Charles had always been a spiritual person. It was one of the things that attracted me to him. I used to think, 'This is someone who takes love seriously. He's not going to run off with another woman like Alan did.'"

"No, he just decided to run off with God," Laura said dryly.

Arden shook her head. "And God is pretty serious competition."

"The thing is," Deborah continued, "I could never bring myself to dislike him, let alone hate him. I mean, to be left because a person wants to devote his life to prayer and community service? That's a good thing, isn't it?"

"Still," Laura said, "it must have been a blow."

"Yes. I felt as if I was losing my mind. At first, I wondered if Charles was lying to me about the monastery, that maybe there really was another woman somewhere just waiting for him to leave me. I debated contacting his mother and the friend who'd stood up for us at the wedding to see if they had any insight into what was going on, but I felt it would be wrong to go behind Charles's back so I didn't." Deborah sighed. "In the end, his intentions proved to be genuine. At least I hadn't married a liar."

"What did you do then?" Laura asked, shaking her head.

"What could I do? I agreed to the divorce and that was that. A mere blip in my life. I'd been working in retail since I'd graduated from college, but at that point I realized I needed to reinvent myself."

Arden nodded. "Reinvention isn't easy."

"Tell me about it! Anyway, all my life I've been drawn to the idea of land ownership, something tangible a person could call her own." Deborah shrugged. "So, I chose to work in real estate."

"Real estate is a pretty competitive business," Laura said. "You must have to be a bit—well, I won't say cutthroat—but seriously focused and determined to make a go of it."

"True. And yet, like I said, there are moments when I feel overwhelmed by the challenges and tempted to give it up, but those moments pass and I recommit and press on."

"Do you know what became of Charles?" Arden asked. "Is he still a member of the cloistered order?"

Deborah shrugged. "As far as I know. But it's funny. I have the feeling that one day he's going to show up in my life again. Honestly, I'd welcome it. I think. He was a very special person."

"You don't still love him, do you?" Laura asked.

"I think in some way I do, though I'm not in love the way I was. Still, I did renew my earlier vow never to marry again. If either of you ever sees me weakening, I want a full-blown intervention."

"Don't worry," Laura assured her. "I'll bring the restraints."

"Thank you for sharing your story with us, Deborah," Arden said feelingly. "We've spent so much time this summer going on about the Smith and Aldridge drama, I fear we might have been ignoring our friends."

"Not at all," Deborah said. "We're in this crazy thing called life together. Sometimes one of us needs more attention than the other; sometimes one of us is happy to retreat a bit. I'm just grateful to be sharing my journey with you guys."

Laura reached for her mother's hand; with the other, she took Deborah's. "Through thick and thin," Laura said heartily.

"Through thick and thin!"

Chapter 72

That evening, Arden had prepared a dinner of New England–style clam chowder, served with a green salad, and a sourdough boule she had bought at Chez Claudine.

"I seem to remember saying something earlier in the summer about getting fat living here," Laura said as she helped her mother clear the table. "I think I was right but I don't much care."

Arden laughed. "You don't look at all different than you did when you arrived. You're just not used to the feeling of satisfaction one gets after a homemade meal."

"Ain't that the truth!"

When the kitchen had been put away, the women settled in the living room for what had become their almost nightly talk. Ophelia made herself comfortable on Laura's lap. Prospero and Falstaff were curled up together at one end of the couch.

"It won't be long before I have to light a fire," Arden noted. "The kitties will be very happy."

"It's only August. And don't you get an Indian summer in this part of the world?"

"Sometimes, yes. But things get chilly pretty early here on the whole and stay chilly—and damp—until well after spring has sprung in most other New England states. Deborah carries a pair of gloves with her until June."

"It's not quite so bad down in Connecticut. Besides, I like the cold weather, as long as it goes away by April."

Arden smiled briefly. It had already occurred to her that Laura might not want to live in Maine year-round, and not only because of its notoriously late spring. The thought saddened Arden, but Laura had never promised to stay on after the search for the truth about what had happened to her father had come to an end. And only that afternoon Laura had expressed a very reasonable desire to return to teaching and maybe even to graduate school.

"Ever since we met," Laura went on, gently stroking Ophelia's silky fur, "I've wanted to ask what it was that finally made you run away from Port George. Was there one thing that tipped the scales?"

Arden had half expected this question from her daughter but hadn't allowed herself to truly imagine the moment of telling. Did it need to be told? Would it be kinder to keep the ugly details from Laura?

"Arden?" Laura frowned in concern. "You okay?"

Arden nodded. Her mind was made up. Laura was not a child; she deserved the truth. It was what she had come to Eliot's Corner to learn.

"There were two things that forced my decision to leave. I told you about that accidental meeting with Frannie Smith, the one in which she accused me of having kept Rob's child a secret. The encounter shook me badly. I began to think I'd never be able to leave the house again for fear of running into Frannie or another one of Rob's family, eager to accuse me of wrongdoing. But suddenly, I began to feel angry. Until then I'd felt so beaten down, so resigned to what had happened. I decided to seize that anger and make it work for me by finally confronting my father about the adoption."

Arden paused. Laura's expression was one of rapt attention.

"I found him alone in his study after dinner one night. He wanted to know why I was there. He was busy, he said, and didn't have time to waste." Arden shrugged. "Maybe he said time to spare, but in my memory he used the word *waste*. Anyway, I took a step closer to the desk and began to speak. My voice was trembling, but I demanded to know where my baby had been taken. He refused to tell me. He said it was for the best that I not know any details. I said, 'For whose best?' He seemed surprised that I had the nerve to talk back to him. Instead of answering my question he pointed out that I had agreed to the adoption. I argued that he had pressured me, that I was a victim of coercion."

Arden paused for a moment. "He said nothing in response, just kept staring at me stony faced. So, I said that I would get a lawyer to find the child and prove that the adoption wasn't legal. Then, he spoke. He told me not to be ridiculous. He pointed out that I had no money of my own and that he certainly wouldn't pay my legal bills. And suddenly, I froze, intimidated into silence by his coldness. My father looked down at his desk then and told me to go to bed. I remember turning and walking sort of mindlessly toward the door. Then he said, and this is an exact quote, I'm sure of it, 'Close the door behind you, now there's a good girl.' I felt about three years old at that moment, dismissed like a toddler."

"I'm so sorry." Laura's voice was low; if she was angry, she kept the anger to herself.

"After that disaster with my father, I thought things couldn't get any worse than they were. I was wrong. A few nights later, my parents gave one of their popular parties and pressed me to join the guests. I was to answer questions about my first year at Blake College—all a lie, of course—and make small talk like I had been trained to do. I dutifully put on a dress and smiled politely, but I was absolutely miserable. My life had been violently turned upside down by Rob's disappearance and the theft of our child. And yet, my parents seemed to expect me to go on as if nothing had changed, to be the same obedient, passive little girl I'd been before I'd met Rob."

Laura shook her head. "I'll say it again. A Gothic novel set in the twentieth century."

"I couldn't stand the people my parents socialized with. They were a soulless bunch, only interested in making money and showing it off. The only decent people at that party were Ted Coldwell and his parents, though at the time I could barely look at Ted without wondering if he had had something to do with Rob's disappearance, if he had been my father's partner in crime. Poor Ted tried to talk to me at one point. He was his usual friendly self, but I couldn't believe that his show of friendship was genuine. I remember turning my back on him. That was the last time I saw Ted Coldwell."

"He mentioned that night to me. He remembers."

"I wish he'd forget." Arden sighed. "Anyway, not long after that, I managed to slip away from the melee of drunken partygoers. The women's teased and lacquered hairdos were beginning to droop, their lipstick to slide across their faces. You could hear the sound of booze sloshing out of glasses. The men were all worse for wear, too, their ties askew or gone entirely, shouting insults at each other across the room, bellowing with laughter. My father was one of the worst of the bunch. He was downing Scotch like it was water. The whole scene repulsed me. I went out into the garden for some fresh air. I could still hear the chaos inside but at least I wasn't breathing all that cigarette smoke. At the time, there was a gazebo in the center of the back lawn. I thought I'd take refuge there for a bit. It was very dark away from the house; someone had forgotten to turn on the security lights. It suited me just fine."

Arden paused to gather her courage. Again, Laura nodded silently.

"But when I reached the gazebo, there was my mother, half-conscious, having sex or very nearly with the husband of one of her friends. Maybe I should have cried out for help, forced him to stop, but I didn't. I was overwhelmed with feelings of disgust and anger, and before either of them could become aware of me, I ran off to my room. No one came looking for me. Eventually, the party wound down, and by three in the morning the house was finally quiet. I remember lying on my bed, exhausted but wide-awake, knowing that I would die if I went on living in that house. Two nights later, I ran off for good. I had no plan. I just knew I needed to get far away from my parents. I took what cash and jewelry I could, and, well, I simply vanished."

Tears were shining in Laura's eyes. "You were so brave. Truly courageous."

"Was I?" Arden shook her head. "I didn't feel brave. I felt forced to run away from home as the only way to save my sanity. I have no idea if my parents bothered to search for me, then or later. It wouldn't have been difficult to track me down. So, I had to con-

clude they had decided to wash their hands of their troublesome
daughter. No doubt my mother retreated again into pretending,
telling herself I was back at college or living a glamorous life in the
south of France."

Laura silently shook her head. "It's hard to believe. . . . I'm so
sorry."

"I was frugal with what little money I had. To that point in my
life I'd never had a paying job, so learning how to be an employee
was a shock, especially an employee hired to do menial tasks,
something I had been taught was beneath an Aldridge. But I'm a
quick learner and I had never shared my parents' attitudes toward
what was honest work, so I adjusted. Later on, as you know, I
changed my name. For a while I lived in Vermont, and later, New
Hampshire. Mostly, I was content. I was so relieved to be away
from Port George and my parents' killing influence."

"You must have been terrified though. Completely on your own
at such a young age."

"There were some scary times," Arden admitted after a long
moment. "More than a few. But I wasn't the first young woman
who was compelled to make a living without the support of friends
or family, and I know I won't have been the last."

"Too true," Laura said quietly.

"And then"—Arden deliberately fast-forwarded over the years
of wandering and dislocation—"when I was about forty, I came
back to Maine and landed in Eliot's Corner. Honestly, I took one
look at this charming little town and decided this is where I would
stay, finally try to put down some roots, if people would let me.
And, yes, I was aware that Eliot's Corner was only two hours away
from Port George, but in a strange way, after all those years on the
move, that nearness held an appeal. Later, I learned that it's not at
all uncommon for a person to need to be close to a place where
something monumental had occurred to her, even if that something was traumatic."

Laura nodded. "A version of a criminal needing to return to the
scene of his crime?"

"Maybe. Anyway, I found the job at Arden Forest, and Margery
became my mentor and my guardian angel. When she passed away,

leaving the shop to me, I felt as if I'd been given a great gift, something I could nurture and protect and take pride in." Arden smiled, though she felt tears burning in her eyes. "Like I might have done with my daughter had I been allowed the chance."

"You truly are the heroine of your life." Laura wiped tears from her cheeks. "Succeeding against all odds, fighting for justice for that young girl you once were, fighting for her right to a self-determining existence."

"I just did what I had to do to survive. As I said, mine is a pretty common story. Maybe the details of my story are more colorful than average—a disappearing fiancé and parents with outrageously outdated ideas about a daughter's independence—but that doesn't make me any stronger than any other woman who's fought the good fight."

Suddenly, Falstaff lumbered to his feet and let out a great wail, sending Prospero leaping from the couch and causing Ophelia to appear supremely annoyed at the interruption of her nap.

"What's wrong with him?" Laura cried. "Is he hurt?"

Arden laughed, glad for the dramatic distraction. "He just wants our attention. We've been ignoring him for too long."

"Well, he's got it now!"

Chapter 73

"A letter for me?"

"It was left at my office after hours," Ted told Laura, "slipped through the mail slot. It's addressed to 'the woman asking around about the summer of 1984.' I don't know how the sender knew I'd be able to reach you; word must have gotten around that you'd been to my office."

"How odd. Would you open the letter and text me a photo of it?"

While Ted went about doing just that, Laura put her phone on speaker and told her mother what was transpiring. Ted's text arrived a moment later.

"The handwriting is pretty bad," Laura noted, "but here goes. Ted? Can you stay on and read this with us?"

"Sure." First, Ted greeted Arden—it was the first time the two childhood friends had spoken since 1985—and then Laura began to read aloud:

" 'To the woman with that podcast. I know something that might interest you. I worked as chauffeur and mechanic for Herbert Aldridge from 1982 to 1984. My name is Steve Penn.' "

"I remember him," Arden interrupted. "He always had a smile for me."

"But you can't say if he was trustworthy or not?" Ted asked.

"No. But he's not lying about employed by my father."

"He goes on: 'I still live in Port George, on the outskirts. Last year I retired from my job at a car repair place. Anyway, I might be able to help you if you're still interested in that boy who went missing and was never found. Call me any time at the number below. Yours truly, S. Penn.'"

"What do you think?" Arden asked. "Ted, should we give him a call?"

"I don't see why not. Let me know what you find out. I've got a client coming in so I've got to go."

When Ted had rung off, Arden suggested that Laura place the call to Mr. Penn right away. "I'll listen silently, of course."

Mr. Penn answered on the fourth ring, sounding a little out of breath.

Laura introduced herself. "Thank you for contacting me. You said you might be able to shed some light on the disappearance of Rob Smith back in August 1984."

Mr. Penn cleared his throat. "I told you that I worked for Herbert Aldridge as chauffeur and mechanic. They had an '81 Plymouth Reliant at the time and a 1962 Cadillac Coupe de Ville. Wouldn't be surprised if they still had that Cadillac. Mr. Aldridge treated it like it was his own child. Anyway, not long after their daughter went off to some college, about the start of September '84, I was fired, just like that. Mr. Aldridge didn't give me a reason, just handed me a letter of recommendation along with the money owed me, and I was sent packing."

"Are you saying you think your firing relates to the disappearance of Rob Smith?" Laura asked, shooting a glance at Arden.

"Well, I'm not sure if it does. But here's what happened. One night a few days before Rob was declared missing, I was in the garage and I heard some noises coming from the construction site on the property. A clanking, like, and an engine of some sort. I wasn't supposed to still be at the house, but I'd stayed late that Sunday to finish a chore. I wondered if someone was trying to sabotage the construction—Herbert Aldridge wasn't the most generous of employers—and I thought about checking it out, but in the end, I did nothing. I was pretty tired, and honestly, I didn't really care if the

Aldridges were robbed or what have you. He wasn't a nice man at all. She could be all right, but mostly, she was out of it. She was taking some sort of pills. It wasn't a secret, either."

"But when Rob was officially declared missing, why didn't you come forward?" Laura asked, struggling to keep a note of accusation out of her voice. "You could have done it anonymously, told the police what you heard that night."

"I suppose I could have, but at the time I didn't connect what I heard that night with Rob's going missing. But with you asking around town about those days, I started thinking and putting one and one together and . . . And besides, life does strange things to you, doesn't it?"

"What do you mean?" Laura asked. Her mother's face was ashen.

"Well, see, about two weeks ago my grandson, he's twelve, he got into an accident out on a boat with his friend's family. Came close to drowning. He was in the hospital for three days, and I can tell you those three days were the worst of my life. I guess coming so close to losing Hank got me to thinking about what those Smiths must have gone through, losing their son like that. So, I thought I would tell you what I know." Mr. Penn paused. When he went on, his tone was almost apologetic. "Which isn't really anything, is it?"

"No, no, you've been very helpful. I appreciate your contacting me."

"You know," Mr. Penn went on, reanimated, "now you've got me wondering. Maybe the reason I was let go so sudden was because Mr. Aldridge thought I might've been hanging around late that night, maybe seen or heard something. I mean, if he was the one making the noise, he or someone working for him, and if the noise did have something to do with young Rob Smith. But if that was the case, wouldn't it have been safer to keep me close and treat me right, in case I got it into my head to blackmail him? Assuming I'd seen or heard something damning, and I hadn't. At least, I didn't think I had."

Laura shared a look of frustration with Arden. "I can't say what Mr. Aldridge thought or didn't think," Laura said carefully. "I doubt we'll ever really know."

"Probably right. But you won't tell anyone I got in touch with you, will you?" Mr. Penn sounded genuinely worried.

"I promise." Laura wondered if Steve Penn could still fear Herbert Aldridge. "Thanks, again."

"Not much, is it?" Arden said with a frown when Laura had ended the call.

"Yet more soft evidence, but it's helpful—possibly—in painting a picture of corruption under the sweet surface of small-town life. I'll pass the story on to Ted, and he can put it with the other circumstantial and downright flimsy evidence we've uncovered." Laura rubbed her eyes. "I feel more frustrated than ever. I feel as if we're beating our heads against the proverbial wall."

Arden sighed. "I know we've talked about this before, but how bad would it be if we never learned the truth about what happened to Rob the day he went missing from Port George? I know we both want to know, but what if we never can?"

"It would be bad," Laura said after a long moment. "But not the end of the world. At least I finally know something of my birth father. That he was one of the good guys, well loved and respected. That means a lot."

"And when we tell Frannie and her family who you are, you'll have gained kin."

"Assuming they believe me." Laura smiled ruefully.

"We could prove it if we have to. You could take a DNA test."

"Then what? They might still want nothing to do with either of us." Laura sighed. "Still, we owe it to my father's relatives—to my relatives—to tell them that I exist."

"And once the Smiths know, it's inevitable that my parents will learn that I'm still alive. That their scheme to keep me apart from my child failed in the end."

"They might attempt to contact you. Or me, for that matter."

Arden shook her head thoughtfully. "Even if my father was the one behind that threatening letter you received earlier this summer, even if he's the one who had you followed, I doubt he'll continue to be a bother to us if he sees we've stopped trying to find out the truth behind Rob's disappearance. But if he does make contact—"

"I'll protect you from your parents," Laura said fiercely. "You'll never again be at their mercy. I know you've done a fine job of taking care of yourself all these years, but now that we've found one another, you have me to rely on."

"I don't want to be a burden on you, Laura. I—"

"You're not a burden. I choose to be here. You've chosen to let me stay while we travel this journey together. This relationship is mutual." Laura swallowed hard. "Isn't it?"

Arden opened her arms and Laura went to her. "It is. We're here for one another for the rest of our lives."

Laura had never felt happier.

Chapter 74

Deborah was poking around the shop on the hunt for a birthday present for the administrative assistant in her office. Phil exclusively read nonfiction, specifically histories of war, a topic about which Deborah admitted she knew next to nothing. "I know we won the war against the British back in the eighteenth century," she had told Arden earlier. "And I know that the Allies won World War Two and that all war is terrible. Beyond that . . ."

To make Deborah's search more difficult, she had no idea what books Phil already owned. Arden, who had sold so many tomes to Phil over the years she had lost track of their titles, suggested Deborah give her colleague a gift certificate, but Deborah was determined to make an effort.

While she fretted over biographies of Wellington and comprehensive surveys of the Vietnam War, Arden was silently suffering agonies of guilt—something she had been dealing with since telling Laura what she had witnessed in the gazebo that night back in June of 1985.

There was no doubt in Arden's mind that she should have stopped that man from completing his attack, but the thought—even in retrospect—of shy, dominated, beaten-down Victoria Aldridge having the nerve to shout, to scream, to pull on the arm of that disgusting man, to face the exposure that would follow, to have her story denied—as it would have been—or spun entirely out of recognition . . . It was impossible to fathom.

For all Arden knew, her mother might have been in the habit of having affairs with the husbands of her friends—with Herbert's colleagues. If you could call what had happened in the gazebo an affair. Those men might have known that Florence Aldridge could be taken advantage of when she had had a lot to drink. Having sex with a friend's wife behind his back was exactly the sort of power play that group would relish. Or, what Arden—what Victoria—had seen that evening might have been an isolated incident. Come morning, Florence probably wouldn't have remembered what had been done to her.

Which didn't change that she had been violated, and that her own daughter had let it happen. The whole thing was enough to make Arden feel sick to her stomach. She was still surprised that she had told Laura, her child, not only the horror she had witnessed that night, but also, more important, her failure to take action. Yet, Laura hadn't accused her mother of neglect, hadn't pointed a finger of blame, hadn't berated her for her lack of courage. Laura had accepted everything Arden had told her this summer with compassion and understanding.

Still, Arden thought, her daughter's generosity didn't erase that Victoria—that Arden—had walked away from her mother, a woman in distress. No one else must ever, ever know about that moral crime. The shame would be unbearable.

Deborah reemerged from the stacks, a frown on her face. "I give up. I'll get Phil a gift certificate after all. I mean, I don't even know which war is his favorite, if you can have a favorite war. Does he like the old ones better than the contemporary ones? Knights in battle armor or soldiers in tanks? Ugh."

Arden was glad that her friend had stopped by. Deborah's dilemma was a nice distraction from her own dark thoughts. "How much do you want to spend?" she asked, reaching below the counter for a new box of gift certificates.

Deborah shrugged. "Let's say twenty-five dollars. Oh, I love these," she exclaimed, taking up a suede-bound notebook from the spinner rack closest to the counter. "Especially this purple one. Too bad I only use my phone to keep track of my life."

"You could change that."

"I'm not so sure. Since going all keyboard and screen, my handwriting has really deteriorated. Every time I have to sign my name I panic. Hey, what's on your mind?" Deborah asked suddenly. "You look, I don't know, down or something. Are you still disappointed by the fact that the guy who worked for your father didn't have something more concrete to share?"

"No. I really didn't expect he would be able to help us."

"So, what then?"

Arden took a box cutter from a mug of pens and pencils—it was a new one; Brent had insisted they toss the old one that was always jamming—and sliced open the box of gift certificates. "It's just work stuff," she lied.

Deborah groaned. "Oh, come on, how long have we been friends?"

"Okay," Arden said after a moment. "I'll tell you what's on my mind." *If not all of what's there,* she added silently. "I've been thinking a lot about my mother. I've often felt bad for what my leaving home the way I did might have done to her already-fragile mental state. Remember I told you how she felt responsible for the death of her first child? Well, I can't help but wonder if she also felt responsible for my running off and suffered because of it."

"She *was* responsible for you leaving. At least partly."

"Yes, but I don't like to think that my actions punished her unduly."

Deborah was silent for a moment, her expression thoughtful. "Be honest," she said finally. "Wasn't there an element of revenge in leaving home like you did, without even a note? Or did you really believe that neither of your parents would care that you were gone?"

Arden put a hand to her head; she felt deeply troubled. "Honestly," she said after a moment, "I didn't run away to punish my parents, not consciously at least. I did it to save my sanity. I didn't give any thought at all to what my parents might feel when I was gone." Arden sighed. "But my running away must have had enormous emotional and psychological consequences for my parents. It had to have. It was totally selfish of me."

"Your act was one of self-preservation. There's a difference. Besides," Deborah went on matter-of-factly, "there's nothing you can do about it now. What's done is done. I don't mean to sound harsh, but it's not in the least bit productive to take on a load of guilt so long after the fact. And don't forget that you were provoked. I could go on if you need more reassurance."

Arden managed a smile and began to fill out Deborah's gift certificate. "Thanks. Enough about me. What's happening with the Coyne property?"

Deborah's face lit up. "There's been a turnaround! The deal is almost locked up. Almost. I don't want to jinx myself by getting too excited."

"We'll have to celebrate after the closing."

"Don't make assumptions!" Deborah scolded. "I'm superstitious!"

"Sorry." Arden passed the gift certificate across the counter for her friend to sign. "But I have a good feeling about this." Arden paused. "I don't know why I'm telling you this now, after the fact, but Gordon offered to loan me the money for the roof repair."

Deborah's eyes widened. "Whoa. And?"

"And I turned him down. I didn't want to complicate our relationship."

"Because your relationship is more than a friendship, or could be if you let it. Don't look so surprised. It's no secret."

"Yes." Arden was oddly glad that Laura wasn't the only one who had sensed Gordon's interest. "Do you think I did the right thing?"

"Don't ask me. With my relationship track record? As long as you feel good about your decision, that's all that counts. Anyway, Gordon's not the type to pout and feel all rejected. So, how *are* you going to pay for the roof repair? Has the loan been approved?"

"It has, but I haven't signed the papers yet."

"What are you waiting for? A big fat check to appear out of nowhere?"

"Of course not. I'll call the bank first thing Monday morning."

Deborah nodded. "Good. Hey, how about you, me, and Laura—and Gordon, if you want to ask him along—take a picnic out to Eliot's Field tomorrow evening. Take advantage of the warm weather while we can."

"That's a wonderful idea," Arden agreed enthusiastically. "I'll make crabmeat sandwiches. But let's keep it we three women."

"Greater freedom of conversation! I'll bake a dozen of my infamous chocolate cupcakes with caramel icing and we'll go wild."

"A dozen?" Arden asked, eyes wide. "For the three of us?"

"Yeah. Do you have a problem with that?"

Arden laughed. "Not at all!"

Chapter 75

Laura winced. Guilt was perhaps too strong a word to describe what she felt at the moment. Still, she had been neglectful. This text from her friend Sara confirmed that.

She had met Sara in graduate school. They were studying different disciplines—Sara's focus was art history, particularly American art of the nineteenth century—but they shared much else, such as a love of nachos (well, of anything with melted cheese) and an abhorrence of reality television.

Sara had been maid of honor at Laura's wedding. Soon after, she had left the East Coast for a teaching position in Oregon. That lasted for a little over three years before Sara missed her native soil and came home to Connecticut, where she met and married a man twenty years her senior, a renowned illustrator of children's books. Laura liked Oliver a lot. Jared had disliked Sara and had downright loathed Oliver.

Sara had been 100 percent supportive of Laura's desire to seek out her birth mother and had promised not to hound her with questions on her progress or lack thereof. But that promise had been made weeks and weeks ago. Laura didn't blame her friend for wanting to know what was going on.

I can't stand it any longer. What's been going on? Did you find your mother? Your father? When are you coming back? Are you coming back? This enquiring mind wants to know!

Laura, who was sitting on a bench outside Eliot's Corner's tiny library, briefly filled Sara in with a promise for the full story at another time. Sara's last two questions she left unanswered. Not that they weren't fair questions, just difficult ones to answer. When *would* she be ready to let go of the search for the truth of what had happened to her birth father? Maybe never, not entirely, but she couldn't stay on in Eliot's Corner forever, not with a career to revive. Laura considered herself a reasonable person. As much as she wanted to see a culprit—if one existed—brought to justice, she was not ready to abandon the possibility of a fulfilling future just to satisfy what some might call a grudge. Maybe if her mother hadn't recovered from the trauma she had endured and hadn't been able to make a good life for herself, Laura might feel more of a do-or-die attitude about her quest.

The better question to ask might be, When would she be ready to say farewell to the mother she had only just found? It wouldn't be a farewell forever, only a temporary goodbye. She and Arden would continue their relationship; hopefully, it would deepen over time and bring them joy and a sense of security as they grew old. But it would be a long-distance relationship, as were so many family relationships these days.

Dismissing the mood of melancholy that threatened to descend upon her, Laura got up from the bench and continued her amble through the town she had come to love this summer. From across Main Street, Ben and Marla Swenson waved, and Laura returned their greeting. She stopped to examine the display in the window of Re-Turned, the vintage-clothing boutique; Michael Brooks, the owner, had a knack for the whimsical, and this week's display featured a trio of teddy bears wearing vintage hats and costume jewelry while enjoying a tea party. A few minutes later, Laura ran into Jeanie Shardlake and Martha Benbow, coming out of Chez Claudine. Both women had been at the "Star-Crossed Lovers" event at Arden Forest. The three neighbors chatted pleasantly for a while and then took their leave.

Finally, Laura turned toward home. She was already fairly well known in Eliot's Corner, Arden Bell's daughter, who had miraculously returned from wherever she had been all those years to reunite with her mother. Laura had been accepted without prejudice, and while a few famous busybodies were no doubt still itching to know every gory detail of Arden and Laura's past, the majority of people in town seemed content (at least, on the surface) to let Laura Huntington and Arden Bell be.

Yes, she would be sorry to leave Eliot's Corner, this charming little town that in so many ways time seemed to have kindly forgotten. She would visit, but visiting wasn't the same as inhabiting, just as meeting on FaceTime or Zoom was a poor (but sometimes needed) substitute for meeting in the flesh.

Laura turned onto Juniper Road. Juniper End waited, just ahead. And there was Arden, standing in the tiny front garden, waving to her daughter. Laura hurried her pace and once again gave thanks to Cynthia Huntington, the woman who had made this miraculous development in Laura's life possible.

Chapter 76

The evening picnic in Eliot's Field had been a highlight of the summer for Arden. Her sandwiches had been a hit. She had eaten two of Deborah's decadent cupcakes, and Laura had scarfed three. The bottle of prosecco was gone not long after the three women had settled on Deborah's colorful picnic blanket. They hadn't seen another soul in the park, and by seven o'clock the breeze had taken on a slight hint of autumn, so that by the time Arden and Laura reached Juniper End they were pleasantly chilled.

It truly had been a perfect evening, Arden decided. As if by silent agreement, the conversation had remained light with almost no mention of Deborah's impending sale or Laura's search for the truth about what had become of her father, a brief respite from the woes and challenges of life.

"Gosh, I'm so bad at this," Laura muttered. It was the following day and mother and daughter were attempting to make headway with a puzzle Arden had found at a yard sale. "I haven't done a jigsaw puzzle since I was a kid, and I wasn't very good then."

Arden, who had an uncanny skill with jigsaws, smiled. "Relax. It's not a contest and you'll improve over time, I promise."

Laura didn't look convinced. "I'm surprised you can manage working on a puzzle with three cats leaping around." She eyed Prospero, who was standing at attention not far away.

"People say you can't train a cat. I've found the way to do just that with these three. If they leave the puzzle pieces alone, they get a bit of fresh ham when I'm done."

Laura smiled. "I congratulate you! Oh, wait! I got one!"

As Laura was placing a piece of the puzzle—an image of a flower-filled English garden—Arden became aware of a weak knock on the door of the cottage.

"Who could that be?" she said, rising from her chair.

"I got another one!" Laura cried, just as Arden opened the door.

The automatic smile of welcome and inquiry that had come to her face fell.

"Mother."

The woman nodded.

Physically, Florence Aldridge had deteriorated badly. She was noticeably frail, very thin, and her skin was slack and heavily lined. She looked almost clown-like, overly made-up, and wearing a big-shouldered cobalt-blue silk dress Arden remembered from the summer of 1985. It was, in fact, the dress Florence had worn at the party where Victoria had come across her drunken mother in the arms of a friend's husband. The dress hung off her. Around her neck was a thick gold chain, and on her earlobes were large gold disks, also vintage 1980s. Her hair was pure Joan Collins circa *Dallas*, but pathetically thin, with roots that were a dusty gray.

Arden continued to hold on to the edge of the door. She felt slightly sick to her stomach. It was as if her mother had been stuck in a time warp, as if she had stopped participating in the world outside her big house on the hill once her daughter had left Port George.

The large black car Arden remembered so well sat in the drive like a physical threat. Someone was behind the wheel. Arden could tell that it was a woman but not much more.

"May I come in?" Florence's voice was as weak as her knock had been.

Silently, Arden stepped back and gestured for her mother to enter. Arden had almost forgotten that Laura was there but now turned to her daughter. Laura stood abruptly, knocking over the glass of water from which she had been drinking. Water spread across the partially completed puzzle.

"Does Father know you're here?" Arden asked, looking back to her mother. Was Florence Aldridge in Eliot's Corner to plead on Herbert's behalf? To threaten Arden and Laura to give up their search for the truth, to keep their mouths shut?

"I came here on my own." Florence's eyes shifted to Laura. "I've followed your daughter's—progress—in the past weeks. It wasn't difficult to trace her to Eliot's Corner."

"Who drove you?" Arden asked. "Who is it in the car?"

"Clarice Brown. My companion. My friend." Florence's tone was almost defiant.

Laura had not yet said a word. Her expression seemed a terrible combination of shock and fury.

"So, why did you come here?" Arden asked.

Florence answered promptly, "To apologize."

Laura made a sound that was difficult to interpret. Was it impatience? Disbelief?

Arden took a deep breath, though it didn't help much in calming her, and finally closed the door behind her mother. Laura now came around the table, closer to the other women.

Florence touched her face with her bony right hand; it still wore the heavy diamond rings Arden remembered from long ago. "When I first learned that someone was asking around about what happened to young Rob Smith in the summer of 1984, I was—surprised. I hadn't thought of that summer in so many years. At first, when I tried to remember what had happened, I couldn't. It was all a blank."

Florence swallowed hard. Arden waited. She both did and did not want to hear what her mother would say next.

"You see," Florence went on, a bit pleadingly, "over the years I had largely succeeded in forgetting what I had done. When I did remember bits of that dreadful day, they seemed more like things I'd read in a book or seen in a movie, not something that had actually happened. But this time it was different. This time, I began to recover my memory. Slowly at first, just fragments, like bits of a dream remembered the morning after. Then, suddenly, it all came back."

"What all came back?" Arden demanded. "What are you saying?"

Florence didn't answer the question. "I began to be worried that—"

"That I would uncover the truth," Laura interrupted angrily. "So, you sent me those threatening letters."

Arden looked to her daughter in surprise. Letters? Had there been more than one?

"Yes," Florence said.

"What *did* happen that day?" Laura pressed. "What do you remember?"

Florence swallowed hard again. "Your father had bought me a gun, for protection when he wasn't around. I was always so frightened, you see. I had gotten used to carrying it with me in a silk pouch tied around my waist." Suddenly, eyes bright, she turned to Arden. "You remember that pouch, Victoria, don't you? It was blue, a peacock blue. It was made in Paris. I don't know what happened to that pouch. . . ."

Arden did recall the silk pouch. She hadn't known it had been used to carry a gun. "Mother, what happened that Sunday?" she demanded again.

Florence frowned. "Your young man came to the house to see you. You must not have heard the bell. Maybe you were asleep. You slept a lot in those days. So, Rob walked around the house. He found me on the patio. I didn't recognize him; I'd only ever glimpsed him as he worked on the pool with the others. He was a stranger to me."

"What happened next?" Arden urged, surprised her voice was so steady.

"He told me who he was and said he wouldn't leave until he had seen you and talked to you. He wanted to know that you were all right. He said he was worried because he hadn't heard from you in days."

"Why didn't you let him see your daughter?" Laura demanded. She took another step toward Florence. "Why did you continue to keep them apart?"

Florence startled and put her hand to her throat.

"Laura," Arden said sharply. "Go on, Mother. It's all right."

"Your father was out playing golf," Florence went on in that pleading tone of voice. "The staff all had the afternoon off. I was all alone. You have to understand! He was so young and strong. I told him he couldn't see you, that you weren't at home. He said he didn't believe me, and that's when he came toward me. I was frightened and I . . ." Florence shook her head before going on. "And then the gun was in my hand. I didn't mean to shoot. I didn't want to. I just wanted him to go away. I thought he was going to hurt me. And then he was on the ground. He was dead."

Arden couldn't speak. For so long she had so desperately wanted to believe that her mother was innocent of any wrongdoing. And all the while her beloved Rob was being threatened with a gun, she had been mere yards away, knowing nothing, oblivious of the danger.

"How could you be sure he was dead?" Laura demanded, her face dark with anger. "You might have saved his life if you'd tried, called 911, shouted, anything!"

Arden felt her heart break for her daughter, Rob's child. She wanted to go to her, offer comfort, but found that she couldn't move.

Florence didn't answer Laura's question. "I don't remember what happened next," she went on, almost wonderingly. "The next thing I remember is being in my bedroom and Herbert telling me that it was all taken care of, that everything was going to be all right. He brought me down for dinner. It was the three of us, like nothing bad had happened. I began to wonder if I had imagined it all, or if it had just been a bad dream."

"But it was all too real," Arden murmured.

"Your father and I never spoke of it again. I managed . . . I managed not to think about what had happened. Eventually, it all went away. Until you—Laura—showed up in Port George and started asking questions."

Laura literally snarled. "You killed my father."

"It was an accident. But no one would have believed me. I would have gone to jail."

"That shouldn't have mattered!" Laura cried. "You should have gone to the police immediately!"

Florence seemed to sink into herself. "I'm so sorry," she said, her voice high and thin. "Please, it's not as if I didn't care. I did. If it's any consolation, I knew in my heart the moment I saw you in Port George that you were my granddaughter."

Laura laughed wildly. "It's no consolation whatsoever. You threatened me in those letters! Your own flesh and blood."

"I was only trying to protect you," Florence pleaded. "You have to believe me."

"Protect her from whom? From my father?" Arden pressed.

Florence turned to her, and the look of shame in her eyes struck Arden like a blow to the heart. "From all of it. From the truth."

"You had me followed," Laura went on unmercifully. "Was it your friend, the one who drove you here today?"

"Yes. I just wanted to know that you were all right. I'm sorry if I frightened you."

Suddenly, Florence's face turned gray and she began to crumble. Arden darted forward and grabbed her mother by the shoulders. As she took the weight of the woman who had given birth to her, she felt a rush of what she could only describe as maternal instinct. The daughter had become the mother.

It was the way of the world.

Chapter 77

Laura stood absolutely still as her mother helped Florence into a chair and then dashed to the kitchen to fetch a glass of water. As Laura watched impassively, looking down at the bundle of bones that was her grandmother, she felt ill at the thought of having to touch this woman. The very idea was repulsive and Laura was ashamed of herself, but she knew she could not deny that strong reaction against her own flesh and blood.

"Why are you telling us everything now?" Laura demanded when Arden had returned and Florence had managed to take a few sips of water.

Florence sighed softly. "I'm tired, so very tired. I want to put an end to all this."

"You should be ashamed of yourself." Laura ignored the look of reproach her mother shot at her. Maybe she was being self-righteous. So be it.

"I am," Florence replied matter-of-factly, looking Laura directly in the eye. "I thoroughly despise myself. I have forever. Remembering that I was responsible for that young man's death only confirms that I was right all along. I'm despicable. I killed my own son through neglect, I forced my daughter to give up her baby, and I killed the father of her child."

"You didn't kill my brother," Arden said soothingly, "and it was Father who forced you to send me away."

"But she *did* kill my father," Laura retorted.

A pitiful wail broke from Florence then. "Poor Joseph," she cried. "But your father took care of everything. I didn't mean to shoot him. I loved the poor boy."

Suddenly, like a surprising rain shower on a sunny day, Laura's attitude toward her grandmother shifted. The woman was ill. She was sad and hopeless and old. She had endured much. She was to be pitied, not punished. Maybe once, but not now.

Arden gently put her hands on her mother's frail shoulders. "It's all right, Mother," she said softly. "You don't have to say anything else."

Florence shook her head. "Oh, but I do. A long time ago I became very good at not seeing what I couldn't stand to see, in not believing what I couldn't stand to believe. Ask your father. He knows what I am. Not that I asked to be this way. But I've always been too weak to be better."

Suddenly, Florence broke from her daughter's gentle hold and lurched from the chair. In spite of the pity Laura had felt for her grandmother only a moment earlier, Laura cried out and recoiled from the withered old woman. Florence Aldridge seemed like a macabre figure from an M. R. James ghost story, her eyes wild, her skin gray, her face a mask of crumpled linen.

"Mother!" Arden cried, dashing after Florence, who had torn open the front door of the cottage.

Laura forced herself to run after the two.

Clarice Brown was climbing out from the driver's seat of the old black Cadillac, her face drawn with worry. Laura recognized her at once as the woman who had been following her around Port George.

"Florence?" the woman called out, taking a step toward her friend.

Florence shoved hard at her companion, and the woman cried out as she fell heavily to the ground. With an ease that startled

Laura, Florence got into the driver's seat and started the engine of the big old Cadillac.

"She shouldn't be driving!" Clarice shouted. "She hasn't had a license in years. Stop her!"

But it was too late to make a grab for Florence. Instead, Laura dashed forward to where Arden knelt beside Florence's companion. Arden grabbed the woman under her arms and pulled her a safe distance from the car, which was now careening wildly in reverse. When it reached the paved street, it swung around, nearly flattening the mailbox, and tore off.

"Why didn't you stop her?" Clarice cried as Arden helped her to her feet. Her stockings were torn and her knees scraped, as were the palms of her hands. Otherwise, she seemed unhurt, if distraught.

Laura dug her phone from the pocket of her jeans and called 911. She had made a note of the Cadillac's license plate long ago, back when she had first seen the car in Port George. It was not a number she was likely to forget.

"What is your emergency?" the dispatcher asked briskly and dispassionately.

Laura opened her mouth and, for a moment, simply did not know where to begin.

Chapter 78

Clarice gave Arden the name of a friend in Port George who could fetch her. She refused to go to the local emergency care facility, though she silently accepted a warm wet cloth with which to wash away the worst of the dirt and bits of gravel that were sticking to her scraped knees, and she didn't protest Arden's assistance with affixing a bandage over the deepest of the scrapes.

After turning away an offer of something to eat or to drink, Clarice waited for her ride, sitting absolutely silently and motionless in a chair by the front window, her hands folded in her lap. Arden wondered what the woman was feeling. Anger at having been thrown to the ground by Florence? Worry for Florence's safety? Possibly a combination of both and certainly something more. Arden had no knowledge of the relationship between the two women, nothing that might enable her to hazard a better guess.

"Nothing yet from the police," Laura said, when Arden joined her at the table. Idly, Arden wondered if they would ever resume their puzzle. It didn't seem important now.

Arden took one of Laura's hands in her own. "I'm sorry. I'm sorry you were subjected to that . . ."

"That confession," Laura said quietly. "I'm not. It was awful, even terrifying, but I believe that Florence didn't mean to kill my father."

"I believe that, as well."

After that, Arden and Laura fell silent. Two interminable hours later Clarice's ride pulled into the drive. Clarice stood abruptly and Arden saw her wince in pain. With her knees slightly bent she began to walk toward the door of the cottage. Arden easily caught up with her, and with a hand on the woman's elbow, she guided her out to her friend's car. The friend did not introduce herself, but scowled as she helped Florence Aldridge's companion into the front passenger seat of the vehicle. Neither woman said a word of farewell.

Arden returned to the cottage and sank into a chair. "Something's become clear now. Remember Florence saying that my father brought her down to dinner the night she—only hours after she killed Rob? Until now I couldn't get the timing right in my head. I remember a night when she hardly touched her food but drank more heavily than usual. After about twenty minutes or so she stumbled upstairs to her room. That must have been the day Rob—died."

"I'm so sorry," Laura said feelingly.

"It was that night, after my mother had gone to her room, that my father told me he'd reserved a room at the Two Suns. He said it was a 'fine establishment' where I'd receive the best of care. He told me there would be minimal contact with the outside world and that he and my mother would not visit during my stay. It would be too upsetting for her, he said. He told me I'd be leaving Port George the following week. I just sat there, listening to his words, numb. . . ." Arden almost laughed at the awful absurdity of it all. "And all the while, Rob's body was somewhere on the property. . . . We don't know what happened to him before my father 'took care' of things, do we? He wouldn't have acted before nightfall."

Laura shook her head. "No, he wouldn't have. He would have hidden my father's body until he could safely . . . until he could safely get rid of it."

"And the very next morning Rob's family reported him missing. I didn't learn that until a few days later when my father told me that Rob had run off, left Port George and me behind. I didn't want to believe him, and because I didn't have access to the outside world, I didn't know what other people were saying had happened. For all I knew my father was lying to me and there had been a terrible accident and Rob was in the hospital, wondering why I didn't come to his side. It was so frustrating, the not knowing."

Laura shook her head. "And not having anyone to talk to."

"I didn't tell you this before now. I guess I've been embarrassed to admit the depth of my cowardice. After I'd told my parents that I was pregnant and before Rob's disappearance, I *did* try to reach out to him. Late one night I snuck down to my father's study where the only landline was kept, determined to call Rob at home, beg him to come and rescue me." Arden shook her head. "Oh, I don't know what I hoped would happen. I was such a child, so naïve. Anyway, I got only a step into the study when I heard a noise. I was sure someone was approaching. I panicked and fled back up to my room. I don't know, maybe I imagined the sound. It's possible. I was so afraid. It took so much courage to sneak out of my room in the first place, down the stairs, and into my father's study. I knew that if he found me wandering around the house in the middle of the night, he'd know I'd been trying to contact Rob."

Arden, who continued to hold her daughter's hand, looked for any shred of blame in Laura's eyes and, yet again, found none. It gave her the strength to carry on. "I feel such guilt for not having tried again. If I'd gotten through to Rob . . ." Arden took a calming breath. "Even if it turned out that was the last time I heard his voice, at least he'd have known I still loved him. To think he might have died assuming I didn't care . . ."

Laura shook her head. "No. I know he believed in your love."

"It's too late to know for sure," Arden said sadly. "If only I'd heard the doorbell that Sunday. If only, if only!"

Both women startled at a loud knock on the cottage door.

"I'll go." Slowly, Arden walked to the door and opened it to find two female police officers.

"Arden Bell?" the taller one asked.

"Yes." Arden felt Laura's hand slip into hers.

"I'm sorry to have to tell you that your mother, Florence Aldridge, is dead."

"How did it happen?" Arden asked steadily. She realized she had been expecting this news.

"It seems she lost control of her car, went off the road, and hit a tree. The initial finding is that she most likely died on impact. She wouldn't have suffered."

Arden nodded. "Thank you."

When the police officers had gone after what Arden supposed were standard proceedings when informing a family member of a death, mother and daughter settled in the living room. The cats, who had been absent since Florence's arrival, now returned and settled at Arden's feet as if to offer comfort.

"Are you okay?" Laura asked gently.

Suddenly Arden knew that she wasn't okay. She wasn't okay at all. "My mother . . . ," she began, but could go no further. Wracking sobs erupted from deep within her and she buried her face in her hands. Perhaps wisely, Laura said nothing but simply came to her and placed a hand on Arden's shoulder. The cats shifted closer, and through her terrible sorrow Arden could hear a calming purr.

After a time, Arden raised her head and gladly accepted the tissues her daughter offered. When she spoke, her voice was thick with emotion. "I loved her. For a long time, for all my childhood, I truly loved her. And now . . ."Arden sighed tremblingly. "Now she's gone and I realize that I love her still."

"I know," Laura said softly. "I'm so sorry. I truly am."

Arden raised her swollen eyes to her daughter. "She died not knowing that I forgive her. It's awful. I—"

"If she didn't know in—in that moment"—Laura took her mother's hand—"she knows now. She knows that you forgive her. I'm sure of it."

Laura returned to her seat and the two women sat in silence for some time. Arden felt her breathing return to an almost normal rhythm, and eventually, tears ceased to leak down her cheeks.

"I suppose," she said finally, "that an autopsy will determine if my mother suffered a medical incident that made her lose control of the car or if she . . ."

"Yes. I suppose it will."

"Remember what she said about being so tired, about wanting to put an end to it all. It's just too awful. My poor mother, so desperate, so despairing, all on her own—" Arden felt her throat constrict again and pressed a tissue to her eyes.

"Please," Laura begged. "Whatever happened this afternoon was not your fault. You must believe that. Please, for my sake if not for your own."

Arden nodded. "For your sake, I'll try. I promise I'll try."

Before Laura could respond, Falstaff, still at Arden's feet with his friends let out an ear-piercing yowl.

"My God!" Laura cried. "What was that about?"

"When life ends for one," Arden replied with a small smile, "it still goes on for others. Falstaff is simply reminding us that it's time for his dinner."

Chapter 79

The next morning, a Monday, Arden and Laura enjoyed a breakfast of strong coffee, scrambled eggs, and toast. The cats were remarkably restrained in their efforts at snatching bits of butter and egg.

Laura had slept remarkably soundly given the emotional chaos and shock of the previous day. No doubt the double shot of brandy she had taken after dinner had helped. Maybe it was also the reason she forgot to remind her mother to call the bank that morning to make an appointment to sign the loan papers.

When the breakfast things had been cleared away, Arden turned to Laura. "You said letters, plural, when my mother was here. You said she sent you letters."

"Yes. I'm sorry. There was another one after the first. I didn't tell you because I didn't want to worry you even more than you already were worrying. I did show it to Ted though, and he agreed with my feeling that the writer might not be trying to threaten me but to protect me. And I guess in a way we were right."

"Yes, you were."

When her mother had gone off to her bedroom to get dressed, Laura found herself thinking again about what Florence had said that day before, about wanting to put an end to it all. After so many years of being passive, of being protected and told what to do and to say and to think, the idea of Florence Aldridge finally making a decision of her own was, in a way, remarkable. But suicide was sad and horrible. It was born of despair, not of confidence. Florence could not be admired for taking her own life, if that's what she had done, but she could be pitied. A guilty conscience had eaten away at her reason.

Laura's cell phone chirped. "It's Ted," she said to Arden, who had just returned.

Arden nodded; her mouth tensed.

"Hi," Laura said, bracing for whatever news her mother's old friend had to impart.

"I just got off the phone with the chief of police," Ted said without preamble. "Herbert Aldridge voluntarily admitted to the police that he paid someone to bury Rob's body, his bicycle, and the gun used to kill him. His wife's gun. And he confessed to having bribed the chief of police and a few other bigwigs to cut short the investigation into Rob's disappearance."

Laura swallowed hard. "My father . . . Where is he?"

"Rob's body is . . . It's at the bottom of what was once the swimming pool. I'm so sorry, Laura."

Laura's head began to whirl. She recalled what Steve Penn had said about hearing noises on the Aldridge property that long-ago Sunday evening. She turned away from Arden and lowered her voice, though she knew that in a few moments she would have to share this news. It was, in a way, what they had been hoping to hear, but it was dreadful all the same. "There'll be an—" What was the right word? An excavation? An exhumation?

"Yes," Ted confirmed. "It's being arranged. I'll let you know when as soon as I find out."

"Ted? Did Herbert reveal the name of the person he paid to—"

"Yes. It was Jake Barber, but Herbert swears he had nothing to do with Jake's death the following year. Anyway, I'll let James know later today. I don't know if it will bring him any peace or not."

"Thanks, Ted," Laura said. "For everything. You've been very kind to my mother and me."

"I'm sorry, Laura. I wish this whole thing had turned out differently. I wish that . . ."

Laura swallowed a lump in her throat. "That's all right," she whispered before ending the call.

Laura turned to face her mother. Arden was standing perfectly still. Her stance was almost unnerving, a perfect contrast to the picture of frantic determination Florence had been as she ran from the cottage to her death.

"You might want to sit down."

"What is it?" Arden said firmly. "Just tell me."

Laura did. Arden reached behind her for the arm of a chair, and Laura dashed forward to help her mother sink into it.

"Can I get you some water?"

Arden shook her head. "Will there be—"

"Yes. Ted will let us know when."

"I want to be there," Arden said fiercely. "I need to be there."

"We'll talk about that later," Laura said soothingly. "Just rest now. You've had a shock. We both have." Laura moved away from Arden's chair and sank into one of her own.

"Those weeks after I came back from Two Suns," Arden said in a tone of weary disbelief, "I was living only yards away from the body of the man I loved. It's too macabre."

That was one way to put it, Laura thought. "And it's probably the reason why your parents never moved. New owners might have had the idea of digging up the yard to lay a foundation for a new structure. And then the ugly truth would be known."

Arden simply nodded.

How, Laura wondered, how had Herbert and Florence Aldridge ever squared their consciences living so close to the body of the young man they had killed? Because essentially, at least in Laura's mind, both had pulled the trigger of that little mother-of-pearl-handled gun. Both were culpable.

But in the end, Florence's conscience had gotten the better of her. Had Herbert's, too? Had the desire for genuine confession and absolution been the real reason for his speaking up now?

"I can't believe my father confessed," Arden admitted, as if reading Laura's mind. "After all these years. His reputation, what might be left of it, is completely shattered now. Everything that mattered to him—status, influence, power—all gone."

"You've said that your mother mattered to him."

"Yes," said Arden thoughtfully. "She did. Maybe that's why he finally dropped the charade. Without his wife, he has nothing left to live for."

"You've always said that your parents were in love." Or, Laura added silently, codependent. But was there much difference in the end? And did it matter? Life was difficult. People got through the best they could.

"Do you remember," Laura went on, "that earlier this summer I said quite firmly that I would never forgive the person who hurt my father? But now . . ." Laura paused, momentarily choked with emotion. "Now that I know it was Florence, that deeply sad and troubled woman, well, I think that like you, I *can* forgive her."

Her mother smiled. "I'm glad. Truly. I'm not saying she should be absolved of all responsibility for her actions, just that she needs understanding."

"You know, we should tell the Smiths about me—and about you—as soon as possible," Laura said after a moment. "Before they hear the truth via the Port George grapevine."

"Yes. I wonder if they've already heard that my family is to blame for Rob's death?"

"Even if they have heard, they probably haven't heard that Rob's child is alive and well. That news needs to come from us."

"Gosh, I'm nervous," Arden said with a shaky laugh.

"Me, too. But there's no time like the present. I've got Frannie's number in my notebook." While Laura looked up her aunt's phone number, her mother sat with her hands folded in her lap.

"Hello," Laura said, when a woman's voice answered her call. "Is this Frannie Armitage? . . . This is Laura Huntington. We spoke recently about research I was doing for a podcast. . . . Thanks, I'm fine. Look, I have something very important to tell you. Are you alone? It might be best if someone is there with you, your husband maybe or one of your children."

After a moment, Laura nodded. "Good," she said, her heart beating so loudly she could hardly hear her own voice. "I'm glad Mr. Armitage is there. My name really is Laura Huntington. But I haven't been in Port George researching a podcast. The truth is that I was trying to find out what had happened to my father back in August of 1984. You see, Frannie, I'm your niece. Your brother, Rob, is my father. And I'm here in Eliot's Corner with my mother. Victoria Aldridge. May I put you on speakerphone?"

Chapter 80

Spring 1984

Victoria had no specific reason for being in the Port George Public Library that afternoon. She had almost finished writing her end-of-term papers, and only a few days before she had checked out two novels she had been eager to read, both by contemporary writers. But even on a warm and sunny day in May, when the majority of people might prefer to lounge on a grassy lawn, Victoria Aldridge was drawn to wander through the stacks, reading titles, opening certain volumes, exploring sections she had been ignoring during the school year, planning future studies.

She found herself regarding works concerning the geological history of the earth. Why not? She reached for a copy of Charles Lyell's *Principles of Geology*, and suddenly—a tectonic shift?—found herself jostled roughly.

"I'm so sorry!" Victoria cried, automatically taking the blame for someone else's clumsiness. Only then did she look to see who had crashed into her, dropping several chunky books at her feet.

"It's not your fault," the young man said hurriedly. "I'm the one who came barreling around the corner. Are you okay? I'm really sorry."

The look of genuine contrition on the young man's face caused Victoria to blush. "I'm fine." She crouched to help him gather his books, and a moment later the young man's arms were once again full.

"Thanks. Excuse me, but aren't you Victoria Aldridge?"

Victoria nodded. "Yes. How did you—"

"Everyone knows the Aldridge family." The young man smiled.

"And you're Robert Smith. "I—Someone pointed you out to me once."

That was true. She and a classmate had gone into town after school one afternoon for an ice cream at the North Star. "See that guy?" Maggie had whispered just as the girls were about to enter the diner. "The one getting out of that green car? Isn't he gorgeous?"

Victoria had only nodded. The guy truly was gorgeous, and so far in her life, Victoria hadn't been particularly impressed by the looks of any guy in Port George.

"That's Rob Smith," Maggie had gone on. "He's supposed to be super-nice, too. Everyone wants to go out with him, but from what I heard he's really picky. He's only had, like, one girlfriend and that was a few years ago."

Before the girls could ogle any longer, Rob Smith was gone. Victoria hadn't given him much thought after that first sighting. Why should she? She wasn't often in town, and since she had never seen Rob Smith before, it wasn't likely she would ever see him again.

But now, standing just a few feet from this super-nice, gorgeous guy, Victoria wondered how she had ever forgotten him, even for a moment.

Rob was smiling. His eyes were soulfully dark. "That's me, but you can call me Rob."

Victoria's grip on the shoulder strap of her pocketbook tightened. "Okay. So, what are you doing here? Well, obviously . . ." She laughed nervously and nodded toward Rob's armload of books.

"I'm enrolled at the community college. I need these for a final paper. I'm taking this class on the history of psychology. It's fascinating. I mean, even though people started thinking about the mind and behavior and all that stuff in ancient times, psychology didn't come around as a separate science until the late nineteenth century. That's, like, yesterday in terms of time."

"The class sounds really interesting," Victoria said earnestly.

"I think so. A lot more interesting than what I'll be doing this summer, which is working for a construction company." Rob dipped his head a bit before going on. "We, ah, I think we're going to be at your place, actually. Your parents are putting in a pool, aren't they?"

"Yes, but I don't know why they want one." Victoria half laughed nervously. "Neither of them swims and I prefer the ocean."

Rob smiled and shrugged. "Maybe it's the hot thing to have these days, the way to impress the neighbors." Then his eyes widened. "I didn't mean—"

"That's okay. It probably is the reason we're getting a pool, to impress the neighbors, though why anyone would care is beyond me."

In a moment of awkward silence Victoria gazed at Rob and he gazed at her. She had never before found herself in a situation like this, so close to a guy, face-to-face. . . .

"So, you go to Wilder Academy?" Rob asked suddenly. "I mean, your uniform . . ."

Nervously Victoria touched her white uniform blouse. "Yes. I'm a senior. I'll be going to Blake College in September. It's in Massachusetts."

Rob nodded. "Right. I'll still be here in Port George. Not that it matters. I mean it doesn't matter to you, it matters to me, of course." Rob shrugged and laughed. "Sorry. I'm babbling."

Victoria smiled and felt her heart flip. "So, what else are you studying besides psychology?"

"Well, right now I'm mostly taking basic courses, you know, core requirements. But when—if—I transfer after two years to a four-year school, then I'd like to major in economics."

"What do you mean if you transfer?"

"Well, if I can afford to continue," Rob said easily. "We'll see what kind of financial aid I can get, maybe a scholarship if I'm lucky. My parents aren't in a position to help, you see." Rob smiled. "My sister Frannie thinks I'm nuts wanting a college degree. Mom and Dad have done okay without one, but I don't know. I'm one of those oddballs who actually likes school."

Victoria smiled. "I'm one of those oddballs, too."

"I guess oddballs need to stick together."

Victoria's smile widened. She felt a strong urge to put out her hand to shake, one oddball with another, anything to be able to touch this person. But before she could act on that wild idea, a discreet cough caused her to turn her head. A woman about her mother's age was looking directly at Victoria and Rob. Before Victoria could determine if she recognized her, the woman looked away.

Everyone knows the Aldridge family.

Victoria's stomach tensed. She was doing nothing wrong. It was not a crime to chat with someone in a public place. Still, she felt guilty. Her parents would not be happy about her spending time with a young man who would soon be working as a laborer on their property.

"I've got to go," she said suddenly. "I mean, I'm expected—"

Rob nodded. "Okay. It was nice to meet you. Guess I'll see you around. I mean, here, in the library. I'm kind of here a lot. I'm surprised I haven't run into you before." Rob winced. "Not that I intend to literally run into you again."

"I know. I mean, sure. I'll see you. Bye."

All curiosity about geology abandoned, Victoria hurried toward the stairs that led down to the ground floor. Her mind was in a whirl. She hoped she hadn't insulted him by hurrying off, because he was as awesome as Maggie had said he was. And imagine, he would be working at her house that summer. Well, not at the house exactly, but on the property. Not that she could have anything to do with a work crew. She couldn't exactly hang around watching for him. . . .

At the top of the stairs, Victoria stopped and looked over her shoulder. Rob was still where she had left him. He smiled, and after juggling the stack of books to free one of his hands, he waved. Victoria smiled and waved in return. As she fairly bounced down the stairs, she vowed to find an excuse—it wouldn't be difficult— to visit the library again tomorrow.

Let everyone know the Aldridge family, she thought. To heck with them!

Chapter 81

Arden hadn't slept much the night before; she doubted that Laura had either. Both were sporting bags under their eyes. Neither had been able to stomach breakfast, other than a cup of coffee. Arden was glad that Laura had volunteered to drive. She doubted she could stay alert enough not to—Arden squirmed. She had almost thought, Not to drive them into a tree.

The morning was dismal. Gloomy. Chilly. An appropriate day, Arden thought, for the somber and solemn task at hand. If the sun had been shining, the air warm and scented with the sea, it would have seemed a mockery of what they were setting out to achieve. The recovery of a loved one.

At eight o'clock, they left Juniper End and Eliot's Corner for the journey to Port George. "Music?"

Arden shook her head. "Do you mind silence?"

"Not at all."

The drive was both endless and over in a moment. By the time they entered Port George, Arden was feeling greatly unsettled. She hadn't set foot in the town since the day she had run away and had never thought she would be doing so again, especially under such odd and dreadful circumstances.

At the foot of the long drive leading to the Aldridge house on

Old Orchard Hill, a group of locals was gathered. They had a pent-up energy about them that further upset Arden.

"Eager for a glimpse of something macabre," Laura said darkly. "Like a body."

"Or for a glimpse of us. The long-lost daughter and grand-daughter."

"Don't make eye contact." Laura steered the car past a police officer charged with keeping the curious from further invading the property.

Arden sighed. "I think I recognized a few of the bunch. Some faces don't change."

Laura was directed to park in a makeshift lot, alongside two police cars, an ambulance, and a few noncommercial vehicles.

"Ready?" Laura asked, turning to Arden, whose expression was set and grim.

Arden nodded.

When they got out of the car, another police officer directed them to a cordoned-off section at the back of the house, a good way from the paved area that had once been the site of the pool. Work had already begun. A large digger of some sort, helmed by a man in a hard hat, was loudly scraping and lifting away layers of concrete and soil. Arden wished she had brought a pair of earplugs. It hadn't occurred to her that this—process—would be so noisy.

Almost more disturbing to Arden than the terrible noise was the presence of the house in which she had spent the first eighteen years of her life. It had seen so little happiness since the Aldridge family had moved in. She almost felt sorry for it. One day, hopefully, laughter would ring through its many rooms and real love would reanimate the pile of stone, brick, and wood. One day, hopefully, the house would be a home.

Arden sighed and instinctively shrank into her rain jacket. "I haven't been back here in over thirty-five years. A lifetime ago."

"It must feel very strange," Laura said quietly.

"It does. In some ways, I hardly recognize the house. It feels foreign. Alien."

"Probably a good thing."

The weather was growing worse. The skies were a dull gray, and a harsh chill in the late-summer air hinted at the long winter to come. A drizzle began, adding to the gloom into which those gathered were already sunk.

Arden pulled her rain jacket more tightly around her and shivered. Maybe, she thought, she shouldn't have come here after all. It wasn't too late to go back to the car and wait for news. She wished that Laura hadn't decided to be present; Arden prayed that if Rob's remains were found here today, Laura would not catch even the tiniest glimpse of shredded cloth or—or of anything else. But Laura was standing tall, her expression unwavering. If her daughter could stand the strain of this moment, Arden thought, then she, too, would be strong.

"Frannie is here," Laura whispered. "To our right."

Arden briefly glanced in the direction Laura had indicated. Yes, that was Frannie. She was heavier now, and her hair, what Arden could see of it under her rain hat, was, as Laura had mentioned, entirely gray. Her face was, also as Laura had told her, greatly lined. Maybe the lines had been etched there by grief.

Though Frannie would have recognized Laura and therefore known that the woman standing with her was Arden—Victoria— she didn't seem interested in making any contact. Arden understood. There was time for reconciliation later. Once . . . Once they knew for sure.

Arden looked back at the small team at work on this somber project. She wondered if the man operating the big digging machine, or the ones charged with descending into the ever-widening and deepening pit, had ever worked on such a job before. Were they frightened of what they might unearth? Would they feel disgust or repulsion if Rob's badly deteriorated body was indeed discovered? The thought saddened her.

Suddenly, something, a feeling, made Arden look around at the house. She wished she hadn't. Quickly she turned back to the scene of work before her. She had seen an old man standing behind a curtained window in what Arden remembered had been a pantry. The old man was watching. He was Herbert Aldridge. How much he could see from his vantage point Arden didn't know. Had he recognized his daughter? Why did he feel the need to witness this moment? What was going through his head as he waited for the body of the man his wife had killed to be recovered, for the body of the man he had had so ignobly buried to be found? Was he distraught, grief-stricken, overcome with guilt? Defiant? Exhausted? Maybe all of those things.

After what might have been an hour or a moment, Laura grabbed her mother's hand. "They found something," she whispered.

"It's a bicycle," Arden said in a choked voice, as a dirt-encrusted metal object was lifted from the earth. The bicycle looked so pathetic, like a creature that had once been as alive as its owner. If Rob's bike—and who else's bike could it be?—had been found, then it was a sure bet that . . .

Arden glanced quickly toward Frannie Armitage. The woman was as still as a statue; a man Arden assumed was her husband tightened his arm protectively around her shoulders.

The men continued to work, while the silence of the people gathered to witness the moment deepened. Then, one of the men in the pit of churned earth and stone called to a man who stood on the edge of the raw cavity. Arden assumed he was the foreman.

"I can't make out what he said," Laura whispered. "Did you hear?"

Arden shook her head. She watched as the foreman gestured to a man in a dark suit to join him, and suddenly she knew. "They found him," she murmured. "They found Rob."

Laura let out a small cry and put her hand over her mouth.

After speaking quietly to the foreman, the man in the dark suit approached Frannie and her husband with an air of respect and formality. Immediately Frannie's knees began to buckle and both her husband and the official helped her away from the scene.

"Remember that old expression?" Arden said, her voice oddly calm in spite of her agitation. " 'Truth is the daughter of time.' "

"Yes. And thanks to the passing of time, the truth is finally out."

"Arden?"

Arden turned. "Ted," she breathed. "I didn't know you would be here."

Ted Coldwell had aged well. He had been a handsome young man; now he was a handsome and distinguished-looking man of about sixty. He was dressed for the weather and the occasion in a classic tan trench coat over a suit and tie. His sturdy dress shoes were of the kind no professional businessman in New England was without.

He took the hand Arden offered him in both of his and smiled. In his warm brown eyes, Arden saw the native kindness she remembered so well.

"I know we spoke briefly on the phone just the other day," Ted said, "but I still feel surprised—very pleasantly surprised—to see you in the flesh. I'm just sorry our reunion is taking place at such an emotionally difficult moment."

Arden hastily wiped a tear from her cheek. "I'm so sorry, Ted, that I ever thought you had something to do with Rob's disappearance. I must have been temporarily mad."

"No, just grief-stricken. And no apology is necessary. Please accept my deepest condolences on the death of your—"

"He was my fiancé," Arden said proudly.

"I can't thank you enough for all you've done for us," Laura added.

Ted shook his head. "I hardly did anything. It was Laura who spearheaded the search for the truth. Honestly, I wish I could have done more, and a long time ago."

"Like you said, no apology is necessary," Arden replied with a wobbly smile.

When Ted had moved off, promising to be in touch soon, Laura, who until that moment had remained remarkably in control of her emotions, finally broke down in sobs.

Arden put her arms around her child, Rob's child, and whispered. "It's all right. It's finally going to be all right."

Chapter 82

Laura's breathing was slowly returning to a normal rhythm. It was both what she had wanted and what she had dreaded. The recovery of her father. Well, of his earthly remains. His spirit, Laura was sure, lived on in the people who still loved him.

But for a brief moment when she and her mother had first arrived at the Aldridge estate, seeing that group of nosy locals eager for a thrill, Laura had doubted yet again the wisdom of her quest for the truth about her father's disappearance. What pain had she wrought by opening old wounds and poking at old sorrows? What tangible good would any of this do Rob's family, his parents and siblings, the woman who had agreed to be his wife, his child?

Now that her father's body had been recovered, Laura knew for sure that she had done the right thing in pursuing the truth. Every person deserved a respectful send-off, a kind and careful farewell to the vessel that had provided a home for his or her soul here on earth. Now, finally, nearly forty years after he had been so unceremoniously put in the ground, Robert Smith would get the burial he deserved.

"I'm okay now," Laura said, assuring her mother with a watery smile. "Let's check in at the bed-and-breakfast."

Before her mother could reply, some strange impulse made

Laura turn toward the house. She wished she hadn't. An old man was standing half-concealed behind a curtain in a room on the ground floor. Her heart began to beat madly and she felt blood rush to her cheeks.

Herbert Aldridge.

"He's been there the whole time," Arden said. "I saw him earlier. Watching."

"Come on," Laura said firmly. "We're leaving this place. Now." *And I,* she vowed, *am never coming back here again.*

Chapter 83

Not two hours after the women, emotionally exhausted, had gotten to the Lilac Inn, Herbert Aldridge's attorney was on the phone. Mr. Aldridge, he told Arden, requested a meeting with his daughter.

"He would like it if you could come to the house," Bill O'Connell went on, "but if that's not possible, he's willing to meet you here, at my office."

Arden, who had been on the point of telling Mr. O'Connell that she would prefer to meet her father at the lawyer's office, surprised herself by saying that she would meet Herbert at his home. A time was arranged for the next day.

Laura was not happy. "He doesn't deserve any courtesy from you," she stated firmly. "And do you really think he's going to apologize? People like Herbert Aldridge never apologize. They never admit they've done anything wrong."

There was more in the same vein, all of it understandable, but Arden's mind was made up. She had to confront her father face-to-face, in spite of her fears and misgivings. And there were many. But she reminded herself—forcefully—that she was well beyond the grasp of her father. He could do nothing to her now that would hurt her more than what he had done to her when she was a teenager.

Arden Bell was in charge of her life in a way young Victoria Aldridge had never been.

Arden arrived at the house on Old Orchard Hill promptly at eleven o'clock. There had been no curious crowd to hinder her progress up the long drive, and by parking outside the house, she was able to avoid even a glimpse of that awful gaping hole out back.

Mr. O'Connell opened the door to her. He was a short, rather chubby man, with a boyish, unlined face that contrasted wildly with his shock of white hair. His suit fit him beautifully. He shook her hand and said he would wait for Arden in the living room.

When he had gone off, Arden took a deep breath and glanced around the front hall. It looked exactly the same as she remembered it with one glaring exception. The portraits of Joseph were gone. On the wall were faint outlines of where they had once hung, but those imagined faces were no longer looking down at her. Maybe now, Arden thought, her brother could finally rest in peace.

She straightened her shoulders—her parents had been sticklers about good posture—and knocked on the door to the study.

"Come in."

She hadn't heard that voice in decades, the voice she would never forget. Arden knew that she could turn around and leave, tell Bill O'Connell she had decided not to meet with her father at any time or in any place. But she wouldn't run away. Not again.

Arden opened the door to the study and stepped inside.

And there stood her father.

Up close, he looked even more deteriorated than he had seemed through the window of the pantry the day before. His once vivid blue eyes were dull; his formerly thick mane of hair was pitifully thin; his famed broad shoulders were fallen forward. Try as he might to rule and command every aspect of his world, Herbert Aldridge had not managed to ward off the ravages of time. He had proved human after all.

Unlike its master, Herbert's study had not changed in any major way since the last time Arden had been within its four walls. It was still a decidedly old-fashioned masculine space, like something you would find in a gentlemen's club in London, with built-in bookshelves lining three of the walls; an oversized, tufted brown leather couch; a center rug in dark colors; a globe on a brass stand. Even the old black rotary phone was still in place on the desk, the phone with which Arden had attempted to make that one call to Rob's home so many years ago.

Father and daughter did not shake hands or even attempt to.

"Would you like to take a seat?" Herbert gestured to the guest chair in front of his desk.

Arden sat. Herbert remained standing at the side of the desk.

"The portraits. They're gone."

Her father nodded. "Yes. I had them taken down yesterday. With your mother no longer here, I was glad to see them go."

"You had them destroyed?" Somehow Arden already knew the answer to her question.

A look of pain passed over her father's face before he said simply, "Yes."

For the first time in her life Arden realized that those imaginary paintings, those fantasies of what might have been, had caused her father real torment. Perhaps he had not only tolerated them as one of his wife's pathetic attempts to pretend that life had not been cruel to her firstborn; perhaps he had also been tormented by them.

But now was not the time to start feeling sorry for Herbert Aldridge.

"Why did you want to see me?"

Her father didn't immediately answer her question. Arden was not surprised. Herbert Aldridge had always done things in his own good time.

"I knew that the woman asking questions around town was your daughter," he said at last. "I could see the resemblance immediately. To you. And to Rob Smith. And I guessed that if your child was in Port George, then there was a good chance she had found you, or, at least, that she had discovered the identity of her birth mother. I realized there must have been a leak in the adoption process. 'Well,' I thought, 'no plan is foolproof forever.'"

Arden took her time in responding. She wasn't sure she believed that he had known Laura's identity immediately. Her mother, yes. Her father? "So," she said finally, "you guessed that I might be alive."

"I've always known you were alive."

Again, so long used to mistrusting this man, Arden wasn't sure she believed him. "How? Were you having me watched all these years?"

Herbert allowed the tiniest evidence of a smile, gone as quickly as it had appeared. "No. I just knew. And when your daughter turned up, I thought, 'Now maybe I will see her again.' *My* daughter." Herbert cleared his throat. "Your mother hadn't been well for a long time. She'd grown increasingly confused and disoriented. I wrongly assumed that she was too ill to be aware of what was happening in Port George, to know that someone had returned looking for the truth. As for myself, I felt oddly resigned about what might be revealed in the end. 'Let them find me,' I thought. 'Florence has been punished all along. I'm the one who now deserves punishment for all I've done.' So, I let your daughter pursue her quest and put no obstacles in her way."

"Did you know that Mother sent two threatening notes to Laura? She was trying to get her to stop asking questions. She was trying to protect Laura from the truth."

Herbert blanched. "I had no idea." His voice was momentarily shaky. "I swear."

"Mrs. Brown, her assistant or companion or whatever she was, helped Mother by writing the notes in her own hand and then by mailing them. She also followed Laura, keeping Mother informed of who Laura spoke to and of where she went."

"Clarice Brown has quit," Herbert said quickly. "The very evening of the day she drove your mother to Eliot's Corner. She was in fact a paid companion; she had nursing experience. Her résumé and references were solid. I couldn't have known she would aid your mother in such a misguided enterprise."

A misguided enterprise? Nothing, Arden thought, like the misguided enterprise her father had undertaken in August 1984. "I know you confessed to convincing people in charge to put a premature halt to the search for Rob."

"Yes. I did."

"It was wrong."

Herbert Aldridge didn't answer that charge.

"I never changed my will," he said abruptly. "You are and always were the sole heir to my estate. To ours, your mother's and mine."

Finally, Arden thought. *We get to the reason for this command performance.* "Why?" She laughed in disbelief. "Why are you leaving everything to me after all that happened? I ran away from you. I'm sure that sent a pretty clear message that I was done with being an Aldridge."

Herbert walked around his desk and gripped the back of the big chair as if for support. "Because you're my rightful heir," he said forcefully. "My child." He paused and a look of despair darted across his face, gone as quickly as it had come. "I think you should know that your mother left your room exactly as it was at the time of your—departure. She insisted nothing be changed. She kept the room clean herself. It's all there, your clothes, furniture, books. Just as you left them."

Arden felt tears prick at her eyes, but she commanded them to stay away. She would not cry in front of her father, even with this moving evidence that her mother had cared, had perhaps always hoped, deep down, beyond the reach of her dubious denial mechanisms, that her daughter would return.

"I see," Arden said after a moment.

"In addition to what will come to you after my death—the house, the land, everything—I want you to have this."

Her father opened the top drawer of his desk and withdrew what was clearly a check. He placed it on the far edge of the desk, facing Arden. "This is to help you and Laura now, before . . . before I die and probate is settled."

Arden leaned forward to pick up the check. Twenty-five thousand dollars.

"Where were you when I was young and entirely on my own," she said with a bitter laugh, "frightened and desperate? Why couldn't you have helped me back then?"

Herbert cleared his throat. "Please, take my help now. I hear you have your own business. An independent bookstore. It can't be easy in this day and age."

Arden thought she heard a note of pride in her father's voice—his daughter, a successful businessperson—but maybe that was wishful thinking. The money wouldn't make up for all Arden had suffered, but it could help now in a practical way. And she would sell the big old house in Port George as soon as her father was gone. That, too, would provide financial security for herself and her daughter.

Arden looked at the man who, along with her mother, had given her life, and in that moment she felt genuine pity for him. All that money and power and what was he left with at the end of his life?

Not much.

"Thank you. I will accept this check. As for the estate, that, too, I will accept." It was, Arden thought, her due.

Herbert nodded. "Thank you. Mr. O'Connell will handle everything for you. He's a good man." Herbert smiled. "The first honest lawyer I've ever hired."

Arden couldn't return her father's smile. She doubted he was a thoroughly changed man. Still, any effort toward honesty and transparency was a good thing.

"I suppose it's pointless to ask to meet my granddaughter?"

"Laura has made it clear that she has no interest in knowing you." For a moment, Arden considered adding, *I'm sorry.* But she didn't.

"That's all right. To be honest I'm not sure I could bear to look her in the eye and see . . . Did you hate your mother and me so much you had to change your name to distance yourself from us?"

"I didn't hate you," Arden said honestly. "I don't hate you. But I was scared of you, Father. I wanted to leave it all behind. I knew I would never forget what had happened to me, but I thought that if I could start over in new surroundings, I might be able to live each day without—reminders."

Herbert nodded. "I understand," he said quietly.

Arden wondered if he did. Did it matter at this point? Not to her.

"I'm sorry the boy died," Herbert said suddenly. "Very sorry. But I'm not sorry I kept your mother's name out of it all."

Arden shook her head sadly. "You didn't do her any favors in the end. You didn't help her to get well by keeping her crime a secret."

"It was too late by then for her to change."

"That wasn't your decision to make," Arden said, her voice rising in anger.

For a brief moment, the bright blue eyes that Arden remembered so well seemed to spark to powerful life again. "Wasn't it?" her father said forcefully. "I knew her better than anyone did, better even than she knew herself. I knew what she was and was not capable of enduring. And I did what I had to do to keep her reasonably content. I loved your mother. No one can say otherwise."

"I believe you," Arden said after a moment. "Father? Do you believe she drove into that tree deliberately after confessing her crime to me?"

Suddenly, the life that had sparked in Herbert Aldridge's eyes went out. Arden almost regretted she had asked the question; she was not here to torture her father. She remembered the conversations she had had with Laura about the nature of Herbert and Florence's relationship. It had been a loving relationship. Had it also been a codependent one? Abusive? Had it been all three? And what did any of it matter to anyone but Florence and Herbert?

"In the beginning," Arden's father went on, ignoring her last question, "I convinced your mother that we shouldn't go after you. I convinced her that you had probably gone on to Blake College and would be just fine. It wasn't difficult. You mother loved you, but she was so ready to believe a bright and shiny story, rather than have to deal with the ugly reality. It wasn't long before she began to paint elaborate scenarios of your life outside of Port George." Herbert Aldridge swallowed hard. "Thankfully, she spoke of them only to me. From the day you left home, her life outside this house virtually ceased."

Arden sat perfectly still, though that uncomfortable feeling of guilt regarding her conduct toward her mother was once again making itself known. Perhaps neither Herbert nor Victoria Aldridge had done the right thing by Florence. But what was done was done, no matter how unfair it had been to all of them.

"After a few years, I was tempted to look for you," Herbert went on after clearing his throat. "But I didn't. To be honest, I had no idea what I might say to you if I found you. How could I explain what I'd done? What your mother had done?"

Again, Arden received this information in silence. Strangely, she believed that her father *had* been tempted to locate her, maybe even to ask her to come home. But she was not surprised to learn that he had conquered that temptation.

"Before you go, I have one more thing to give you." Herbert again reached into the drawer from which he had taken the check. "All of your mother's jewelry belongs to you now and will be delivered as soon as probate is done. But I know this piece was always your favorite. I wanted to give it to you myself."

Arden immediately recognized the worn red leather box in which her mother had kept the Victorian snake bracelet that had come down through the Montgomery family. She wondered how her father knew the bracelet was her favorite piece. Had her mother told him? How much had Herbert Aldridge known about his child in the years she had lived under his roof? Maybe more than Arden had assumed. Maybe less. She would never know.

"Thank you," she said, accepting the heirloom.

"Your mother told me once that snakes were a symbol of eternal love. Florence was a romantic woman." His tone was fond, without a trace of criticism or mockery.

Arden rose from her chair. It was time for her to leave. Again.

"Goodbye, Father."

Herbert Aldridge nodded. "Goodbye, Victoria."

Arden didn't bother to correct him.

The check and the heirloom in her bag, Arden carefully closed the door of the study behind her.

It was over.

She knew that she would never see her father alive again.

That was all right.

When Arden got back to the bed-and-breakfast, and finding Laura out for a walk (she had left a note explaining her absence),

Arden collapsed onto her bed and slept deeply for almost two hours. When she awoke, she felt remarkably refreshed and unburdened.

"You scared me." Laura was perched on the edge of her own bed, her face drawn. "I came in from my walk to find you dead to the world."

"I'm sorry." Arden smiled fondly, stretching her arms over her head. "I think I kind of was. I don't remember dreaming at all. I don't even remember falling asleep. But I'm awake now and I want to show you something."

Arden got up from the bed and retrieved her bag from the top of the dresser. First, she withdrew the case that contained the Victorian bracelet.

"This is the piece I told you about, the one that belonged to my maternal grandmother." Arden handed the case to Laura. "Before that, it belonged to her mother and grandmother. My father gave it to me earlier. He said he knew that it was my favorite piece of Florence's."

Laura gazed down at the bracelet. "It's beautiful. But isn't it tainted for you, knowing how cruel your grandmother was to your mother about Joseph?"

"Oddly, no." Arden took the leather case from Laura. "It seems I've been very successful after all in removing myself from much of the negative emotions surrounding my family."

"So, the meeting with your father went well? Clearly, it didn't leave you traumatized."

Arden smiled and sat next to her daughter on the edge of the bed. "I don't know where to begin, but I can say with all honesty that I'm glad I agreed to meet him."

"Even in that big old house?"

"Interestingly, once I was inside, I ceased to feel intimidated."

"And he was polite? He wasn't abusive in any way?"

"He was polite. Formal as always, but there were a few emotional moments." Arden paused before going on. "It could have been far worse than it was, but I'm glad it's done with."

Laura smiled. "Me, too. I was really worried that you'd be left feeling emotionally battered."

"There's something else." Arden now took her father's check from her bag and held it out to Laura. "This is for you."

Laura took the check. Arden couldn't read her daughter's expression as she stared down at it.

Finally, Laura softly said, "This is an enormous amount of money. But it's made out to you. I don't understand."

"I'm giving it to you."

"What about the roof of the shop? You haven't signed the loan papers yet. You could take this check and be done with the repairs and have money left over."

"The roof is my concern," Arden said firmly. "This money is for you. And there's one more thing."

Laura shook her head. "I don't know how much more I can take!"

"My father is leaving the estate to me. He never changed his will. I've remained his heir all along."

"Sheesh," Laura cried, "what a turnup! Ah, so *that* will certainly take care of a new roof!"

"When my father dies, of course." Arden frowned. "I don't want to start talking glibly about his death."

"I told you there have been rumors about his poor health for some time."

Arden nodded. "You know, on my way back here I remembered a conversation you and I had not too long ago, about accepting money that might not have been earned honestly. We said, half-jokingly, that a conscience was a burden. Now, I have absolutely no proof that my father earned at least part of his fortune through underhanded means, though I know it's generally suspected. Maybe this makes me an unethical person, but I don't feel bad about inheriting the Aldridge estate. I'll put it to good use. It won't be wasted nor will it ever be used to harm anyone. The estate is the least my father could give me considering all he took away."

"I agree. Don't spend a moment more worrying about the ethics of accepting."

Arden paused. "Before I left, my father told me that he was once tempted to look for me. But he didn't because he had no idea of what he would say to me if he did find me."

"No idea what he would say?" Laura exclaimed. "How about an apology for one? I think his saying that was just a low-down bid for sympathy from a man who knows he doesn't deserve it."

"Maybe it *was* a bid for sympathy, but what's wrong with that? Maybe it is the thought that counts after all."

"Thoughts don't always count. Actions always count. Actions speak louder than words."

"Let's agree to disagree about what measure of forgiveness my father deserves or doesn't deserve."

Laura nodded. "Fair enough. Hey, I'm starved. It's a bit early for dinner, but we could go someplace and have a cocktail and some nibbles first."

"Go out in Port George? All eyes will be upon us."

Laura smiled. "Let them be."

"If this is going to be a celebratory evening, then I'm wearing my bracelet."

"And dinner at Enio's"—Laura waved her grandfather's check— "is on Herbert."

Chapter 84

Laura let out of whoosh of air. It was a pleasant afternoon, the air warm but not sticky, but Laura was having difficulty breathing normally.

"Are you as nervous as I am?" Arden asked.

Laura managed a smile. "If you're ready to turn tail and run, then yes. I am. But here goes."

She knocked on the door to the small house.

A moment later, it was opened by Frannie Armitage. "Come in." Her smile, Laura thought, was genuine, if brief. "My sisters couldn't be here, but they hope to meet you both soon."

Laura and Arden followed Frannie inside. Laura was terribly conscious of how difficult this meeting would be for her mother. Laura would do whatever she could to make it bearable; if they were met with the slightest degree of anger or animosity, she would take Arden's arm and leave. A reunion with the Smiths could happen in stages or it could fail to happen at all. This was a choice.

"My mother, Geraldine," Frannie was saying, as she helped her mother from a chair.

Laura swallowed hard. This was the woman she had seen with Frannie earlier in the summer. Her grandmother.

"Hello," Laura said awkwardly, stepping forward but unsure if she should extend her hand or embrace the woman. "It's . . . It's incredible to meet you."

Geraldine smiled. "It most certainly is. Now, let's have a hug."

When Laura was released, she stepped aside to allow Arden to greet Geraldine.

"Victoria. After all these years."

"Mrs. Smith," Arden said warmly. "It's so good to see you again, it really is."

Frannie then turned to her father. "And this is my father, Rob senior."

Laura struggled to contain a sob. Her grandfather was sitting in an armchair, a crocheted blanket over his legs. The father who had so cruelly lost his only son. She thought she could see a strong resemblance between the two, if the few photographs she had seen of her father were a good indication of what he had been like.

Mr. Smith didn't rise from his chair but he reached for Laura's hands. "My first grandchild," he said, his voice husky with emotion. Then he turned to Arden. "Vicky Aldridge. You were all Rob could talk about that summer."

Arden silently embraced the elderly man.

"Please," Frannie said. "Everyone have a seat."

Laura sat next to Arden on the couch. The cushions were almost flat with use, but clean.

"The old woodstove," Arden said. "I remember it so well."

An awkward moment of silence followed, until Frannie said to Laura, "I liked you immediately when we met at the café, but I didn't recognize you as my flesh and blood. I stopped hoping long ago that one day Rob's child might show up and claim her heritage."

Laura smiled. "I liked you, too, and I thought you had suspicions about my identity. The way you looked at me at one point. Maybe I was imagining it. Maybe I hoped you'd recognize me right away so there would be no need to go on lying."

"Why, exactly, did you keep your identity a secret for so long?" Frannie asked.

"I truly am sorry for that," Laura said feelingly. "I hoped to be able to give you some definitive news about what happened to my father the summer of 1984 before coming out as Rob Smith's daughter. And I worried that if it was known that I was the child of Victoria and Rob—and that Victoria was alive and well—someone would try to stop the investigation again."

"Someone being my father," Arden added softly. "And to be honest, I was afraid that real harm might come to Laura if she dug too deep. Claiming to be an impartial researcher seemed safer."

Frannie nodded. "I understand. We all do."

"And I apologize for not having told you about the baby." Arden looked from one member of the Smith family to another. "My parents were—very forceful. And with Rob suddenly gone, I felt I had no one to whom I could turn. I went along with the adoption not because I wanted to give up my baby, but because I felt I had no other choice."

"You were a child," Geraldine Smith said soothingly.

Frannie nodded. "I'm sorry I gave you such a hard time when you came back to Port George that next summer. But I was just so angry. I knew something bad had happened to my brother and I needed to punish someone for it. You were there and you were vulnerable."

"I understand," Arden replied. "I really do. And you were right all along. About the baby and about my family's involvement in Rob's disappearance. But I swear to you I knew nothing about that at the time." Arden paused and looked to Laura. "I had a feeling, but nothing more."

Laura took Arden's hand and gently squeezed it.

Mr. Smith spoke to his daughter. "Show these two young ladies the album."

Frannie reached for a photo album that sat on the low, round coffee table and handed it to Laura. "Pictures of Rob as a baby and as a little boy. There are more albums, too. You can have a copy of whatever photo you want."

Laura realized her hand was trembling ever so slightly as she opened to the first page to find a faded photo of Geraldine holding a baby, a toddler by her side. The baby had to be Rob. The toddler, Frannie.

Quickly she closed the album and laughed nervously. "I guess

I'll have to take this slowly. I feel . . . overwhelmed. But I want to know everything there is to know about my father. Every detail, his hopes and dreams, his favorite foods and television shows, what music he liked best. What he didn't like, too. What he found funny and what left him cold. What made him angriest and what made him happiest."

Frannie smiled. "That will take some time."

"I'm not going anywhere. Not now that I've found my family."

Mrs. Smith rose from her chair with the aid of her cane. "Frannie, would you serve coffee? I want to show Arden something upstairs."

Frannie went off to the kitchen as Mrs. Smith and Arden left the living room.

Mr. Smith pulled a cell phone from the breast pocket of his short-sleeved shirt. "Let me take a picture of you," he said to Laura. "How about this new phone Frannie got me? Takes pictures as good as a camera!"

"Then let's take one of you and me together," Laura suggested. "Grandpa."

Chapter 85

Arden had never been in Rob's bedroom. Mrs. Smith hadn't allowed girls in her son's room or boys in her daughters' rooms.

"We've kept the room pretty much as it was," Geraldine explained. "One of the younger girls could have moved into it, but neither could bear the thought."

Arden glanced around the simple room, noting with tenderness all that was left of a young man. Books. Posters of bands thumbtacked to the wall. A baseball mitt and bat. Records. A closet full of clothes. No, she thought. Not all that was left. The woman who had pledged to be his wife was alive, as was his daughter.

Geraldine went to the scarred wooden bureau and opened the top drawer. From it she removed a packet of envelopes, tied with a dark blue ribbon, and handed it to Arden. "No one knows I have these. I found them a few days after Rob went missing."

Arden sat on the edge of the bed and carefully removed the ribbon. The envelopes were slightly yellowed. She opened the first, glanced at the pages inside, then hurriedly peeked into the other envelopes. "They're letters and poems, addressed to me. But why didn't he send them?" And then she thought she knew. They would have been evidence of the relationship. Even giving them to Victoria in person would have been too risky: What if they were found by her parents? Maybe Rob had intended to give them to her once they were married. They would have made an extraordinary wedding gift.

"When I realized that the papers were personal," Geraldine explained, "and had nothing to do with Rob's going missing, I tucked them away. I didn't want strangers to get their hands on them. I suppose I intended to give them all to you one day, but before I was ready to pass them along, you had left town and no one knew where you had gone."

Arden retied the ribbon around the bundle and held it close to her heart. If Mrs. Smith *had* given the papers to the police, it would have become known that Victoria and Rob had been a couple; it would have given the police reason to look closely at any involvement by the Aldridges in Rob's disappearance. But the police had been in the pay of Herbert Aldridge. Rob's papers would have been destroyed.

"You've given me a real treasure," Arden said earnestly. "Thank you from the bottom of my heart."

Mrs. Smith shook her head. "I can't imagine how difficult this all is for you, knowing your parents are responsible for, well, for taking Rob away from you. The bond between a parent and child is so precious. To have it severed by betrayal . . ." Mrs. Smith shook her head. "At least now you have the opportunity to be a parent to your own child."

Arden looked fondly at the woman who would have been her mother-in-law. "What did you think all those years ago? Did you have any suspicion that I might be pregnant?"

"I did wonder if there was a child on the way." Geraldine sat now next to Arden on Rob's bed. "But, for better or worse, I never attempted to confront your parents and ask for the truth. They were—"

"Yes. I understand."

"Frannie, though, she fought as best she could for access to Herbert Aldridge and for justice for Rob. But her best wasn't good enough, and my husband and I didn't know how to help her."

Arden took Geraldine's hand. "I'm sorry. I truly am."

"I felt very bad for you. I liked you and I was glad you and Rob had each other. Maybe I should have tried to reach out to you. . . ." Geraldine shook her head. "We should get back to the others. Rob will be boring young Laura with tales of her father's Little League days or some such."

Arden, holding Rob's gift close, followed Geraldine from the room and back downstairs.

Laura, Frannie, and Rob senior were drinking coffee from mugs. When Arden took her seat next to Laura, Frannie poured another cup and handed it to Arden.

Arden gratefully took a sip of the hot coffee. "I can't thank you enough for allowing Laura and me into your lives. I—I wish I could make up to you for what my family did to yours. But there's no way I can, is there?"

"Being here with Laura is a good start," Frannie said firmly.

"And with you, Vicky," Rob senior added.

Arden smiled. She remembered how her father had called her Victoria the day before. So much of a person's identity resided in the memories of others. Victoria. Vicky. Arden. She was all of those people.

"What will happen to your father?" Frannie asked. "Now that he's admitted to his crimes."

Arden looked to Laura and shook her head. "I really don't know. I've never been close to a criminal case before."

"Like you," Laura said, looking to Frannie, "I want to see justice done for my father."

"Punishing a sick old man won't bring back our Rob," Geraldine said.

"We'll let people in the know sort it all out," Rob senior added with a firm nod.

Frannie looked as if she was going to argue with her father's statement, but when she spoke, it was to say that the family had decided to hold another memorial service for Rob in September. "The whole family will be coming to Port George. We'd like the both of you to participate."

"We would be honored," Arden said through tears.

Laura nodded her assent, clearly too moved to speak.

Geraldine gestured to the plate of cookies on the table. "Please. Have one. I baked them only this morning."

"Rob swore that his mother made the best chocolate chip cookies in the world," Arden said after taking a bite. "He was right."

"Is the recipe a secret?" Laura asked.

Geraldine Smith smiled. "Not from family."

Chapter 86

Before leaving Port George, Laura had arranged a meeting between Arden and Kathy Murdoch, to whom Laura had sincerely apologized for her earlier deception. Kathy had seemed hurt for about a minute and had then rallied her usual good temper and assured Laura she completely understood why Laura had kept her connection to Victoria Aldridge and Rob Smith a secret. The reunion of the former Wilder Academy classmates was properly emotional; there were tears but there was also laughter. Kathy renewed her promise of making Laura—and Arden, too—her famous mac 'n' cheese with bacon when they returned to Port George to visit the Smith family.

Later that afternoon, Laura had driven Arden to Miss Thompson's house. This reunion was more profound. After a few minutes, Laura left her mother and Miss Thompson on their own and went for a coffee. She was briefly tempted to visit the Aldridge estate again, but she could discover no good reason to do so.

The next morning, Laura and her mother had set out for Eliot's Corner and were home well before noon.

"I've never been happier to be in this cottage than I am at this moment," Arden had declared when their bags had been unpacked and the kitties properly fed and feted. Deborah and Gordon had taken good care of Ophelia, Prospero, and Falstaff, but the cats were happy to have Arden home.

Both women slept soundly that night and woke feeling more refreshed than they had expected to feel.

"The first day of the rest of my life," Laura had announced to the three cats, which she found lined up and waiting for breakfast when she came downstairs from the loft.

The cats continued to stare, unimpressed.

"Okay," Laura said with a laugh as she went into the kitchen to open a can. "I get it. I'm not the important one here!"

"That bracelet really is gorgeous," Deborah said, for what had to be third time in the past fifteen minutes. The friends were gathered in Arden's little yard, enjoying a late-afternoon cup of tea.

Deborah was referring to the Victorian snake bangle that had once belonged to Arden's mother. Laura agreed that the workmanship was superb, but admitted she had passed on trying the bracelet on her own wrist. Snakes were snakes.

"Have you started to read Rob's letters and poems?" Gordon asked Arden.

Arden nodded. "Slowly. It's a bit overwhelming. I can almost hear his voice speaking the words. We were both so young, so naïve, and that's reflected in Rob's writing. It's almost amusing, in a tender sort of way. I'll cherish each page always, but honestly, I don't think I'll be reading them often."

"And in case you're all wondering," Laura added, "no, I haven't asked to read my father's papers and I won't. They're private."

Deborah frowned. "Rats. That means I'll never get a peek at them! Oh, I've got some big news for you all. I made the sale! I'm now eligible to become a full partner in the agency."

"And you've been sitting here all this time saying nothing," Arden scolded. "Deborah, that's excellent news, congratulations!"

"You rock, Deborah," Laura told her.

"I'm glad all that hard work paid off in the end," Gordon said.

"Me, too," Deborah admitted. "It wasn't much of a restful summer for me, but then again, I'm not sure I'd know what to do with too much downtime."

"It hasn't been a restful summer for any of us," Gordon pointed out. "Any word from Port George?"

"I talked to Ted the other day," Arden said. "He told me that there was no memorial of any sort for my mother. I'd already guessed as much. I'm sure I would have been informed if it were otherwise. Maybe if the postmortem hadn't so strongly suggested my mother's death was suicide . . ."

"So, um, where is she?" Deborah asked.

"My father had her buried in the Montgomery family's plot, next to her son. My brother. I believe that's what she would have wanted, what she probably instructed in her will." Arden looked to her daughter before going on. "And there's more news. The night before last my father suffered a major stroke. He isn't expected to live through the end of the week. I didn't tell you right away," she added hastily, "because I needed some time to process the news."

Deborah sighed. "I'm sorry, Arden. I truly am. A life is a life. It's sacred, even when it's been wasted or mishandled."

"I'm sorry, too," Gordon said. "Losing a parent is never an easy thing, even one from whom we've been estranged."

"Thank you both. Mr. O'Connell, my father's executor, told me that funeral instructions are in place, and I'll honor them. You know," Arden went on after a moment, "I don't believe my father would want to live now that my mother is gone. They were so intertwined, so invested in one another, through thick and thin."

"Isn't that what marriage is supposed to be all about?" Gordon noted. " 'In sickness and in health, for better or for worse.' "

Laura rolled her eyes. "Unless it drives you mad well before death!"

"Hear, hear!" Deborah cried.

Gordon winced. "As a fellow divorced person, I guess I shouldn't preach the storybook line. Reality is a lot more complicated."

"I don't think I can handle being at Herbert Aldridge's funeral," Laura said suddenly. Until that moment, she hadn't given it much thought, but now she knew for certain.

"It's all right," Arden assured her. "You do what's best for you."

"I'll go with you if you, Arden, if you want me to," Gordon offered.

"Thank you. I would like that."

Laura shot a glance at Deborah, who nodded almost imperceptibly. Yes, a look of genuine fondness had passed between Arden and Gordon. Good. After all the years on her own, Laura thought, Arden deserved a worthy companion.

"There's another bit of news," Arden said now. "My father's estate will come to me when he dies, and when I'm gone, it will go to Laura. In the meantime, there's plenty for the two of us to share."

Deborah slapped a hand over her heart. "Whoa!"

"It was a huge surprise to us both," Laura told them. "We'd assumed Arden had been cut out of the will years ago."

"At least you can relax somewhat now," Gordon said to Arden. "You've been working so hard for so long."

"It *will* be a relief to have a cushion beneath me for once," Arden admitted. "And now I don't need a loan to get the roof on the shop fixed before winter weather destroys what's left of it! The roofers start work next Monday."

"How does it feel to be an heiress?" Deborah joked.

"Weird." Arden laughed. "It was weird when I was a kid and it's weird now. But I'll adjust."

Laura had never been overly materialistic, but she would be lying if she said that the idea of finally being free of Jared Pence's remaining debts didn't warm her heart.

Suddenly, her mother turned to her. "Laura, I know you were planning to go back to Connecticut, but what about staying here in Eliot's Corner? You might be able to get a part-time teaching job in one of the local colleges, and you yourself said there are reputable online degree programs. If you're willing, you could earn your PhD online."

A shocked silence descended on the group of friends.

"That is true," Laura admitted after a moment. "About good online degree programs."

Deborah cleared her throat and looked from Arden to Laura. "I hope you don't take this as my interfering, but Laura could move into my place if she decides to stay in Eliot's Corner. I've got a big spare bedroom, and there's a second bathroom as well. We wouldn't be living in each other's pockets, and Laura could come and go as she pleased while I continue to do the same."

Laura looked to Arden, who was smiling.

"The bedroom is big enough for a nice-sized desk," Deborah went on, "or you could use a laptop anywhere else in the house. And there's definitely free shelf space for your books."

Gordon nodded. "I think it sounds like a grand idea. Not that my opinion counts."

"I wouldn't say that," Laura told him. "And if I stay on in Eliot's Corner, I can be at your opening at the Fry Gallery." Laura then turned back to her mother. "And I could join the Arden Forest book group."

"As long as whatever decision you make, to stay in Eliot's Corner or to go back to Connecticut, to move into Deborah's or to remain at Juniper End, isn't unduly influenced by anyone else," Arden said firmly. "This has to be about what's best for you."

What was best for her. Laura knew the answer to that question as certainly as she knew that Falstaff had a penchant for fresh tuna. "I would love to stay on in Eliot's Corner. And, Deborah, I'd be happy to move in with you. We'll talk about compensation when it's just you and me."

"I don't expect—" Deborah began.

"I'm not a freeloader. And now, like Arden, I have a bit of a cushion. As much as I'm loath to admit it, the fact is that Herbert Aldridge—my grandfather; there, I've said it—has made it possible for me to make this decision. And being in Eliot's Corner will allow me to see the Smiths as frequently as I like. I haven't met them all yet. There are Rob's other two sisters and all my cousins and maybe even aunts and uncles."

Arden was beaming. "This is truly a matter for celebration."

"I'll run home and grab a bottle of champagne!" Deborah cried.

"Why the heck not?" Laura wiped a tear from her eye.

Chapter 87

"What's this?" Laura pointed to a large cardboard box sitting unopened on the dining table.

"Bill O'Connell sent it," Arden told her. "It arrived this morning."

"Do you want to open it now or wait until you're alone?"

"No. Let's open it now. I'm sure there's nothing you shouldn't see."

The box contained several photo albums. A brief note from Mr. O'Connell stated that her father had selected the contents the day before his stroke; he had left a note instructing his lawyer to send the box to Arden as soon as possible. A second delivery, consisting of Arden's personal belongings, was forthcoming.

Arden opened and quickly glanced through each album. "These are photos from my childhood. It looks as if there's nothing here past 1979 or '80. Who knows what else I'll find in the house when ... when my father passes away."

Herbert Aldridge was still lingering, but death would visit him before long. Arden found herself praying for a swift end to whatever struggles might be taking place in what was left of her father's mind. Certainly, his soul had to be in torment.

Maybe.

"Did he ever say anything to you about those creepy portraits of your brother?" Laura asked.

"I can't believe I forgot to tell you! I noticed right away that the portraits were gone. I asked my father about them and he said he'd had them destroyed after my mother's death. It dawned on me then for the first time that those paintings probably caused my father serious distress. After all, he had lost a son, too."

"You're probably right. I can't imagine anyone living in that house would be immune to the mood set by those what-if pictures."

Arden again opened the first of the albums and smiled. "This one"—she showed the photo to Laura—"was taken when I was three. My hair was so white blond! That's definitely a color you don't see naturally on an adult."

"Quite the fancy pink dress, too. Black patent leather shoes and purse. Bow in hair. You're picture-perfect."

Arden smiled. "Maybe on the outside. Look, here's my first-grade class picture. As you can see, I towered over the other girls and most of the boys. My mother told me I had an enviable frame for clothes. It didn't make up for being teased and called String Bean and Beanpole."

"Kids can be idiots."

"As can adults." Arden turned another page of the album. "Look at this! I remember the afternoon Mrs. Clarke took me to the October Fair hosted by the Chamber of Commerce."

Laura laughed. "My word, you were awfully cute! Did she win you that teddy bear?"

Arden smiled. "She did, and you're prejudiced."

"I also have eyes to see." Laura paused. "Were there any photos of your brother? I mean, there must have been, but did you ever see any?"

Arden shook her head. "No. But like I said, who knows what I'll find when I go through all of my parents' things. Gosh, what a daunting task that's going to be."

"There's no deadline. And I'm here to help you."

"Look at this photo. I must have been eight or nine. I vaguely remember that dress. It had a scratchy lining."

"You look so solemn and serious," Laura said after a moment. "Poor little lost girl."

Arden smiled at her daughter. "That first night you were here, I so badly wanted to watch over you as you slept, a vigil I was denied as a young mother. Of course, I didn't leave my room. Can you imagine what you might have thought if you woke to find me staring down at you?"

Laura laughed. "It might have been just a tad unsettling! You know, if I ever have a daughter, I'll name her Victoria."

Arden's eyes widened. "You're planning on having a baby?" She had never dreamed of being a grandmother, not when the role of motherhood had been denied her.

"Who knows? With my family's support, I might just be able to now."

"Would you consider adoption?"

Laura nodded. "Yes. Of course. But I'm not making any big decisions yet. I'm still reeling from the discoveries we made this summer."

The two women turned again to the photo album. "Here's me with my mother," Arden said softly. "Easter 1977. I remember that hat of my mother's, and that handbag. They were the loveliest shade of blue, periwinkle I think you'd call it."

"Florence was truly beautiful."

"She was. You know, her signature perfume was Joy by Jean Patou. Ironic, as she was such an unhappy person after my brother died."

"Maybe Florence was unhappy even before your brother died. We know so little of her."

"That's true. I'm just sorry she wasn't able to laugh more in her life."

"Look," Laura said suddenly, "I've been wondering if you'd like me to try to find Alice Davidson, your old friend from Two Suns. I'm hardly a professional detective, but I think I've developed a few sleuthing skills this summer. And maybe Ted could help."

"I'll think about it. I suppose if we do find Alice, she has the choice not to respond."

"Exactly." Laura took her mother's hand in hers. "You and I have become so close. It's more than I ever hoped for. I mean, you hear these stories about children finding their birth parents and things not going well at all. And no one is really at fault. The past is the past for a reason. Things change, people change. So, this relationship we have is a bit of a miracle really." Laura paused. "To be honest, I'm not sure I'll ever be comfortable calling you Mom, but that doesn't mean I don't love you as my mother. Oh, how could I have forgotten! Wait here."

Laura dashed off to the loft. When she returned, she was carrying a large rectangular box. "I'm afraid it's not wrapped. I was afraid of disturbing the packing."

"What is it?" Arden asked as Laura placed the box flat on the table.

"Your birthday present. I know, I gave you the scarf, but like I said, that was a placeholder. I wanted to get you something more personal, so I contacted a former classmate of mine from grad school. Her family have been in the antique-book and print trade for generations and she was able to find this for me. I had it sent to Deborah's house so that it would be a surprise."

Arden reached for the kitchen scissors and carefully cut through the heavy tape and layers of Bubble Wrap. What was revealed was an excellent reproduction of Branwell Brontë's portrait of his three sisters, painted in the 1830s.

"I don't know what to say," Arden breathed. "I've always loved this. Do you know what Elizabeth Gaskell said about it?"

Laura shook her head.

"She knew Charlotte, and she said this was a 'good likeness, however badly executed.' I'll hang it in the shop where everyone can see it. Young Tami, for one, is going to love it."

Laura laughed. "I'm so glad you like it. Maybe we could do an Arden Forest event around portraits of our favorite writers and what, if anything, we can learn from them."

"That would be a lot of fun." As Arden gazed at the portrait of the three brilliant sisters, she thought about how along the way she had given up any hope of happiness or adventure. She had been content to make do with peace, and peace was all well and good as long as it didn't slip into complacency or apathy. But there was no chance of a complacent or an apathetic life now, not with Laura by her side.

"Hey, was I imagining it, or did I see a significant look pass between you and Gordon the other day?" Laura asked suddenly.

Arden looked up and smiled. "You're not imagining it. I think I'm ready to . . . I'm not going to throw myself at Gordon, I'm just going to let him know, subtly, that now might be the time for us to take things a step further."

"Ditch the subtlety. You're not getting any younger, none of us are. And now that I'll be sharing a house with Deborah, you and Gordon will have all the privacy you need!"

"You're assuming Gordon will say yes to my proposal."

Her daughter just rolled her eyes.

Acknowledgments

In memory of Elizabeth (Betty) Wall and also of Betty (Miss Elizabeth) Smith, two dear friends who are much missed and who will never be forgotten.

Thanks to John Scognamiglio and the entire team at Kensington, who have always gone above and beyond for their authors. And cheers to Rusty Donner and to Phyllis Arcidiacono, who against all odds are back home where they belong!

Please turn the page for an
author Q&A with
Holly Chamberlin!

Q. Arden Bell, née Victoria Aldridge, one of the main characters in your latest book, *Barefoot in the Sand*, considers the gift she was given on her eighteenth birthday, an old edition of one of her favorite novels, her most prized possession. Tell us about any books in your collection that hold a special place in your heart.

A. So many books mean the world to me, but I'll tell you now about one in particular. My father, Joseph, was always on the lookout for interesting old books and prints, both for himself and for me. A long time ago he gave me a 1905 edition of *Villette* published by Thomas Nelson and Sons as part of the New Century Library. It's in excellent condition and it means an enormous amount to me because it was a gift from my father, from whom I got my passion for reading (as well as from my mother!).

Q. *Barefoot in the Sand* is in part a mystery. Was this the first time you've written a novel with a strong element of whodunit?

A. Yes, it is, and though the mystery element is minor compared to the emotional story at the center of the book, it took me quite a lot of time and mental effort to make it coherent. I'm in awe of how writers who specialize in mystery and detective/procedural stories do it! Their brains are definitely way bigger than mine!

Q. You were writing this book during 2020, a time when the entire world was grappling with COVID-19. How did this affect your storytelling?

A. COVID hit my family hard; both my stepmother and a cousin were very sick and, at times, not expected to live. Luckily, both recovered, but it will take at least a year for them to regain full strength, and who knows what long-term effects might appear? My husband and I remained in strict isolation, and the strain of that—not seeing our friends and family—was at times enormous. That said, I chose not to deal with the pandemic in this book. Honestly, I don't know how to write about what we've experienced and are still experiencing, and as far as was possible, I wanted this book to be full of love and forgiveness and coming together and healing. I think we need those elements now more than ever.

Q. Besides writing *Barefoot in the Sand*, what other projects or activities helped get you through 2020?

A. Walking. And more walking. Until bad winter weather got in the way, I took long walks as often as I could manage. And I took photos and drew pictures. And I watched tons of old movies from the 1930s through the 1950s. I mean lots. And I ate cheese. Lots of cheese.

Q. What's next up for Holly?

A. My next book will once again be set in Eliot's Corner though it will focus on a new cast of characters. However, Arden Forest and its book club will play an important role for my heroine!

BAREFOOT IN THE SAND

Holly Chamberlin

ABOUT THIS GUIDE

The suggested questions are included to enhance your group's reading of Holly Chamberlin's *Barefoot in the Sand*!

DISCUSSION QUESTIONS

1. Several versions of the older-woman / younger-woman dynamic make an appearance in this novel. Talk about some of those variations as mentioned here: the loving adoptive mother (Cynthia) and her child (Laura); the older mentor/guardian angel (Margery) and her younger friend (Arden), and, to a lesser extent, Arden and Tami; the birth mother (Arden) and her long-lost child (Laura); the dedicated teacher (Miss Thompson) and her pupil (Victoria); the nanny (Mrs. Clarke) and her charge (Victoria); the employer (Arden) and her employee (Elly); the mentally/emotionally damaged mother (both Florence Aldridge and Regina Montgomery) and her daughter (Victoria and Florence).

2. As an extension of the first discussion question, consider the two mother/son relationships represented (if briefly) in this novel, namely, Mrs. Teakle and her son Brent, and Florence Aldridge and her son, Joseph. For all he suffered as a child, Brent is a well-balanced and functional adult, largely, we assume, thanks to his mother's having bravely defended him against his brute of a father. What sort of mother to a son do you think Florence might have been? Admittedly, this question is nearly impossible to answer based on the little we know of the young Florence, so be the author for a moment and use your imagination!

3. Lines and passages from *Villette* often come to Arden's mind as she faces trials and tribulations. (We all find ourselves turning to favorite stories and characters for comfort or inspiration!) Here is another line from the novel for us to consider in relation to *Barefoot in the Sand*:
   Man cannot prophesy. Love is no oracle.
   What are your thoughts about the future of Rob Smith

and Victoria Aldridge, assuming they had been allowed a future? Do you think their relationship would have continued and survived, and if so, under what circumstances? What if Victoria hadn't gotten pregnant? How might that have changed things for the couple? Would Victoria have gone off to college that fall and continued to see Rob long distance? Would her expanding world have made the idea of a life spent in Port George, married to Rob Smith, seem less desirable? So many first/teenage loves fade and come to a rather inglorious end. But not all.

4. Here's another line from Charlotte Brontë's 1853 novel, spoken by its heroine:

   "The negation of severe suffering was the nearest approach to happiness I expected to know."

   Compare this statement to what Arden tells us early on about having abandoned the expectation of excitement and adventure in favor of achieving peace and contentment. Is this a negative thing? Where does hope for positive change fit into this scenario, if it does? Is it possible to live for any length of time without some degree of hope in a better/changed future? At the end of the book, Arden feels that with her daughter by her side, excitement and adventure are now possible—that active happiness has indeed come her way. Do you understand what she means by this?

5. When Laura appears on Arden's doorstep, Arden knows her instantly. (In a sense, Laura is Arden's "pearl of great price.") She has loved her child for thirty-six years without even knowing the child's name. How do you love someone you know nothing about? Can love be entirely instinctual, spiritual, heart based, without what is commonly held to be knowledge or information? Or is this notion mere sentimentality or wishful thinking?

6. Arden and Laura host a bookshop event around the theme of star-crossed lovers in literature. Both women admit that to different degrees they were prey to the darkly glamorous myth of fated or doomed romance. We know that not only women have succumbed to the dangers of a story that ignores the daily, pedestrian, but no less wonderful aspects of love. How has modern culture kept this unhealthy myth alive, and how has it worked to erase the allure of love as a sickness, a dynamic all about suffering and sacrifice? What do you tell your daughters—and sons—about true love, soul mates, and devotion unto death? Why do we need—if we do need—stories of grand passion to inspire us?

7. Twenty-one years after leaving her hometown, Arden settles in Eliot's Corner, a town only two hours from Port George—the place where she had known and loved Rob as well as the place where they had been so cruelly separated.

   Consider this passage from *The Scarlet Letter* by Nathaniel Hawthorne, a classic story of two doomed lovers, Hester Prynne and Arthur Dimmesdale, in relation to Arden's choice:

   But there is a fatality, a feeling so irresistible and inevitable that it has the force of doom, which almost invariably compels human beings to linger around and haunt, ghostlike, the spot where some great and marked event has given the color to their lifetime, and, still, the more irresistible the darker the tinge that saddens it.

8. Though Victoria/Arden suffered at the hands of her parents, she continues to defend them as "not evil," as well-meaning in their own way. Laura has trouble understanding her mother's emotionally generous view of Herbert and Florence Aldridge. What do you think of this

difficult, problematic pair? Do you share the sympathy for Florence that both Arden and Laura come to feel by the end of the story? Do you think Herbert's handling of his wife's fragile mental state was indeed well-intentioned, performed out of love? How morally culpable is he in the killing of Rob Smith?

9. Arden tells us about the night she came across her mother and a family friend in the gazebo on the Aldridges' property. She feels great guilt and shame about not having acted to stop what she saw as an assault. And she comes to realize that her running away without leaving a note of explanation was cruel, no matter how necessary it seemed at the time. What are your thoughts about Victoria's actions/nonactions that summer of 1985 when she was eighteen years old?

10. When Florence Aldridge nearly collapses in Arden's cottage, Arden steps forward to help her and experiences a rush of maternal feeling. The mother, she tells us, has become the child; it's the way of the world. Talk about your own experiences with the dynamic that comes to those of us who care for a sick or simply an aging parent.